REPORTS
TO
AMFORTAS

JOHN MENKEN

Order this book online at www.trafford.com
or email orders@trafford.com

Most Trafford titles are also available at major online book retailers.

Printed in the United States of America.

ISBN: 978-1-4907-2289-4 (sc)
ISBN: 978-1-4907-2290-0 (hc)
ISBN: 978-1-4907-2291-7 (e)

Library of Congress Control Number: 2014900131

Trafford rev. 01/07/2014

Trafford. www.trafford.com
PUBLISHING

North America & international
toll-free: 1 888 232 4444 (USA & Canada)
fax: 812 355 4082

Dedicated to the late Alan and Nibby Bullock of Oxford, U.K., and to my late wife, Reina Attias Menken, who all urged me to finish and publish this crazy book.

And also to the memory of my mother, Esther Adelson.

ACKNOWLEDGMENTS

Great help was rendered by the late Marthe Macmillan, the late Karen Hack, and the very alive Ruth McKee of the Mesa Public Library, Los Alamos, New Mexico; David Windham and Kerry Owens of Big Star Books, Santa Fe, New Mexico; and Maida Henderson, Rebecca Ahrens, Rhonda Black, and Michael Zurovitch.

INTRODUCTION

This is a book about stories. Plato described Socrates saying, "Remember the stories for they will save you in the end." And it's about stories within stories.

And it's about forgetting. About losing, remembering, and finding. A Native American once told me a story of going through the woods, finding a fork in the trail, and deciding on one of the paths. He discovered that the trail ended nowhere and that from there it's best to go back to where the fork was, rather than to try and find your way from where you discovered an error, which is very much like a well-known Middle Eastern story of Nasreddin, who when a neighbor found him crawling in his front yard looking for something and asked him what it was, he said it was a key. The neighbor joined him on the ground looking for it. And for a long time, not finding it, he asked the mullah, was he sure he dropped it here? And the mullah said, "Oh no, I dropped it in the house." The neighbor said, "Why are we looking for it here?" The mullah replied, "Oh, it's too dark in the house."

And it is also about language. How do we decide what a word means and how it travels from one language to another?

The great storyteller Leo Tolstoy, when setting himself the task of understanding the story of the Gospels and looking at the first sentence of John, "En arche en o logos," and noting that logos has either eleven or thirteen chief meanings (which could boil down to four that are possible in the context), and then finding what he could use in Russian, used *razumyenie* since it actually can carry those four possible meanings. So we can see the undertaking might be quite complex.

There is a tendency among us to pooh-pooh stories. Jews describe some as grandmother's stories that can be ignored. In describing the current situation of humanity and how we got here, the paradigmatic teacher of the twentieth century George Gurdjieff summed it up by saying, "Grandmother forgot."

So storytellers have a kind of madness. Which I share.

And since this is an introduction or the entry to the book, I will open the tent flap using the formula for beginning a story favored by the ancient Armenian storytellers, the *ashougs*.

> I pray for mercy,
>> Mercy on Amfortas and his friends;
>
> I pray for mercy,
>> Mercy on Merlin, Bors, Lama;
>
> I pray for mercy
>> Mercy on David, Lancelot and Dzovinar;
>
> I pray for mercy,
>> Mercy on Asaph, Percevel and Marya;
>
> I pray for mercy,
>> Mercy on Ali, Kali and Shakespeare

I pray for mercy,
Mercy on Paracelsus, Madelein and Feirefiz

I pray for mercy,
Mercy on Trevrizent;

I pray for mercy,
A thousand mercies on the departed of the listeners to this tale.

CHAPTER ONE

Merlin

Now that they have all gone on, I am compelled to publish their reports. They were not delivered in the dark, in some musty enigmatic room, like those caves where bats twitter their secrets to entranced latter-day Druids. All the transactions in this book, all the working ideas and experiences recounted by members of the Society Amfortas, took place in the open light under an intelligible sun.

All of us, though, before we met, had been stained by terror. But this was not unreasonable.

Our meeting in Olivet took place roughly ten years after the Nazi depravities had become public. Still, after ten years, the augury of that defection, a licensed defection from humanity, had not really reached deep into the general psyche of the human family. Oh, of course people had felt shock, outrage, revulsion, and guilt; and there were some who even felt shame. I will hazard to say that the depth of terror in which "mankind" had implicated itself during those years had not yet come near "zero to the bone."

For us, we had in common an apprehensiveness that bit deep into our minds. And there it burrowed like fervid yeast to agitate the cosmic presumptions on which we had build our lives.

The Society Amfortas was founded by chance.

Articles would turn up in small journals . . . articles that bore the imprint of an author approaching life from an odd angle. It was in the nature of things that such an article spoke to the condition of some reader attuned to this rare temper . . . who would in turn respond by post. In this way, rather tentative communications among a widely scattered assembly began to take place. Before long these people, people who had not known each other but who shared a profound disquiet, initiated an association based on the need to know others similar to them. At first the community existed only through the medium of the worldwide postal delivery system. Ideas held us together. Ideas, plus the price of a postage stamp, were the only glue.

Before our first meeting, only a few of us had met face-to-face. And that meeting took two full years of preparation. We had chosen as the site a small college campus in the state of Michigan in the United States. Our membership comprised sixty persons of which men outnumbered women at a ratio of about three to one.

The school was between the summer and fall terms, and so we were able to lease their whole facility. Olivet was one of those red-brick rural colleges of which many had been built during the nineteenth century in the midst of fertile black-earthed farming country throughout Middle America. Early settlers had named the hill on which it was set *Olivet*. On the north slope of the hill, a road led down an even but steep grade into the village proper. In the center of the campus crowning the hill was a large well-kept but undeveloped tract of land given over to grasses and a dense miniforest of oak trees. In 1868, a college wit had named this wooded portion *Broceliande*. These were very old oaks standing with random ease on top of the hill like attentive shaggy watchmen.

The college buildings were set as though to follow the Celtic custom of avoiding hubris and the lightning. They were set back and below the crown in a square around the small wood. A wonderful old timber-and-rough-rock Congregational Church on the northeast corner of the square housed our full society convocations. For smaller meetings or working teams, we would use offices in the combined administration and classroom building on the square's west side. This was the oldest building on campus and creaked like it.

In the soft summer evening, the sounds of the lowing dairy herds in surrounding farms were reassuring. They nightly confirmed us in our purpose. They spoke to us of the worth of our undertaking.

Three weeks had been allowed for the meeting. Members had been asked to deliver short papers defining their cardinal areas of interest during the first two weeks. By this I do not mean their arena of work or specialty but refer to those questions which caused them to twist and turn in the night. We had planned the final week for the boiling down of these diverse problems to several key subjects of study.

We hoped to put into place an instrument whereby we could pool our resources and help each other. It fell out, as so often happens with collective efforts, that we were unable to follow this straightforward agenda. Events happened at the meeting which could not have been foretold. By the end of the first fourteen days, only thirty of us remained. The other half of the assembly had taken themselves off in some form or other of "high" indignation.

Over the years that followed, those of us who remained in the society have kept in touch; and when it seemed natural to do so, many of us became friends.

Right now I think it is proper to say that by no means were we any sort of secret society. That we are scarcely known outside our own circle is due more to the fact that very few people found our company interesting than from any desire on our part to be hidden. What we asked of ourselves and what we sought did not exactly "turn others on." We wanted a way of thinking and feeling both rigorous and imaginative. We needed food for our souls and satisfaction for our conscience. No form of power was ever on our agenda as a society. We are not a *politico-religio* event as was the Rosicrucian phenomenon of the seventeenth century. And we were not, as far as I know, connected to any ancient and venerable brotherhood of tradition. Most of us had more than a "full plate" of worldly obligations. And so it is truly hard to say what it was that kept our fellowship together.

At the beginning of each member's association, he or she was asked to submit a short self-description. And in a spirit of play, each of us was invited to choose a "pen name." Mine, for example, is Merlin. I picked it without much thought. I grew up until my twelfth year in the village of Drumelzier on the Tweed River. It was natural for a boy-child running and balancing in those regions known of yore as Celyddon and Goddeux to become enthralled with the legends surrounding our local bard and mage.

You will find at the front of each report from our members in this volume a slightly retouched version of that person's "vita." I have kept the emphasis of each and interfered only slightly with their style.

They are all gone, as I said. For some years now, I have been the corresponding secretary. Now I too stand facing a deep unknown. Or rather, I am approaching a land . . . a country whose language I have been almost too late learning. Yet it is with satisfaction that I fulfill the geis . . . presenting to the world this volume of reports from members of the society.

The book in your hands, the first, contains some of the material submitted to us by those members who chose to investigate the "out of the way."

I cannot attest to the literal veracity of any pieces in this book, for consider: when a person is asked to write down what one has learned that may be of value to one's fellows, how will they do it? But my opinion is that most of our contributors have represented more or less actual encounters and real traditions. I think, moreover, that they have also described flesh-and-blood individuals, though perhaps with some small and deliberate disguise. The one clear exception to the rule is most likely the report from "Paracelsus." And I think he has adequately warned us by calling his piece "The Difficulty of Telling the Truth."

My own association with this "community" was a direct result of an article I had written to probe the relationship between "eidolon" and "eikon." For some years, I had been troubled by the role of mimesis in the "Gerasene" impulse of human herds to throw themselves over a cliff by persecuting others. Were people following a commanding "idea" or were they enjoying the thrill of identification? Were they imitating an idea or their picture of the desires of their "role models" when setting about to destroy other living and sentient beings? Flowing from this question comes another. From where or what do ideologies/models derive their power and authority? The piece was never published, but it did attract the attention of a senior editor of the journal to which it had been submitted. The person turned out to be a member of Amfortas.

When I look back quietly at the years of my association with our fellowship, I am deeply moved by recognition of the great good it was for me. Through this very rare undertaking, I met my wife whom I soon will be joining again after a year of separation. But all my colleagues were special and rare people. To honor this fact, I have ventured a personal reminiscence about each at the head of their chapter. It would be cheating the reader to not provide some sense, some impression of their irreplaceable quality and presence.

I wish the thirst for truth did not so often drive men mad. But neither the quest nor the "truth" produces the madness. At least I do not think so. I think it comes from forgetting who we are, where we come from, and where we are going. To each of these questions, for each of us . . . there is a doubled answer. And neither dimension of the doubling do we dare ignore all the long way. I think it is like this: The Society Amfortas came about on such and such a certain day. After a fashion, it had its own mothers and fathers. When we close our books, it "will be no more." So it is with we individuals, whether we like it or not. Only at its peril would Amfortas forget this basic biographical reality. Yet there is another "biography" which as a society or as individuals we could not forget.

One day when I was about eleven, I remember sitting by the River Tweed with a book on my lap and my lunch in a bucket by my side. The smells of my mother and father were deep in my clothes. I could taste my mother's salt sea flowing from a small cut in my mouth and feel my father's turmoil in my pulses. Deeply rooted in my "biography," I reached for a sandwich, my eye falling on a verse in the book before me:

> The Prophet Johannes called me Myrrdin
> But now all kings know me as Taliesin.

And so I thought a name reaches roads past easy reckoning. I took a short nap after eating. When I woke up, I read further:

> I was in many shapes before I was released;
> I was in a slender, enchanted sword . . .
> I was in rain-drops in the air; I was a star's beam;
> I was a word in letters; I was a book in origin;
> I was lanterns of light for a year and a half;
> I was a bridge that stretched over sixty estuaries;
> I was a pat, I was an eagle, I was a coracle in seas.

Then came the description of a battle, not without humor, among the trees of the wood, followed after by another voice or perhaps the same one singing:

> Not from father or mother was I made
> As for creation, I was created from nine forms of elements;
> From the fruit, from the fruit of God at the beginning;
> From primroses and flowers of the hill;
> From the bloom of woods and trees;
> From the essence of soils was I made;
> From the bloom of nettles, from the water of the ninth wave.

Further along, my eye lighted on this stanza:

> I have been a blue salmon;
> I have been a dog, a stag, a roebuck on the mountain;
> A stock, a spade, an axe in the hand;
> A stallion, a buck, a bull . . .
> I was with my Lord in the heavens
> When Lucifer fell into the depths of hell;
> I know the stars names from north to south.
> I was in the fort of Gwydian,
> In the Tetragrammaton . . .

While sitting there, I thought, I listened to thoughts deeper than words. I could hear the water rushing over the smooth river rocks . . . it was early spring. That seems so . . . but who, then, am I?

All this is by way of advising the reader to not waste too much dear time trying to figure out who anyone in this volume really is. But also, I assure you, it is not a fantasy. For some of the material, I have found possible corroborative sources and, to make the going easy, have provided notes.

At the founding of the society, we assumed the name *Amfortas*. This seemed to catch something of the essence of our "meaning." Almost all histories of civilization later than the Paleolithic sound somewhere in their entrails unmistakable intimations of lamentation. Where explicit, the legends call out for a "deed" that will rectify and heal. In our time, this call and this deed became its own ultimate perversion. It was as though humanity's guardian angel had been dealt a fresh, nearly mortal wound.

In the stories about the Fisher King, the wounded Amfortas languishes. The castle and the king are waiting for the "right" person to arrive and to ask a question. Almost to a person, those who remained of our fellowship say this in a special and similar way. Each of us is a bearer of this "right person." But the weave of our private world renders him or her mute and foolish . . . like that "true person of no title" whom in the Zen tradition is set upon by teachers in order to rouse toward hearing and seeing and saying.

We were not deceived. We knew a question alone will not redeem the wasteland. Surely questions were continually being asked. The "wrong" person was asking. The questioner was that one with all the answers, that dweller in a dead world. Furthermore, Amfortas was of no help but was "himself" problematic for he was surrounded in his castle by a symbiosis of serving girls and boys. He ought to have been surrounded instead by the glory of God, the Shekinah.

During the meeting at Olivet, some of us came to the conviction that the instruments of "thought" hammered out by Hephaestus in the employ of the "secular city" were inadequate for making the difference. The group that parted company with us after the second week, roughly half our number, felt ferociously otherwise.

After the splitting up, those who remained of us spent the first day in considerable angst. All meetings were cancelled. On the crown of Olivet Hill, among the oaks in Brociliande, we set up a large table. Shakespeare, always an efficient organizer, hired several local widows to provision the table throughout the day with coffee and tea and abundant food. Our stomachs free from care, small groups of us continuously walked among the shaggy trees debating how to best proceed.

The next day, we convened in the reassuring rocky church. To a person we had awakened convinced that we each had sufficient first-hand experience to validate the presence in us of a spiritualized subjectivity. But we were all too vague. We made a pact to explore further and write reports on our findings for the benefit of our companions. Surely we each could find the form and the "know-how" to convey our private convictions. The depth dimension which encompassed us and, which though unseen, permeated our lives ought sure as daybreak to be communicable. The "right person" could be led forth to ask the question.

So it is that a question is embedded in each report to Amfortas. But the *form* is not that of a question.

Approach the volume like an archaeologist. After all, we are now of a past. As I said, for all practical purposes we are gone. But avoid that nineteenth-century method of archeological research which is addicted to vertical penetration. The current century's French school has amply demonstrated that the horizontal approach will yield the most fecund results. As I understand it, the axion of intelligence is turned "ninety degrees." The contiguous layer is regarded as a single text. Then the digger proceeds to the next deeper plane. According to this twentieth-century school, the rotation of the digging axis unveils otherwise hidden patterns.

For example, when I was trying to comprehend seriously why I chose Merlin for my pen name, my attempts at introspective penetration came up barren. But by casting my net wide and catching hold of my "figure's" horizontal shapes in the names— Myrrdin, Taliesin, Leu, Lailoken, and Suibhne Geilt—I got results. As my good friend Shakespeare describes in his report about archery, indirectly the target aligns itself.

In sum, the question is an answer that remains a question. When the prophet Isaiah insists:

> Sing to God a new song.
> Praise from the ends of the earth,
> You who go down to the sea and all in it,
> You islands and all who live in them.
> Let the desert and its towns raise their voices . . .

What is a new song?

CHAPTER TWO

Bors

Known generally as Abbie, Abigail Cook was born and "raised" in Rhode Island. Practically from the time she started reading, her twin passions were literature and history. By the time she was twelve, if she were missing from home, her family knew she could be found either in the Providence Public Library or the library at Brown University. The dilemma of twin passions was solved in her characteristic fashion by undertaking in succession two separate doctorates. She earned her first PhD in history under Carl Becker and immediately assumed work on another in literature, which was conferred by Columbia University. Now thirty-two years old, she took a teaching post at a small Midwestern college.

During a vacation which she spent at Cambridge, England, her gifts brought her into the orbit of British prewar efforts and she was recruited for work at Bletchley. She stayed in England for the duration of the war. Immediately thereafter, she returned to the States and resumed her teaching position.

Intelligence work had brought her attention to the unholy marriage between certain mysticisms and political power. Thereafter, she spent each summer in Europe probing into the nature of this recurring type of alliance. She is a founding member of Amfortas.

*   *   *

I was having a late supper with Bors at the Stouffers in Shaker Heights, Ohio. I remember very well the round large room of the restaurant but not how or why we were there. Even before I started on the excellent martini, I began to enjoy the peculiar discomfort Bors always aroused, and she must have caught something in my manner. She leaned over and lightly put her hand on mine.

"Dear Merlin, do discover what you want."

How long we sat like that I do not know. My wits were stolen by her smile. She continued to look with deep sympathy into my eyes . . . my ears were pounding. After a considerable silence, she leaned back, lit a cigarette, and told me a bit about herself. Though she thoroughly enjoyed the company of men, early in her life she had decided to not marry. Not worthwhile. "Other fish to fry."

Always disconcerting, always a mere ten minutes in her presence changed my breathing, my skin temperature, and pulled my capacity for attention to tatters. Quite a few of our company shared this experience I describe. Whether men or women, it made little difference. She smoked incessantly. At the Olivet meeting, she was past fifty-five years old.

On this night, I finally realized she was expecting an answer.

"What I want at this moment totally overrides what I believe I want."

"I know about this moment. What about the other?"

"I said it is overridden . . . gone—"

"Then it is of no consequence . . . Merlin, my dear, do remember who you are . . . it's now or never."

Somehow I managed to blurt out that I wanted her friendship. To my eternal good fortune, it was now.

Notes on a Visit
Bors

Exuberance piled on exuberance, the roses in the monastic garden are a mass of thorny bushes impossible to gain access into, yet they seem pruned. Since I do not see how anyone could have gotten in among them, they must have grown that way. Pythagorean roses tuned to the fifths.

To explain how I got here, we must back track a few weeks. I had given myself a breather from my customary summer activity in order to indulge an interest in Saint Anthony. Some women are touched by those men who most need to repudiate us, those who are driven by love and attraction to hate and struggle against even the thought of us. So I was in Yugoslavia.

This day I was trekking along the Dalmatian Coast. Official literature placed the site of Anthony's first illuminatory cave not too far away. It is a glorious, rugged coastline. The sun beats off the Adriatic, its rays reflectively caught in the moist air and bouncing off multiple rock faces appearing to surround me in a moving field of light. In this blaze I had gone on for two miles this morning along a rock path. It had rained the night before. Along some patches the footing was treacherous. But spicy smells of wild flowers and herbs growing along the path now and then gusted into my face. They display some valor to grow here because there is a lot of salt spray.

As I rounded an outreached rock, I came upon a ragged individual sitting and seeming to doze in the morning sun, his head on his knees. My progress on the path must have had some good crunch to it because he instantly looked up and smiled widely (I thought, at the time, crazily). He was pretty tall and took a lot of unwinding to stand fully up. After some study, he greeted me in a difficult Serbian dialect. I had a hard time at first to make out what he was saying. He simply wanted to know why I was here. When I mentioned Saint Anthony, he stared and then laughed. Then he asked where the cave might be. I showed him the map I had with me.

"Nah . . . this is the cave of poor Linus. He was a minister of Emperor Leo who fell into disgrace some say. He spent the last years of his life there, where you have that mark. Either he spent them in disgraceful seclusion or spiritual isolation . . . who knows . . . The cave of Anthony is really over there . . ."

He pointed to a small dark patch about half a mile further up the path. When I asked how he could be sure, he shrugged and started toward the cave. I followed along. At any rate, it was in the direction I was headed.

To shorten a long story, after we had reached it about an hour later and had hunkered down near each other and shared some bread and cheese I had with me, he convinced me of his familiarity with the region and its history. By now it was midmorning. He gave me some water from a skin he was carrying. It was a fine moment. Then he told me about the community he belonged to and urged me to visit. I could feel the nerve endings, which the past year had grown raw, healing in the warm sun.

They, the C—brotherhood, had been founded long before the birth of Anthony. They saw part of their charter to be the maintenance of scrupulous records. He was unable to make it plain to me at the time, but somehow they deemed this activity essential to their mode of Christian life. He went on to explain that my scholarly credentials prepared me perfectly well to visit them deep in the midst of Montenegro. The authorities now classified the monastery as a museum. He explained further to me how to arrange for a visit and how to get there. He winked and told me the government would fall over itself to pave the way for an American scholar to visit their "museum." When he was satisfied that I fully intended to give it a try, he stood up, bid me goodbye, and walked off. Left alone, I pondered what had happened.

So, in this way some days later, I found myself standing in the monastery garden. Government officials acted as he predicted and issued me the appropriate travel permits with only a few restrictions. Primary was that I was to let them develop any film I might expose during the trip. But I never carry a camera, so that was easy.

The garden was amazing. In a way the rose bushes stood like a small storm of fiery thorns guarding the way to the Abbot's quarters. And who is an abbot but a guardian cherub?

He was a bleak man. He kept me standing while he pored over my credentials far longer than necessary or tolerable. Finally, without yet looking at me, he took his eyes off the papers and dropped them to stare at a burl on his chestnut desk.

"You're the one Vlado found prancing in the rocks near Anthony's cave."

Prancing was not quite the word, but I admitted it. Then he looked up with very mild eyes and explained gently that women were a distraction to their lifestyle. However, since in recent years the government had put them under the jurisdiction of a female cultural commissar, they had become accustomed to occasional women around the "museum." I was granted permission to walk around the grounds, the church, and to make use of the library. He insisted that I avoid the men's private quarters. He asked me to return here to his study for lunch.

I went directly to the library. The librarian, a young, almost winsome man, flashed me an ingratiating smile and offered me any help I might need. I told him that first I wished to be able to context their "brotherhood" in history.

Long before the arrival of Christianity here, this place had served as a special site for meetings every six years. The clans of what is now called the Alfold Plain, the Walachian Plain, and the Dinaric and Transylvania Alp-sconce held council of mountain, hill, and plains peoples where the present "museum" stands. It most likely was a place of special veneration, sacred to the Great Mother. Since these peoples had always accepted the presence of garrisons without hostility, the Roman Empire supported these regular clan gatherings. The region, in Roman eyes, was a convenient buffer against barbarian tribes from the northeast.

Christianity arrived as an outcome of a memorable visit by Saint Bartholomew to one of their sexennial meetings. The record is silent about the content of their discussions. But a small parcel of land was given to a band of Christians, and a charter was signed permitting them to build a little church. The present-day chapel of the Virgin is reputed to be on this precise site. Generations later, an event occurred that had major consequence for the C—.

Their pastor, in a rare journey, went to witness the Council of Chalcedon. The events and the intrigues surrounding the council precipitated a crisis of faith for him. After three years pondering his experience, he set forth a directive for the community. Hereafter, although they were to sincerely maintain an attitude of friendliness toward all ecclesiastical authority, they were never to inwardly choose the side of any bishop of Rome, Greece, Egypt, or Asia Minor. He put successive generations in a difficult position. With time it became very difficult since the bishops of Rome were geographically close and began to exercise more and more political power among the churches.

As their rule evolved over time, it did not insist on lifetime monasticism for the brothers. They based their life on the rule for Nazirs in the Old Testament. Members of the community were dedicated for very exact periods of time. I found this fascinating, but very little was explicitly described. I resolved to enquire of the abbot about this.

The C—s had a very low status in the church. Often they were considered a pariah community . . . the off-scourings. For periods of time, people in the surrounding areas who had been baptized and confirmed in the church at C—could not marry Christians of other communities without special considerations. At times, after the late Middle Ages, they had to undergo what amounted to a conversion. But there were other periods when this was not the case. All in all the community weathered the vagaries of political pressure and changes in empire with little more than ordinary disruption.

That morning there was nothing I found to hint at the highly original and profound tradition which Vlado alluded to in Dalmatia. Lunch time had arrived, and I left the materials on the table and eagerly left the library.

To my delight, when I arrive at the abbot's study, my mysterious friend from the cave I found was joining us for lunch. Although my host had mentioned him, and often during the past several weeks I had thought of him, I was nearly convinced he was made of air. Without saying hello he greeted me with sarcasm.

"As usual I suppose you have been looking in the wrong place for the wrong thing."

"Like hell! That's not my usual way."

"What ought to catch your attention is the fact of the history . . . not the facts in it . . ."

Mildly the abbot intervened:

"Our rule is and has been always to maintain as impartial a record of events that happen to us or that we become aware of as is humanly possible. You will notice that church historians such as Eusebius and Ireneus are classed under literature."

With this flat assertion the subject was dismissed, and we sat down to lunch. I asked them about the Nazir rules and drew from them bemused glances and no comment besides a shift of conversation toward world politics, changes that seem to be happening to the world's weather, and the march of fickle new fashions. I had decided to return to the library when the abbot held me for a moment with those mild eyes.

"If you have any questions you can't answer for yourself this afternoon . . . please feel free to return in the morning. If you would care to join us for lunch again, we will try to respond."

Clearly, they did not welcome female guests at supper.

The afternoon proved fascinating. I began to get a sense of the scale, the vastness of the C—'s historical effort. But nothing intrigued me until at day's end, while gathering myself to leave, I noted a scribe's marginalia alongside some lists of material and personnel consumed during the struggle between the Crusaders and Saladin. It caught my eye because it was so strange and unexpectedly in colloquial Greek:

> Lancelot weeping for the ladder's loss. Wavering, true to character around the perimeter of the city what a laugh the timid Lion. The job was botched in the cradle. Harry and Eleanor had picked his heart to pieces . . . Mater and Pater had cast their lots for the rags and indentured the future.

The dates of the records were from the early 1190s. Certainly it was referring to the incomprehensible tactics of Richard Lion Heart when presumably trying to regain Jerusalem. The city had been seen metaphorically as the "ladder" or entry to heaven.[1]

The winsome librarian, under the influence of the clock and "punching out time," had become less charming and was glowering at me. This at least smelled promising, and I decided I would after all return in the morning.

When I got back to the neighboring village where I was billeted, I felt great. Here was a place of ravishing and simple beauty. Whether through the manipulation of the Yugoslavian government to preserve certain memorials of a more innocent national past or through plain accident, I could enjoy a mountain village of an earlier time. Like a Balkan "Brigadoon," I was in a town that seemed to breathe an air untouched by the assassination at Sarajevo.

Supper was at the inn and afterward I went for a stroll about the town square and then over the local "museum" church. The adjoining cemetery was very old. There were old markers on some of the graves with English, or Frankish, or Germanic names graven into them. This shook loose a bit more of my memory, and I began recalling details of the campaigns of Richard toward the close of the twelfth century.

In 1187, Jerusalem fell to Saladin. All Christendom bitterly lamented the loss. In 1192, Richard Lion Heart fought very successful battles and three times had come as close as six miles from the city. All three times his resolve wavered and he seemed reluctant to attempt the recapture. It never seemed true to the character of heroic Richard to waffle like this. The scribe, with a pre-Freudian incision, seemed to suggest that our hero had been eviscerated by some "beak sharpening" on the part of Eleanor of Aquitaine and Henry II. Well enough so far . . . but the intriguing idea of identifying Lancelot with Richard was a stunner. If the entry was contemporary with the record, then it phased nicely with Chrétien de Troyes composing his Comte de Grail and Robert de Boron his Joseph . . . and well before Wolfram. In all the "Grail poems," Lancelot came near but was unable to actually approach the Grail? What a splendid track to open up. When I returned to the inn, the thoughts were buzzing so furiously that I had a hard time getting to sleep.

As early as decent, I drove up the next morning to the monastery of C—. Vlado was waiting for me outside the library. An astonishing man! He was out of his "habit" and fitted out in an excellently tailored suit. His mustache, which I barely noticed while he was in rags or in monk's garb, now seemed to charge at one—it was so neatly trimmed and waxed and turned. He didn't wait for me to speak.

"My dear lady, I see something has caught your interest. Good. We would like you to leave here with something of value for your work. But the way our archives are arranged, you won't be able to follow it through very far without help. Could you say what caught your interest?"

I explained what I found and how I had interpreted it. He was standing with his back to the rose garden. He waited long enough to fit a cigarette into a fine amber holder before he answered. I had the chilling thought that for some reason I was being maneuvered by a KGB agent. After all, first I had met him clambering in rags among rocks, then at lunch he wore the monastic habit, and now he was standing framed against an unforgettable glory of roses on an early morning and dressed with impeccable continental dash. I couldn't contain my sudden nervousness and barked:

"What are you . . . some secret agent?"

"I understand your confusion . . . but no, I am not. I am what I said. I was hoping though, that later this morning you might reciprocate our kindnesses to you and give me a lift to Z—. I have some business there. These are my city clothes. Come, let's go into the library and see what we can find that helps."

While we were raising a small dust storm going through long undisturbed volumes, the librarian was busy duplicating material from a list Vlado had given him. It wasn't until later that day when we were in the town of Z—that he began to pull all of our morning's work together.

First he wanted to show me some entries in a chronicle held in the Provincial Museum in town. Though it did not meet hard scientific criteria, it convinced me that there were reference points outside the monastery that at least lent credence to some of their claims.

The C—base their world view on a unique reading of the Gospels . . . a Gospel epistemology. By insisting always that their work was merely historical and not doctrinal, they managed to steer free of those crags of controversy that have sunk many bigger ships than theirs. Their scholarly time was spent trying to understand chronologies, epics, and particular events in the light of their "plain sense." They claimed no interest in subtle doctrines, nor did they ever espouse heretical or "Gnostic" teachings. They survived.

Their exemplary interpreter of Scripture epistemology is Jesus as Logos. In the Gospel narratives, he often explicates the Teaching, the Prophets, and the Writings. That Jesus functions as *interpreter* par excellence in no way detracts from their acceptance of him as *interpretation* of Scripture.

As mentioned above, they charted a course that kept them out of the whirlpools following the Council of Chalcedon in 451. This doctrinal debate was, they held, a "red herring" to mask the real issues, which were struggles over the location of church authority. Logos as discriminator always was laying bare these kinds of bones.

They demonstrate that throughout the Gospels Jesus manifests this activity. Each time he was being tested by others concerning his "understanding" of the Teaching (their translation of Torah, "The Law"), he showed subtly and sometimes not so subtly that behind the exchanges contests were going on over the seat of authority at that time . . . in that place. Since they are followers of Jesus, having been founded by Bartholomew, the C—have felt themselves perpetually tasked and mandated to apply this kind of critique to all matters.

Mysticism is a means to arrive at the condition they consider to be the human birthright. Described simply, this is a balance of the human endowment so that divine reason can become active. They make a necessary distinction between certain "states," "forces," and "spiritual flashes" which, though seeming similar, may have opposite results. The C—succinctly define these as that which *blinds* reason and that which *illuminates* reason. As Christians they do *not* equate Jesus with other prophets. However, a certain posture vis-a-vis the world is "shared." Using a slight turn of sign, they can say that Christ as teacher is present in the long ago as well as the today. What is shared—and this is surprising among the religious—is the "skepticism" of all great teachers. Moses, Zoroaster, Laotze, Confucius, Buddha, Muhammad, and, of course, Jesus were skeptics in relation to the world systems they were born into. They were skeptical of the received religions practiced and understood in *that* world. The C—do not feel free to cast aside this responsibility.

Now that Vlado had prepared the background, he proceeded to become specific. My gate into their lore was what had caught my interest, namely the "ladder's loss." He now employed this period of history to show the nature of their practical activity.

In those days, the C—were strongly censured for their position about the Crusades, their neutrality. But they felt that eagerness to fight wars had led to dishonesty in the highest places. At the beginning of the fifth Crusade, Pope Innocent III called the Germans to war with an unconscionable distortion of the nature of faith. Prior to the Pope's dereliction, it had been customary for several centuries that the propagandists introduced slight changes into the weight of language in support of the feudal system. Innocent III formalized and lent sanction to this deliberate misunderstanding. *Fideles*, believers, became weighted to signify *vassals.*[2] Language and propaganda had altered the terms of belief from believers *in* Christ to vassals *of* Christ. This was profoundly unfortunate because the force of emotion becomes shifted from faith to loyalty. Loyalty connoted killing in behalf of one's party. The C—at this time could not translate their ancient faith into an oath of political allegiance. If the appeal had been made on grounds of politics or justice, they may have answered it. But they could not, especially in light of their Gospel epistemology, perjure their souls. The purport of the pope's statement was that those who did not fight would be accused by Christ of "unbelief . . . and of lack of loyalty to their liege lord."

"De ingratitudinis crimine vos damnabit, si ei quasi ejecto de regno."

Vlado's brotherhood could neither swallow it nor encourage those who sought their advice to swallow it. He turned the harmonic of his discourse up a spiral of fifths. He now wished to discuss "that marvelous mystic," Meister Eckhart.

Vlado had two reasons for this to be the springboard of our discourse. One was that much of his work is now readily available and, to the attentive student, quite accessible. The second reason was more important. This great man's work had been appropriated by the detestable Nazi mystagogues. Vlado wished both to protest the violation and provide an example of how the absence of skepticism can derange our reading of the past "masters." Any history can be distorted by current authoritarian claims.

He took out of the folder we had brought from C—the copies that had been made in the library. There were records of communication between a monk of the community and Meister Eckhart. There were spirited discussions of literary works of the period. Then he showed me a much earlier letter. One of the monks, it seems, was a friend of Wolfram von Eschenbach. With the loss of Jerusalem, the spiritual geography of the Christian world had changed profoundly. He urged Wolfram to strive to establish a "new geography," one that could be inwardly discovered by the reader. It was clear that Jerusalem in the physical sense would no longer be able to embody the European longing for the "Grail." Wolfram started work on Parzifal during 1203 or 1204. And his challenge, as set forth by the monk, was to work on its inner significance and find a "geosophical" location for the "Grail" in the West so that meaning could be redeemed for Western civilization. Vlado turned to a group of documents from the 1260s. It seems that a successor to the above monk's activities, a Brother Marcus, had established relations with a certain Albrecht while the monk was in his early years of training. This Albrecht was none other than the author of *Titurel*. Many years later, Brother Marcus made a journey through the Rhineland as an itinerant preacher. At this time, Meister Eckhart was still a young man and was quite taken by the flair of the older, eccentric, "non-attached" friar. Taking this opportunity and sensing the younger man's potential, he impressed upon the young Eckhart the value of the symbolisms developed by both Wolfram and Albrecht. Some of the material I was shown was of fairly technical nature regarding the nature of poetics. The work of the above poets was fairly well-known to all persons familiar with middle-high German and the "symbolisms" had percolated thoroughly through the "mass culture."

In time, Eckhart came to see how the judicious use of the "symbolism" could bring his own "conceptions" into contact with the deeper intuitions of the people. He determined that it was possible to recapture for individuals the transcendent implication of "place." Usually at this time, notions regarding the "uncreated" dimension of the human soul were associated with metaphors of "light" (the scintilla). Eckhart set about to harmonize these intuitions with such homely metaphors of *place* as *castellum* and *burglein*.

At this time, I interjected. As he had been developing this theme in far greater detail than I am representing it, I became furious. I told Vlado that he was going far toward supporting the Nazis' appropriation of Eckhart. Didn't he recall that it was not only Eckhart whom the Nazi beast claimed as prophet but also Wolfram and Albrecht? I pointed out to him that though his "ancient history" was pretty good, his grasp of modern history was lacking.

A) Both Eckhart and Wolfram had been appropriated by the mythology of National Socialism to provide legitimacy for their ideology.

B) Alfred Rosenburg, the Nazi theoretician, had called on the "Aryan" to find their ideal in the glorious "Eckhartian man."

C) Almost all German scholars and academics rallied to support those conclusions.

D) Eckhart had been "drafted" to provide spiritual legitimacy. Wolfram and Albrecht, as distilled through Wagner, had provided the emotional material for the persuasion of the German masses.

He was not happy to be reminded of this, but he accepted it. Furthermore, it was directly on course toward the theme he was developing. No matter how genuine, how deeply valid, religious, and cultural material may be, if it is not faced and studied with a correlated critical attitude and healthy skepticism, it can become twisted into its opposites. He became heated, and I remember the words he used, because at one point they became uncharacteristically purple:

"In the hands of those who worship themselves . . . those who would offer sacrifice on the defiled altars of their own greed, ambition, and sickness . . . yes, then lilies fester worse than weeds . . . the true, the good, the beautiful becomes the handmaiden of evil."

He admitted that at times he wondered if the C—did not have some share in the culpability. They had projected some of their ideas into the currents of the twelfth and thirteenth century life of Europe. In the twentieth century, the very mediums they had employed were in their turn appropriated to evil. But then we must remember that this phenomenon relentlessly occurs. Even the root classics such as the Bible and Koran have at times been appropriated to wickedness. Were it not that this particular case illustrated a general law, he would be tempted to stop any apostolic work and spend the rest of his life in penitence.[3]

Vlado went on. What is important to grasp is the importance of *thought:*

"Thought is what we are about."

After a long silence, he explained that all those who exploited Eckhart had ignored his thought. They bought what he stimulated them *to feel.* Could the Nazis have taken him to their bosoms if they had realized that he was a profound student of the Jew, Maimonides? How would they have accepted that he used a text from Maimonides for his defense against the charges of heresy that had been brought against him? I had to confess that I was unaware of this. Vlado said that it could be found referred in Eckhart's defense to Article 23 of the Papal Bull of Condemnation.[4]

We cooled down, and Vlado proceeded with his presentation.

C—tradition always looks toward balance and completeness. Eckhart earns their admiration because he, like themselves, had kept firm in the face of the warring parties of the time. In simple terms, the contending factions were the Thomists and Augustinians. Again in simple terms, this can be seen as a continuation of the contentions between Platonists and Aristotelians. Eckhart accomplished this by not evading the issue but by pushing his feet down through both viewpoints to reach undisturbed ground from where he could accept and incorporate both schools of thought. His accomplishment by doing this was to transvalue them and to achieve, contrary to common views of this work, a life-affirming and world-affirming mysticism. Those who would mine Eckhart for their own private mythologies always turn a blind eye to his Thomism and Aristotelianism. Also, they will avoid careful study of his unusual language. But in fact, Eckhart reveals that Plato is the proper digestive juice for Aristotle and Aristotle for Plato.

Vlado now wished to turn toward the "magic" mentioned above whereby Eckhart made interior *place* as well as *light* work as a metaphor of the *uncreated*. Both the poets and the philosophers were engaged in the common task of recovering meaning for Christendom after the fall of Jerusalem. In Eckhart's second sermon, the topic is Luke 10:38. Literally translated, the Gospel text reads

". . . he entered a certain village, and a woman there named Martha welcomed him to her home."

But Eckhart renders it

". . . which is translated so: Our Lord Jesus Christ went up into a little castle and was received by a virgin who was a wife."

(A digression is in order here. The "place" of the Grail in the poetic traditions was a small castle. As far as qualities, the Grail for Chrétien emitted light, for Wolfram it radiated heat. At the time Albrecht composed *Titurel*, he held to the earlier qualities but combined them into a "fire and water crystal." Church artists of the time were making the following representations in their altar art: ". . . a little Madonna knelt under a 'glory' of fire in a Gothic chapel," i.e., in a little castle).

In Eckhart's sermon, this "castellum" is the place of the human person which is free and wherein God is received and the "Son" begotten. He had employed all the elements that over the past few generations had become part of the discourse of his audience. By doing this, he was able to connect his words and the activity of Logos with the great streams of feeling liberated by the Grail romances and impart to them a certain direction. As a great teacher, he was scrupulous to do this "magic" with consummate lightness. He employed the harmonics of structure and relationship rather than burdening the listener with literal material images which would have been inappropriate in the context of his sermons.

The C—hold that the study of Eckhart, either by design or by "accident," discloses and re-elevates the intentionality of the Grail poems. By the same "sea-change," the poems give substance and impetus toward the study of Meister Eckhart. The *rough magic* needed for this "opera" is found in the passion toward the fullest possible comprehension of a real historical contextualization of the twelfth and thirteenth centuries. Hence the dedication of the C—to preserving the widest possible historical record.

The effort faces a recurring problem intrinsic for Western humanity. Scholars continuously are biased toward either romanticism or reduction. They find their footing either with ideology or abstraction. Partiality toward any party eats at the trunk of their healthy and skeptical faith.

The afternoon in Z—was intellectually dazzling. But even more stupefying was what they have to say about Patristics and the development of the Christian faith. That would require at least a volume to open up the subject. Remember, the above discussion rotates merely about one sentence of translation. And even that is touched superficially.

Upon our return to C—, I was pleased to discover that I was expected to join the community for supper. Everyone was in their best habits and very cordial to me. The atmosphere was very special and festive.

After the meal, I learned that the real reason for the festive atmosphere in the refectory was that a new evolution of the community's function had been initiated. A full one-third of the brothers were being sent "into the world" on various missions to countries of both East and West. Vlado was among those to be sent forth.

Notes

1. *De Perigrinante Civitate Dei* by Henry of Albano described the place of the Cross and Tomb; i.e., Jerusalem, as the ladder which might lead to the heights of spirituality.
2. I have found an argument very close to this in Helen Adolf, Visio Pacis, p. 47-48.
3. A ghastly example of this indiscriminate human tendency occurred near the very region of Bors's visit. During World War II, according to some estimates, seven hundred thousand persons of Serbian Orthodox national faith were liquidated by Croatian Roman Catholics. The leader of this intrafaith pogrom was Pavelic, the Croatian dictator whose regime was hailed at its inception with enthusiasm by Archbishop Stepinac of Zagreb. Oddly enough, it seems that the Orthodox Christian victims were offered the choice between death and conversion to Catholicism. It is peculiar that so very few were either able or willing to take advantage of the offer. Furthermore strange (though obviously not according to Brother Vlado) is the fact that apparently the Croatian Franciscans were in the forefront of the crimes. It certainly requires a specially tendentious reading of *The Little Flowers of St. Francis* to find therein a program for murder. Apparently, any differences, not merely mystical or philosophic, are sufficient cause for this kind of behavior.
4. Eckhart's answer to article 23 of the *Papal Bull of Condemnation* can be found in Raymond Blakeney's *Meister Eckhart*, p. 289. "A hundred men are many and numbered; a thousand angels are many and without

number; but the three persons in the Trinity are neither many nor numbered. If they are many they would not be one. It must be said that this is true, according to I John 5:7, 'these three are one.' For deprivation is the beginning of number, but the beginning of multiplicity is negation, but in God there is no deprivation nor yet negation, since there is fullness of being." At this time, Eckhart also produced a text from Maimonides regarding the "substance of God." See Schurmann, *Meister Eckhart*, Indiana University press, Chapter 3, Note 33. "Echod, One, in whatever way you consider it; under any examination you will find to be one, indivisible in all its modes and in all regards; and you will find multiplicity neither inside its intelligence nor outside its intelligence."

CHAPTER THREE

Lama

"Lama," or Marshall Davidson, was born on the East Coast of the United States. His family were wealthy ethical culturists. For that kind of upbringing, his early years were normal. However, while an undergraduate at Yale, he became an anglophile and moved to England to pursue his studies. He took firsts in Classics. He had already joined the Royal Navy with some fellow classmates when World War II began. Under the pressure of the circumstance of *this* war, he rediscovered his Jewish roots and, when he could, spent whatever time came available to study his "tradition." Access to special information during and after the war revealed shocking mendacity among all concerned, which led him into a long involvement with Far Eastern religion. It proved a blind alley for him. He regained his American citizenship and returned to the States where he assumed a position at a small Iowa college.

He published an exceptional article in *Speculum* about the influence of Virgil on Chaucer. This captured the attention of an associate of Amfortas. A year later, a piece titled "Shakespearean

Nekiya" led to a correspondence which brought him into membership with the society.

*   *   *

His most arresting quality was his voice, in spite of the fact that he looked utterly unique. Lama was taller than average, always superbly dressed, and he was topped off by flaring wild hair, reminding me of nothing so much as of a tangled corn husk's crown. Now his voice was always measured, and the words he spoke seemed to hang far from the ideas they expressed. To listen to him speak placed the listener square in the Augustinian paradox of a time somehow stretched between the soul's *intentio*, *distentio*, and *extentio*. One could not but heed him. I often thought it must have been a remarkable experience to have served in the Royal Navy under his command.

Our encounters were usually in Chicago, because I traveled on a tight schedule and it was hard to get Sioux City flights with any flexibility. He found the occasions of value because he could take the opportunity to look through some odd bookstores and visit the Art Institute where he enjoyed their exceptional Oriental collection.

Lama had a great power of abstraction. In a restaurant, for example, if he was following a train of thought, he could seem to vanish before one's eyes. Also, and I suspect it is related to this feature, he had an uncanny intuition of events happening at a distance. Part of the agreements made by members of Amfortas was never to question another about extraordinary gifts or experiences unless invited to do so. He never invited. However, on occasions I know of from others and one personal experience, he managed to contact members of the society who were on the verge of some dangerous exposure and to warn them to avoid certain acts. Through his intervention, fatal accidents to three of our fellows were averted.

According to the Order of Melchizedek

Lama

[The following is a nearly verbatim transcript of a conversation on a spring afternoon in a suburb of Toulouse. I have chosen to assign the name Ephraim Lunel to the rabbi I interviewed because it was in the town of Lunel that a major kabbalistic work, _The Bahir_, was first published. This, of course, is not the rabbi's name.]

Toulouse, March 30
The Study of Rabbi Ephraim Lunel

Lama: We thank you, Rabbi, for agreeing to this interview.

R. Ephraim: Is this a form you have to follow?

Lama: What do you mean, sir?

R. Ephraim: This "we thank you . . ." and the rest. Also I do not respond well to "sir."

Lama: Rabbi, I came to interview you about your views about religion.

R. Ephraim: Does it interest you?

Lama: Of course.

R. Ephraim: Why of course . . . ? That is never of course. Do you always wear a hat indoors?

Lama: No . . . I thought . . .

R. Ephraim: You don't look authentic in it, you know. Why not try to be yourself?

Lama: Very well . . .

R. Ephraim: Much better . . . don't you feel more normal?

Lama: Yes.

R. Ephraim: Good . . . Now, you were saying, "about religion?"

Lama: Yes, in America recently several books have addressed themselves to the growing conflict between Reform, Conservative, and Orthodox denominations.

R. Ephraim: Do they call them that . . . denominations . . . like money?

Lama: Sometimes we do, sir.

R. Ephraim: Hmmph . . .

(A long silence.)

Lama: Do you have an opinion?

R. Ephraim: That subject is not worth the trouble of an opinion.

Lama: But sure it is one of the most pressing issues in the contemporary Jewish world . . .

R. Ephraim: Not in my Jewish world.

Lama: Your world, as you put it, has been referred to by some authorities as heretical, by some others as the world of an ignoramus. In a recent publication you have been called a latter-day Kairite.[2]

R. Ephraim: That is rather encouraging . . . oh, no, not that I am called names . . . but that you are easily provoked.

Lama: How so?

R. Ephraim: Why do you suppose?

Lama: I have no idea.

R. Ephraim: A good start.

Lama: I see . . . you wish the interviewer to have no ideas.

R. Ephraim: That is impossible. But to say one has no idea could be the beginning of manners.

Lama: Well . . . how do I begin?

R. Ephraim: Begin.

Lama: What do you believe?

R. Ephraim: Ahhh . . .

(A long silence.)

I believe that at the beginning of God's creating of the heavens and the earth/the earth was tohu va-vohu/darkness over the face of Tehom/Wind of God hovering over the face of the waters./God said . . . "be light . . . and there is light."

Lama: You believe in the Bible . . .

R. Ephraim: I believe in God . . . Tell me, why did you want to interview me, of all people?

Lama: I heard some of the attacks on you as I mentioned. I am intrigued. You contributed a piece to *Annales*[3] about marriage contracts in the region of Troyes at the time of Rashi . . .

R. Ephraim: Did you read it?

Lama: No . . . I read a review of it . . .

R. Ephraim: And—

Lama: You were called simultaneously excessively "Talmudic" and "non-Jewish."

R. Ephraim: And this intrigued you?

Lama: Frankly, yes . . . How do you understand this kind of reception?

R. Ephraim: Merely that readers tend to ignore the contexts within which I may nest my discourse. Years ago I was careful in delineating it . . . but I soon discovered that it made little difference. So now I play a game with myself. I bury the contextual signifiers like a dog buries his bone. Look, Mr. Interviewer, I am a rabbi by ordination. I make no pretense of pastoral calling. Also, I have no doubt that I am exactly everything I've been called . . . at least from the viewpoint of the accuser. My lineage of study is a very small, barely perceptible school of thought never comfortable within the mainstream of Judaism. Nevertheless, like the other so-called normative divisions, my "school" is of great antiquity and to my satisfaction of profound trustworthiness.

Lama: I didn't know that.

R. Ephraim: How could you?

Lama: Are you an observant Jew?

R. Ephraim: I do observe that you are still uneasy that I am wearing a hat while you aren't. You don't have to blend in, you know . . . this isn't the Roman army. Come, why don't you ask the questions that really interest you? If you don't . . . how will I have the chance to discuss what interests me . . . ? And *my* beloved time will have gone into that place the Americans call the Bermuda Triangle.

Lama: Yes . . . how can one live a life toward God?

[Rabbi Lunel looked at me speculatively. He pressed a small button on his desk and nearly instantly a young boy poked his head through the door. The rabbi asked for tea and pastry].

R. Ephraim: I like the question. I warn you that I will answer it in my own way, in my own form and sequence . . . Because what I have to say is not really *in* the words. Still, after the sentences have done their work and the discourse has vanished into time . . . the words will remain. For example . . . if you publish this no one will believe that I have said what I will be saying. Apart from your own sense of "sureness" you, yourself, will not be certain that I in fact mean anything I say. I will not verify my saying . . . you will have to verify.

Lama: Agreed . . . the conversation is open to question
             before it begins and the meaning will be open to
             question after the conversation is over.

R. Ephraim: Excellent . . . now your question could be shortened
             to "what is the way." Mr. Buber was perceptive
             when he said somewhere, "if it is not *toward* God it
             is not a way . . ." or something like that. Now bear
             with me while rather than bury, I will explicate the
             context of my views.

Lama: Of course.

R. Ephraim: We call ourselves the "School of Shem." You recall
             that Shem was described in Genesis as the son of
             Noah. In the laconic style of that text the nature of
             the knowledge of our school is hinted at through
             the formulation, "Blessed be YHWH/The God of
             Shem."

Lama: But all Jews are descended from Shem.

R. Ephraim: Genetically true. Knowledge, though, is not
             exclusively genetic any more than language is. Even
             in the Talmud students are signified . . . "sons." For
             us, students are called sons even if they are women.
             According to the text, Shem lived six hundred
             years. In those days when the system of sexagesimal
             mathematics was the style . . . six hundred meant a
             complete number. Then if we reckon up the numbers
             literally, it would appear that Shem was still living
             at the time of Abraham. On this point "normative"
             Jewish tradition and ourselves agree . . . namely
             that at that time Shem was called Melchizedek, the
             King of Shalem.[4] We assert that this refers to the
             existence of the school in Jerusalem at that time.
             For us then, Abraham's journey out of his "father's
             house and land" was a returning upward toward the

spiritual homeland of his ancestral teaching. Out of biology . . . into biography. Since those days much as happened. But still, as in the days of Abraham, the school of Shem exists . . . off the beaten track.

Lama: Not credible . . . you expect me to believe that a school exists now dating from the time of the Flood?

R. Ephraim: Recall our premise. I'm not expecting you to believe anything.

Lama: Very well. How come it is so unknown?

R. Ephraim: That depends on what *you mean* . . . unknown.

Lama: What are its main tenets?

R. Ephraim: The relation of language to thought has certain outcomes; language is a kind of spell. In most languages those who think and speak are enthralled to a tightly constrained conception of "Being." Everything said, thought, averred, and necessarily everything conceived is bound into the netting of the verb *to be*. The essential building block whether of description, exhortation, or whatever, is . . . *is*. To us this means that a kind of "shell" forms around all thought . . . and *that* shell precisely *is* the limitation created by our notions of "being." In most language this fact is veiled as though by a sleeping potion. To disrobe this condition calls for a major effort of reduction. Furthermore, in almost all tongues, the word for God is not the word or, if you will, not the sign of "being." Therefore people have to add on and say such thing as "God" exists, meaning by that, "God is." From the start then God is conditioned . . . in trying to think "God" . . . by Being. To escape this constraint, the thinkers of some cultures have had to postulate "nonbeing." But however they slice it, the dialectics of "nonbeing" are sill hinged firmly to the shell . . . they represent admirable attempts, through the given system . . . to go beyond it. In the formulation I mentioned earlier, YHWH, the God of Shem, something quite different is occurring. The letters YHWH comprise themselves the very elements of the verb "to be" through all its usages. So then, Shem's "god" is discovered in every thought one can think with language. This being so it is not in any way able to be exhausted through language. Follow me . . . since the "name" comprises the essentiality of language, there is no way it can be defined, named, explained, nor pronounced. In fact, to call it the "unpronounceable name" is a tautology. Since the letters composing the name are in addition both vowels and consonants, pray say how it could be pronounced? Regrettably in making this assertion we are again caught in the net of "thinking being . . ." but considering my words only hints, one can say that the "name" points toward all possible modulations of being, time, space, and what is *not* that . . . etc. It points in short to beyond "being."

Lama: Is that any different than to say that God is unknowable in essence as is held by both Christianity and Islam?

R. Ephraim: That question has already been answered. Think about it.

Lama: I must say that I am becoming a bit irritated and angry.

R. Ephraim: Ahh . . .

                    [There was a long silence and, if my memory serves me, it covered two events. One was a genuine look of surprise on Rabbi Ephraim's face, the first such look I had seen. The second was the arrival of the boy with our refreshments].

Forgive me. It is a fault of mine that I often provoke anger in well-meaning people. I seem so sure of myself in areas of some fragility for others. Please bear with me. We *are* headed, believe it or not toward an answer to your primary question. But I think it is a good moment to draw back from this kind of examination to another.

Lama: Really, I apologize for being so touchy. It's not like me . . . I don't really understand myself.

R. Ephraim: It's fine . . . devash. Let's take a light subject and look at what strange things happen to simple thoughts. Consider the rainbow. For normative Judaism the rainbow acquired the aura of ill omen, it was only the fortunate who did *not* see one. Much later, another world, another time the famous Cotton Mather described it as the sign of evil and even as an emblem for the "devil." And now I understand that in America his descendents are accusing those children who have chosen this very sign for their "banner," of dereliction and wickedness. How can this be? Where is the sense? After all, in the Scriptural story of the Flood it was placed in the skies as a testimony of God's intrinsic Alliance with Noah and all earth. But it must infuriate people. Was it too full of glamor or, as Socrates may have said, "too Gorgias?"[5] I find it particularly unfortunate that between the fifteenth and the eighteenth centuries, Noah was a person denigrated by the "normative" branch of my own tradition in many homilies and interpretations. I must ask why the figure of Noah and the sign of the Alliance is so troublesome?

Lama: I had never thought about it.

R. Ephraim: It is not easy to think about.

             [He took the occasion to pronounce the blessing
             over the pastries, and we spent a few moments
             quietly eating].

R. Ephraim: We believe that the difficulty people have with an
             adequate relationship to the narrative of Noah is
             that this particular section or "breath" of scripture
             is charged with the soul of sublime common sense.
             And it is the common sense embedded in the sign of
             the rainbow, the "body" of Noah, and also through
             the fibers of the school of Shem that is exasperating
             for people.

Lama: I feel that we are skirting absurdity if not obscurity.

R. Ephraim: Follow me a few steps here . . . we obviously cannot
             today exhaust the section . . . by its nature we
             cannot. But we can bear some interesting ideas. In
             the line usually translated in English or French as
             "make," "establish," etc., . . . that is the line, "The
             sign of the Alliance which I *make* . . ." etc., . . . the
             word is actually in Hebrew, *berithi*, which literally
             means "give." This should be the starting point of
             our thinking about it. The "giving" is the sign of
             the Alliance. Nothing else quite like it occurs in
             scripture . . . a giving that is set in the clouds. Now,
             the act of giving and receiving is always *prior* to any
             "consciousness of" . . . It is prior to schematization
             or thematization. It *is* an accord prior to thinking
             about it . . . it is a *chord* sounded and struck before
             the harmonies are discernible. It is an "octave," if
             you will, set into the clouds of heaven by which I
             receive the other. In this act, humanity, the earth, and
             all that dwell therein take on a meaning one for the

other. Proximity is established, and with proximity always arrives responsibility for and to the other. In short, it is evidence of an alliance. Then we have here an identity that does not coincide with itself. Please make it real to yourself . . . the event is an irreplaceable identity signified and set into the world of meaning, into heaven by "giving to the other."

> [I motioned for him to stop a moment as I found this hard to follow. And I played it back for myself several times until it made some sense. Then I nodded and Rabbi Ephraim continued].

The rainbow in the clouds is like the psyche in the soul. It is the way a relationship between uneven terms, without any common time, arrives at relationship. It signifies non-indifference.[6] Scripture puts it this way:

> When the bow is/in the clouds,
> I will look upon it/and remember the
> everlasting Alliance
> between God/and every living creature
> all flesh/that is upon the earth.

Yes, sublime non-indifference. How can people make of this an "evil omen"? Through the absence of common sense.

Lama: I like what you are saying! I really do, if I understand it. But it seems that for a school to exist, there must be something to transmit that is not "prior" to consciousness of . . . there must be a content.

R. Ephraim: True . . . and content there is. To communicate we have employed systems of thought, cosmologies, traditions. At times we have fostered schools of "art" and the "arts" of meditation, prayer, and ritual. Always it is firmly grounded in common sense. And the ground is shareable without recourse to mystification. It is common ground intrinsically but not easy to always get to. This stated, I must affirm that we nevertheless hold the view that religious truth is revealed.

Lama: That's a hard one.

R. Ephraim: Entertain it, please.

Lama: It seems to fly in the face of common sense.

R. Ephraim: Touche! Have some more tea before it gets cold.

[Silence.]

Our task is to see that the "knowledge of YHWH" does not vanish from earth.

Lama: With humanity's record it seems futile.

R. Ephraim: It's good you say "seems" . . . The adventure has its horrors . . . and some beauties. We must remember the Alliance, you see. By common sense, an alliance calls both parties to remember. Obviously God cannot forget. But if we forget, the result must follow . . . in our view it may be that the earth, even without flood or fire, may face simple cessation . . . a shadow of habit without substance.

Lama: More people are "remembering" God than ever.

R. Ephraim: Does it seem that way to you? Perhaps. But they are not remembering the God of the Alliance. Let us say that the representative of this, of YHWH, in the soul is the very common sense I mentioned. We can find it in all the chords of non-indifference . . . as conscience, the sense of truth and beauty and goodness. It is as common as the clouds, as the light and air and water and earth which form the matrix for the "bow in the skies." No one is void of it . . . for all were included in the giving and receiving. People can face away from God toward a self-generated "god" they wish to remember. Wouldn't it be a pity? So *then* we are called to critique, to remind, to warn, and even at times to threaten. If we are lucky, we live in a time when the call is more positive . . . to evoke, to inspire, to awaken. When truly lucky, we may be called to demonstrate beauty, truth, goodness, and even a kind of holiness. Thank you for being kind enough to listen to my polemic. Shall we turn to some content?

Lama: Absolutely.

R. Ephraim: Excellent.

> [Rabbi Ephraim stood up. I hadn't noticed before, but he was surprisingly small. During the above exchange, he had seemed tall, and as it went on, he appeared even loftier. I recalled my first impression. I was standing and he was seated and he then looked deep. Now as he stood by the chalkboard, he appeared an ordinary and quite small gentleman.]

Lama: Do you mean like "J," "P," and "E," in the Documentary Hypothesis?

R. Ephraim: Hah! Well, in a sense they were on to something, but their method was trying to beat at an omelet to unscramble it. To use two or three parties as the whisk doesn't help. The Bible is a book of a *people* . . . many pens, many inks.

Lama: And many sources. The story of the Flood was not exactly original.

R. Ephraim: A good starting point . . . but where does it differ?

Lama:	The names . . . Noah in the Bible, Utnapishtim in the Gilgamesh epic.
R. Ephraim:	Not yet enough information to use common sense.

[Here he rapidly wrote out three names on the Chalkboard:

NOAH-UTNAPISHTIM-ZIUSUDRA.]

The hero of the Sumerian flood epic is called Ziusudra. The hero of the Babylonian is called Utnapishtim. In the Bible it is Noah. However, if I write on the board the concept *one who brings comfort* or *with whom is rest*, then I would find that all three names fit under that rubric. It is a case where names sound different but point at the same meaning. Furthermore, let me write down their lineages. Nine kings before Utnapishtim, and nine world patriarchs before Noah.

Lama:	You seem to be undermining your own position . . .
R. Ephraim:	Apply your mind! We are dealing in content. So the differences will appear in the *materials* in the narratives. In these two, we have *boats*. In the story of Noah, we have a *tebva*, a rectangular vessel. It is not the word for boat. It occurs twice in scripture . . . in the Noah section and in the section about the rescue of Moses. Exodus II 3-5. We see that both the meaning and the method of surviving the Flood have changed from the Sumerian and Babylonian versions. We don't have the time to unpack this section, but for our purposes, it was a good place to start.
Lama:	The obvious place . . .
R. Ephraim:	Your word . . . obvious for what?
Lama:	The preservation of life and knowledge. Ahhh . . . Of course, Shem carries the knowledge of YHWH.

R. Ephraim: *That* kind of life, *that* kind of knowledge . . .

Lama: Something is continued with a direction imparted by the Alliance . . . Continuity in a good spirit.

R. Ephraim: Not too bad. Let's follow the association.

[Here he wrote CONTINUE on the board].

Since we can't follow every strand, let's follow that one. Do we have a person's name that relates to this?

Lama: Joseph.

R. Ephraim: Can you cite it?

Lama: Rachel said . . . "God continued me a son . . . she called him Joseph."

R. Ephraim: Not too bad . . . you *have* studied on occasion.

Lama: You also said that the word, *tebha*, is used only once again, in the deliverance of Moses from drowning.

R. Ephraim: Quite good . . . the footprints do show up. Now we don't have time to delve here too much since I am all the time attracted to your original question. And all this is by the way of coming to an answer. I would like to add one thing about this word which later you might find interesting. The substantive, without the feminine ending, means "bird cage."[8] In all of these, there are allusions to the nature of continuity.

Lama: I confess I feel out of my depth. My knowledge is not adequate to the exercise . . .

R. Ephraim: That's very good . . . what are your instincts?

Lama: What do you mean?

R. Ephraim: Where would you like to find clear footprints of Shem's school?

Lama: The time of David.

R. Ephraim: Better to see it as a chord . . . Jesse-David-Solomon.

Lama: Hmmm . . .

R. Ephraim: Much material evidence here. In a spirit of play, let's look a little, shall we? Jesse can be understood to refer to substance.[9] Surely in the three generations he initiated very substantial steps were taken. Look at the matter of the "story." A kingship is established, territory is relieved and secured, and at last a temple is built. In addition, tradition holds that much of the Book of Psalms was composed in this time as well as the three books of Solomon. Since the school of Shem-Melchizedek was located in Jerusalem, it was natural that it, rather than Hebron, becomes the capital and locus of the temple. Let's return to the literal concept of continuity. The seventy-second Psalm is entitled "Of Solomon." At its conclusion the statement is found, "end of the prayers of David son of Jesse." It also forms the closure to the second book of the Psalms. The third book begins with Psalm 73 and is called "a psalm of Asaph." In a way, this is all very curious. What can it mean?

Lama: I haven't a clue.

R. Ephraim: The full citation of naming of Joseph bears the clue. "God gathered away (asaph) my disgrace. So she called him Joseph in order to say may YHWH . . . continue (yoseph) another son to me." The relationship of antinomies and contrapletes is a primordial concept of the human mind. I don't know why I should do your work for you, but reflect a moment. The second large unit of the Book of Psalms ends with a psalm *of Solomon* and concludes by saying "end of the prayers of David son of Jesse." The succeeding large unit begins as *a psalm of Asaph*, begins under the sign of gathering away but implies the presence of continuity. Asaph was described in tradition as a chief counselor of Solomon and a leader of the makers of music. Continuities proceed by discontinuities. Music itself teaches that. Giving and taking. Out of the presenters of notes, from their being gathered back into the silence and new notes given, music comes to be. It is the continuance of discontinuance. It is the interaction of Asaph and Joseph.

Lama: Astonishing!

R. Ephraim: Only if the music is beautiful.

> [Here is a very long silence on the tape. I do not recall what we were doing.]

Lama: Elijah!

R. Ephraim: What?

Lama: Elijah is another example. Wherever tradition ascribes events to the activity of Elijah may be evidence of "the school."

R. Ephraim: It seems you are thinking by *type* of activity. Often "tradition" doesn't know what it is reporting. In some cases, yes, but in others of the same type, no. I think what you are seeing is an Elijah *type* activity common also to Christian and Muslim lore. Not that good an instrument here. It is better to discern the melody. Then you can recognize the variations that are genuine even if *against type*. When we hear the melodic line of the school of Shem . . . its continuity of discontinuity . . . then there comes a breaking in of recognition. An example: In the European Middle Ages, we produced a garland of quotations from Bible and Misnah. It is even found today in some prayer books called "Chapters of Song." We regret that it is not found in many. I guess serious people don't consider it worthy. Would you be willing to listen to a few sequences of its arrangement?

Lama: Of course . . .

R. Ephraim: The heavens declare the glory of God
                  And the firmament showeth his handiwork
                  The earth is the Lord's and the fullness thereof
                  The world and they that dwell therein . . .
                  Let the floods clap their hands
                  Let the mountains sing for joy together
                  And whether they sing or dance
                  All my thoughts are in thee.
                  Those are the beginning and concluding verses of the
                  first chapter.

Lama: How many chapters are there?

R. Ephraim: Six.

Lama: Naturally.

R. Ephraim: For you a portion of the third chapter . . .
                  How long wilt thou sleep, O sluggard?
                  When wilt thou arise out of thy sleep . . .
                  Open thine eyes . . .
                  It is time for God to work
                  For they have voided Thy teaching.
                  [Here is another long silence. Some throat Clearing.]
                  For he hath satisfied the throat of the soul
                  And the hungry soul he hath filled with good.

Lama: Rabbi, I am troubled. If what you say is true then . . .
                  then what can one believe? People don't even know
                  what they are studying. Is everyone roaming around
                  and groping in the dark?

R. Ephraim: We are approaching your question. The one you
                  have just asked is a fragment of your primary
                  question. I think we all are groping somewhat . . .
                  except of course those with *all* the answers and who
                  are merely blind. Your question holds your answer.
                  Believe what you *can* with a good heart. No more
                  and surely no less. Listen, my friend, God's world is

very big . . . would it not be churlish to cut it down in our minds to our own size?

Lama: But if all traditions have *missed the boat!*

R. Ephraim: I have not said that. They have not. But forgetting leads to forgetting. Because common sense is so uncommon and at the same time not good enough for people, magic becomes mistaken for seamanship. When that happens, one can say that, in a way, God's Law has been voided . . .

> [At this moment Rabbi Ephraim sighed. A minor detail and impossible to communicate is that the whole study seemed to disappear for an instant.]

I think the most common error is the confusion between manners and law. Each household has its own construction of manners. When the host enters, stand . . . when he sits, don't rise . . . and so on. Well, when that sort of thing is considered to be law and teaching, matters have fallen either into the realms of "magic" or of "politics." An assembly of people thinking this way is a gaggle of apprentice sorcerers. Not only in religion. It could be those seeking to become academic gods as sociologists . . . sociology is a field very much like sorcery. But this condition should not be permitted into the spiritual life. For prayer is a gift of the Almighty. When it becomes a technique for achieving "altered states" . . . then what is it? Toward whom is it? This error is the root of so much rot. Like the proverbial "tenth of an inch at the beginning," it leads to further and further elaborations. First to falsity . . . then conceit . . . then fanaticism . . . and inevitably to that causeless hatred which continually is destroying the Temple. I wanted to trace for you the bleak and terrifying *lawfulness* of this progression, this continuity. *It* is not the song of Shem. Returning to your question . . . believe what, with a good heart, you can believe. The way I just described cannot be followed with a good heart. For you I simplify. Believe what you can. Have the faith you can.

Lama: Thank you.

R. Ephraim: You are welcome.

Lama: I have strayed from the path of our inquiry.

R. Ephraim: It was thoughtful of you to do so.

[Another long silence. During it, he returned to his desk and summoned the lad to remove the dishes and cups.]

Lama: Elijah . . .

R. Ephraim: Yes . . .

Lama: His appearances in Scripture and in Lore have just that quality of discontinuity and continuity.

R. Ephraim: Yes . . .

Lama: He appears . . . he goes. He breaks through the fabric of events. But the breaking through is continuation of an essential layer behind *that* and under the event . . .

R. Ephraim: Or above it . . .

Lama: Yes . . .

R. Ephraim: His shape, whether it is here or there, gathers and emerges beyond our school's work. We can't very well talk of that. In retrospect, we say he came . . . he went . . . the wine was tasted. His song is not ours but not different either. You said in your letter that you are a teacher of English. In that history and literature can you hear our melody?

R. Ephraim: That is something to think about, not answer.

[The tape ends here.]

Notes

1. Lunel is the name of a contemporary French historian whom I looked up and met while researching the background of this report. He had no knowledge of a rabbi by this name.
2. Kairite is the term for a Bible-centered, anti-rabbinic sect founded in the eighth century.
3. *Annales* is a French Journal representing a specific school of historiography. Perhaps the most representative product of this school is Fernand Braudel's work, *The Mediterranean and the Mediterranean World in the Age of Philip II*. I was unable, however, to find any articles on this subject in my edition of *Annales*.
4. Even normative Judaism does have this tradition. I found this in Aryeh Kaplan's translation of *Meam Lo ez*, Maznaim, Volume 2, p. 68:

   > Translator's note: Malchi-zedek is none other than Shem, son of Noah. Salem (Shalem) is Jerusalem, which was already (the time of Abraham) an important place of worship; it is written . . . "in Salem was set His Tabernacle, his dwelling place in Zion" (Psalms 76:3). When the city became large enough to require a government, Shem was crowned king and given the title Malchi-zedek. This title actually means "king of righteousness."

5. The term "gorgeous" seems to derive from the human flaw exposed in the Platonic dialogue "The Gorgias."

6. I have found some of the above formulations in Emmanuel Levinas's book *Otherwise than Being*, Martinus Nijhoff, The Hague, translator Adolphus Lingus. Rather curious coincidence, I thought. Levinas is definitely not a rabbi.

7. Genesis 6:14, "make yourself an ark, *tebha*, of gopher wood." Exodus 2:3, "She took for him an ark, *tebha*, made of bulrushes."

8. He must be here referring to the Egyptian (a Semitic language) word for a chest or box *ḏb3.t* , the substantive of which without the feminine ending, *ḏb3*, means, indeed, a bird's cage.

9. *Yesh*, substance. *Yesha*, David's father.

10. *Pirkei Shirah.* About this portion of the Jewish Prayer Book, both Rabbi Hayim of Volozhin (1749-1821) and Rabbi Abraham Issac Kook (1865-1935) speak very highly. Of course, Rav Kook's training was in the Yeshivah of Volozhin, and so this may signify some kind of localized tradition.

CHAPTER FOUR

David

Yanos Tepekzevich, on his arrival in America, changed his name to John Tepek. David is the name he chose for Amfortas usage. Both of his parents were killed during the German "occupation" of Yugoslavia. He was, at the time, fourteen years old. Almost immediately, he began to serve as a courier for the partisan forces of Joseph Broz. At fifteen, while bicycling across a meadow with important messages, he was intercepted by a German officer known in the village as a rapist of young boys. He killed the predator. At the war's end, he immigrated to the United States under sponsorship of relatives living in New York City. He studied architecture at Pratt Institute and, after graduating, took a job with the New York Port Authority. After several years of steady advancement, a profound interest in the work of Josef Albers "seduced" him to undertake a master's degree at Yale. He was always attracted to large-scale projects. Feeling himself unqualified for his goal, he pressed on to another degree, this time in civil engineering. After becoming qualified, he accepted a job with a firm offering travel and the chance to participate in the building of a water and sewer and road system for Basra, Iraq. While in the Near East, he began to experience a rapidly accelerating series of "paranormal" events. The "overlay" of this set of conditions on top of an already keenly developed awareness of a dislocation between the overt world and his own reality kindled an interest in what is euphemistically described as hidden matters. His entering the orbit of Amfortas came as a result of an exceptional piece he published in the British journal *Psychical_Research* entitled "Color_Induced_Hypnosis."

*   *   *

He was short and swarthy and continually worked up about one thing or another. Why David chose to live in Phoenix, Arizona is an imponderable. In this smooth and bland city, he seemed utterly out of place. I dreamed up the excuse that in that city there was plenty of work for an engineer specializing in water management. However, he assured me I was wrong. He liked it there, he said, because of the city's minimal psychic activity. This environment suited his private requirement for conducting his favorite types of experiment.

He and his family (which included three children) lived in a house of his own design on the north slope of Camelback. The children went to public high school. His wife was a mainstay of the Phoenix Musical Theater. He enjoyed golf and swimming. The family attended the Greek Orthodox Church, and they were apparently an ideal unit of the simple, wholesome, American life.

If we set this context for an individual who could hypnotize a full table of people by merely shuffling colored napkins and who believed completely in the close presence of a world of spirits and reincarnation, then we sense something of the paradox he represented to me.

At the Olivet meeting, after an interminable polemic by a disgruntled member, he walked up to the podium to congratulate him. Gently taking the speaker by the elbow and talking animatedly all the time, David led him out of the church and across part of the campus directly into the college's swimming pool.

Implications of a Redemption Myth in China
David

> Let China's civilization become spiritualized and she will lead
> the world into a surer and better civilization than it has ever
> known. Who saves the soul of China will save the world.
>
> Flewelling

China's old water systems are wonders of the ancient world.
But a lot more goes on there. When I read Edgar Snow's account
of the "long march," I knew a lot was going on that could not fit
into words. The narrow escape of the "red army" at the Bridge of
Tatu and their subsequent progress through the territories of the
LOLO People fired my imagination. The "official line" that the
"reds" behaved better than Chiang Kai Shek's forces to both the
white and the black LOLOs is not adequate. Everybody behaved
better than *them*. The explanation explains but does not help me
understand. I am still convinced the miraculous had a hand in the
events. So when an opportunity came for me to work in China,
the idea of this "other" system of causes made up my mind for me.
As I said, their ancient water management systems were great. But
they really needed some current technological transfer to deal with
vast arid but arable regions.

In the more familiar English spelling, the province I was hired to
work in was called Sinkiang. Our office was set up in Shache. This
part of Central Asia sometimes belonged to China and sometimes
did not. Now it is far from the center of things, but in the old
days it was very far—a good two-thousand-mile land journey to
Peking (Beijing). No straight lines in surface travel. Every time
China lost the territory, intense and successful efforts were made

to regain it. Jade magnetized the Chinese to always come back to this country. Like gold, jade is found in watercourses like natural rivers, creeks, and arroyos in the form of pebbles. But also like gold, the largest deposits were not found by hunkering down and panning. Pebbles and rocks of jade were just the throwing off, the effluvia of the basic sources which had far denser roots. And here at the sources, jade parts company with gold, which has its roots deep underground. The primal slabs of jade are found high up in the mountains. To the Chinese, it is a heavenly material.

Now I want to set up a "lattice" to try and capture an elusive meaning.

In the Occident, we have the idea of a "fall of man." Over millennia, it became a pretty sharp doctrine . . . I mean this as though I were saying a sharp photograph. It comes to stand out from the surrounding ideas in which it grew. It is like an aerial photo of a wide terrain in which only one acre was given high resolution. Naturally, it is hard to know where it started, just as in the photo it would be hard to see a pond's origin. It seems to precede early parts of the Bible in which it does not really carry the "sign" of a fall. An expulsion, yes, but not a fall. Now, the expulsion idea resembles a fairy tale with several options. The fairy tale version goes like this:

> An offspring of a monarch is exiled. In exile he gathers a force and attempts a revolution.
> The revolution: Fails because he was unrighteous in his rebellion . . . or . . .
> Succeeds because the Emperor had been misled by sinister courtiers to exile the Prince.
> The latter version has more narrative potential.
> > A) The rebellious prince restores the kingdom and the emperor to their right place.

B) The rebelling prince does not attempt a revolution but establishes a new and more profound kingdom in exile.

C) The most subtle version is that it was a conscious royal act designed to create conditions for . . . and stimulate the growth of . . . an excellent unforeseen but possible culture.

King Lear is a dark inversion of the structure. The outcomes are in proportion to the "value" assigned to the emperor-father. Also, they are related to the way the individual and society fit together . . . the way cult and culture governing authority mesh together. Another ingredient is the "hot" concern of the epoch.

Here is another "line" of the lattice:

The ancient Chinese have a singular view of the origin and cause of the suggestibility of the human mind. In the Kuo Yu, it says:

> What is meant when the book of Chou says that
> Chung and Li succeeded in bringing about that there would
> no longer be communication between
> Heaven and Earth?

It goes on to give the familiar song that, once upon a time, divine beings and people kept properly distinct realms. But:

> People and spirits became confusedly mingled and things could no longer be properly distinguished.
> Ordinary people then performed the sacrifices and each family had its own "Wu" who were utterly lacking in the necessary qualifications. The people exhausted themselves in the rituals without coming to know the happiness that truly attends such . . . people disregarded their solemn vows and were without a sense of awe.

Then it goes on to say that Chung and Li managed to rectify this confusion by cutting off communications between realms.

My acquaintance with Ch'en Pao-shen brought these three lines into a square.

He lived in a small house past the city edges of Shache. Americans would call him of indeterminate age. He was old enough to get some state assistance in living out his remaining years. At one time, he had been an active scholar. Now and then the government "organs" would send manuscripts to him for his evaluation and comment. He "owned" a small though fine library and several rare jade pieces.

Some say that he was related to the grand tutor of the last emperor of the Manchu dynasty, the unfortunate Hsuan T'ung, and in violation of all custom had given to him the tutor's name to perpetuate "his memory." Others believe he was actually *that* Ch'en Pao-shen himself and had learned the secret of longevity. Once a year, he is visited by his daughter and his son-in-law who are both physicians in Fukien. There were in their sixties when I worked in Sinkiang. All managed to survive the cultural revolution.

How I met him is a short story in itself. Shache was so remote that recordkeeping never became the *religious* activity it was at the center of the empire. I could find no reliable records of flooding in the foothills, and there were scant indications of any reliable record of rainfall in the past decades. I could find no way to get a "fix" on hundred-year or fifty-year rain or flood cycles. This data is needed in my trade. Without it, planning becomes a nightmare.

Originally I had thought my China assignment heaven sent not only because of my interest in the obscure but also because of my interest in the visible. I knew that the Chinese people had been great record keepers for thousands of years. Though political history had been constantly tampered with, I was led to believe that the archives of the interior ministries were inviolate and thorough. Data on the height of water in the wells was as important and sacrosanct as their records of astronomical phenomena. But here in the far West, of course no such luck.

I got a letter of introduction and a map to the house of Ch'en Pao-shen from an archivist in the local, skimpy Hall of Records. He believed that this gentleman might be able to help me. His house was "beyond" the telephone system. I arranged to visit around 11:00 a.m. so not to surprise the gentleman too much.

When I drove up, I found him waiting. Li, the archivist, had sent ahead a messenger to inform the old man about my visit. He brought me eagerly into his small house. Soon he had a kettle of water boiling furiously. He let it boil for ten minutes. In nearly unaccented English, he made me understand that this particular tea, Li Chi, reaches its full value only when the boiling water has been made thirsty for oxygen. Tea should always be prepared according to the hexagram "Fu" . . . return renewal, etc.

While we drank the tea, Ch'en Po-shen told me he was a fake and probably could not help me much.

> "Good old Li knows I get bored. In his kindness he sent you to lighten my time. But in principle I *may* be able to help. Jade speaks in a way. During flood years, much ore comes down the mountains. We can read the history of the river and creek beds. We can tell from how high up in the range a piece of jade came."

I really liked the man. In my bones I knew he could teach me about what really interested me. Our association lasted the duration of my time in Sinkiang; about a year and a half. He told me he would teach me what he *could* about the Ch'en clan's culture. He would do this because I was helping his country.

All the minerals have their place both in the heavens and in the psychophysical nature of human beings. This was one of the many ways in which correspondence between the *three realms* has a "material" base. But jade is the most special of them all. He claimed that the use of jade for ornament and emblem began at about the time of the Chung and Li I mentioned above. At the time communication between the human realm and the divine realm was cut off, jade was given as an earnest of eventual rehabilitation. The subtle patterns and veinings in the stone were hieroglyphs of eternity and the *long body of heaven*. Pattern is conceived by the Ch'en clan as *of* the essence of all reality on the hither side of T'ai Chi, or the Great Limit.

To demonstrate *pattern's* relation to the psyche, you may remember my article about color by hypnosis. Well, that depended always on temporal patterns. But I have a first-rate example from a group I lived with and observed for a time in Iraq. They used *raw pattern* . . . line. They have a specialized knowledge of this for healing or at least reducing the suffering of "mental illness."

The healer makes a study over a short but *definite* period of time. He studies carefully the sufferer's eye movements, body movements, repeated postures, etc. After a careful subjective preparation, he develops a design. He executes it as a seal or die graved into one of the wide variety of metals and imprints this *pattern* on a number of daily use items. The patient is sequestered in a small hut that is "saturated" by this design. After three days, he or she usually recovers. The *daily use items* are given to the patient for a permanent property as an "emblem" of the healing. Also, the recovered person is given an amulet carrying this device as an ornament and a reminder. The way this works was explained to me as being based on a contradiction.

The sufferer has been "spellbound" by the way they had grown up. Events, favorable and unfavorable, have happened to them throughout their life. The tendencies of the individual have been "bound" by two poles that develop. On one side is a condition like a deep, seemingly bottomless pit . . . a hole. On the other pole has grown a compelling and closed system. Neither "exist" except in the mind of the sufferer. The healer discerns the *plan* of the patient's spell. This is something like a circuitry blueprint (a Freudian-type reader may grasp the idea better as a plan for plumbing infrastructure). The healer reproduces this "plan" with a few very minor and undetectable variations of pattern. These variations harmonize with the larger world, the non-private world. By being for a definite period of time in an environment of which the external visible reality *is* the spell, the system begins to collapse on itself. During daily life, whenever the sufferer's spell had begun to collapse, he or she had moved toward the other subjective pole, namely the hole . . . a terrifying place but, nevertheless, a place for retreat. But now, in this new circumstance, the patient's retreat is caught by the variations of the pattern and is led through them to suggestions of a world of content. By intensifying the pattern of the spell for a precise time, this tribe has found that they can dissolve that spell. I have found that their results are very successful and contradict Western assumptions. For example, the cures are achieved without unreasonable suffering unless the illness has grown out of the patient's own criminal acts. The time of the healing is very short.

Now is a good time to look at how the work of Chung and Li led to suggestibility. The time-space mentioned above, when there was "communication between heaven and earth," was in fact an environment of understanding. The premise was that the psyche and spirit of human beings were ineffable. They were resourceful to the nth degree. The human was a "whole" and cited as *part* of a larger whole, i.e., the universe. This is formulated, "Anthropos forms a third with Heaven and Earth." In our wholeness as *persons*, we were in fact the actual *field* of communication between heaven and earth.

[Ch'en, in his fashion, raised the question whether above-mentioned time "exists in past or future."]

When unqualified Wu, in order to keep food on their plates, began meddling with this demanding system of knowledge, the integrity of the human spirit was threatened. Chung and Li did the needed thing and cut off the communication. They substituted a system of *as if*, which is well documented in the Confucian Analects.¹ The world of "as if" opens up the great potential of human beings to suggestion and, hence, suggestibility. Not wanting to leave people as hanging prey, the corrective was also developed. This was the establishment of the whole science and art and its study . . . of pattern. Pattern from metals to music.

Let's work back to his second lattice line . . . the "fall." The "return of the exiled" relates with the arrival of a heavenly person, a messiah, a Saoshant, a twelfth Imam, Maitreya, etc. The Ch'en do not venture to guess whether this is a literal return or an entirely new event. Is the condition of communication between heaven and earth a past to be regained or a future to be grown into?

And threading in the "first line," Ch'en Pao-shen says that jade tells the story. Here is his version:

In the Persian classic *The Conference of the Birds*, we find the verse

> It was in China, late one moonless night,
> The Simorgh first appeared to mortal sight.
> He let a feather float down through the air,
> And, rumours of its fame spread everywhere.
> Throughout the world men separately
> Conceived an image of its shape, and all
> Believed their private fantasies uniquely true!

> (In China still this feather is on view, whence
> Comes the saying you have heard no doubt,
> "Seek knowledge, unto China, seek it out).²

The feather corresponds to the nine-chambered diagram, which was borne by a "dragon horse" and brought out of the river by a tortoise and presented to Fu Hsi. This same "feather" was borne out of the Lo River at the time of legendary emperor Yu. It was a piece of jade with special data graven into it. Jade is the medium and matrix. What was *on* the chart came from a far past or a far future. On the far side, that is of the separation between the divine and human.

An outing with Ch'en Pao-shen proved a turning point for my understanding. I had been in Sinkiang for six months. By using a lot of pressure on myself and others, I had gotten the basic surveys completed. Without being too specific about the region where I was preparing a water-management plan, it was in the southern part of the province.

The territory was watered by runoff from the Kunlun Mountains. The only part of the Sinkiang that had adequate rainfall was far to the north, north of the Tien-shan range. On the slopes *south* of the Tien-shan and closer to us . . . north of the Kunlun and Karakoram, it is possible, without high technology, to fan out the water from the mountains through the irrigation and develop excellent oasis. However, there were two aquifers divided by a "blue clay" barrier. The "blue clay" varied from three hundred to a thousand feet thick. The streams charge the upper aquifer, and the subsurface runoff charges the lower. In the middle of the basin, created by the Tien-shan and the Kunlun ranges, is the vast Taklamakan desert. It is about two hundred miles wide and perhaps four hundred long. All the streams run out here to vanish. My plan was to multiply the available oasis by fine tuning the management of the water coming off the Kunlun. In some areas, I was engaged in persuading the authorities to undertake a drilling program in order to exploit the deep aquifer, because this continually recharges from the mountain runoff before the beginning of the "blue clay" barrier. One of the constraints on former irrigation systems here is the rapid water loss from evaporation in the exceedingly dry atmosphere and through fast downward percolation in the sandy and gravely soil. The local people were fine and willing workers and in the given local conditions and requirements—terrific water managers. But the ruling idea of my mandate was to improve the conditions for agriculture in Sinkiang toward its becoming a granary for all China. New technologies were required. Though they grasped the problems quickly enough, they were not trained to give me much help in putting the data together in the direction I aimed at. Only six months into my assignment and I was worn out.

On this day, word reached me that the old man Ch'en wanted to see me fast. I had grown attached to him. It was a toss-up whether I put him off or put off a day's work. I dropped everything and went to see him.

He told me a great tiger had been sighted in an easily reached part of the Tien-shan. He beamed. We were going on a tiger hunt. I thought he had lost his wits. I was swamped with work and also did not like the idea of killing tigers. He solemnly told me it was a "once-in-a-lifetime" moment and I agreed. Also, the hunt, he said, was not "to kill but to see."

Our party comprised about fourteen men of all ages. A local cooperative provided us with several ancient but worthy trucks. On our fourth day of driving through a passable stretch at the far western end of the desert, we came to a road head. The Yarkant River had sliced a thin band of negotiable terrain. We started off on foot and by nightfall had pitched camp at our destination. The next two days we were all holed up in a scattering of cunningly devised blinds among huge boulders in the Tien-shan foothills.

Our company had found the tiger. The hunt was a success. We watched from concealment while this magnificent beast carried out his daily tasks sometimes at a distance from us and at other times close. On the morning of the second day, he came unnervingly near the blind I shared with Ch'en. Later that day, he loped off toward the northeast and disappeared.

That evening we all celebrated and shared our feelings and thoughts. For the first time on this excursion, we had a full meal. It was a feast. Someone had contrived to bring live shrimps in huge barrels of water spiked with local wine. So we indulged in "drunken shrimp." Another person had prepared a Mongolian dish of lamb, fruit, and an assortment of sweet and hot peppers. There was superb marinated duck. We washed down the substances with five different kinds of wine and finished off with the great spirit "Inkapay." Somehow I did not get drunk.

Later Ch'en and I walked slowly off and found a convenient table rock where we sat down. The night sky of dizzyingly large stars came as close to us as we to it.

He pointed to a region of the sky with few visible stars. He dropped his arm vertically down and pointed to a barely noticeable notch in the Tien-shan.

"That's the way the tiger went."

Straight as a die, he again raised his arm to the dark patch.

"That region there . . . along a line we could draw from T'ai Chi[4] through the 'Weaving Girl' . . . and three thumbs over at this time of year we call the 'Gate of Heaven.'"

After a long pause, he went on and, bringing his hand down along a line from his forehead to his belly and then back, said:

"It exists also in HSIN.

[This word does not translate well. It signifies both the heart and mind of a human being. It carries a diachronic as well as a synchronic meaning. The heart of the mind and the mind of the heart].

We sat looking at the stars quietly and finished a bottle of wine Ch'en had brought to the rock with him. Then leisurely we strolled back to camp and went to sleep. Early the next morning, we started back along the way we had come. After about an hour, he took my hand and squeezed it tightly as though to be sure I would remember.

"These past days . . . all six of them are Ch'an. This excursion has been . . . *days of Ch'an.*[5]"

Back at work, pieces of our task began at last to flow coherently together, and most members of our team began seeing creative solutions to what had been "gluey thickets." Proper locations for diversion of streams seemed to present themselves right off the maps and confirm themselves in the field. It was uncanny.

When I mentioned to Ch'en the abrupt jump forward of my work, he agreed it was "quite wonderful." But he thought it could be more wonderful if I would comprehend what had happened.

The River Diagram and the Lo Writing

We were in the garden of his small house, and he drew into the sand some characters.

His explication was elegant:

> A tiger hunt is to bring to meet the *shu* of the tiger and the *shu* of man. It is a useless undertaking. But it partook of *li* (理), which was disclosed as shape through *hsing* (性). Intrinsic to every step and act along the way was *te*. The "virtue" manifested human form, *li* (禮), by the *non-apparent dance* of our activities.

It must have come about that by bringing my life and work into harmonic alliance with this obscure but vast weave of ways spontaneously changed its constitution. What does this add up to?

> When the tiger eats, the ox grows fat.

Ch'en Pao-shen then almost solemnly intoned:

> We believe that the expected savior, the Jade Angel, at the end
> of time is humanity itself fully grown into its rightful status
> and place. It is the time-space when communion between the
> divine realm and the human realm is "reestablished." This
> will be on a fresh footing . . . different from the *transactions*
> of ancient times.

Then he asked that I ponder the chapter of Chuangtzu entitled
the "Happy Excursion." I conclude my report by quoting from
this section in the translation of Fung Yu Lan. Ch'en said that
when our hsing has learned this, the Gate of Heaven appears.

> Chien Wu said to Lien Shu, "I heard from Chieh Yu some
> utterances that were great but could not be justified. Once
> started, there is no end to his tale. It seemed to be as boundless
> as the Milky Way. It was very improbable and far removed
> from human experience."
>
> "What did he say," asked Lien Shu.
>
> "He said: 'Far away on the mountain of Ku, there lived a
> spirited man. His flesh and skin were like ice and snow. His
> manner was elegant and graceful as that of a maiden. He
> did not eat the five grains but inhaled the wind and drank
> the dew. He rode on clouds, drove along the flying dragons,
> and rambled beyond the four seas. His spirit is compact. Yet
> he could save things from corruption and secure each year a
> plentiful harvest . . .' I thought all these sayings were nonsense
> and refused to believe them."

"Yes," said Lien Shu, "the blind have nothing to do with beauty, nor the deaf with music."

* * *

Hui Tzu said to Chuang Tzu: "The King of Wei sent me some calabash (gourd) seeds. I planted them and they bore fruit as big as a five-bushel measure. I used it as a vessel for holding water, but it was not solid enough to hold it. I cut the calabash into two for ladles, but each of them was too shallow to hold anything. Because of this uselessness, I knocked them to pieces."

"Sir," said Chuang Tzu, "it was rather you who did not know how to use the large things. There was a man of Sung who had a recipe for salve for chapped hands. From generation to generation, his family made silk washing their occupation. A stranger heard of this and proposed to offer him one hundred ounces of gold for the *recipe*. The kindred came together . . . they said: 'we have been washing silk for generations. We gained not more than a few ounces of gold. In one morning we can sell this art for one hundred ounces . . .' So, the stranger got it. He went and informed the King of Wu. When Wu and Tueh were at war, the king gave him (the stranger) the command of the fleet. In the winter he had a naval engagement with Yueh. Yueh was totally defeated. The stranger was rewarded with a fief and a title. So while the efficiency of the salve to cure chapped hands was in both cases the same, yet here it secured him a title . . . there, nothing more than a capacity for washing silk . . . Now you, sir, have this five-bushel calabash; why did you not make of it a large *bottle gourd*, by means of which you could float in the river and lakes? Instead of this you were sorry that it was useless for holding anything. I think your mind is wooly."

Hui Tzu said to Chuang Tzu, "I have a large tree which men call the ailanthus. Its trunk is so irregular and knotty that a carpenter cannot apply his line to it. Its small branches are so twisted that the square and compass cannot be used on them. It stands by the roadside but is not looked at by any carpenter. Now your words, sir, are big but useless and not wanted."

Chuan Tzu answered, "Have you not seen a wild cat or a weasel? It lies crouching down in wait for its prey. East and west it leaps about, avoiding neither what is high nor low. At last it is caught in a trap or dies in a net. Again there is the yak, which is as large as the clouds. But it can't catch mice. Now you have a large tree and are anxious about its uselessness. Why do you not plant it in the domain of otherwise than being . . . in a wild and barren wilderness? By its side you may wander in non-ado; under it you may sleep in happiness. Neither bill nor axe would shorten its existence. Being of no use to others it would be free from harm."

I think there is matter here for Amfortas to chew on for a time.

My project in Sinkiang was satisfying to both the Chinese agricultural authorities and myself. Now, I hope in this report to you, it meets the need.

Notes

1) Lun Yu III, 12: He sacrificed to the ancestors *as if* they were present. He sacrificed to the spirits *as if* the spirits were present. Fung Yu land, *History of Chinese Philosophy*, Vol. I, p. 58.

2) I used here not David's translation, which was from the Chinese translation of the Persian:

> In China, moonless night.
> Simurgh revealed to the living.
> Feather form floats down.
> Word of it runs to the world edges.
> Each man, each woman, each place
> Saw shape they thought . . .
> Each thought their thought
> Their dream of it the true "this"
> Still can see in China the feather
> From this say
> Seek knowledge as far as China.

3) The account of the signs is rudimentary. For a fuller version, see Joseph Needham, *Science and Civilization in China*, Vol. 2, p. 220-230.

4) T'ai Chi is an old name of the Pole Star. Weaving Girl is the constellation that seems near it.

5) Ch'an or, more familiarly, Zen, means apparently "meditation."

CHAPTER FIVE

Lancelot

Lancelot, thoroughly American, was given the Christian name Wesley, as are so many good Methodists in that country. The family name of Adams claims distinguished antecedents in New England. His immediate family were successful farmers near Evansville, Indiana. When it came time to enter college, he surprised and disappointed his parents by choosing the University of Indiana in Bloomington rather than Indiana State. From his teens onward, he had a passion for folklore and pursued it at university, where earned he a doctorate in European Folklore of the Middle Ages. He again surprised his family when, upon completion, he returned to farming. Very quickly he made it into a far more successful enterprise than it had been. The "handwriting on the wall" convinced him that even well-run farms like the Adams's were doomed in the face of real estate development and industrial farming conglomerates. With a few turns of luck and superb timing, he secured for himself and his family a small fortune for their property. He guided reinvestment so that each family member could in their own way pursue their chief interests. He moved to Wisconsin where he began a highly specialized small farm for himself.

He sustained a dilettante interest in folklore and in pursuit of it traveled widely throughout Europe. Marya's article in *The Journal of the PMLA* caught him up into a spirited exchange of letters with other respondents to the piece on Merlin, among who were members of Amfortas. Within several years, he had formally associated himself with the society.

*   *   *

Lancelot was a huge slab of a man. Though I am not short, whenever we were talking he tended to lean over and try to shrink himself. Contrary to his intention, the effect was unsettling, as though a rock slide was poised before my face. He was addicted to puns, and even the worst of them could set him roaring with laughter.

With very rare exceptions, the only place he would meet with any of us was at his own small farm. We usually paid for disturbing his quiet by helping with some of the chores. Once he tried to show me the correct way to use a scythe for mowing down some huge stands of unwanted growth along the roadside. Though my flesh was willing, I was obviously lacking some of the desired spirit.

"Gads man! Just pretend you're Francois Villon!"

During a rare meeting with me near my own ground in England, we managed to have a splendid time for several days tracking ley lines. On our return to the city, we decided to go into the slums of northeast London and see what we could of Canonbury Tower, the old digs of Francis Bacon. We spent some time poking about. He only had one thing to say as we left the tower: "mmm."

Lancelot was a truly gentle person and unusually patient in listening to others . . . he was slow to judge either pro or con. His hobby was falconry.

The Tree of Seth
Lancelot

Ladies and Gentlemen of Amfortas:

As you know, I had almost decided to forget and ignore any relations I had with the society after the abominable nonsense at Olivet. I do not like scenes. That was an ordeal for me. I agree, however, that the membership took the right course. Still, at the time, I had decided to repudiate the geis of filing a report. God only knows what *you* would consider significant enough.

Well, I made the decision to reverse myself after an extended trip to Europe. I had come back through Chicago and rented a car to drive back to my digs near Madison. I hate freeways. I chose to thread my way out of the city with my mindset like Robert Frost's—to "out-walk the farthest city light." Driving as much like a walker as imagination permits—from clump of commerce, through darks of residences—I caught a glimpse of their city, which appeared that night as diabolically circuited as Dante's Inferno. I changed my mind and decided to report after all.

Let me tell you . . . while writing this, as I am now, looking out over the Wisconsin River here near Mazomanie . . . nothing seems more outlandish than what I am doing. To raid my memory like this and plunder tons of notes to tell you about something I scarcely believe is painful. This is a record of an insanity that in the writing is saner than my day-to-day drudging routine. So far the only auditor of this material is a porcupine that visits my south field in the evenings.

Several years back, I had been pillaging the resources of the former Benedictine Monastery at Brevnov Chechoslovakia. I ran across some stuff that kept me tracking clues for a few years. Originally my game had been to track down legends about *healing trees* in Central Europe. Someone at the grand old university in Prague finally fobbed me off to Brevnov. He dangled the promise of a batch of letters by an abbot to an address in Detroit, Michigan. They had been written (and copied) during the period when the mad king Ludwig of Bavaria was chartering Benedictine foundations in the Middle America, circa 1850. The letters were *not* about the trees.

What I found was evidence of a totally unknown undertaking assumed by an unknown league of men and women. I am inclined to start off my story after the fashion of a Hungarian folktale:

> Once upon a time, far, far away . . . beyond the Seven Seas and even further, there lived behind the crumbling walls of a ramshackle oven, in the seventy-seventh fold of an old woman's skirt—a white flea . . . and in the middle of its belly, there was a magnificent planet called Earth.

And on this Earth flourished thousands and thousands of clubs and nowhere more than in a place called North America. There were Hutterites, Swords of the Lords, Doukhabors, Mennonites, Catholics, Sons of David, Baptists, Oneidians, Know-Nothings, Jews, Odd Fellows, Keepers of the Flame, Harvards, Yales, Parity-ites . . . and on and on . . . and on.

The Sethian Fellowship, of all these clubs, appears in no clerk's records. They established themselves here mostly during the nineteenth century. Prior to that time, all their "branches" except one were in Europe. The one exception had founded itself in America right before the French and Indian wars and quietly sustained a small membership during the birth pangs of the United States. During the War of Independence, the headquarters of this original club on American soil was in a small house in Brooklyn Heights. The origin of this fellowship on the planet is asserted by them to be antediluvian.

I think I should give you a general view and go on to the particulars. These gleanings are my own interpretation of some discussions. Their spiritual ancestor is not the Seth of Egyptian myth but that first *substantial* son of Adam and Eve as appears in the West's Common Bible. With rare exceptions, such as I will show later, they make every effort to remain unknown and invisible to the public eye.

As I said, it was not until the nineteenth century that the majority of Seth houses moved from Europe to America. The reason for the move was to try to preserve the original intention of the founding of my country. They see the United States as one of the most important experiments ever undertaken since the migrations of people set off by the nightmare of the "Tower of Babel." Should "these States" degenerate toward the opposite of their original idea, the tragedy would be one of cosmic proportions, and a greater tragedy for the whole world than for America itself. This they resolutely believe. The political instruments designed by this country to dissolve the chains of the *master-slave* relationship that at the time were endemic worldwide were only the initial stages of larger program. A major item in the long range was to restore the appropriate balance of Earth's biological continuum—namely, to reach proper relations between men and women.

Sethians are utterly convinced of the eventual healing or balancing of the human species on this planet. They context our world within a much larger stream of life, which includes the Milky Way. And as our informant put it, widening her eyes . . . "beyond that." They take a radically long view about everything. Individual members know that they will not live (as we understand living) beyond a small slice of this long view. But they believe it is only this kind of perspective that provides them a context adequate to making sense of *any* contemporary conditions. Their undertaking requires them to monitor the *purport* of any time or place. They think that without this kind of view, they could be easily duped by the drift of the meaning of ideas from place to place and time to time. To illustrate the problem, an example was provided by my informant, "only for its exotic flavor, taken from the Orient." The fellowship pays little or no attention to the East.

In India, both among Brahmanic devotees and Buddhists, the concept "meditation" refers to *keeping an idea or an image in mind*. They may visualize the universe as space or greater than space or smaller than a grain of rice. Sometimes part of the idea is the visualization of the features of a deity to its minutest detail, etc. In Japan, however, this same "idea" is quite the opposite. There, ideally, meditation has no idea, no concept, no image. This is an obvious and convenient example to show how societies change the content of *key ideas* in order to suit persuasions that are bound by locality or time.

In the West, which as I suggested is the permanent theater of Sethian action, this propensity has been equally virulent. The "house" of Seth always finds itself *thrown* into various present times. Their long view keeps them sober enough to be able to find where they are.

Now, with pleasure, I will approach some particulars. One could guess that a search for legendary "tree" material would lead to some people gathered under the name of Seth. Most rood tree and healing tree motifs in the Western world can boil down to ancient legends of Seth/Enoch and the Tree of Paradise. Admittedly, some strands of this material resolve into a special and sacred oil. But I do not think anyone could have guessed from the available data what the content and program of such a group actually turned out to be.

The Prague librarian sent me to Brevnov because he had heard that the letters kept there referred to a certain "league of Sethians." Naturally, it seemed in line with my inquiries. He assumed as did I that the groups were connected to lore concerning the rood tree. What I, in fact, found led me after some detours to a generous but modest house on a quiet street in Highland Park, Michigan. Here a circle of "fellows" descended from those correspondents of the abbot of Brevnov met at irregular intervals. After considerable screening procedures and certain earnests required of me for assurance that I would in no way divulge anything which they did not permit, I met the club's president.

As above mentioned, rarely does one of their numbers produce work for the public. The intervals between such emergencies varied between three and eight hundred years.

I liken the intervals to the life span of a moderately long-lived tree . . . shorter lived than the Bristle Brush Pine and longer than the Russian Olive.

The woman was gifted with a breadth of expression. She could be frostily civil or raucously vulgar and most of the stops in between. It turned out that William Blake was the most recent member to publish, so she chose his work to provide an entry into the world of the Seth League. Apropos of this, it was apparently Blake's work, which convinced the clubs of Europe about the primary importance of the experiment in democracy under way across the Atlantic.

Her account of his opinion of America is interesting. When Blake met Tom Paine by the Liverpool docks to discuss the purposes and implications of the American Revolution, its vital necessity dawned on him. He could see that the world needed somewhere a nation with enough "space" for an idea of individuality that was not swallowed into a presupposed pattern. Whatever drawbacks and failures might come from this were minor compared to the benefits.

At the time in Europe, infinity could only be seen as a system . . . a tightly constrained Newtonian system. This, Blake thought, fed the hungry "satan" in man by supporting in "him" the delusion that a total hegemony was not merely desirable but was possible. It led to the supposition that death could be *averted by growth*.

And hence it became an intoxicant of what Blake termed "the inner worlds." The risk represented by the United States had to be accepted, because hopefully the horizons of humanity, both inner and outer, could then come closer to a truer infinity.[1]

> I turn my eyes to the Schools & Universities of Europe
> And there behold the Loom of Locke whose Woof rages
>   dire
> Washed by the Water-wheels of Newton . . . cruel Works
> Of many Wheels I view, wheel without wheel, with cogs
>   tyrranic
> Moving by compulsion each other; Not as those in Eden:
>   which
> Wheel within wheel in freedom revolve in harmony &
>   Peace.

My notes indicate that here I began to have my doubts. Everything was too pat. The quotes from Blake were *too* appropriate. I voiced my skepticism.

She was a handsome, magnetic woman in her forties. When she stood up after my question, the rustle of her dress was electrical; it startled and aroused me. She went to the cupboard and mixed a couple of drinks and brought them back to where I was sitting. After we clinked glasses, she asked, "Who do you think we are?"

"I really don't know."

"But we are something or other, yes?"

"Sure . . ."

"Well, what then . . . some New Age freaks before the New Age?"

"Things can't be that deliberate . . . I mean to impress me you must have memorized those passages."

"My dear sir, not the passages . . . the poems."

"Not possible!"

I wished I had not said that. She flashed me a wicked smile as in the Russian proverb[2] and began to recite the entire poem *Jerusalem*. I had to listen. I began to feel near the middle that another stanza, another line, would kill me, wring me out like a worn-out dishrag. It was nearly impossible to bear. She concluded as fresh as a morning glory and smiled that same smile at me.

"Now, sir . . . with that out of the way, you are probably at an adequate pitch of fatigue to benefit from our talk. From here on, no notes. Put the pad away. Let's get to the heart of the matter."

You have now read a pretty fair account of the surfaces of the garment of Seth as told me and as taken from on-the-spot notes. It entirely misses the lining. That I have to reconstruct from jottings I set down after this memorable talk.

I had resolved to get somewhere at a table immediately and start scribbling. It was not to be. When the woman showed me out of the house, the presunrise light was already brightening the street. I walked over to my car across the street and, the moment the key went into the ignition, I fell asleep. A police officer woke me up and hassled me. I got abusive to him and wound up at the Highland Park station house where it took me the better part of the day to wrangle my way out of the mess. I was so beat that evening when I left the police station that I checked into a motel, conked out, and did not wake up until first light of the next day. Only then, after coffee, was I able to start scribbling to reconstruct the "heart of the matter." Here is a reconstruction of that reconstruction

The Symbols
The Horizontal Rod and Diagonal Stylus

The rod is the "rood tree" in its manifestation as the contexting principle of the universe when it is shown horizontally or being carried at the side of a person. The diagonal stylus is the "rood tree" in its manifestation as the informing principle of the universe. The metaphor to which this most obviously relates is the horizontal tablet and the scribe's stylus . . . or the parchment and brush, or paper and quill or pen. Sethians understand writing and designing and related activity as properly human expressions of a synchronically natural and divine principle of the great universe. When used as a sign set not to the forty-five degree angle but with the "tree" rod at sixty degrees, it indicates activity of the informing principle operating from a dimension beyond our comprehension. On rare, extreme occasions, this emblem has appeared in human culture. It might show up "out of the blue" much the way gypsy signs might show up on certain doorposts. In keeping with the theme above, William Blake is a pertinent example. His use of "crosshatching" was in defiance of all the rules of engraving. At a time when "flesh" was being debased, he managed at times to transform the grammar of representation of "flesh" into "lattices of light." It appears on certain of the Gothic cathedrals. It was the mark of the "righteous" in the Book of Ezekiel . . . Other examples exist.

The Three Realms

Of cardinal concern to the work of the League of Seth are "three realms." Through the ages, their activity centered upon the preservation and fostering of these "realms" or values. They are childhood, old age, and youth.

Childhood

The league struggles to assure that children will be able to pass on a living tradition to new generations of children. Games, puzzles, rituals, and songs are communicated for hundreds of years among the young. Usually by the age of twelve or thirteen they are forgotten. The forgetting secures their transmission. Every few hundred years, conditions in a given culture may change and require the gradual introduction of new materials and the dispersal of the old. For example, hopscotch has been good for four hundred years . . . cats and mice has transformed to streets and alleys with police and thieves in just the past seventy-five years . . . and so on. The principle remains constant, i.e., to establish a base in the psyche that enables the later adult to suffer their way back to unity. "Suffer the little children to come unto me."

The modern world is a severe challenge to their effort. Widespread dislocations due to war and politics added to top off the ubiquity of the media sever, the usual childhood into bits. The decay of traditional safeguards have left them often alienated from their own kind and make them prey to such adult madness as childhood sexual abuse. In former times, no matter how hard times were, children could get away into their own lives. Now, since the Industrial Revolution, it has become increasingly difficult.

Old Age

The application of influence has been directed toward assuring that cultural and political systems, which are often allied to the retrograde human tendency of heedlessness, do not ignore the old people in their midst. In earlier times, it was possible through religions and superstitions to see to it that old people would be respected and not trampled under. The activity of poetry and philosophy were constantly enlisted with success. They kept the conscience alive *enough* to prevent the persistent human tendency for substituting *honor* in the place of *respect* from overtaking the day-to-day life of people. "The very young and the very old are lords of the atmosphere." [3]

Youth

This "value" or realm has constantly stimulated the Sethians to their most creative and delicate activities. It has required them to sustain and continually provide evidence that humanity does *not* have all the answers. Youth is not a chronic period of life. It is diachronic and synchronic, a condition of flexibility of mind and feeling. In a properly functioning person, this value is present throughout "old age." Death is most graciously met wearing a worn-through body but bearing a youthful mind, heart, and soul. The league holds that religion and science both are essential for youth but that their "value" is upside-down to common understanding. Religion and science serve humanity best when they present unseen vistas for which "answers" are palpably inadequate. However, both endeavors become addicted to certitude which they each in their own way hope will plug up all gaps. It is natural that "ordinary" people tend to characterize both religionists and scientists as "old." It is a pity that they do, but it shows a sound instinct. Only if mind and feelings are inwardly open and not encysted can Time be for people the high value it truly is. Seth clubs protect the "gates" to new theoretical structures in both religion and science. They work at this not for the sake of novelty but to deliver communities from the delusion of having all the answers. In the past several hundred years, the passion to "close up" the universe has again become so great among people that the

League of Seth finds this an unremitting and taxing endeavor. They are now seeking another avenue to accomplish the task of protecting youth. They consider it possible that if human beings would understand that each and all of them could die at any moment, people might wake up to youthfulness. But their research is not yet conclusive.

In sum, the very young, the old, and the youthful refer to realms outside the language grid on a plane of existence which is a lining of our apparent world. *What* they hold these "energetic values" to be is Sethian lore still unavailable to me.

The Mandate

Before the "flood," no persons or groups accepted the natural and logical human sense of responsibility for others. Seth was born in the "image" of Adam. Adam was created in the likeness of the Creator. Seth *should* have encouraged and stimulated responsibility throughout the young world. He was rendered regrettably heedless by "whatever . . ." According to the principle of "to whom much is given, much will be required," he bore a heavy responsibility. Several hundred years before the flood became inevitable, he vowed to assume an indefinitely long task of rectification. The charter for the League of Seth was established. Members never assume the role of prophet, leader, etc. They make every effort to assure that the moral, intellectual, and spiritual supports needed by such *actors* are available to them. The actors are understood to have their own soul force.

The path of the human adventure extends throughout the universe all the way "until God," who also is in *every* "where."

Now, the *mandate* threw me. Certainly it is a metaphor. But what a tangle twisted one it is. There are few indications where to find adequate referents. Did they mean to say that Seth stood for a "type" or a "group" or what? As I drove westward across

Michigan, these were the directions of my thought. I had planned my trip to reach the town of Marshall at lunchtime. There I could treat myself to a good meal at Wyn Schulers.

I sat there later enjoying one of America's reassuring restaurants and reflecting on Olivet only a dozen miles to the north. I came to the conclusion that in "true-blue American fashion" I had been had. This being *had* by one movement or another is by now an ingrained part of the American way.

After lunch, I took the short side trip up to Olivet. The term was in full swing. Students were bustling in and out of buildings, young couples were strolling among the huge oaks . . . it was altogether like a recruitment poster. I went into the old rugged fieldstone and wood church . . . the one where Amfortas had its larger meetings and sat down. In the stillness, I was able to build up a plan to confirm or deny the Sethian mirage. Was their game, I had been thinking, what they claimed . . . or a highly original delusion on the part of some intelligent and resourceful people?

Then and there I broke off my trip home. I drove directly to the Detroit airport where I took the first available flight to New York. Subsequently, my itinerary led me to the address in Brooklyn Heights, which incredibly enough was still a Seth house. From there I went to Europe where I was able to prove to myself one thing. Though it is hard to get an adequate fix on the level of literal versus symbolic truth which motivates the Sethians, they are not delusional.

To tell the truth, my decision to report was not only due to my despair in the face of the Dante-esque circuitry of our civilization but also a hope. If they are real . . . and they may be . . . then so may we be real.

In Brooklyn Heights, it turned out I had been expected sooner or later. A white-haired man with bushy eyebrows handed me several typed sheets of paper. Later when I read it, I could not help remembering the president of the Highland Park Club grinning at me.

The Awakening of Personhood
Four Essential Conditions that People Today Try to Avoid
Memory   Fear   Conflict   Faith
Memory.

Memory is a human capacity individuals must develop in themselves. It is through memory the various separated and oft fragmented dimensions of the person can be brought into initial contact with each other. Ultimately then, when memory is developed, these fragments arrive to lively, mutually nourishing harmonies. Let us say that the unconscious stores all events and impressions a person experiences holographically. If we consider the unconscious more inner than what we call conscious . . . then to re-elevate from the unremembered to the remembered establishes a provisional contact between inner and outer. This kind of contact either through memory or otherwise is an irreplaceable part of being human. Furthermore, if an event is lived with an intense level of awareness, as well as merely being *undergone*, it becomes part of the "hologram" with an *extra* circuit—a circuit which relates the event to one's life in a memorable way. Thereafter, even if "unremembered," it will bring a flow and vitality to the souls. Then the principle continuity begins to become established as a fresh dimension of human life. Only when a person has this quality of flow and tenuity is that person able to hold and work toward a living ideal. Otherwise, "ideals" become entirely something else. There are varied kinds of memory, kinesthetic, affective, sensory, mental, etc. They all require a process of integration and correlation.

As persons alive, we carry in our body and psyche the stream of heredity, the stream of the soul's humanity, and the stream of the "divine dispensation." These are the innermost flows of memory and are a human birthright. The plane of our life is a context which may be called outer. But it is integrally connected to the above-mentioned streams through family, culture, civilization, and religion. As a person develops inborn nature, these aspects of inner/outer can be brought into musical contact. It is a pity that in a person or culture without the strength of continuous tenuity, it often falls out that this latter contact can be explosive and hazardous. For this reason, it is important that the capacity for personal remembering is brought at least to the plane of kinesthetic and affective continuity.

Fear

Fear is multidirectional and multidimensional. Perhaps it is the archetype of polysemy. The perfection of fear is a rare and priceless accomplishment. If a person has not brought their memory into their private structure as an active and vital part, unconscious, rudimentary fear can in one day obliterate it. Properly developed, however, the powerful momentum of fear becomes a supporting and strengthening pillar in the elaboration of memory. On the path to human stature, one of the initiatory trials is the production of a condition called great fear.

Contrary to most teachings of the present era, we believe the ardently sought state of "fearlessness" is pathological and nearly incurable. The first step toward perfection of fear is discrimination between figment fears and natural fear. For in some countries it is un-sane to be fearless of the police. In others, the fear of police is an excessive response where the more natural one would be a certain wariness.

A young child finds in his or her family good soil for the growth of natural fear. But at the same time, the family encounter creates all the predispositions toward the growth of a person's later figment fears. Because of this intrinsic connection between an embodied life's earliest experiences, when an excessive and unperfected fear begins to rage memory may be wiped out. In such a case, terror goes through a person's unremembered life like a tornado; it touches ground all the way back to earliest childhood. This is a difficult but not "final" situation. The intuition of it forms the "fear of fear." Because of this "fear of fear," there are certain systems of "human development" which, through a procedure akin to hypnosis, create a condition of "fearlessness." As a result, they cut off their clients from the reality of their past. Regrettable. People who are *advanced* in this way do remember, but much like shades. After years of work, the capacity to fear is no longer a cause igniting the impulse of flight. It becomes, then, the force that evokes the wish to understand the incomprehensible. Finally, it matures to become what is called in the Bible "the fear of God." Hence it is called the *beginning* of wisdom.

Conflict

We prize conflict as a great good. Like almost all the dimensions of experience, it is both an inner and an outer condition of life. The early steps toward the spiritualization of conflict are gaining the skills related to conflict within oneself. This is a vein of alchemical gold. Each such conflict is a nodal point in a human constitution . . . what Freud called a *knotenpunkt*. It is only natural to wish to avoid, repress, or transcend such knotenpunkt. But our mathematics show that when this is attempted by large masses of people, the results are lamentable, often leading to vast cultural conflagrations such as wars or inquisitions. Over the centuries, our fellowship has labored to establish an accessible basis for inner conflict in whole cultures. In children's culture all over the world, games and fairy tales help to develop an exuberant imaginary life for the individual child. Children can see, however, that life as it is . . . is not like that. These early "conflicts" set down beachheads of intelligence in the child. Thus it works: arenas of struggle are engendered between the world of daydreaming and fantasy . . . and the child's view of themselves (usually more accurate than anyone else's). In the arena is also the confrontation between both the above and the "actual" world of family and school. Right here begins the seed points of creative intelligence. This is a priceless situation unless the child finds themselves in such a hazardous position that their only survival option is a retreat into imagining or outer conquest.

In later life these "knotenpunkt" call us to face them in a different ways. If evaded, they create the field of conflict with others. But skill applied at this level is the beginning of self-knowledge. When people in their ignorance try to dissolve or transcend these nodal points, not only do they lose important beachheads of their personal evolution but they may even become a cause of grief to others. In order to remain free of conflict and contradiction, often such people strive to become *conquerors* of themselves or of others. They cut rather than untie the Gordian knotenpunkt.

Clearly the above three qualities are not on anyone's shopping list for spiritual development unless it is to wish themselves rid of them. We understand this contemporary feature though we do not approve of it. Our fourth condition, however, would have everyone's approval. But the fact that we consider the above three the royal highway to the fourth will, I am sure, draw hisses.

Faith

Some Frenchman said of faith, "after we have exhausted knowledge and exhausted the will . . . we acquire from within, the faith such that even if we wished not to believe we would be unable to not believe."

Faith is a force prior to knowledge and will. In the adult, it calls for cultivation. It demands a person's maximum effort to know, understand, live, and wish. Without this, the person is not keeping faith with their own nature as human. The leap of faith does not come on the near side of the quest to know. It comes at the exhaustion of one's knowing. Still, thank God, while we live we are never without faith. Our goal is to arrive at a truly grown-up faith, a blossom, fruit, and seed that comes through great understanding to a simple perception which "passes understanding." The way of memory, fear, and conflict brings a person to the discovery of this faith.

We oppose making faith hinge on *contemporary* conceptions of love. Because of the way the Western psyche now is, this can only lead to headaches or worse. Faith is the center line of our work with the "three realms." Baldly stated, it was the confusion and misdirection of this force that led to the flood.

> [I was reading this on the plane to Europe. At this place in the paper, the face of the lady president was so vivid to my memory that I thought she had sat down in the empty seat next to me . . . tigerishly showing her teeth.]

Look now under the skin of the world's faithful. All so full of "loving faith," and see there the dead men's bones rattling for power.

Faith is the heart of the human spirit, and marrying it to power corrupts without remedy. The Book had put it this way . . . "and all flesh had corrupted their way upon the earth."

You now have my report. As I said, the decision to file it came under some kind of compulsion. I think Amfortas would do well to look at the short sections about fear and conflict once again. Obviously at Olivet, very few, if any, had gotten to first base here. I would rebuke the adversary who seemed to think himself a "Galahad." He bore a more striking resemblance to a Spectre generated by Urizen.

Getting this posted relieves me of an oppressive burden.

Notes

1) My interpretation of this rather dense passage is that Newton's system was theoretically graspable. This made the world into a potential field for aggrandizement. It became feasible to imagine that men could control and therefore *possess* reality. The next all-too-human step would be to attempt to swallow up what was *other* into one's feeling to self-satisfaction. Thereby one subjectively converts the other into the same. Hence, if one could keep on *saming the other*—fattening on the illusion of growing until coming to the end—why, one then would not have to *face* death.

2) Probably the Russian proverb made famous by Federenko at the United Nations. But actually he was quoting a Chinese proverb learned while working in that land. "When the tiger shows her teeth, it does not mean that she is smiling."

3) I believe this is an ancient Egyptian proverb. Or at least I found one much like it cited as such in C.S. Lewis's *The Abolition of Man*.

CHAPTER SIX

Dzovinar

Mazda Djilas was brought up with an elder brother by an aunt and uncle living in Tiflis. Natives of Yugoslavia, they had been sent to Georgia for safety from a particularly bitter outbreak of conflict between Montenegran patriots and some remaining Turks. As a child she was deeply religious and so was quite naturally unhappy in the USSR. Her brother was able to make use of the chaos during the second World War to escape with her. They made their way across Asia to find refuge with other relatives living in Shanghai. During the brief period of fluidity following the war, she met and married a US citizen working there as a director for UNRRA in northeast Asia. When the Chinese civil war broke out, she was evacuated with agency personnel and families. The premature loss of her husband compelled her to strike out on her own as a weaver. A unique flair and prodigious capacity for work catapulted her toward the front rank of world-class textile artists. She contributed to the *The Personalist*. An article in this journal entitled "The Person as Artist" caught the attention of Amfortas.

She was very reticent about becoming associated with any sort of "group," and it was not until three years had passed and much serious correspondence that she actually became a member of the Amfortas Society.

* * *

The last time I saw her was seven or eight years after our Olivet conference. We had arranged to lunch together at the Plaza during one of my trips to New York.

Her hair was still black with a striking streak of grey, and it was drawn back behind her neck and gathered with a clasp. The gravity of her face still touches me all these years later. I was fascinated watching her enter the lobby. She walked with a firm, secured footstep and a free stride that conjured visions of a woman walking alone through a meadow. Dzovinar's handshake was direct, dry, welcoming, and electric. The contact set us loose from the swirl of banality around us.

Toward the end of lunch, I told her a joke. Her face broke free of its gravity . . . a flash of ocean surf on a bright morning. Her laughter and joy in her eyes were so beautiful it could break one's heart.

Whenever I met her, and particularly this last time, I felt myself in the presence of a beneficent force of nature.

In the late afternoon, one day during the first week of the Olivet meeting, she took my hand and insisted we walk a little ways. Just behind the small administration building, the hill sloped to the west and there was a small cemetery. She indicated a bench for me to sit on and took for herself the butt end of a log lying nearby, setting it down in front of the bench. She sat on it facing me . . . holding my eyes with hers.

"What do you think of this cat's cradle of evasion and justification entangling our meeting?"

"I think we have to end it or it will end us . . ."

"Exactly so . . . how?"

"I'll think of something . . ."

"Don't think of something . . . do something."

This was her way.

The Art of the Science of Personal Movement as Taught by a Nontraditional Vedic Community

After the odd meeting of Amfortas in Olivet, I decided to revisit some places that had deeply affected me while I was traveling as a refugee with my older brother, Milovan. May his memory be a source of blessing. It took me several years to arrange the details.

A weaving is an intention and an intimation . . . a line becomes a plane. It is a celebration of ambiguity . . . where the visible, by a kind of art, becomes the agent of its own invisibility. The weaving has gathered it into a new but shifting appearance. As such, it approximates a paradigm of the path of persons.

Certain threads of my experience called constantly to me . . . called and sent tremors of intimations . . . demanded that I "examine" the texture of my life.

Fortunately, our federal government was wise enough to provide substantial tax advantages for me to travel and study weaving techniques around the world. From the confluence of such streams, I was enabled to return to some scenes of my girlhood.

The title of this "report" is misleading . . . as are some colours. How can a "Vedic" community be nontraditional? Only through my definitions. For I use the word in my own way to signify those who follow the thread.

Which thread shall be the basis of the weaving?

On spindles before me are blue . . . gold . . . red . . . green . . . white, and of course there must be black. Do we unravel or do we weave . . . loop and knot or braid?

Vedic because the thread is red.

Not the red of the Soviet.

The red blood.

The red of certain moments of life . . . of sunrise, of sunset, of awakening to love, of a special rose, of the dyed skins of the desert tabernacle . . . of the square of sincerity.

*   *   *

1943. A special morning. We knew we had arrived in Persia and it was May. The war zone lay behind us. Milovan has steered us this way. Our first thought had been west. But we heard that refugees there were being stopped and sent back. Milovan had quickly sensed the nature of the chaos and chose our road to the east.

Weeks went by as in a dream. Then one morning, this morning I called special, we woke up and knew we would be safe. As though they had been silent until now, I heard the singing of birds. We were on a roadside among a buoyant stand of hollyhocks. Most of the blossoms were red. There was hope. Cocks were crowing.

A few miles farther on, we found a stream. Fresh water! Our feet sore and wounded smelled worse than sewers. We took the opportunity to bathe ourselves and wash our filthy clothes. In no time, the morning Persian sun dried our garments and we were on our way. Then we heard the faint, high chimes of bells and before long found ourselves among a small flock of goats and sheep and the children who were herding them. With a strange speech, a language pleasant as birds, the children chattered to us. Seeing we did not understand, the tallest among them, a shapely girl, took me by the hand . . . We went to the right and over a small rise. Before us beyond the rise was the lovely sight of a small village of white-washed mud houses. I began to cry.

I arrived in Teheran with my papers in meticulous order. The Shah now was at the height of his vainglorious power and the country was in snip-snap shape. Ransacking my memory, I had only managed an approximate idea of the location of the village I sought. Twined more vividly were hollyhocks and sunrise, cleanliness, hope, and humanity.

Provided I stayed clear of certain military installations near the border of Russia, wide-ranging travel arrangements had been made for me in the northern parts. The villages seemed countless. In each of them, dutifully I sat with woman, girls, and boys . . . taking my notes and studying their way with the wool. Having been on the run once, I knew to ask no questions and say little. Elliptically I would now and then probe about "my village." To most of those I did ask, it seemed I followed some fantasy. In Tabriz, one greybeard looked at me while cocking his head to the side and murmured, "Hurqalyavi." [1] Timidly smiling, he confessed to never having seen a place like that.

A week later, I found my village.

I was the guest of a wealthy merchant in Sari. He encouraged me to use one of his horses for a ride by his house. He assured me that since I was an excellent horsewoman and clearly wore Western riding clothes, I would encounter no difficulties.

Golden thread . . . delight . . . delight of purposeless pleasure . . . pleasure unknotted from need . . . the pleasure of beauty . . . that pleasure which when it is given we must take or commit a crime against the universe. Here, now only several leagues south of the Caspian, among thickets of wild yellow roses, I rode gratefully, easily, without haste, and found my bells and long-haired goats and the village of whitewashed houses.

"So, after all these years, you have returned to visit us."

These words were spoken by the tall, stately woman who, as a child, had been the first friend I discovered on our flight from Tiflis. Now she was grown and a woman of rank in the community. We were sitting in her house after an evening meal of lamb and rice. Word had been sent to my wealthy host that I would be staying in the village overnight.

"It could not have been easy."

"No, it has not been easy."

"You are married?"

"I am widowed."

"Ahh . . . as am I."

"In America, where I live, I attended a meeting of colleagues . . . Questions came up calling for an answer. I could only answer by trying to revisit some special laces."

"Do you have a profession?"

"I am a weaver."

After a night of refreshing sleep, Daina woke me. We washed but took only water . . . no food. Then she instructed me to be silent where she would be taking me this morning. We went to a building that I had noticed when here as a child but had never been inside. It was a low rectangular structure. Within, the earth had been dug away to expose a space deeper than the building was high.

Established on the deep ground was a very large loom holding a huge tapestry more than a third completed. A dozen or so young people were at their posts before the weaving. Over on one side, a goodly proportioned timber frame was set up with a gamut of sounding stones and metals suspended along the frame. On the other side, a drum was being struck and a flute was played by two very old men. For unpredictable lengths of time, the drum and flute fell silent; and during the stillness, a short, barrel-chested man with a leather mallet ran along the wood, stone, and metal gamut and struck tones. Sometimes he struck the same tone but on different stones or metals and hence of different timbres, over and over. The result was nothing like what we are accustomed to call music—more like a not-unpleasant arrangement of unrefined noise. Correlations stood out sharply at times between the figures of sound graven into the silence and the lines of thread worked by the weavers.

This work went on without a break until, as though by arrangement, it stopped and everyone put their stations in order. Daina led me out of the building. I had been so absorbed in the performance that I was surprised to find the world still there, the blue sky arching above . . . the bird song present . . . and in the distance, the bells of the herds.

Daina rested her hand lightly on my arm and turned me to face her.

"My dear friend, we will have food with my mother and father . . . and then, though it breaks my heart, you will have to leave."

I was hurt. I could think of nothing to say. My thoughts reminded me of the former time I had been here. I wished then to stay here forever. I could have now stayed here forever. That time, Milovan and I had stayed for several weeks until we had regained our strength.

When we walked into the house, Daina's parents smiled at me with such welcome that it confused me. After all, I was feeling hurt. They were rugged, seemingly simple folk. The mother, deciphering what must have been a bitterly conflicted countenance of grief and surprise, spoke to me straightforwardly.

"Our strength and our way of life is possible because we have become near unseen. No one pays attention to us. You are from a far country. You know the headman of the neighboring town. Everyone hereabout knows more or less where you are. We, my dear, must not ever become objects to the curious or powerful. Please consider the situation. Be generous and gracious with us."

As simple as that, I was convinced that neither because of inadequacy nor of dislike was I being sent away. The weight lifted

from my heart. I shared this one marvelous and essential meal
with them cheerfully.

Nevertheless, when later I was flying to India, sorrow like a
spring frost bit deeply into me.

*   *   *

After Milovan and I had left the village some weeks
behind, we were having a hard time getting food on our
own, and we knew we needed some traveling companions.
Steadily we were working our way south, hoping to find
country where we could safely spend the winter in the open.
South, almost as far as Shiraz, on a gentle mountain pass, our
bodies seemed to give out on the dusty road. We came to on
the road again among a ragged troop of metalsmiths. To this
day, I remember the name of the pass because of the irony.
"Gardeneh-ye Kowli Kush . . ." Gypsy-killer pass. All the
passes in this part of the world are named to kill someone.

Falling in this with company was amazing good fortune.
How different it was living among a weaving community
where we had been (I believe this is true whether the group is
settled or nomad) and the life in the atmosphere of a moving
camp of metalworkers.

The songs, the camp animals, the vibrating edges of the
people . . . all are a different world. The roaring, rustling
sound of the forge fires, the hammering, the agonizing
grinding wheels were emblems of a differing celestial
mechanics. Particularly so when the families had a lot of
work to do and blossoms of sparks kept spilling from their
work into the sky at night . . . seeming to merge with the
stars. I sat and became enthralled by the fibers of relation I
sensed between the sparks, the embers of the forge fires, and
the stars which appeared to take these minute particles to

themselves exultantly with respect. I thought I could hear the stars singing.

Yes, we had done well to join ourselves to a group like this one. Always there was the burble of enthusiasm and excitement around us. Only the leader at times assumed an air of gravity when a dispute arose and he had to rule solutions for the problematic. We had plenty of food, and the tribe saw to it that both Milovan and I put in hard days' work every day so that we "could enjoy our meals."

*   *   *

This revisitation of the mansions of Providence called for me to land in Delhi. There was a journalist couple, both of whom were Hindu, who knew of my work as a textile artist and were eager to help me get into a particular region of Rajasthan. I had my reasons. They, in a rare moment of intimacy, shared with me theirs.

Several times in their lives, they had been "brought back to their senses" by an apparition. A small family in the characteristic white Rajasthani garments had appeared to them seemingly out of nowhere, vigourously strode by them, and then gone on. They were haunted by these events. On one occasion, they had been in a particularly fancy restaurant . . . sitting on the terrace and celebrating a glamorous job offer in New York City. They were enjoying their dreams of proffered wealth and of life "near the center of things" and the envy and respect of their colleagues. Then they saw this small group of figures emerge from the distance, pass in their radiantly white clothes under the terrace, and continue out of sight. They looked at each other and realized they really had no desire to leave their homeland. There were several other occasions. Though they had visited Rajasthan several times on assignment; this time, free of professional obligations, they hoped for something. They did not know what.

Both my expectations and theirs were fulfilled when after some travel we arrived in the village of K—. Something here was very different. I call it the "blend." Lives here, I sensed, were braided in a unique way. The dignified Rajasthanis were mingling quite easily with traveling flute makers and a recently arrived band of minstrels and smiths. I felt we had been dropped into a movie set before the action, *before* the cameras started and players assumed their parts. Someone unfamiliar was staring at me. I searched the crowd and noticed a short, wiry, grey-haired woman who looked away the moment I caught her eyes. A few moments later, she was gone. Soon after, a gentleman came up to Narayan and invited the three of us to follow him and meet an old man of the village. The ancient seemed of so little weight that any stir of wind would pick him up to a roof or treetop.

"You come on a good and auspicious day. Today our smiths have returned from a long journey. We are glad to see them again."

"We are glad to see you. You (indicating me) have also been here before."

"Possibly."

"You know why you have returned?"

"Yes."

"Then surely you can leave now, don't you think?"

"I think so."

"Your friends should stay for a time. But you are needed."

My friends were startled. I understood. After I spent some time clarifying matters with the ancient, arrangements were made for my return to Delhi.

Human life . . . Time . . . Space . . . Radiance . . . Darkness. Lines of heredity . . . lines of evolution . . . lines of essences of becoming. Momentums of the soul, momentums of the mind . . . momentums of body and feeling.

Distaffs and shuttles . . . warps and woofs . . . forces and hammers and anvils . . . the tongs of the days and nights.

The returning metalworkers had validated rumors which had been heard for so many years. There had been a vast number of murders of Gypsies and Jews. Some black thread had wildly found a willing "slave" to weave a slab of time across history, a slab as solid as ice, like black ice at the crossroads. There had indeed been migrations of peoples over the face of the earth and death in diabolical furnaces. I remembered conversations between Milovan long ago and the old man. Milovan had told him of the events in Europe. The ancient had conceded that there may have been a miscalculation in the Hindu calendar. They could have erred in charting the dance of Durga. But it was not something to correct lightly. The elders of the people of K—had sent reliable persons and groups westward into Turkey and Romania and also into Italy and France with the charge to verify Milovan's account beyond doubt. Then the investigations had to be repeated and repeated. Now, twenty years later, the final confirmation was brought. The events *had* happened and in such a way that the calendars of the village required extensive correction. To put it lightly in our terms, some decimal points were in the wrong place. Rather than being at the beginning of a frighteningly long "Kali Yuga," we were at the closing dramas of one shorter by a multiple of ten.

People were needed where they were. Where they were is where they are part of a fabric of relationship. It was urgent that the human race move onto the ascending plane.

To explain . . . this is understood as movement on a plane of evolutionary growth. A line of development utterly departing from hereditary limits could no longer suffice. The line of motion had to move with sufficient force to lift the threads around it. People "in movement" were no longer free to "ascend by detachment . . ."

They *were* attached. The direction of movement in this time is ascent in attachment. Freedom lies in the absence of *intoxication* with the fabric of heredity and social context.

I remembered years ago our pain at being sent from this haven as we had been sent from the village in the north. It had then been bitter, I told the old man. He explained that we each carried a world, actual and potential, in our souls. Abdication from our destiny was unthinkable to the people.

Each person comes into the world, in their view, with an inner world . . . a portion of the world of the soul that can be woven and built into a world of beauty. This is our birthright. Humans are free to neglect it. Religion is non-neglect.

There are hazards in our condition. Sometimes we will encounter individual and even collective evil. Among the "materials" of our inner world, we have a black thread . . . this is not evil but, as the materiality which can absorb light and life, it is an absolutely indispensable material. This *can* become the baseline for any internal structure able to pass through physical death. This thread is *neutral*. Within the inattentive or the possessed, it can become monstrous. The connection of the human being to the *virtu* of the black thread is through the textuality of identification. However, it can also become the medium for obsession and possession. Properly proportioned, the process is the sap of life. Out of scale and proportion, it is poison. For those in "motion," attentiveness is the nervous system of the inner world.

At times in individual and collective life, the evolving pattern of the inner world becomes imbalanced and can even become infected by what can only be called evil. The ensuing struggle is of high seriousness.

The people of K—have an unusual approach to both initiating and fostering movement along an ascending plane, a world. One must be very clear that this is differentiated sharply from motion along a *line*, which is the way of the sannyasin and monk.

In a rug, the number of knots per inch create its density. The more dense, the more fine. By its own nature, the material of the thread establishes the limit of the knots. Coarse wool has different limits from fine wool . . . both are different from silk. Another factor influences outcome also. What is the level of destruction wrought on the source of the material?

The K—imagine a weaving in which the density is created by depth and variety of knottings . . . by layers rather than repetitions. The fibers are at once light and reflectors of light. Many layers of this open weave, many varied loops of knots, are the means for achieving both fineness and density of illumination. The more free is each layer to move while embodying relation with the others, the more excellent the artistry.

That is how they describe the birthright of the person, the human life, and of the society in which the life is grounded. The pity is that we have very partial and limited ideas of unity . . . in linkage with these notions, we try to stitch the various layers together until they cannot move. A person is already an implicit unity, a loose unity. But we aspire to a tightly congealed unity of individual or group because of fear. So we break the intrinsic into fragments that have lost their relationship to the whole. The fear is a fear of the looseness of the material on any given level; it is fear of being *too* available to the winds, fear of the infinity of light and apparent finitude of time. Rather than endure the vulnerability and the openness to God's presence, we prefer to be able to call on "God's name." People prefer to be rugs instead of human beings. Surely Amfortas can understand the implications of the K—people's theory of development.

* * *

While I was sitting in the Delhi airport, I came to grips with the need to visit one more place. I had avoided thinking about it.

I needed to see the place where Milovan had met his death . . . where his unmarked grave lay. My brother had been the light and solace of my life. His good cheer, intensity, wit, and his sturdy good faith had been the only substantial presence between me and some unutterable terror that lay beyond the circle of our small lives.

*   *   *

Before we left the village of K—, the two of us had several conversations with the old man about our futures. During the many talks Milovan had with him, I was usually excluded because of my age. But now, since it was *my* life at stake, I was permitted to join them.

The old man was of the opinion that though our best chance for "survival" was to throw ourselves on the mercy of the British, it was not a solution offering good chances of *survival with meaning.* He thought our original idea the best, namely that we continue and try to reach our relations in the European colony in Shanghai. He offered positive reasons of which I remember very little. They had to do with "pressures of light and shade." The negative ones had more force for me. He was convinced that the current mood in India could lead to a couple of young people like us ending up as merchandise. The British, though outwardly courteous, would be of little help to a couple of youngsters from Soviet territory. To cross China, on the other hand, offered us a much better chance at a real future, a future along a path. Milovan and I were very tired, and the thought of extending our journey another several thousand miles on our own was awesome. But the old man had a strong influence on my brother, and my brother had a strong influence on me. Before long we were attached to a caravan of nomads who again were heading north. The total journey, which was not by any imagining straight, took us well over a year. We crossed many borders, were immersed in many languages, re-crossed many borders. The caravans considered us good luck. The old man no doubt had started a rumor about us and this, more than any wealth could have done, protected us. The journey itself was not at all the ordeal we had feared. We felt ourselves always surrounded by friends. The physical demands had become easy for us by now. Only once did we encounter real fear, and that was near the middle of our journey.

A caravan of Kazaks was taking us across Western China on their route to Ulan Bator. We were skirting the north edge of the vast Taklimakan Desert following the Yarkant River. One night a sound came with the wind that was blowing from the south across the sands. It was as though we were along a sea shore, and we could hear the water clawing and sucking at the rocks. Images of foam and flecks of kelp and amber crowded into my mind. The campfires kept trying to go out. The Kazaks said nothing, huddling in small groups and smiling uneasily at us. Their speech is a form of Turkic spoken by many people in the region of Tiflis, so we could make out the gist of what they were saying. They feared the spirits of the Taklimakan Shamo. The wind came across from where their capital city had been many, many thousands of years ago. Whether we caught the fear by contagion or sensed real presences, I cannot to this day say. Soon Milovan and I were terrified out of our skins and spent the night awake while continually scavenging twigs, dried grasses, and rare pieces of deadwood to keep the tiny fire fed. Toward daybreak, Milovan and I seemed to have the same images, for we shared them. They brought a measure of tranquility to our hearts. We thought we could see a city by the sea. Well-dressed stone steps went down to the water all along the seafront. The water heaved in long swales, and there were occasional glimpses of stately women emerging from the foam and ascending the stone ramps and stairways. When day broke, we greeted the sunrise fervently. I, personally, have never at a deep level been afraid of anything since then.

*   *   *

While sitting in the airport, the memories had become so present to me that I decided to cancel my departure to the States and try to make whole my brother's memory. My attention had been riveted by a small Rajasthani family, which entered the waiting lounge at the far end and walked calmly through it, passing very near me and continuing to exit at the opposite end.

Summons of the ascending world.

Insane difficulty of getting into China.

Weeks of waiting in Delhi. Weeks of government offices and the presentation of purposes and credentials.

Finally an opening in the wall appeared. An official somewhere had recognized my name from a review of an exhibition of my work in Florence. In exchange for several lectures at the Fabrics Institute, a series of tours and talks before collectives that produced wool or silk, my wish to visit Kaifeng would be honored. I was required to commit to complete avoidance of politics . . . particularly Middle Eastern politics. They seemed to have assumed that I was Jewish.[2]

*   *   *

The last caravan Milovan and I were with followed the Yellow River cut from far to the west to the town of Hun Po where some seasonal boat traffic began. Great merchant families had maintained wharves here for moving goods by boat toward the population centers in the east. Despite the war, some traffic still went on. We two "kids" were granted passage along with the goods our caravan had sold.

On the approach to Kaifeng, the river becomes as wide as a lake. A chunky middle-aged gentleman, whom we had noticed in an almost continuous doze during the last several days of the trip, became suddenly alert. Very graciously he approached us and began to talk about this and that. If we wanted to see real boat traffic, we should see the Yangtze . . . but we were quite right to be here because for him *this*, the Huang, was *the* great river. Sensing our limitations due to age, he spoke to us in a recognizable Turkic dialect:

> *Te* is strongest here, and with it, surrounding it, interpenetrating it, is Tao. The Huang is a membrane both stitching together and defining the faces of the desert and the monsoon. This river has borne all the stress, all the vitality of the reconciliations of the ethers of the mountain, the desert and the jungle.

I found the above quite interesting, and I have set it down more or less as I remember him saying it. He offered us the hospitality of his house in Kaifeng. We did not refuse.

His name was Wu. I remember him fondly, but the memory is streaked with darkness, because it was while we were guests of this gentleman that Milovan died. A stomach problem had been bothering my brother on and off for the past six months. It suddenly flared up and in a sudden rage of infection and fever that the best physicians Mr. Wu could hire could not stop. This malady took his life, took this rare young life. As soon as possible afterward, Mr. Wu arranged for both passage and bodyguards to deliver me to the home of my distant relatives in Shanghai. The bodyguards were now necessary because I was a girl who no longer was a child . . .

* * *

The government guide assigned me in Kaifeng, to whom I described where I vaguely remembered I wanted to be, brought me finally to a neighborhood far less vital that I remembered. Still, it was familiar. My body remembered more than my mind. My heart began racing, and my feet seemed to lead me toward the right where we came upon the small cemetery. It had been preserved as a relic of the past. The park, according to my guide, had been the private preserve of an important family of Hunan province. The place was much as I recollected.

When I saw the grave, I recalled the small stone had been carved with the ideograms Tao, Ming, and Li, which still were visible, unblurred by time or element. Mr. Wu had taken it upon himself to bury Milovan in his families' ancestral ground. He would not flaunt tradition to the extent of marking a grave site with a name not only of different family but of barbarian lineage. He had his reasons. I began to weep.

The embarrassed guide turned away. There was a whirring of a flight of birds over my head. Instantly an ancient with a white flowing beard, a seamed but young face, and garmented in a luminous robe that brushed the ground was standing there. He stood just beyond my brother's gravestone and swayed as though on shipboard; a small nod and he vanished. He appeared and then was no longer there. Where he had stood, I noticed a very small pebble on the ground. Wanting something material to remember the moment by, I hurried to the spot and, picking it up, dropped it into my purse without thinking about it. I then walked up to the guide, who was still turned away, and touched his arm, indicating my readiness to leave. Noticing my streaked face, he handed me a small handkerchief and again turned away. I was grateful for his delicacy. Without looking back, he led the way out of the cemetery. I followed.

Early the next morning, just inside the door of my hotel room, I found a cloth pouch tied with a red thread. Inside was a note and a letter. The note indicated that the pouch was intended for the keeping of the pebble, "for it deserved respect." The note also introduced the letter as one to be given "to Mazda, when she returns to visit her brother's grave."

Mazda:

If you are reading this, you rejoice many worlds. I owed to you this testament. Your brother was an excellent young man. He brought into my desperate life certain needed thoughts. He told me of the ideas of the headman of the K—. They spoke probity to my condition. It ordered my mind and brought meaning to my life. Perhaps, though, the ideas were Milovan's . . . after he worked through the headman's.

Before I met the two of you, I was a follower of the Tao Hseuh Chia [(道 學 家)][3], which originated here in Kaifeng when it was the capital city of the Sung. For me, buried deep in the teaching was a bolted door. What Milovan told me threw back the bolt. Through this I became able to truly bring respect to my ancestors and the departed of my clan. For this reason I was able, with a good heart, to open my families' ground for the remains of your brother.

After I had sent you to the East and had ample time to think, I vowed to offer prayers for your welfare. Also, I vowed that if you remembered your duty to visit the grave, I would tell you what I learned. A form of will and testimony. It will not matter if you think you do or think you do not understand what is written here. It will not matter if you think it relevant or irrelevant to your concerns. As I now have come to believe, either way, reading this will bring you much good.

You ought to know that I was able to keep informed of your life for some time while I lived. With gladness I learned of your marriage. With sorrow I learned of your path among the tall widows. With satisfaction I learned of your accomplishment as an artist. If as an artist you choose to be a blessing and not a curse to humanity, that will be good fortune. Then Tao will be the ocean and Ming and Li will be the streams of your talent. In our lands, we describe the expression of wisdom as a loom with work on it in progress. A classic is called "ching," literally a *warp*. The ongoing commentary to the ching is called "wei . . ." literally a *woof*. But Milovan opened to me another depth to this. He told me how the people of K—play an entirely different kind of textual weaving. An additional direction is set forth so that the loom of wisdom does not entangle its weavers but opens the weave to heights and depths.

Our people have suffered conventional wisdom's greatest pitfall. It is a bitterness that our people, our Han people, have been hypnotized for eight hundred years by our most illustrious philosopher, Chu Hsi. He performed a "brilliant" reduction of our inheritance. From his time to ours, our thinkers have seen and pondered our "wisdom" through his spectacles. We did not understand they were not of clear glass; they were in a sense prescription lenses good only for him and his own private problems. They helped him live and walk, but they blinded us so that from the end of the Sung time till today we have been coasting downward on a spiral plane

One evening when you were my guests, Milovan told me of a fable told to him several times by the old man of K—. It was a picture of how followers with the "best intentions" betray teachers. Milovan did not understand it but repeated the laconic formula of the tradition:

> Long ago a student turned to ruins the teaching of China. He turned the ends of the loom . . . and making the 3, 2 brought ruin. Chou Tun I, those brothers of stature Cheng Hao and Chen I . . . in heaven they are grieving. When Chu Hsi made

simple the meaning of Chung the world was destroyed.

When I heard this, I trembled. It was like hearing the decree of heaven. When Milovan saw my face, he was troubled and said it probably had no meaning. I assured him it meant a great deal. He went on to say that the old man was given to these mystifying statements. To lighten my burden, he related a tradition of the

K—that was about another time and place:

> The One is a trap . . . the Two is twice a trap. The trap of the Odd and the Even destroyed Troy.
> When brought by Iskander it destroyed our own land. It now threatens to destroy the land of our adoption.

He asked if I understood what was meant by this, and I had to answer that I did not. The second riddle did not succeed in displacing the distress I felt from the first.

I went to my ancestral shrine and prayed that my mothers and fathers would help me to clear my understanding. That night I had a dream. Two merchants were playing at "odds and evens" with their fingers. A man whom my dream announced to be Pythagoras came and poured a kettle of cold water on them. Instantly a band of squat gnomes armed with staves attacked him. Smiling sadly, he retreated over the horizon. I pondered the meanings till morning.

When I saw Milovan, I told him of this and of my thoughts. This kind of counting in the game comes from an error in Li. It shows those who cherish commerce and its excitement as their *highest value*. The figure of Pythagoras tried to wake them up. But already the "counting" had become philosophy. It had become lifelessness, it had become politics and tyranny . . . it had become art and insignificance, it had become religion and oppression. From that day, my thinking took a new turn.

Mazda, at the time when the three lamenting founders of the Tao Hseuh Chia were still on this earth, before the time of Chu Hsi, they were residents of this province and the cities of Loyang and Kaifeng. And also at this time, Kaifeng was the home of a respected Jewish Community. My family preserved some traditions of their relations with this community. A particular idea of theirs is relevant here. They spoke of a One before heaven and earth which is *not the one of counting*, not a one or two or many. Like the Tao of Chuangtze, *this* is neither this nor that. But not entirely like his Tao either. In our life on earth, *this* is the additional direction of the loom. Through *this* we make looms. Extending our apprehension of *this* through the surfaces of light, the surfaces and knottings of time and space, we come to the origin of the weave of the people of K—.

I will specifically demonstrate the ruin brought on the Han people from the reducings of Chu Hsi. You will note how such matters and such flaws of understanding may not be limited to my own black-haired people. Before Chu Hsi, there was a book, considered to be a "ching," which described centrality. It had been called according to the theme of its first chapter, Chung Ho Ching.

The Classic of Central Harmony:

When the passions of joy, anger, grief and pleasure have not been awakened there is a state of chung, centrality. When the passions have been awakened and all are in tune, there is a state of ho, harmony. The chung is the foundation, the ho is the highway, Tao, of civilization. Once chung and ho are achieved the universe becomes a cosmos.

But Chu Hsi could not bear the contradictions . . . he could not embrace plurality. He ground his spectacles so he only regarded highly the theme of the second chapter. And in his preface to his new edition, he framed his lenses in this way:

> Chung denotes being without inclination to either side; yung denotes admitting of no change; by chung is denoted the correct way to be pursued; by yung the fixed principle regulating all things.

The book became known as the Chung Yung instead of the Chung Ho Ching. It is no accident that the most spirited of the English translation of this new and corrupted conception was done by the pathetic fascist, Ezra Pound. He called it the Unwobbling Pivot.[4]

Mazda, do not let his happen to you. Be of great range. Your brother saved me by bringing with him the key that unbolted my ancestral chapel door. Avoid the pitfalls of such timid reductions of meaning as was perpetrated on my culture by Chu Hsi. Be a woman of Central Harmony, of Chung Ho.

-Old Man Wu

I took the stone without looking at it and put it into the cloth pouch and retied it with the red thread. The letter I placed in a special pocket that I had in the waistband of my shift. They are with me now in my home near New York City.

I read the *New York Times.* I now outline work I need to do in preparation of a new weaving I intend . . . inspired by the Shakespeare play *The Tempest.*

My mind is troubled by reports in the newspaper about street crime and the seemingly endless cycle of two-dimensional action and reaction that governs the world of politics. What a multitude of shrines our species has set up o the altar of "odd and even." And the ambitions of church and state are so palpably *unthreaded* to the light.

This morning, it puts me in mind of Omar's quatrain:

> In path of faith to either shrine we start,
> The one on earth, the other in the heart;
> Try, if you can to reach a human heart,
> One heart is more than thousand shrines apart.

I hope the members of Amfortas will be patient with my sentimentality. But I look at the "stone" which I picked up at Milovan's graveside. It is utterly common and ordinary. I did not ask for bread . . . but that is what the stone has become.

Notes

1) *Hurqalya* is a term of great significance to certain schools of Islamic mysticism. See particularly H. Corbin, *Spiritual Body and Celestial Earth*, Bollingen Series XCI:2, Princeton University Press. From the above book, a quote from Shaikh Abu'l Qasim Khan Ibrahami, p. 240:

> Roughly, the word Hurqalya refers to the *mundus archetypus*, the world of Images (alam al mithal), the world of autonomous Figures and Form (alam al suwar). Although strictly speaking, the Heavens of this universe are what we designate as Hurqalya, whereas its Earth is referred to by the names Jabalqa and Jabarsa, philosophers sometimes refer to this universe as a whole, with its different planes and degrees as Hurqalya.

2) Probably because Kaifeng was once the center of a vital Jewish community, it had been a nodal point of the Silk Road.

3) The School of the Study of the Tao. This is the proper name of what is known commonly in the West as neo-Confucianism.

4) This is a very rare interpretation of the "drama" of Sung philosophy. I personally have been able to find only two writers, neither Chinese, who have come to similar conclusions as "Old Man Wu." One of them is GI Gurdjieff, who in the metaphor of the "Alla-attapan," *All & Everything*, First Series, p. 822-855, describes in

cognate terms a very "similar" Chinese reduction. The other is from an unpublished doctoral dissertation by Dr. Roderick Scott. Dr. Scott had been a resident in China from 1911 until the end of World War II. It is titled *The Personalistic Insights in Ancient Chinese Philosophy*, University of Southern California, 1946, particularly p. 116-121.

CHAPTER SEVEN

Asaph

Abraham Rose grew up an Orthodox Jew in Portland, Oregon. While still a young student in a Talmud Torah, he became keen about psychology. Rather than enter a rabbinical school, he prevailed upon his parents to permit him to attend Yeshiva University in New York City where he soon switched his allegiance to mathematics. Subsequent to his graduate degree, he accepted a post teaching in a small New Jersey college. One of his students, a member of a nearby Mongolian-Tibetan community, was intrigued by his obviously traditional lifestyle and invited him to visit his family. Assured that, though as Tibetans they had dispensation to eat meat, on this occasion they would abide by strict Buddhist requirements which would be kosher, he accepted the invitation. Here he met several families, among whom was the student's uncle, Tenpa Tenzin. The two became fast friends. They shared a common hobby—the construction of mathematical games and entertainments. One of their most successful was published in the *Blaisdell Journal* of Claremont, California. Another was placed

in the little-known British journal, *Cipher*. Both games had to do
with the flows of fluids and the flows of events and the phenomena
at the boundaries of each. A British correspondent of Amfortas
engaged them in lively discussion for over a year. Soon they were
among the very few participants at the Olivet meeting who, prior
to it, knew each other.

*   *   *

Asaph bubbled. There is no other way to describe his curious
presence and the impression he made whether in a group or
one-on-one.

I remember once being his guest for a Sabbath dinner with his
small family in Watchung, New Jersey. I had taken a bus from Port
Authority and was waiting for him to pick me up on the street in
front of the bus stop. Just about the time I was getting anxious, I
sensed a commotion further up the street and watched a battered
car come weaving and wheezing through the rush-hour traffic. He
finally cut directly across the path of a taxi to somehow land his
Ford at the curb in front of me. With no ceremony, he urgently
waved me in and we rattled off.

His small house hard against some low hills was a haven of
peace. His wife, a small Belgian woman, came to the door to greet
us. Two children hung shyly back. The tranquility had no effect
on him.

After a fervent and enlightening celebration, we sat up into
the late hours discussing every philosophy under the sun. The
next morning when I was due to return to New York, he flashed
me a mischievous grin and told me I was on my own. "Get back
any way you can, old man, I can't drive today." His wife came to
my rescue by describing the way to walk to the local bus service,
which would drop me off where I arrived.

Although I am fairly convinced of the authenticity of the material on which he based his report, I would guess that the translations, true to his character, are highly idiosyncratic. I have no idea how he arrived at a term like "bizarre" to describe sixth century Near-Eastern politics. The text probably used an adjective like "difficult," "dangerous," or even "wicked." But Ali told me that Asaph's intuitions on translation were impeccable. He wished that the Western followers of his religion would throw out all the translations heretofore made into English and then throw Asaph's intelligence at the texts. It would thoroughly renovate our understanding of Tibetan Buddhism.

One time Asaph came to deliver a paper in London. He took the occasion to visit me at my residence in Wells. We went to visit the cathedral which he had heard so much about. After much time roaming about, we stopped for a time in the central court where a huge, venerable tree shelters the birds. It was a fit "object of contemplation."

Asaph was of medium build, wiry and muscular and, like Walt Whitman, wore a hat, indoors or out.

History as Present Time
Translation and Short Comments on Several Nestorian Texts
Asaph

Partiality rules history. Written by the "winners," does history mean we should believe that all the "losers" were bad? A hasty step to think so. Our whole narrative has not been told. We may be in the early events of a hundred-thousand-year story, the middle point of that story, or of a shorter one. We may even be, as some hold, at the end near the third-act curtain. Since we don't see the ocean into which our river empties, we don't really know *where* we are or which tributaries are carrying the strongest essences. As a Jew, I certainly know better than to rely on the histories written in Christendom. And I have a passion for things thrown up by events . . . coins, letters, bill of lading . . . these things have broken loose from the river banks and appear suddenly in our nets, in our hands . . . and they present an intimation, the faces of the many "losers," of unnumbered struggles and conflicts. Losers who have been dismissed, painted over, buried in a bog or left to rot on the islands of the past, like Philoctetes, may have another story. And also, since the *winners* are on the verge of becoming the architects of the greatest loss ever, perhaps matters are a trifle upside-down.

The Case

What we are taught to call the Nestorian Church was by their own membership called the Church of the East, or simply, Christian. I have a problem. What shall I call them in this short report? Will you know of whom I speak if I call them quite simply Eastern Christians? Since the greatest howl of this appellation will come from their fellow Christians of slightly different hue and cry, I shall risk it. After all, members of Amfortas are able from time to time to put prejudice aside.

They flourished for nearly a thousand years in Asia. We have in hand a document which was discovered neither at Tun-huang nor at Kao-ch'ang. As a matter of fact, the manner of our acquisition would throw doubt on its reliability among strict academic circles. But to you, my colleagues in the society, let me simply state that both myself and Ali are convinced of its genuine character.

The documents were found when the monks of Hsuan-miao Kuan monastery in Wuzhong of Nigxia province were digging to expand their housing complex. They discovered ruins which were unmistakably of a Ta-Chin (Christian) monastery. A relative of Ali's, the monk Thubten Norzang, known in Tibet as a Terton (gTer-ston), was traveling the region and stayed with the above-mentioned Taoist community in order to explore the ruins. It was he who found the material—a large collection from which I selected only a fraction for this particular investigation.

The discovery was in 1937. Large portions were in Syriac, and so Thubten Norzang never had been able to decipher the complete transmission. It was only recently that he was able to get copies into Ali's hands. The two of us then prepared a complete translation into the Tibetan tongue and sent that on to Sera Monastery, now in India, for their archives.

Let's jump right in:

> Attention: There is One, true and firm, *Who* being uncreated is the origin of origins, *Who* is ever incomprehensible and invisible, yet ever mysteriously existing to the last of the lasts; *Who*, holding the secret source of the origin created all things, and

Who surpassing all the holy ones, is the only unoriginated
Sovereign of the Universe—is not this our Eloha, the triune
mysterious Person, the unbegotten and true Sovereign?

This formulation is not unique to our collection. It shows up,
for example, on the stone monument presently resting at Hsian-fu
in the place know as Pei-lin, or the "Forest of Tablets." It is a pretty
fundamental expression of Eastern Christian doctrine expressed in
Chinese script. I want to call attention to the fourfold repetition
of the word "Who." After this repetition, they affirm this to our
"Eloha." In all discovered cases of this "sutra," three Chinese
characters are used to transliterate the four Syriac characters or
Eloha. Some scholars have reduced the idea to the abbreviation of
the Hebrew Elokim. But in the context here, conclude differently.
The first two letters do refer to the name Elokim . . . but they
intend the final pair to harmonize to the "active"[1] two letters
of the Tetragram, i.e., the "yod" and the "hey." The fourfold
repetitions, above is the key to the significance of the concept and
is combining the witness of *seeing* with the witness of *knowing.* In
the fourth section below, I shall elaborate this a little bit.

At this stage in the discussion, however, I think it is useful to
sketch out some little-appreciated history of this church. In their
heyday, they encompassed twenty to twenty-five ecclesiastical
provinces. Each province consisted of between eight to ten episcopal
sees. This adds up to somewhere between two hundred and two
hundred fifty bishoprics. The territory, in their own words, was
"The East," from Kurdistan and the Euphrates to China. Prior to
the rise of Islam, churches were throughout the Arabian Peninsula.
At one time, they were strongly represented in India.

It is very important to our purpose to recognize that the great
house of learning, so decisive for Arabic Civilization that was
founded in Baghdad by Caliph al-Ma'un in 830 CE, was staffed
primarily by members of this church. Their commission was

the translation of the scientific and philosophical works of the Greeks from the Greek and Syriac into Arabic. They also were the dominant practitioners of the medical arts. A tremendous debt is owed by Islam to the Dar al Hikmah and its most illustrious dean, the Eastern Christian (Nestorian) Hunayn ibn Ishaq.

Section Two
A Letter

Brothers and Sisters:

What began as a curse upon us from our brethren in the West has become the source of great blessings to our Church and the cause of truth. But now our blessings our success and our growth has caused us to be hated by many of the peoples among whom we have lived and worked. Perhaps we have encouraged this by allowing ourselves to become puffed up. We easily forget that the One from whom blessings flow is the source origin and goal of them.

Each time we founded a Bishopric according to our ideas, with its school, library, and hospital and thereby raised the level of the Province, have we not prided ourselves as benefactors? And have we not demoted the Benefactor? Are we not obliged to remember that we are the means by which God's gifts of faith, learning, and health are given to God's children?

I take this lesson: What we have learned, what we have found most helpful to our lives in faith . . . should be taught to others whether they "join" our church or not. Let us not endlessly remain victims of the foolishness that separated the Churches in the West and in the East of days gone by.

Does God care about our endless justification for our own divisions by the numbering of divisions in the Nature of God? We should long ago have given this up.

Let the Church of the West continue to decide matters of life and death in this way. If they must, they must.

We cannot help them. But let us help our neighbors here in Asia. Let us proceed without quibble to communicate the Word of the Way to our neighbors, or our brothers and sisters who are near at hand.

We have determined that certain teachings will be helpful to all regardless of membership. What do we mean by the "dual nature" of Christ? Like a seed, this *idea* carries the means . . . and is the gate for the necessary rebirth of the human being. The mentality system of the human being needs to be turned over. Our teaching on this "dual nature" can lead to his metanoia, this return to God. Our schools must show how, though words are not meaning, they are a divinely given way to communicate meaning.

To this end it is time to reveal our teaching about the constitution of the human nature . . . how the human

"body" is the field of reconciliation. The divine nature is without definitions that can be provided by our inherited

"Adam"—our mentality system. It is without references. To our minds it is therefore *empty*.

Reaching to here it is a simple step to reveal that the Saviour of humanity is necessarily always present next to us on earth.

A saying has come down to us. When Adam and Eve fell from Paradise to the Earth, it was a fall from unity to division. The unity of the mind and heart fell to separation between mind and heart. The saying is that temptation came from *two* spirits. One is the spirit of the snake and the other of the peacock. After the fall, what had been four rivers of Paradise, became four houses of the heart.[2] In each person, each of the four chambers houses one of these spirits, thus: one housing

Adam; one housing Eve; one housing the snake; one housing the peacock. The heart is the fallen paradise.

Fortunately for us, each house is still dependent on its river in the supernal paradise. We still can come under the influence of the heavenly rivers.

But, where does this all take place?

The *place* of this is spaciousness beyond spaciousness. *Space as we know it* is evoked in the realm of emptiness. Therefore there is no time that the Saviour is absent. We become absent. The Saviour is present.

Does this correspond with your understanding?

If so, do not be concerned that our brethren in the West wish to insist that Mary is the Mother of God.

Let us be silent and not argue. We are talking in different tongues. Let us assume that they mean by this something very different from what we would mean by this. Let us assume that their meaning is for the Good.

What we can do is bring many here in the East to God. We can bring them to know and see that the turning at the bottom of our mental system is not merely a metanoia but a returning to our God and our birthright.

If what I have said touches you agreeably, I urge you to send us one of your number who is of good memory and wide learning. Here, around our monastery by the frontier of the Swat region, the peoples are at peace.

Without distraction we can organize our thoughts so that a teaching of coherence and universal application can be developed. Perhaps in a year or two, we can begin.

Your brother in Christ,
Shimon.

Ali and I disagree about the probable date of this letter. He argues for the seventh century on the premise the letter was sent *to* the monastery that was uncovered. He reasons the town and monastery were founded during the early Tang since that dynasty had strong relations with the frontiers. I hold that the letter was written much earlier and brought by one of the Christians who founded the center at Wuzhong. Either way, the author was writing from a fairly remote area, some kind of frontier near the Chitral.

Elegant forms often develop at the boundaries of events. Mark the fascinating ingredients in the letter. After Adam and Eve "fall," they each reside in the divided human heart. Also the agents of the "temptation" hereafter reside with them to make a curious kind of family. Namely, Adam, Eve, Snake, and Peacock. All hearts, whether gendered female or male, acquire these tenants.

Mark that the author attributes some of the church's problems with neighbors to a "puffing up." Recall the stress Paul made in *his* letters on the flaw of puffing up, the activity of "leaven." Mark that of all birds, the peacock excels in puffing itself out as though it had been suddenly charged with a very active yeast. So I read their figure to indicate that the resident in the heart, apart from the gendered natures, is a spirit that exalts itself and a spirit that goes on its belly eating dust. All of this is a conceit which, unpacked, suggests a highly intriguing psychology. The expression "mentality system" in the Chinese text reminds one of Buddhist psychology. It is conceivable that, as in many boundary situations, the forms I have described as "elegant" may be the outcomes of reciprocal flows across the frontier.

Section Three

[We were informed that the following was originally not part of the collection but was found in a bottle gourd in the wall of a building being scavenged for construction materials. Many frontier settlements in the north were built from ruins of Christian communities.

Quite a number of Mongol clans or, as they are called, "Banners," were Ta Chin. When they fell, the materials were used without much delay in the building of new settlements. Amusingly, if I can use this word in this context, many *stretches* of the Great Wall are made of material from "Nestorian" communities.]

Last Words for No One
A Will:

I am ashamed as I near the end of my life. There are no visions. I no longer have even the language for religious talk. I am pressed by a demanding clarity when I read backward into our Scriptures and our Church history.

I am old like a child. It seems so simple to me that Jesus taught one thing. He came to deliver us from our inflexibility. For this he lived his life and died his death.

Inside we are this chain of inflexibilities. We are bound up in a chain of shells like the armor of insects. This is the world inside us. We shine out into the world reflections of the hardened surfaces and make a middle world where we live our lives. It is a kingdom of reflected powers and hierarchies from which we form our picture of heavenly order. The heavens and the earth take on the shapes of these inflexibilities in us, which endure stubbornly in us like a die. It was by living his life against this and dying in a way opposed to this terrible pattern (the text has Li (裡) that Jesus tried to give a new pattern 理, which has a more cosmic significance) to the world. But neither dumb faith nor brilliant changes of mind could reach deep enough into us to unbind the shells. These inflexibilities remained. How sad! Merely the old shells gleaming with the new names and costumes became the spectacle and order of the Churches. I pray for deliverance

from these artifacts before I die. May I meet God as God is.
That is all I can do now.

> The eighty-six-year-old monk, Li Ho.

Throughout my translation, I have chosen to use the English "inflexibilities" instead of the more familiar "bonds" and "bondages." It could be either. But both Ali and I agree that the force of the term in context far more strongly suggests a situation of the "subject's" will and decision than it does one of external coercion. Supporting this translation is the likelihood that the Ta Chin monks were touched by Taoism. Taoists were near neighbors at this location.

The "will" implies that it is with the complicity of the individual that these inflexible structures persist. Human nature, one could say fallen human nature, set these down into place. It follows then that persons can by some kind of inner activity or non-activity alter the topography. Could he be implying that the system can be changed from rigid shells to supple spheres? I admit this is not as dramatic as calling it "release from bondage." But it can have, as a working idea, strongly persuasive and far-reaching subjective results. The way the monk has set up his discourse, the results would then become synchronically "objective." He puts before us a vision of our tyrannical enthralling mirror system. The world we create and its institutions are a middle ground, neither real nor unreal, in which we satisfy our inner inflexibility by making it "outer." We fashion an "external" world that does not threaten or contradict our internal configuration. By a kind of feedback loop, this world of mental artifacts now transformed into the material of society and technology supports and gives "virtual life" to the inner shell-like conditions which innerly enslave us. For this reason, I am satisfied to render the translation as I did. Mark this from the Lao Tzu book, chapter 76:

> When Man enters life he is supple and weak

When dead; inflexible and hard.
All things, the grass as well as the trees
   are tender and pliant when they live
When they die they are dry and stiff
Therefore the inflexible and hard are companions of death
The flexible and tender, are companions of life.

We think the old man was advising that we choose life.

Section Four
[A letter or copy of a letter]

Friends, Brothers, Sisters:
   We have arrived safely in Kerala, God be thanked!

As we hoped, the members of the old community here were very helpful and they have provided us with enough for our needs. The province has gentle rulers whom, long ago, it is said, conferred upon we Christians a high place in their caste system. The system itself goes against our beliefs, but it is too complex to explain. We were shown charters inscribed on copper plates confirming our status here. They now are already several hundred years old. You can understand how this made us feel welcome. Though the script of the writing is unknown to us, the signatures were in a Hebrew script of the Persian language.

My purport however is not to satisfy curiousity. I wish to strengthen you in your resolve. Yes, the arguments will go on about one and two and three and four. They will go on and on. Do not be anxious about this. Was not Paul struggling against this among the Greeks of Asia? It is in the Greek temperament to number. Is it any wonder they excel in commerce? But despite this they are good and devout and are to be loved as fellow Christians. I have my doubts about

Rome. The bishops of Rome gained and secured their power so much like the Caesars. I must remember whenever I think of them that we are enjoined to not judge. Their style may be simply a bad inheritance of character. They do not get dazzled by numbers, at least. Except as instruments of rule, they find them of little use. Then it is possible that because they do not understand the speech of numbers, they may become too intolerant of those who do. They are irascible and impatient. Truly, were it not for you, I would not waste precious time thinking about such matters. But you, living so near the Church of Antioch, cannot avoid these concerns.

I urge you to take no sides in the arguments about these numbered and geometric explanations of God's nature.

Remember, there are usually two motives behind the arguments that God's nature be numbered according to this or that scheme. The first and most obvious is the process of constructing an idol. An idol, as the prophets said, is made to measure by man. Number is the instrument of measure. The second motive, more sinister because more deliberate, is to set up a "system of such and such an outline." Always people will disagree about an outline. The sower of division and discord can then conquer.

Now let us look soberly at the uses of the speculations about the one and the two and the three and the four.

You see, our minds cannot approach to think the ineffable without some kind of device. The mind requires signposts. *We u*se the discourse about numbers to arrive at an intuition of a Unity that is not used up in number . . . a Unity that is not a uniformity and without reference to counting. But since the mind will count, and the heart will color the numbers of counting, they must be used as all kinds of tropes and figures of speech are used.

Now, if the persecutions become too severe, do not lose your life for vanity. I know that our people have been accused for causing the massacre of the Monophysites in Persia. I am aware of the hypocrisy of politics within both the Empires that surround you. They can soon use this slander as an excuse to attack you. They are pack of wolves. Packs have this in common, my friends . . . if one of their number is slain, the others feel more strongly their solidarity. They mistake this feeling for brotherhood. It is only the intoxication of uniformity. In the swell of this feeling, they will rage and destroy whatever questions their pack-ness. So be on your guard. This madness has certain signs. People will imitate the expressions of each other. There will be a similar glare and brightness in their eyes. They assume a uniformity of posture and language. When you see such signs among those around you, leave the area. You will know by these signs that the "abomination of desolation" has usurped the holy place in the midst of human nature. First then, take yourselves to the nearby mountains without delay. Then when you have provisioned yourselves, proceed to Seleucia-Ctesophon.

Yours in God,

in faithful fellowship,

Thomas Salman.

When we started to decode this letter, we got very excited because we assumed from the data this it was written prior to the Council of Chalcedon. We interpreted *several* as more than one hundred and less than three hundred years. We also assumed that the copper plates were those now in the Mar Thoma Church at Tiruvalla. The description accords with Tisserant's. According to his account, the plates are scribed in "old Tamil with signatures in a kind of Persian Hebrew script." Indian astronomers date these copper plates between 415 and 450 CE. We were disappointed when we reached the part later in the text referring to the massacre under the Sassanid King Firooz. This date is clearly about 490 CE. Modifying our enthusiasm, we were able to legitimately speculate that the recipient was the renowned poet and scholar Nerses who was known as the "Harp of the Holy Spirit." Nerses founded the first theological university in the world at Nisibis. Perhaps he was encouraged by letters such as this. The dates add up. I doubt that a copy of a letter to a person of lesser stature would have found its way as part of a major legacy to the Mongolian frontier. Naturally, such romantic notions of mine have no hard evidence.

The letter is far more dense with meaning than the disarmingly simple and laconic style suggests. As a matter of fact, I doubt we could exhaust the implications in less than a modest monograph. I will limit the discussion to what I contracted for when I commented on the "creation sutra" in section one above.

The fourfold repetition of the word *Who*: in Hebrew interpretive writing, adverbial relations sometimes carry the burden of "names of God." Sometimes the word for where, *ma*, because of its implicit relation to place; *Makom*, a name of God. But mark that the word "mi," or "who", is particularly freighted with this meaning.

The content of the text in section one can be exposed with the aid of Thomas Salman's letter. The numbering and the attributing in the "creation sutra" resolves consistently back to *Who*. Whether speaking of one (uncreated) or two (origin of origins) or three (holding the source of origin created all) or four (surpassing all the Holy Ones is the unoriginated, etc.) . . . no matter how one piles up the number, it all refers to *that Who*. This is an aspect of the letter writer's insistence that his correspondent avoid the debates rather than cycling and recycling around the number of natures of their savior and the nature of the Trinity. The author of this letter is proposing a thought first put forward in the West by Erigena in the ninth century.[4] In simple terms, it can be described thus:

the distance between human knowing and God is, for practical purposes, infinite. Whatever systems or structures humanity devises to describe or explain reality reflects the needs of the human effort to grasp the ungraspable. Such efforts are needed in order to *think about* God. These descriptions are approximate and must not become idols at the feet of which we either sacrifice others or ourselves. Truth (not in the dogmatic sense) and ethic have a prior claim on the human soul since these virtues refer back directly to that *Who*. For this reason, the person to whom the letter was sent is urged to leave the battlefield of contesting doctrines *before* leading others into the temptation of killing him or her.

Section Five
(an original letter; it bore a seal as signature)

Greetings to you my brothers and sisters: I am amazed at what I have heard of your teaching. You have taken the m*eth*od of a year as the *meaning* for all time. Must I return to you each year? Must I bring a new teaching to you each year?

What I have said is a "sense" and not a decree. Do you find it sensible to forget always the circumstance of what I say and tear off the words that are spoken as though they were holy writ? News has reached me that you are now practicing and teaching certain doubtful ideas.

Is it so, that you teach that there are certain distinct types of men and women?

Is it so, that you or some of you teach that the world in which we live is an inferior creation presided over by "princes of darkness?"

Is it so, that you teach that the created world is a kind of machine and the work of the church is to deliver humanity from existence?

If it is true then you have fallen into bitter error. An error like that of some brethren in Egypt. It is grievous.

Have you forgotten the subject of the teaching when these *exercises* were presented to you? Then you have snatched my fingernails and hair and forgotten my marrow!

The marrow is to love one another. The bones are to be born into a new world. The muscle, tendon, and tissue are the methods by which we accomplish our aim while still among our brothers and sisters.

Listen. How can we love one another if we cannot distinguish one from the other. When my brother is a mote in my eye, how can I see him as he is? When my sister is the desire in my eye, how can I see her as she is? It was to answer this condition that the method of types was invented. In the arena of relations it is to be used like a chariot for love. The theory of types is the entry toward discovering the actual presence of our brother or sister so that we can love them. The study of types is a gate not a path. Through the invention of types, we begin to truly see that one whom we look at is *not* ourselves. Then further along the path, we learn that our companions are different from one another and incommensurable.

This study is not even a real gateway but one that is drawn on the air. But we enter it and begin and again begin and after many beginnings discover that God has created each person absolutely unique.

Also, until we begin to so see . . . this world is truly *like* an inferior creation ruled by a tyrant. The tyrant is our own ignorance and darkness. It is *like* that.

About the machine of the universe. I had recommended that for a period of time you meditate upon the world of which we are part as *though it were a machine*. I suggested that you continually for a time see it that way; like a cart, or a ship, or a blacksmith's forge, or a potter's wheel. I meant it for your m*editation* which when you had penetrated it in a month or six months or a year . . . never more than a year . . . you could put it aside like any intelligent child will put aside a toy that has been comprehended. Through this exercise you could have learned something. But you have taken these tools for thought as doctrines.

What will become of you when I am gone and cannot remind you?

I worry for you because the distances I am now traveling are very great and I am growing old. I am sending this letter with a brother and sister who both have standing among us here. Keep them with you for a year. Though they are younger than some of you, be modest enough to learn from them. Provide for their sustenance even though it may be some hardship for you. The benefit to all of you may be eternal.

This is a copy of the signature seal.

*   *   *

Our *favorite* document. Ali saw it as first-rate Buddhism. I saw in it the explication of certain troubling doctrines of Esseneism and Jewish Gnosticism. We were quite taken by its allusiveness and implications. Here I will restrain my enthusiasm and deal with it on its own terms as much as possible.

Apparently the author refers to a system of human typology. Ancient traditions abounded with such systems. For example, it was taught that the cast of characters in the *Book of Job* represented various "types." For some, the twelve tribes of Israel were the general brackets for a system of types. And, of course, astrology was a highly sophisticated instrument of this order.

But what this author is saying is something quite different. He says that the ability to divide into types is merely a method for *beginning* to educate people in the discernment of differences. We learn that some people are other than me. I am some type but not that. This step or gate is needed because, otherwise, the person under the pressure of spiritual growth might retreat to one of two positions:

A) the need to feel safe while becoming vulnerable can cause the student to try sustaining a "user-friendly world" and hence fall into the position of all are the *same*;

B) the student might become overwhelmed by the illusion of chaos created by a sudden perception of the unaccountable abundance of singular essences and hence feel the desperate need to conquer a place for themselves

The suggestion by the author is that once the scales of sameness and otherness have been loosened from the students eyes by this chemical, i.e., the theory of types, they may come to a gradual awakening. The discovery of the utter singularity of each person we meet within a so-called type will dissolve both the scales and the theory. We ourselves are aware that as we get to know our friends in depth over longer periods of time . . . the deeper we know them, the more singular they become. Instinctively, we sense the folly of trying to type them. Those persons we do not know very well or strangers are readily assigned to this or that type. This group seems to be trying to accelerate the process.

The meditation upon a "mechanical world" was explicated for me by Ali. In early Buddhism, a similar meditation was employed as a "skillful means." If practiced sincerely, it could lead to *paravritti*, a revolution of the mind system in the direction of "virtuous" perception. Perception that is true to the *virtu* of perception can never be the *same* as the meditation itself. If it were, it would be a simple matter of programming. To be more specific, the perception that is an adequate outcome of meditating on the world as a machine cannot be that the world is *in fact* a machine. When the author heard that his followers were teaching that the world was a machine *in fact*, he knew something had gone seriously wrong. The early Buddhists, when they prescribed the machine meditation, added the requirement that the practitioner during the phase of this discipline avoid completely the use of *actual* machinery.

The author's dismissal of the "inferior world doctrine," while affirming it as a useful meditative toy, is quite special. It casts an inquiring light on much so-called "Gnostic" teaching of the Mediterranean basin. The use of *this* meditation would be a help in dissolving a specific and localized reality that had been created by ignorance. Mark this, to the author, it is an actual relative existant . . . but one that is built up, as it were, over each person's head by the fibers of their own or collective thought and held in place by the *force of flight* from recognition of the *other*. It is the force of the habit to cast away responsibility for the other, to fly from love of the other, to deny one's own fragile humanity as one among others.

If the author was not totally unique in his thinking, then among many other groups which had refused to abstract metaphors into doctrines, an exciting psychology was being taught and practiced. It reminds me of William Blake's idea of liberating people from the "mundane shell." One must ask, if this is indeed the case for even a few groups, what happened to cause the defection of so many sects and parties from this exciting eikon and led them to mechanically call their "toy" the truth.

This last question comes near the nerve struck at our Olivet meeting.

This is a good place to wrap up with another question. As a society, Amfortas is on to something genuine. Is there time in the context of the larger human society for our roads to reach?

Notes

1) I don't know how Asaph could have arrived at this unless he refers to some convention worked out between Chinese and Syriac whereby the "sound" of the aleph could be understood to refer to yod. It is true that the means Western translators arrived at the word "Jehovah" did involve a "conventional" mashing together of Elokim and the Tetragram. See some implications of this in chapter four, above, pp. 105-106.

2) In the Islamic book *Umm al-kitab* (Mother of the Book), a similar "mythology" is hinted. See the *Soteriological Cosmology of Central Asian Ismailism*, Pio Filippani-Ronconi. This essay is included in the volume *Ismaili Contributions to Islamic Culture*, editor Syyed Hossein Nasr, Tehran, 1977. Worthy of note that the cosmology described herein bears striking resemblances to the "Panc-tathagata" of Mahayanist conception and this Buddhist doctrine was apparently worked out and formulated in the "Uddi yana-Swat area contiguous with the Shugnan-Wakha-Chitral region where copies of the 'Umm al-kitab' have been found still in use today." Above volume, p. 106.

3) See *Studies in the Lankavatara Sutra* by D.T. Suzuki, London, 1968. He uses this expression as Vijnana system throughout his book.

4) Probably referring to John Scotus Erigena, *Periphiseon, id est De divisione naturae*. The author is dealing with causes here, though, not necessarily divinity. According to Scotus, there is no particular arrangement of number of

causes between the unknown God and his creation. The system and number of "causes" are really *in the mind of the contemplator.*

5) Although Asaph does not mention it here: the nineteenth and twentieth centuries have really proliferated various theories of human "personality types" as doctrine. But we have also expanded the theory in the fields of history, sociology, and psychology as a means of *explaining* events.

CHAPTER EIGHT

Perceval

George Ezekelian was born in Tarpon Springs, Florida, of Greek and Armenian parentage. His family had settled in this community after a few wandering years as refugees following the atrocities of 1915. A born linguist, he learned both of his ancestral tongues and caused some consternation to his family by insisting at the age of nine that they also teach him Turkish. He left home at fifteen to "see America." He worked in restaurants to support his travels. Usually he found employment in the ethnic communities of large cities, adding continually to his store and feel for languages. Especially noteworthy at this time was his acquisition of Yiddish and Lithuanian. On his own, before he reached eighteen, he had discerned the Indo-European harmonies between his native Greek and the nearly Sanskrit roots of Lithuanian. The Franz Werfel novel *Musa Dagh* changed the direction of his life. Two conclusions drawn from reading that novel were the catalysts. One was that Werfel was correct in predicting that the course of German policy toward Jews would follow closely that of Turkish policy toward the Armenians. The second was that America would have to go to war with Germany.

As soon as he was of age, he enlisted in the United States Army. His skills were quickly apparent, and he was sent to language school and subsequently served in military intelligence both before and during World War II. He was among the first to debrief survivors of Nazi concentration camps. After eight months, he suffered a nervous breakdown. A few years were spent in and out of military hospitals. For no apparent reason, he suddenly recovered. When he left the service, he had the rank of major. During the three years following, he journeyed without break and then privately printed a short tract entitled *Why Do the Nations Rage?* He received a number of unsought responses. Several did lead to further correspondence. He is one of the founding members of Amfortas.

*   *   *

Memories of Perceval are so contradictory that simple impressions convey very little. But I must try.

Once we were driving together to attend a folk dance festival in which he was involved. He wore a houndstooth sport coat and a bow tie. His hair was flattened down like a Mississippi gambler. He began to berate the organizations taking part in the event. Strings of curses, colorful, contemptuous metaphors for almost everyone I might be liable to meet, crackled around in the car. Many were funny. I assumed he was venting his frustrations and using me as an accomplice. But when we finally arrived at the arena and he began to introduce me to the various people he had described, he proceeded to use the same language and even embellished on the themes. Almost all of them took his abuse with good humor.

Once when several of us were in San Francisco for a small planning session, he invited me personally to join him while he visited a certain Gypsy fortune teller whom he said he held in high esteem. For this outing, he appeared in a baggy tweed jacket wearing a dark beret over unusually messy hair. He treated the venerable lady with exquisite manners utterly free of any affectation. The encounter went on for several hours in impeccable courtly dignity. For our Olivet meeting, he appeared daily wearing a freshly pressed linen suit with a small red rose in his lapel.

The last time I saw him was in an airport departure lounge prior to his departure on an extended journey. Hs manner was simple and kind. After an awkward silence, he said:

> The way is long . . . Merlin, be of good cheer. We have actually succeeded. You have wondered about the roses. I smuggled them into the college kitchen cooler. A fresh rose every morning . . . wasn't that a nice touch?

Practice of the Momentary and the Eternal
The Teaching of Ashoug Ezekelian

There is nothing that was that is not
Life is a chorus of life . . . echo of the gone ahead.
Life is the echo of death.

These are two of my uncle's countless maxims. My family *acquired* the name Ezekelian during the time they resided by the town of Kefil, near Birs Nimrud, between the rivers Chebar and Eurphrates. Here, according to tradition, is located the tomb of the prophet Ezekiel. We had settled here after a flight by our forefathers from the Roman Empire into lands controlled by Parthia. It was only much, much later, during the reign of a fanatically fundamentalist Muslim Caliph of Baghdad, that we returned to the land of the Hayc, Armenia. Since our time in Kefil, a special teaching has been handed down through the generations in my clan as a unique hereditary lore. The "style" of transmission has been from paternal uncle to nephew.

This was a teaching regarding the nature of time, space, and the relationship of the eternal with humanity. We understand it to be the heritage of the prophet Ezekiel. There is a tradition that this organism of thought was entrusted initially to one Israelite and one Magian family. Considerably, later it also became heritage of a Christian family, and after the Muslim conquest, a Muslim family was also initiated into the "lore." Until at least the twelfth century, the town of Kefil was a place of pilgrimage for all the above religions.

My family calls the teaching, "Tzan-a-tzan . . . Tashn." Roughly translated, it renders as "many times at once," or perhaps more fancifully, "many rhythms . . . one tune." The philosophically minded might call it "the One and the Many." Our prime axiom is that a human being is a human being, neither angel nor devil nor animal nor anything else. In order to come down strongly with this emphasis, as though keeping time with his right foot, Ezekiel used the term ben Adam: one hundred times in his book. That is to say, "son of humanity . . . son of anthropos."

To both the average and the scholarly reader, the scroll of Ezekiel can seem organized as though a bomb exploded in the middle of it. In fact, it is not so. Even it if had been messed up in transmission, it clearly says that the human being relates to time, space, place, the animal world, etc., in a way unique throughout the universe. Angels, for example, cannot be in two places or times at once.

The means by which our lore is transmitted are the methods and forms of dance, music, and literature. Then those learnings are correlated in an activity of a comprehensive nature chosen by the learner.

*   *   *

I was working at the Assyrian-American Club and Restaurant in Chicago during my seventeenth year. It was owned by an Abraham Shimon. A lot of people were in tight financial conditions. Behind a partition in the restaurant, always at least ten card games were going on. When I was not cooking, I had to be sure the players had plenty of coffee, snacks, and cigarettes. If the club had been a true-blue American equivalent, I would have been a pimp too.

One night, to my surprise, my uncle Ashoug walked in. He had learned my whereabouts from my parents. He told me that the two of us were going on a motor trip as a birthday gift for me. He spent a few moments talking to Abraham Shimon. My boss beamed at me and told me to take the next few days off.

The following day we drove northwest out of the city. After a lot of irrational detours, we finally made camp in Wyalusing State Park. This is at the confluence of the Mississippi and Wisconsin Rivers. Uncle Ashoug had brought a cooler filled with food and right away set about preparing our supper. He waved off my help.

"This is your birthday. You cook all the time . . . Worse still, you cook yourself all the time . . ."

It was the first night in years I was not surrounded by electric lights and bustle. All this silence and space was oppressive at first and made me nervous. He said very little. After a while, he explained tersely *where* we were.

"Two great rivers meet here. All around us are the burial mounds of the original inhabitants of this land."

He had brought excellent steaks. The meal was the best I had eaten in years. I began to stop fidgeting. There were a few lights over by the Mississippi, but mostly it was dark.

"Night is God's pledge of impartiality. In all lands of the world, if you have food and a roof, night is good. In the daytime it turns out that the lands sometimes are bad."

I knew there was no need to answer or think about what he had said since among the family Ashoug was known as something of a madman. According to my father, his mind was like a warehouse in a seaport . . . full of unrelated pieces from the old country and meaningless unconnected records. But in the silence, in the nighttime, listening to Ashoug's voice go on and on, it seemed I was entering a new world. Only his voice, like a silver thread, like an axion of light, connected me to the human world as I listened to story after story for the next three days. Though they were of no possible purpose to me, I was enthralled.

After those three days and nights spent in an off-beat sunbeam, I began to read.

*   *   *

I did not see my uncle again for many years. In fact, I did not see him until I had completed my long military service. He was by then quite old and living as a semi-recluse in Fresno, California.

My first call of duty, a pleasant duty, after my discharge was to my family home in Tarpon Springs. After some time with them and learning of Ashoug's whereabouts, I told them I needed to see him. In Tampa I burrowed into my savings and bought a large Cadillac sedan. I bought this extravagant car on the advice of European gypsies I knew during the war. Still a very fragile individual, I drove cross country as fast as possible to reach my uncle's house in Fresno.

It was during this visit that he began teaching me in earnest. As soon as he laid eyes on me, he told me I was a wreck. I told him I knew that. That was why I was there.

"You are a wreck because still you have not learned to *not* cook yourself."

The first material he taught me was series of physical movements that formed a foundation for some of the dance that are part of the lore. To these there are rules for transmission. But he had been getting old, and for years I had been fighting a difficult war. He had taken the precaution to teach part of his inheritance to different people as a means of preserving the "know-how." No *part* in itself was secret. The unique teaching lay in the manner and sequence with which the parts related to parts and hence to the complete part/whole organization or, in his own words, to the "whole mishmash." In all aspects, the principles of Tzan-a-tzan . . . Tashn applied.

A distant niece of Ashoug's had been taught the dance elements as a special branch of her folk-dance studies. When necessary, he would arrange for her to come over to the house for purposes of demonstration.

When I told him I just wanted to learn the essential ideas, he looked at me with some mockery and delivered a talk which I will try to reproduce as faithfully as possible. It clarifies "our" position:

"Yes, you have learned a lot in your life. But I'm going to talk to you like a 'dutch uncle.' You know how it is in restaurants, if you work in Greek kitchens you're fine . . . but in a German kitchen you would have to learn new moves. Isn't that so . . . or pffft? In your disheveled life, I'm sure you haven't found time yet to read Plato. That is a blessing. The way they teach Plato in schools is insane. They gnaw a beetle and swallow a pig. Yes, you are lucky you are disheveled. After today, take one of my Platos. Take either original Greek or demotici. It wouldn't matter if we had one mashed together of both katheravousa and demotic. It would be as disheveled as you. Plato explains clearly in *The Republic* that one must first learn very specific gymnastics. They are needed for years before one can learn important ideas. You see it is between the lines and scenes . . . in the silences where Plato's Socrates has buried the important things. If the gymnastics have not been done, one will miss the living parts, because you will still be cooking yourself instead of the dish."

Despite this, it was more because of my affection and gratitude toward the old man that I submitted to his method. I lacked any conviction that he knew what he was talking about.

A lot of "moves" had to be learned before one could dance. Arms, legs, torso, and head were initially tasked with very simple problems. But since the problems were native to the body, they defied simple execution. I will try to put into words how I understood Plato's comments about gymnastics in relation to what I was learning.

Our bodies, minds, and souls co-exist . . . or find their place of relation within a certain medium. Because of the way we are born or grow up, the medium, which *is* the very intersection of the momentary and the eternal, becomes a kind of animal glue that will not flow unless it is heated. Consequently, neither the parts nor the whole are free to move according to their own nature and receive the "impressions" of the ideas. The medium needs to become "virginal." The simple moves begin the long process of restoring fresh intentionality to the body. This in turn affects the "glue."

According to Ashoug, disciplines like yoga, sacred or meditative dance, etc., . . . are wonderful. But since they do not start from the same premises and do not take into account the intersections of the momentary and eternal, they arrive at different results from those we are after. Tzan-a-tzan . . . Tashn has but one goal: the making of a human being human . . . ben Adam.

Almost all rituals began as fairly comprehensive methods for *steering* human beings along RTA[1] toward a sense of the meaning of the universe or the divine and the human place within and in relation to "it." But in *time*, the chalice becomes a sieve. There is less than nothing between the mesh.

I found that in my practice there were ways I could "engineer" the simple execution of an arm or head move. But Ashoug could see that I had put myself into a state of detachment in order to do it and I would have to unlearn the trick. He insisted that I bring the whole apparatus of my daily state into the move or he considered the effort a waste and "self cooking." A waste in the sense that it could not lead in the direction he wished for me. "Self cooking" in the sense that such efforts merely attenuated or boiled away my substance.

"Better to do nothing . . . Tzan-a-tzan . . . Tashn is not school for schizo-psycho. You have to do it, not a part of you."

After several months, I knew I could go on living. Also I began to glimpse the completeness that lay behind Ashoug's practice. By this time, I was able to do twelve or so sequences of moves that might be called dances. Execution was imperfect, to be sure. But what was far more important was that I could do them *normally* . . . that is with the full participation of my daily state.

I had chosen the demotic version of Plato and began to see what he was talking about. Without stopping the body work, we began the study of literature. Music, as with Socrates, was to be the last field of study.

*　　*　　*

Our literature study began with a pleasant early morning outing to the Ararat Café in Fresno. We sat at a table near the window . . . as though sustaining a conversation, Ashoug chanted softly and, it seemed, directly into my brain:

Again I pray for mercy on Dzovinar Khanoum,
Again I pray for mercy on Sanasar and Baghdasar
Again I pray for mercy on Kerry Toros
Again I pray for mercy on the departed of the listeners to this tale.

Uncle explained that "mercies" like this one were the customary benediction pronounced by storytellers of the Hayc at the initiation of a cycle of legend. In this case, the names are those in our epic of Sassoun, an important national poem in the oral tradition.

"The mercies include the matter of legend and the matter of the present . . . the departed are the present tense of the past . . . We all need mercy . . . all, those who dwell in our memory and those who are actors in our life. How can an honorable storyteller begin except with prayer?"

I began to notice that Uncle Ashoug had this gift, an ability to express himself in flawless English when he chose and veer without warning into his private shorthand according to whim. No doubt he was showing this off upon our entering into the study of literature.

"The sayer of story must make real that the origin of story and literature is God knows where, God knows why, and with whom . . . only God knows."

We ordered our coffees, and he handed me a book. The cover was inscribed with four rectangles of traditional design, each a slightly different composition and sequentially from top to bottom in red, blue, gold, and green. It was Artin Shalian's English version of *David of Sassoun*.[2]

"Read this through as fast you can . . . like those spy novels you gobble up. Go right through it like a horse in a clover patch."

I accepted the book with a twinge of apprehension. I knew by now that doing what he said would not only bear unforeseen consequences but would not be that easy. By taking this book, I was making another "contract" with Ashoug. This time it probably was for the entire course, an avowal. I hoped I was not becoming an Ishmael to his Ahab.

We sipped our coffee in silence. He seemed to fall into his private thoughts. I let myself drift into my own. On the second cup, he asked me about my experiences in the war and afterward. I had not wanted to ever deal directly with these matters. But the coffee both sharpened my mind and loosened my tongue. The whole morning seemed to go by with Uncle Ashoug's eyes drilling into me like black diamond-tipped gimlets. Even when I described my debriefing of death-camp survivors and our "hands-on" investigations of the camps themselves, his eyes never wavered.

As I finished the dismal tale and began a rather puny recitation of the unhinging of my reason afterward and my shame at having insufficient fortitude for my job, he put his hand on my arm.

"It is time to take a break. The way you do this after telling such matters is to say: may the Lord have mercy on their souls, and you dear listeners, long may you live . . . Please say that now."

I repeated the words. It was so. I was able to draw a breath and step a foot back from the compelling power of my associations and memories.

He led me then to a room used for private parties in the back of the café. He closed the door behind us.

"Now, show me how simple . . . how straightforward you can do the first dance my niece teach you."

I composed myself and began. Almost instantly he stopped me.

"No! You leave self behind. That will make you psycho. This cycle of dance is about giving and receiving. If you retreat an inch above your head in order to do . . . what can you give, what receive? Normal state . . . do in normal state . . . stretch from normal to include highs and lows!"

I started again. This time I permitted myself to feel the whole weight of my mess, my life, my psyche. I found that I could base myself in that daily self-sensing as feeling. I started as I said, but even as performing the moves, I began to cry and he sharply said, "Later." Then, when several minutes later I finished, he smiled and said, "Now you weep." Which I did.

Time went by. Then he said:

"That is the first lesson. Giving and receiving is about conscience. Conscience is root of giving and receiving . . . give and take . . . me and you . . . is the root of life. Literature too is about conscience."

Without more ado, I had the impression of being literally scooped up, and the two of us dropped at a table in the nearby McDonald's. We had vilely delicious burgers and fries. This was my first class on the subject of literature.

A few days passed while I gobbled down *David of Sassoun*. Then we went down to Los Angeles. I had finished my assignment . . . had rooted my way thought the twists and gnarls of the epic. It now sat inside me like an indigestible lump of coaxial cable. Ashoug found my expression amusing and muttered, "Tessan 'an." [3] I knew enough Japanese to translate to myself and smile evilly as possible at him while I wondered where under God's heaven he had picked *that* up. He explained our trips to Los Angeles as part of my cure. His picturesque way of putting it was that there was no place on earth more suited to provide me with the hydrochloric acid needed to start my own digestive juices.

"Los Angeles provides for those with that indigestible ganglion a desperate need for the real. Here, anything with weight sinks. Nowhere on earth is the virtual and the real more confounded. Even dogcatchers here must know nothing about dogs. It is a wonderful place!"

We went for lunch to a small restaurant in Beverly Hills owned by a "relative." It turned out that the owner was delighted to see Ashoug and gave us a preeminent table from where we could see everything and "everyone." After we had accommodated ourselves, Uncle asked me:

"How long could Pokh Mehr have walked here?"

Apparently he was going to quiz me on my reading. As I faced the question and gawked at the inhabitants, I began to laugh. He went on while I kept laughing.

"Not even long enough to find a rock to crawl into." [4]

This made me laugh even more. I nodded—it was the best I could do. Then followed a quite intricate and cheerful discussion about the four cycles of *David of Sassoun*.

How was it possible that a spring of sweet water could emerge from the rock in salty, salty Gaboud Dzov? How could Dzovinar drink "a cupped handful and half a cupped handful" of this anmahagan water and conceive from this one and a half twins? Where possibly in this or what alternative universe is Bu-ghun-tzeh Ka-ghak and the land of Katcher?

As we went along in a labyrinthine path of often ridiculous questions and my no-less-ridiculous answers, I sensed the strands of story dissolve their adhesions from the spine of the "lump" and slowly stretch out into fibers and textures of meaning . . . sudden alarms of signs. Throughout there was the profoundly disturbing sense of a significance far beyond the "substance" of the tale.

Now, the restaurant was a place of sheer "virtuality," a system of symbols around the fantasy of fame and food. In the real sense, the atmosphere was so thin that it could barely support the weight of our discourse, much less the substantiality of our first course, a superb lemon soup. We stopped talking while we ate. It was the only honorable response.

After lunch, Ashoug insisted we forget all this. We drove over to Formosa Avenue and took the tour of Goldwyn Studios.

Late that night as I as dropping him off at his house, he gave me my next assignment.

"One week from today, we will meet at the Ararat. During this time, you will ask my niece to teach you the cycles I have labeled number nine and number twenty-two. Also, she is to introduce you to the pattern of moves called 'Anmahagan Sar.' Also, you will procure a copy of the Jewish version, in English, of the Book of Ezekiel. You will read it precisely the way you read 'Sassouni.'"

I had to go back to Los Angeles to get a Jewish version of Holy Scripture. But I did what he said.

*   *   *

[I am compelled in this section to break the code of constraints set out by Amfortas as protocol for these reports. I do this because in Ashoug's teaching, Eros is a cardinal principle regulating the coherence of the momentary and the eternal.]

It was when the "niece" was showing me how to sustain the easy and natural line of forearm-wrist-hand as it hangs simply at one's side . . . sustaining this while holding the arm out, that I realized how blindingly beautiful the girl was. I began to forget everything and stare at her. I do not believe I had actually *seen* a woman since the war. After a few moments of confusion, which I believe she shared, I was able to recover sufficiently to continue my lessons. They became, from that moment on, essentially different. In the silence, the stillness sang.

"Anmahagan Sar" was different from anything I had yet been shown. Overtly it was far simpler. I sat cross-legged on the floor. Very simple, gentle moves of arms and head . . . sometimes correlated . . . sometimes single . . . provided the basic grammar. She told me:

"It may take you fifteen or twenty years of practice to really do it. It's not easy as it seems. I have been working at it for eight years now and feel like I've gotten only the little finger sorted through."

Many changes of internal geography took place during this week.

Tuesday morning. I was sitting at our table at the Ararat Café and Uncle is late. After the passing of my irritations, I began to

worry that something had happened to the old man or that I may
have mistaken the date. Or that I was supposed to pick him up.
I really wanted to see him this day. This day I needed to see him.
Finally, with a broad smile he arrived and explained his
lateness. It seems that a good friend of his, a Jewish watchmaker,
had called him about an excellent watch that he had purchased
from an estate and had repaired. Knowing of Uncle's interest in all
such things, he called Ashoug to offer it to him for a modest price.
He took it out of his pocket and handed it to me.

"It's for you. It's time you got rid of that *Invasion of Normandy*
watch you always wear."

He was referring to the watch I wore that I had been awarded.
Needless to say, I was touched. I removed the old watch and put
it into my pocket. Before I could strap the gift on, he asked me to
look at its back.

"See, nothing on the back."

True, the back was blank. I smiled as though I understood
the immense significance he apparently attached to this fact and
nodded.

Then I told him about the powerful and unsettling feelings I
was having toward his niece. I thought perhaps I ought to work
alone for a while.

"You should thank God you have feelings. Thank God you are
not one who pisses ice . . . or pisses steam. Live with feelings. Learn
with feelings and respect at the same time *nature* of relationship.
Because you long for does not mean you *must* snatch and eat. But
do not cut either heart out or balls off in order to live in peace.
Happiness and suffering are themselves the path to God's world.
Come, now to our work for the day."

I composed myself and declared myself ready.

"What similar did you find between Sassouni and Ezekiel?"

I thought for a moment at what seemed a ridiculous question.
I told him I wasn't looking for similarities but read them both

straight through like "novels." I further said that thinking about it with hindsight, I did not see any.

"None? Aren't both told with words . . . don't they have people in them . . . aren't there kingdoms and treacheries and powers and loyalties? Don't each have seven wicked kingdoms?"

We sat in silence for a few moments, and then he changed his tone.

"Yes, I agree . . . it is hard to see. Another day for that. For now we call 'Sassoun' the 'lorebook' and Ezekiel the 'workbook.' One can throw light on the other. In general, this is the relationship between lore and work books. There are many such in literature. In Plato, it is folly, for example, to read *The Republic* without the light thrown by *The Symposium* and vice-versa. This is achieved by the harmonics of signs and symbols . . . what Tzan-a-tzan . . . Tashn calls . . . *chords*."

Then he expounded in detail certain structural relationships that provide the inner circulation of the Book of Ezekiel. This, as I intimated above, is the key work of our particular heritage. This material is quite technical. I am placing this exposition as an appendix to my report. For those who wish to labor at it, I recommend that they study the appendix at this time with a copy of Ezekiel in hand and then continue. For those for whom the general drift is enough, you can continue without interruptions.

I must say that I found Ashoug's display of erudition and memory phenomenal. He concluded his analysis with a series of seemingly nonsensical statements.

"We are always battling seven wicked kingdoms.

"Only conscience comprehends the One and the Many. Our dances are rooted in the conscience of the body. The literature is rooted in the conscience of the mind and feelings. The music is rooted in the conscience of organization—the sense of duration, extension, hearing, and touch. All together, Tzan-a-tzan . . . Tashn . . . begins the birth of the conscience of the soul.

"If you forget on the day your vow is due . . . you will forget for seven years. But if you are lucky, you then remember . . . then you must travel the ends of the earth and the uttermost parts of the sea.

"Opposing being to nonbeing is the action and fruit of the tree of self-centeredness. It is an advanced stage on the path toward the doom of self-exaltation. Only Eros in the extreme can shatter such a house of mirrors."

After disburdening himself of these statements, which literally seemed torn out of his deepest reflection, he suggested a trip. He thought the three of us—himself, his niece, and I—should make use of my "gypsy wagon" for a tour of California. What he called the "spume of the ocean." We would meet at my rooms seven sharp the next morning.

The trip was an excursion into the mind of America. The motels, the bizarre towns, private museums, the endless repetitions of houses and lawns, mini manor houses, roadside dramas . . . all this is the nature of our land's average appetites. Unmistakable landmarks from the "epics" exposed themselves wearing polyester clothes.

Over and over during the "tour," Uncle Ashoug repeated the words of Socrates:

"The tales have been saved and not perished . . . and so the tales can save us and our souls if we hearken to the words spoken."

Though short, the trip had been intense. It brought together, according to the theory of "seven climates," much of my learning that had been till then chaotic and sealed it in the coherence of love. I stayed in Fresno several months longer and then returned East to the tatters of my life. Over the years we kept in close touch, and I visited him once a year and continued the program that had been initiated in order to restore me to life.

Fortunately for me, he was still alive after the Olivet affair. Immediately after the conference was over, I made arrangements to go to the West Coast and spend several months with him while time allowed. During the intervening years, he had made his home in San Francisco. He preferred, he said, "for his ancient bones to spend their last years in a real Oriental city." He was pleased that I decided to spend enough time with him to tie some loose ends.

The first week was spent dropping in on old and new friends of his in the city. He was a charmer and always found good and varied company for his "public hours." We talked about family matters, politics, the state of ease or disease of people we knew, the latest advances in scientific thought, etc. He had opinions about everything. They could reverse at the drop of a hat. He had hosts of unsettled opinions.

With a sharp pang, toward the end of the week I noticed that he was quite old, quite fragile. Already it seemed he was faced partly toward a different universe, fresh regions of stars. Though my purpose in visiting him was in part motivated by our wrangle at Olivet, I found that my desire to learn anything new or prosecute any further search into our lore had evaporated. I chose merely to enjoy his company while we had the time.

That Sunday we attended an Armenian church service. It was the Sunday of the *Exaltation of the Holy Cross*. St. John Church was on, of all streets, *Olympia Way*. America never ceases to amaze me with its surrealistic coincidences. We had arrived very early. The sun was initiating its grand modulations through the eastern and southern windows of the church. Uncle Ashoug justified so early an attendance in the following way:

"I need time with my Maker before the priestly rabble foul the atmosphere."

I had stolen a sidewise glance at him nodding peacefully off when I felt someone sit beside me and lightly squeeze my hand. It was his "niece." Immediately I was plunged beyond my depth into her smile and her eyes. Recollection came while I drowned. Seven years before, I had privately vowed that I would ask her to betroth herself to me. That also was on the Sunday of the Exaltation of the Holy Cross.

As it took a navy test pilot forty-five minutes of detailed debriefing for the mere eight seconds between the time his plane catapulted off the deck of the aircraft carrier Tarawa and the time he ejected and hit water . . . like that was the density of thought and feeling in the few seconds we exchanged glances. I asked her right then if we could talk after the service. She agreed. I remember nothing of the liturgy that followed.

That Tuesday at breakfast, Uncle Ashoug's face was turned at last toward this world . . . he seemed less frail and grave and far more exuberant.

"So, my dear nephew George . . . shall we get down to the primary shit of our artful science? The polyrhythm of the momentary and the eternal."

Days and weeks were now given over to intense multiple activities. I practiced dances, recited the lore, and exemplified the content and application derived from some of the "workbooks" I had studied over the years. I will now render a useful but by no means complete account of our teaching. I recognize that much of it will be "old hat to y'all." Nevertheless, if you succeed in visualizing the context, you might find something valuable.

Our family tradition can be called, without euphemism, highly enigmatic. There is no school. There is no clear history past a certain timeframe. And there has been no overt dissemination of the method or meaning of the teaching. Still the Ezekelians are under an obligation to carry it forward in time no matter, whether or not any impact is made on civilization. The simple presence of the activity in the world is deemed ample reason to continue.

"Lift up the place on which you stand and you raise the universe . . . Degrade your place and you recycle the fall of Adam and Eve."

As explained, our root workbook is the Book of Ezekiel. From our point of view, the defilements of the temple are abominations in the midst of the human psyche. It represents (again, to our view) an accurate picture of the condition of a priesthood that has found its center of gravity in falsehood. Said in a slightly different way, it pictures forth a "priesthood" which has found its significance and meaning in self-serving representations to itself of the "truth" . . . a "truth" constructed to justify a false way upon the earth.

> [Since we are talking about the psyche, the priests in our age are not only religionists . . . they are psychiatrists, sociologists, educators, media experts, politicians, etc. In short, they are all those holding the keys to the kingdom of the human world.]

When the "book" describes the evidence of their dereliction as presence of "the creeping things and unclean beasts," the language is the usage of the literal imagination of the time and place, i.e., Mazdasyan Mesopotamia. In that context, it was referring straightforwardly to the "works of the lie." Only considerably later were the notions torn from their proper place and turned into a dualistic Mesopotamian religion. At the time and place of the setting down of the "workbook," the surrounding religion had a different conception than nineteenth and early twentieth century historians have credited it. They believed that only God could create. Angra Mainyu could only lie and distort the already created. So, as it says in the book, the elders of the house "were in the dark, each in his (own) image chamber, sending up smoke and incense." Clearly, from such a subjective position, one cannot come to a perception that leads to sighing and weeping for all the abominations. None of them could merit the sign of the Tav in ink on their foreheads because they were themselves the cause and the expression of the oppression of the soul. The heavenly instruction was to the point: "begin at my Sanctuary." But in order for the prophet to see this situation in its full terror, he had to "bore through the wall" . . . And then he had to *say*.

Ezekelians cannot refrain from reproof.

Uncle Ashoug had made journeys to some of the notables of our time and talked like a "dutch uncle" to them. For example, he visited Freud, Jung, Heidegger, Sartre, and many others less well-known over the years. Sometimes the encounter bore fruit . . . more often it did not. The visits were often short and sudden. He usually told his relatives when he vanished for a time that he had fallen hopelessly in love with someone "unworthy." After a time, no one bothered to ask about his disappearances.

To move suddenly and with adequate momentum to arrange good conditions for the meetings is an outcome of making Tzan-a-tzan . . . Tashn real.

God is present in every time and place. Time, space, and human presence create the condition of *site*. The nature of *site* is that it is in God as much as God is in it. Thanks to this possibility in the world, the opportunity is always available for freedom and choice. *Site* opens to infinity and faces heaven. So it is that humans are embodied in the world. But we do obscure the "situation" and may be unwilling to face toward the opening of the *site*. We have a perverse persistence to turn away from our best interests. All religions are calls to the human spirit, calls to remind us of the veiled incandescence of our circumstance. "Willingness" depends on an irreducible level of awareness and knowledge of the possibility. When education has dammed up or befouled the headwaters of hope, it has failed. Seen in this context, religion is an educational organ for humanity. Their responsibility is great. So even when taken literally, the demand "begin at my Sanctuary" is freighted with doom for many.

Uncle Ashoug was awed by my experiences during and after World War II. He said it had caused him to reflect very deeply about how Tzan-a-tzan . . . Tashn may not have done what it ought to have done. Though he had survived the atrocities committed against our own people between 1915 and 1917, he had not been able to sense the abysm of evil it heralded. Through my recitation, he caught a glimpse of how it flowered like the mouth of hell before all our eyes. He glimpsed in this recital a dimension of depravity and evil he had never imagined. He said:

"Humanity now walks with this dimension as a companion for the rest of the human adventure. It is the worst but perhaps the best traveling companion. If we accept this shadowy companion, these facts, as inescapable datum of human evil and indifference, we may yet have time as the medium for living together. If we do not, time becomes the medium for our dying together."

Ashoug called on me to consider that the teaching of Tzan-a-tzan . . . Tashn may require rehabilitation. In the old days, it was possible that one person could cause a tyrant to change the direction of his policies. Our *form* at the time was adequate to the *site*. Today, however, the old way may not do. When I became convinced one way or the other, he urged me to act on the basis of that understanding. He had begun to believe that now there may be a need for very many people with the *authority to reprove*. Many, trained in our way to live in the full discomfort of an active conscience, may now be needed.

A word about the *authority to reprove*: it is sharply other than the ability to turn the world into a mashed orange for the sting of "one's scorpion." The human tendency exhibited in this formulation is the use of intelligence as an instrument for expressing our habitual resentments or vainglory. Such activities have the opposite results in that it merely excites and magnifies the evil.

He felt that we probably should direct our strongest attention to the situation of women. Potentially they have the strongest *authority to reprove*. They are implicitly the mothers of goodness. For eons, "man" had refused to let "woman" be. The consequence is now that the entire fabric of not only the soul but the biological continuum, which is earth's form . . . threatens to shred itself up. By refusing to let women be, men had twisted themselves up in order to force, mold, legislate nature . . . all for the purpose of obliterating women's possibilities of *siting*. And in this twist . . . this reverse "English," by an implacable law of the universe, they have refused to let themselves *be*.

"We Ezekelians have permitted ourselves an inexcusable partiality over the centuries. Try, nephew, to be impartial."

On the side of Practicks, I was learning that the accessibility of the pattern of *Anmahagan Sar* improved with work on the cycles nine and twenty-two. The ratio of progress was ridiculous . . . about a hairsbreadth to a yard. Uncle Ashoug referred to these two patterns as "the valley of dry bones."

They call for multiple and separating rhythms and directions with varied parts of the body. Always they are done without transcending or finessing one's normal state or one's own volition. The normal is not the middle. One does not "do" it from high, low, or middle . . . but straight on to meet the whole dance with one's whole presence. The form becomes a *site*.

For most of us, the force of habit weaves itself with the way of nature into the fibers that connect muscle, tissue, perception, thought . . . etc. This feeds back to reinforce mental habits that inadvertently build up while the human child is constructing a world of meaning. To regain one's "virginity," a decisive loosening of this subtle but binding clamp is a need. Here is where the rationale for Plato's (or Socrates's) call for a dedicated gymnastic *before* undertaking the study of ideas comes in. For some this may not be practicable due to time constraints, but . . .

If the loosening is accomplished through some outside agency, such as professional manipulators, then one's willingness is passive. In the absence of active engagement, the condition of *site* is unobtainable. Then, though it is too bad, the path of good hope forks to the right or left . . . doubling back upon itself progressively . . . endlessly.

> [According to my lights, it is now the time for a short digression. In the old Paleo Hebrew alphabet, the ninth letter was written (𐤈), and the twenty-second was written (𐤕). They are respectively called "teth" and "tav."
> Tradition is explicit that the inked mark on the fore- heads of those with living conscience was a "tav."
> Dismember to disclose conscience is the momentum.
> Anmahagan, which I chose to not translate until now because of the beauty of its sound in Armenian, renders into English as *having the foretaste of immortality.* The quiet and simple exercise I mentioned above could be called "remember the dismembered."]

No day should pass without a taste of the goodness that is beyond being. Every moment carries its intimations. Every act is a potential sowing of this seed, this stitch. Every word to another is an entryway. For many, prayer is the encounter with goodness. When prayer leads to actual devout acts toward others, it becomes the *site* of transformation. A *sar*, a mountain peak, is a designation for this "place." Hence, "Anmahagan Sar."

God is infinite and is infinitely merciful. This goodness is the token and earnest of nature . . . it is the "handkerchief dropped by the Lord." Only a fool or the distracted will not stoop to pick it up.

I trust the members of the Society Amfortas are thoughtful enough readers to make something out of this material. The best use is neither a coat of mail nor a fancy ball gown . . . but something.

When my Uncle Ashoug departed the earth, he left instructions for me to be sure that his remains were entered into the ground of the graveyard of St. Mary's Church in the diocese of Shirak. This turned out to be in the USSR, in the Armenian Republic. It called upon much of the skill I had learned from him to do this simple thing.

Appendix

I do not wish to encumber this technical discussion with long quotations. For this reason, as I said, the serious reader is encouraged to avail him or herself of the text of the Book of Ezekiel.

A word of information: the Atbash cipher refers to a simple and old method of encoding in which the first letter in Hebrew, the *A*, signifies the last letter, the *T* . . . the second letter, the *B*, signifies the next to last, the *Sh* . . . and so on. Parallelism, which is a stylistic device used throughout the Bible, often uses this kind of crossing relationship with larger units, like phrases and sentences.

Using the important vision extending from chapter 8 verse 1 through chapter 11 and verse 25 as the skeleton key, we can discern that this whole unit uses parallelism in relation as an Atbash cipher.

(a) is verse 8:1 ....(a') is 11: 25
(b) .... 8: 1 b ....(b') is 11:24 b
(c) .... 8: 2-3 ....(c') is 11:22-24 a

From our viewpoint, the book is divided into units according to the methods of the singers of epic. That is to say that the units are arranged so that the association of words or ideas simplify the task of committing a text to memory. Ezekiel yields thirty-three mnemonic divisions.[5] What interests the generations of teachers of Tzan-a-tzan . . . Tashn is the internal circulation, which harmonizes very well with the above "skeleton key." The only exception is a special momentary relationship between units 19 and 25. Length of unit is irrelevant. Coherence defines the unit with an assist from emotional weight.

A and A'

Unit 1
Chapter 1 verse 1 through
Chapter 3, verse 40

Unit 33
Chapter 40 through
Chapter 48

B and B'

Unit 2
Chapter 3 verse 16
Through 27

Unit 31 & 32
Chapter 37,
Chapter 48 verse 15
through end Verse 39

C and C'

Unit 3
Chapter 4, verses 1 through
end of Chapter 5

Unit 30
Chapter 37
verse 1 through 14

D and D'

Unit 4
Chapter 6

Unit 29
Chapter 36

E and E'

Unit 5
Chapter 7

Unit 28
Chapter 35

Here now is a great Chord!

F and F'

Unit 6
Chapters 8 through 11

Unit 26 & 27
Chapter 33
verse 23 through end
of Chapter 34

At the following interface or crossover, the node presents some difficulties:

G and G'

Units 7 & 8	Units 24 & 25
Chapter 12, verse 1-20 or	Chapter 33
Chapter 12 through Chapter 19.	verse 1-20

I cannot adequately explore here the harmonics at play between G and G'. One obvious disclosure is that in combination the two units illumine much of the method and meaning of the prophetic tradition. From their perspective, it challenges the customary interpretations of chapter thirty-four. Usually the bad shepherds of Israel are identified as the kings. But this may be special pleading. By placing F over against F', it would suggest that it is religious leaders who are being chastened as "unfaithful shepherds."

Clearly any text is seen against a background set up by the standpoint of the student. Our standpoint, which is a stream not excessively affected by either substructure of the collective unconsciousness or the superstructure of cultures built upon it, is somewhat unique.

Notes

1) A play on the Indo-European root of the word "ritual," rta, which according to some means "the working out of reality." For some it carries the meaning of order or unity of the world. The English words *ritual, right, rise,* and so forth are related to this "root." A rite means the "way one goes." It, hence, is not a *techne.* Doing depends on "rta," which itself has no "worldly" or practical purpose.

2) *David of Sassoun*, translated by Artin K. Shalian, Ohio University Press, Athens, Ohio, 1964.

3) *Iron sour-stuffing.* I found it well explained in Isshu Miura & Ruth Fuller Sasaki's *The Zen Koan*, Harcourt Brace and World, p. 85.

4) At the conclusion of the Sassouni epic, the ground is no longer able to sustain Pokh Mehr and his horse. The earth needs to be reconditioned to sustain the authenticity they represent. Finally he finds a rock known as Akravou Kar, which has come to mean both crow's rock and rock of Van. A cave in this rock is known as Mhery Dour (Mehr's door). This becomes his haven until the earth becomes firm.

> Akravou Kar is your haven
> When the world is destroyed and rebuilt
> When the ground can sustain your horse,
> Then the world will be yours.
>
> Shalian, p. 367.

5) This is quite astounding. Researching it, I discovered the same structural division based upon mnemonic divisions. However, there was no indication of such an interpretation as this based as it is on a "cipher." See Umberto Cassuto's essay "The Arrangement of the Book of Ezekiel," 1946. It is published in *Biblical and Oriental Studies*, Vol. I, The Magnes Press, The Hebrew University, Jerusalem, 1973.

CHAPTER NINE

Marya

Madame Marya Bardi is the daughter of a distinguished East Indian family. Over the past several generations, her family has excelled in public service, particularly in the area of foreign affairs. At an early age, Marya showed exceptional interest, bordering on passion, in matters of the intellect. This did not inspire other higher-caste families to seek her out as candidate for marriage to their sons. Finding this a "blessing in disguise," she intensified her efforts.

Despairing of an ordinary life for their daughter, they gave in to her wish to enter Rabindranath's school at Shantiniketan. Marya attended this school throughout her student years and then continued at Visva-Bharata for a PhD in English literature. Her most intense extracurricular activity was her participation in Shantiniketan's recreation of North Indian classical dance. In this endeavor. the verdict of her teachers was that she achieved a level of performance and understanding just short of mastery.

Marya's contribution to the *Journal of PMLA* on the *Figure of Merlin* inspired heated debate in its pages for over a year. Two of our founding members followed this lively (by American standards) exchange delightedly and soon thereafter contacted her in her native Bengal. Without hesitation, upon being invited to join, she involved herself in our undertaking.

*   *   *

Since I remembered Marya gracefully lighting up the paths of our conference at Olivet in her bright saris, her dark eyes and tawny skin, with her hair black and geometrically braided and clasped, when I met her in Washington and she was in Western street clothes. I did not at first recognize her. It was, I think, the fluidity of her movement that finally made her recognizable. She was exquisite.

We had learned from our colleagues that we were both in Washington at the same time. She was in town to visit her brother who worked at the World Bank. I was there on simple matters of business. This night we were going to indulge her brother who had become an addict of American Jazz. He had planned an itinerary of some little-known clubs. I was looking forward to spending some "informal" time with Marya. The brother was her youngest and her favorite. We were having dinner, to fortify ourselves for the night's agenda. We were at a fine Italian seafood restaurant just off DuPont Circle.

I had just told her how beautiful she looked. She smiled sadly.

"Merlin, your protocol is damnable. Oh, we know you English very well . . . But you haven't an inkling of what drives me. Here, take this and read it. And, Merlin, please let us have a friendly time and enjoy the music . . . and leave the other."

When I returned to my hotel, I found that the paper was a free translation from an address by her former teacher Rabindranath

Tagore in 1940. Apparently she was determined that I try to understand what motivated her and had it typed out and at hand for this meeting.

> History has recorded many catastrophes; scores of monuments of civilization have fallen into ruins through the ages; yet to this day humanity has not utterly lost. On the strength of that assurance, the boat that is sinking has to be saved; it shall resume its voyage under fresh winds. The young do not realize they too are borne forward on the streams of Time. One day even *their* time will pass through frivolous arguments, scornful laughter, pride in a desiccated intellect and their souls stiffened with cynicism will find no peace. Then will start in their life the search for the fountain of nectar which is immortal. We are all travelers on that path of hope. We prepare to sing welcome to the new dawn in that spirit of faith and reverence in which lies essential heroism, the vision of which shall not be clouded by the pitch of atheism . . . and which shall proclaim: I know that Great Person who is refulgent as the Sun beyond all darkness . . .

The next time I saw her, I blushed. Her response was to smile and touch me lightly on the cheek.

Dancing Through the Roots of Life
A study of the lattice of movement in the village of T—
Marya

Since my Bengal childhood, I have been fascinated by the ceremonial life of small villages. Now I see that what was enticing me was the profound interweaving of art and life in the general consciousness of day-to-day existence.

The study of these relationships has long made the bridge for anthropologists and ethnologists into the "language" of their specialty. Admittedly, it has borne "fruit." For in addition to creating a flourishing profession, what my grandmother calls a "growth industry," it has provided its acolytes a kind of knowledge. Masters in the field acquire a detached view of the social structures that inform places that are exotic to their own cultural latticework. Being, as I am, merely a student of literature, I am minimally equipped for the endeavor of this paper. But I will try.

Originally I had planned to base this study on the "Dance of Gnymn" as still performed in a small village near the town of Merthyr Tydfil in Wales. Several elements had caught my interest in this dance. Ostensibly it is the evocation of the drama of nest building among a variety of birds native to the British Isles. Members of the village assume the parts of the crows, owls, hawks, sparrows, wrens, and other more rare birds, such as the wood thrush.

The dance is far removed from its origins. The name Gynmn is the Welsh version of Nimue. Embedded in the elaborations of the performance is the theme of the spell binding of a mage by a female "enchantress." But for me to have found the theme from the performances here would have burdened the members of the society with far more detail than is courteous. I would have had to include elaborate diagrams and statistical digestion of the repetitions of various gestures not only in the performance but in their daily life. Over time the village has come to arrange itself in imitation of the dance itself. For example, the whole method of bringing an oak branch in the performance is the archetype of the method for a certain type of integration afforded "strangers" into the village culture.

Since the vestiges of the central theme have become so attenuated and difficult to access apart from the whole apparatus of sociological sorcery, i.e . . . . kinship structures, lineality, child-rearing practices, etc., I decided to move the site of my inquiry to a region of Southern France.

Just to the east of the region that is the focus of this report, tremendous Papal activity during the counter-reformation obliterated to a great extent what attention had been paid for centuries to Sainte Mary Magdalene. By now in those regions around Grasse and Vence, and in fact even since the eighteenth century, almost all shrines uniformly are dedicated to "Notre Dame" and Holy Family of various aspects.

However, in the less travelled and less accessible areas around Le Beaux, shrines along the intricate lacework of footpaths which link penitential chapels still show some traces of the earlier veneration shown Sainte Mary Magdelene. If one pushes further into forest areas, one occasionally will find odd figures, barely recognizable as (the current version) "Christian," dominating the devotional art. In these cases, the persons of the trinity hover abstractly at the very top edges of the work. They (the trinity persons) are very impersonal, obviously intended to be omnipresent.

Blatantly, in one of these regions, in the village of T—, a special dance drama is performed every nineteen years. It involves almost all the adult and child population of the village. Only the very old and infirm and the mentally disturbed are exempted from the ceremony.

The first step in their "enactment" is the burning of a barn that had been erected nineteen years before in the center of the dancing field. When the barn has been burned, the ground field acquires the outline and significance of an arena with a very gentle grade down to the center. The rocks, which had been stacked as foundation and footing for the, barn are removed, broken free from where they had been mortared, and distributed around the field in precise arrangements. The lore for the arrangement of stones is always passed to two persons of mature age and opposite sex.

The period of time during which the ground is prepared is called "the harrowing." It is used for the assignment of roles and the initial rehearsal of steps. Some people are learning their way in the dance for the first time, others are relearning. Those old enough to have participated in the ceremony twice before are teaching.

The site of the burning is covered with tarpaulins so that no ashes are lost. At the conclusion of "the harrowing," the covers are removed and the ashes gathered and then spread very carefully over the entire dance field. Children and teenagers under the age of eighteen work it into the ground. Using a tool called "the column," which is made of maple with one end shaped something like a duck's bill, the young people work the ashes carefully into the soil.

Sainte Agatha is patron of this activity. Throughout Southern France, she is usually invoked as "protectoress" from lightning. This concluding chord of the preparation is called "the blackening."

For the next three weeks, the whole enterprise is forgotten, except for a continual watch set over the dancing field by older people. It is the time normally of the greatest rainfall of the year. In the evenings, the community spends most of the time in the local church listening to stories from the "matiere de Bretagne." Whoever happens to remember a tale recites it, and the cycle goes on in utter disregard of sequences or repetition. A child told me these were the most precious moments they ever had.

Three years earlier, lumber had been cut and stacked to dry. Now this wood is brought to the field in horse-drawn carts and assembled into a number of small huts. The huts, I noticed, were in deliberate relationships with the arrays of stone that four weeks earlier had been set out. At completion of this "step," called "the firming," the field takes on the semblance of a shanty town or of one of those lakes I have seen in America where people build huts in midwinter for the purpose of fishing through the ice.

Each family has a hut. In the week following, they take time from whatever chores are ongoing to assemble for midmorning and midafternoon refreshment. These family socials are actually the most secret of all the activities surrounding the dance. I was never invited and never told anything about the events of this week except that they were having coffee breaks in the morning and tea breaks in the afternoon.

The Patterns

Let us consider the arrangements of stones. Their pattern dictates the way . . . that is the order of construction and the spatial intervals of their placement. One might say that the stones are the language and the wooden huts the works of language "wherein people dwell."

The general shape of the field, as defined by the outer circle of stones, is egg shaped. Those of you familiar with megalithic stone rings would recognize resonances with Borrowstone Ring and Alan Water. Both of these Midlothian arrays are built up on the principles of "nine-foldness," according to most researchers.[1] In the words of one recent scholar, these two monuments "reveal the subtlety of reconciliation between geometry and arithmetic, the irrational and the rational."

Within this egg shape, there is a larger and a smaller circle of huts. The smaller circle is composed from an arc taken off the radius of the narrow end of the egg and the large from the wide end. Naturally there are two intersections. These circles are made of nine huts each, in effect creating two nine-sided or nine-pointed polygons. Within each are set down a system of huts in nests of three, generating additional double nine or eighteen huts.

I commented to one of my informants that I had thought there were more than thirty-six families in the village. In light of what was to follow, the answer is worthy of note:

"Yes, indeed . . . there are always fifty-four families in the village, but the eighteen not seen . . . are simply at this time not seen."

In the fourth week after "the blackening," the village is ready to perform the "Dance of Firing." The night before the dance, the entire village spends all the hours of darkness on the dance field. Brightly colored sleeping bags are clumped haphazardly about the huts. Always this night is the full moon, so with the many campfires, the whole terrain is a contradiction to the "darkness"; it is highly illuminated.

By dawn the eighteen "unseen" families are stationed around the perimeter of the encampment. Some are on the sturdy, remarkably powerful and ghostly Camargue horses while most are on foot. A goodly number of these people are holding drums or flutes. I must say, the moment is uncanny. I was stationed just below the wide end of the "egg." I am certain I was awake the whole night through and could see everything since, as I mentioned, it was very bright. I was keyed up and attentive. Still, somehow, without discernable movement anywhere, there were these people stationed suddenly about the entire stone ring . . . Between eighty and a hundred people were there seemingly from nowhere. Nobody is ever prepared for their appearance. This was explained to me later as "one of the mysteries of the Esplumoir." [2]

The dance itself is dedicated to Saint Elijah. On the surface, this is irrational. Between "the blackening" and Sainte Agatha, there is a clear connection. But the correlation here with Saint Elijah is difficult. Toward the end of my paper, I will hazard an interpretation.

There were clear skies. On the morning of the dance, the skies are usually clear and the beginning can be straightforward, as you will see. However, their traditions indicate that on rare occasions the skies are cloudy or regrettably dense fog had settle in. The years of our era, 1217, 1312, 1597, 1863, and 1939, are cases of these exceptions. Since the rising sun is the timepiece for all the beginning moves, on such occasions complex means were required to calculate the opening phases of the dance. When such devices are used, there is possibility of wide margins of error.

> [An interesting digression: the people of T—hold that the drift of humanity to measure time first by the sun, moon, and stars, then the clock, then on to the present style of employing the radiation from the cassium 133 atom is a symptom of loss of integral relation with the universe. From their point of view, humanity lives in two times: one is the harmony of celestial movement, the other is the outcome of the attentio—intentio-distentio of the human soul. Time measured by the disintegration of matter troubles them.]

Errors occurred in 1217, 1312, and 1939. In 1939, the cause was fog. The village is divided over whether the fog that morning was a natural event or a diabolic interference.

A series of circles are scored; more correctly, they are ruled into the ground with the use of a rope trammel around each of the eighteen families on the perimeter. In each case, the stretch of rope varies, causing the "ground rules" to be rather elusive for the ordering mind. For example, the first two circles may be one-and-one-half traditional feet from each other at circumference. The next may be a traditional yard and a half . . . and so on. There are seven circles in each cluster.

Younger people are stationed precisely within their group, and as the shadow of a designated participant strikes one of the arcs during the sun's rising, they quickly *walk* into the dancing field to stand at a prefigured location. From any group, only one person moves at a time, and simultaneously a participant of the opposite gender from another group will also start moving . . . their shadow was the signal, it having touched the ground rule of their circle. This phase is very orderly, and when it concludes, only four of the eighteen families are intact within their own ground rules. Each of the entrants will have taken a position marking out the following patterns:

Starting Positions

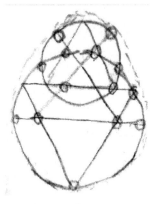

Starting Positions

They now hold their poise (as it were between "sat" and "asat"; I use Sanskrit because English here will not do[3]) with utter stillness while the villagers who have been within the circle all night rise, start their campfires, enjoy leisurely breakfasts, and then strike their camps. The huts are deconstructed, and the materials are carefully stacked outside the perimeter. As soon as everyone is back within the field, the families surrounding it take up willow branches that had been lying by their feet and rigorously brush out the ground rules that they had early drawn around themselves.

A slow song is sung to the time kept by a small hand drum held by one of the horsemen.

During the song, a venerable man with a long flowing beard traces a sequence of steps that brings him in turn to each of the poised standing figures. He circles each one . . . two times in one direction and once in the other. He carries a long staff of blackthorn, and at the four cardinal points of the field, he places the thin end in the ground and draws something. I was never told what he drew, and the distances were too great to make out clearly what it was. Afterward, when I went to inspect the dancing field, nothing remained of these hieroglyphs. Then he goes to sit in the center . . . that place in the egg-shaped design which *was* the center of a circle necessary at the beginning to generate the final egg shape on the proportions developed from the arithmetic nine-foldness.

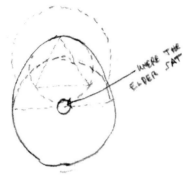

Where the Elder Sat

From this time on, he does not move again. The fourteen "position holders" begin slowly to turn in place.

What is beginning to happen, if I apprehend the event accurately, is like the exercise in Vedic mathematics whereby the realms of three-foldness (the nines) and the realms of seven-foldness dance their reconciliation. Those who had camped in the field overnight divide into twelve units, each unit occupying, at the start, a position on one of the two hexagons. The large hexagon is generated from the arc of the "bottom" of the egg while the smaller is generated from the "top" of the egg. They spin in place and then begin to move *as a group* while simultaneously spinning around one of the young stationary figures. This leaves two stationary figures not encircled by a particular group of dancers but surrounded by the entire assembly.

Time passes.

The rhythm of the singing changes. The "key" changes. The rotations turn in reverse directions. By now the sun has reached a station which throws the shadows exactly half the height of the substances, the human beings. There is a pause of exactly two minutes by the clock. No sound, no motion.

The singing starts up again, changing now from uniphony to polyphony. Each different choir, and there are fourteen of them, sing a slightly different tune to a slightly different time. Each of the twelve circles picks up one choir's beat and tune and performs the subsequent dance in time and with the "feeling" to accord with *that* choir.

The two "free," that is, unencircled young people, begin a very energetic individual dance to their specific choir's impetus. The four remaining families set forth a deep rumbling drone that gathers all the discord into ratio with their baseline configuration.

The duration and force of this portion of the ceremony caused me to expect to see some of the dancers pass out or leave the field, but this did not happen even to the younger or much older participants. The phase lasted twenty minutes by the clock.

During it, a rhythm of flashing lights began. I find this hard to describe. I believe the effect was created by small mirrors that some dancers had attached to the breasts and backs of their costumes. They must at some time have rehearsed to perfection. It demanded that a whole group or system of mirrors would be at the same angle to the sun at precise intervals . . . while, mind you, the circles were rotating at different tempi. The effect is astonishing. From the field comes a regular pulsation of light of a frequency different from what was happening either in space or sound. Superb concentration is needed, which would equal or surpass that of the masters of Yantra in my own land. My instincts tell me that the concentration needed here is greater, because it necessarily involved not simply attunement of the "one" but of the "one" among the "many."

The dance concludes. Everyone holds their place for a short time. By some sleight of hand, the old man who had been sitting in the center is no longer there. (I assume the flashing light affects one's perception like a strobe system and he must simply have walked off the field, as it were, between the pulses.)

The whole assembly shifts modes of action, and now begins the procedure of collectively raising a new barn. In silence, the foundation trenches are dug, the rocks and stones that had formed the context for the dance are taken from their positions and set into the ground. (An exhilarating display of first-rate dry rock masonry.) The hut materials that had been set aside at early morning are now gathered and assembled into walls, trusses, rafters, etc.

The ceremony in its entirety, from its genesis with "the harrowing," through the end of the dance, "the firing," is called "the Esplumoir."

In a sense, the event initiated by the burning of an old barn and concluded with the building of a new one is not present to anyone as a "whole" until it has passed over into the past. It exists as an action only when it is over. Wherein, then, is this action sited?

When it is yet to begin, it does "exist" as a complete expectation . . . and intention and a configuration. Wherein, then, is this "future" sited?

Through the materials and efforts and direction, the new barn enfolds an implicit action that "will have been" performed nineteen years from the date of its construction.

For this reason, it is most appropriate, even an act of semantic genius, to designate the entire instrument as "the Esplumoir." The obvious allusion is to Robert de Boron's *Perceval*, which was probably written between 1190 and 1212. In de Boron's account, Merlin's fate is different from his fate in the British versions. He does not end his days bound into the trunk of a massive oak in Wales, nor encircled in a bower as the victim of a sinister enchantment created by Nimue or Vivian. According to the tradition transcribed in the *Perceval*, he went into his "Esplumoir" in expectation of the time when Arthur will return from Avalon.

I will sketch some hints of a "figure" which will open up the question by affirming that the ritual performed here in the land of "the Magdalene" antecedes de Boron's work. And further, that he may have derived his poetic material from a community kindred to our village of T—.

I present the view that the material of the work is very ancient and derived from a brotherhood and sisterhood of the wise which were active throughout Asia in the epoch of King Solomon. Members of the society resided, among others, in both the lands currently designated as India and Israel. There is not enough space in this short paper to present my whole apparatus, but what I do set down will provide indications where further lines of research can be opened out.

I accept that *The Song of Songs* belongs to the first temple period. Reference to the substances called spikenard, curcuma, and cinnamon, which in those days originated in India . . . combined with reference to South Arabian incense and myrrh, help to validate the dates. For only up until the beginning of the Hellenic period did these materials flow through the kingdoms of Israel and Judah. After this time, trade had collapsed. In my country, we have excellently preserved Tamil songs about the love affair of a young village girl and Krishna that are contemporary with the first temple period. Structurally, these songs are very similar to "the song." It is now also well-known that Sumerian songs are also kindred but of an earlier provenance. In all the above-mentioned lands, the songs are considered to be "esoteric."

Now let us focus on the figures of the garden and the "Esplumoir." The closest Englishing of "Esplumoir" would be a "nest for birds." Certainly at the least it means a dwelling for winged, feathered creatures. The proper location is in a garden. Now let me add a few bits from de Boron. *Perlesvaus*, 2786 ff. the damsel asks Lancelot:

"Ou avez vos la voie emprise?"

He answers:

"Dame, fait il, au Chatl des Armes. Je se bien le chastel, fet la dame. *Li rois a non Messios*, et gist en languer, par il chevalilers qui ont este eu chastel, qui ne firent la bone demande."

Later the lines, 7205 f. are specific:

"El riche chastel que Perlesvaus avoit conqui ne failoit nule rien. Li chasteleaus avloit III nons, ce edit "l'eestoire, *Edem* estoit li I des nons, e li autre, de *Joie*, e li autres, des *Ames*. Por ce ot il a non Chastel des Ames, ce dist Josephez, que onques nus n'I deviia que l'ame n'alst en Paradis."

Another passage worth quoting refers to a river which will be familiar to those acquainted with *Seder Gan Eden*. These are the lines from Perlesvaus I, 7198:

"Il avoit derier le chastel un flum . . . par coi toz li beins venoit ou chastel . . . Icil flun estoit mout beaus e mout plentious. Josephez nos tesmoigne que il venoit de Paradis Terreste, e avironnoit tot le chastel . . . ."

I will rotate the figure a quarter of a turn and emphasize that *among those cultures* which found in their love poems implications of deeply multiple meanings, certain values, ideas, and similarities of design were shared.

The poems employ an ideoplastic imagery of gardens replete with creatures, with good medicine, balm, etc. There is a movement by the lovers along passages and pathways to and fro. Somewhere within this design is a strongly emphasized palace or castle or walled towers. The poems tend to appear in cultures motivated by powerful religious, mathematical, and astronomical interests. They continuously affirm the idea that there is a coherent organic connection among the poises and "scales," or reality, of "sat." Not only do ancient Sumeria, ancient India, and ancient Israel fit the pattern, but I hazard to say that the culture of Southern France between the tenth and fourteenth centuries seem to belong among them.

[I would point out to those aware that the beloved lady of "Song of Songs" is referred to both as garden and wall with towers. Towers in Hebrew is "magdaloth" from whence probably comes Magdalene.]

I affirm that the extended ceremony I witnessed says far more than even the many implications of the reconciliation of the "threes" and "sevens." It demonstrates the fulfillment and means of preservation of a knowledge that is essential to the human endeavor on the earth to become adult. The task, according to those who hold and transmit this thought, occurs within a context far larger than is customarily presumed by most of us. Their undertaking is supported by the continuous aid of "sat." Thank God!

The premise: At some time, forces inimical to human maturity gained great power on this earth. Through the succor and inspiration of Deity, a way was developed to build a "castle and a garden" and to allow therein the presence of a "bird's nest." These figures correspond to other "orders of reality."

To these environs, the "souls" of prophets, sybils, sages, kings, queens, etc., have access in order to continue the long and necessary task of spiritual regeneration. One might call it the "world of spirit . . ." but most likely those who today use this term mean something quite different than I do.

The Ground

I will hazard an interpretation of the dedication of the "firing" dance to Saint Elijah. By demonstrating the disappearance of the "sagely dancer," I think it represents the ascent of Elijah to heaven. Some Jewish traditions say that Elijah dwells in Gan Eden, the Garden of Eden, and can come and go into and from the "Kan Zippor" or "Bird's Nest." Compounding the "burden" of multiple meanings is the curious suggestion implicit in the dance of the village of T—that Merlin retreats (or advances) into his "Esplumoir" with the delightful help (not the sinister contrivance that later Merlin legends suggest) of his friend/sister/beloved Gnymn.

I will try to lead out from the ground how the specific performance enacts the difficult marriage of threes and sevens and by so doing creates a radiance of harmonic energy that is able, by its immanence, to "transcend" the so-called limitations of human nature. In some traditions, this rather bare idea is rendered more poetically as "crossing the rainbow bridge."

Time and space correlate insofar as they are grasped by *stretch* or step. That is, as a *stretch* of time or a *stretch* of space. In human experience, one stretch never can be sensed or thought without the other. Dances and ceremonies lead out their content by the juxtaposition of steps through and along these "stretches."

[I hope someone might follow through on this idea in relation to "Arthurian" studies. I believe that a precise mapping of the adventures of the "knights and ladies" in relation to spheres of time and space will yield surprising results. It could illumine a wide array of seeming irregularities. In these days of sophisticated computer modeling, this should not be too hard.]

Let us retrace the event that breaks through the inertias of "time and space" and leads into the ceremony of the "Esplumoir." Four weeks before the anniversary of the nineteen-year cycle, a barn is torched to the ground. Then once the foundations have cooled sufficiently, it is dismantled and the stones are carried across stretches of space to form the circle and the thirty-six stations of dwelling.

No matter how much time by the clock this operation takes, it is the *identical* space time unit every nineteen years. Literally it is the seed burst which sets the stage and precipitates the action.

[Clock time will vary from event to event because the distribution of physical strength and speed, the soil conditions, and the heat of the fire and the cooling time of the rocks will naturally vary.]

Obviously, were this alone sufficient for the conditions, it would be undesirable. For example, if three-foldness were clutched as the key to knowledge and elevated to the posture of an "idol," it would lead to slavery. Though rich in possibilities, the "threes" can in the end only lead to a cat cradle of immobility. The wonderful engineering term "gone to triangle" intuits this situation nicely. A more pungent description of this pitfall is recorded in the *Book of Revelation*. The author here warns of the dangers attendant on elevating "three-foldness" to divine status. The number 36 is one of the major systems whereby the ancients demonstrated an arithmetical phenomenon called the "square of the sun."

It is characteristic of the number 36 that if you add up the series 1+2+3+4+5, etc., . . . up to 36, the sum is the number 666. They (the author) are saying that, left to itself, worshipped as the key to the enigmas of the universe, the derivatives of three lead to either a cosmic jailhouse or the "beast of the Apocalypse." I am certain that Lama will enjoy reflecting on the implications of Koheleth's "under the sun" from this perspective.

Returning to "the Esplumoir," we find that the principle of threes is established during "the harrowing." It is "the blackening" which introduces the breaking free of this constriction. Ashes are spread and worked into the ground by young people who have never experienced the nineteen-year solar-lunar confluence. Those who are not "virgin" in the above sense are not permitted to participate in this process. The "ashes" establish a *thirty-seventh* location, i.e . . . . the entire dance ground . . . the field. "The blackening" loosens the network of the "given." Sainte Agatha is now presiding over the opus as the resident of lightning. Lightning is both unpredictable and manifests the entire earth perception of the "light field." Far more wavelengths of light are released by lightning than can be perceived from the sun because of atmosphere. Ashes and lightning are in obvious correlation.

With "the blackening" complete, the following three weeks are a kind of rest for everyone. But it is a rest during which memory and the splendor of the human spirit are celebrated. Time is stretched beyond the single lifetime. The grip of "under the sun" is loosened. Spatial boundaries are irrelevant.

"The firming" makes appropriate and balanced use of three-foldness. Properly "placed," the threes become an essential form in the establishment of human habitation. Such balanced expressions are in houses, languages, mathematics, and civilization in general. Here, although there are thirty-six huts, they are distributed in such a way as to relate "threes" to "sevens."

Seven-foldness by itself, if deified, can be as deadly a "god" or "beast" as can three-foldness. In this context, though, as both an a priori and concluding chord, it reaffirms the "rainbow bridge." "The firming" establishes the garden and the walls and towers. If I had been privileged to join a family during the coffee and tea breaks, I am sure I would have learned more of their application for the people of T—.

On the morning of "the firing," the eighteen families, which you recollect had suddenly appeared, are stationed eight families to an arc on each side of the "egg." One each assumed posts at the bottom and top. Seven persons from each side comprise the fourteen dancers who enter the field during the sun-rising. The straightforward walk of these pairs into their positions in tune, with the stretches of time marked by the sun's arc of ascent, pulses against the senses in a way that is truly touching. I was moved, during this quiet procession, to the brink of tears.

They stand quite still as the field breaks up around them into a kind of gentle chaos as the campers arise. Each camper sets about their own particular style of stirring into activity: preparing breakfasts on the many campfires, striking camps, and as a crowning moment, dismantling their huts. All materials, except the earth, stone, ash, and the human presence, are removed. The ground is carefully examined for any stray pieces of food, wrapping, or other debris. A new order reigns over the morning. A pristine order.

Let me remind you that the dance proper has the following players:

thirty-six families
fourteen individuals
one "mage"

Two young people in "free dance . . ." counted as one. This yields forty-nine units in choric movement and one in a unique movement and one in a unique movement followed by stillness.

The old man, the "mage," performs a series of steps and stretches that convey the sense of both binding and loosing. Most of you are aware of the meaning accorded the idea of 49 plus 1 in most old traditions. Here, I think, it is most interesting to look at the enacted disappearance of the "mage," which in this case is a Merlin, into the Esplumoir and the apparent absence of this well-known element, water.

[Having grown up with the fourfold Vedic division of Elements, I had been wondering where the water *was*.]

From my experience in dancing narratives, I hypothesize that the absence of an element of completion and the presentation of a *miraculous* occurrence are related in the realm of the *identity of opposites*.

The best way to think this through is from the public traditional knowledge. Several traditions bluntly state that the fiftieth gate or rung . . . or level of knowing . . . cannot be grasped or attained. This is true in Vedic, Jewish, Buddhist, and Shinto lore. They seem to be saying that the "fiftieth" is not perceivable, is not present to humanity . . . is not *in* nature. This is explained by reference to a fallen state or beginningless ignorance.

Now to step back and fold into this thought the *lack* of water and the idea of opposites. In the domain of color, when all parts of a spectrum are represented except, say, green, the psychological call and desire for green is so insistent that it is nevertheless present . . . by its absence. In the literature which undergirds the garden concept, the gardens are always watered by from one to four flowing rivers. In the case of "the Esplumoir," by renouncing the representation of literal water, attention is called to essential water. *We* are called to provide that which flows, cleanses, refreshes . . . that which possesses the capacity to fill and contain . . . that from which life comes to be. At this level, water is light, wisdom, the flow of divine love . . . time, space, and emanation. In the combined movement of the dance, we can link the missing element to the presentness of the miraculous: the Elijah or Merlin factor. When this factor is present to each of the forty-nine stations, they are each transformed so that the fiftieth emerges as a natural, not an exceptional, outcome. If this factor is, in fact, not present, then the sequences are incarcerated in mere seven-foldness or, worse, in three-foldness.

Our given ideas assign water, even the supernal water, to the feminine dimension. On the surface, then, it is fair to object that in the performance before us, the key player is a "male." This is a long subject also, to which I can only suggest some thoughts. We need to remember that the figures masculine or feminine are not themselves the substances water, earth, fire, air . . . but are each possessed of all. Consequently, they are the bearers of these dimensions, and when their work or dance is done, as in the present case, they are seen no more.

So it is a marvelous effect that when the figure of the mage or prophet has enacted the binding-loosing ritual, that figure remains silent and still as a presence throughout the dance. And then when the dance at last "exists," that is when it has passed into the past; the figure is no longer there to be seen.

Much has been left out. To quote the seeresses: "the wise will understand."

Also, there are many practical considerations which conditions the form of the "the Esplumoir." In principle, the central role could be held by either a man or a woman. The role could take the form of a sage, a sybil, a king, a queen, etc. But politically, in the given circumstances of the village of T—, a free-ranging application of principle could have proved dangerous. Successive witchcraft manias have plagued Southern France. Often it was exceptional women who were the choicest scapegoats. In olden days, they were left as charred and putrid messes bound to stakes. In more recent times, they are often brutally treated and left gabbling in the madhouse. The sixteenth and seventeenth centuries were so frenzied in this activity that I guess much that I saw has either been sublimated or reduced.

So it is very intelligent that the casual visitor to the village would have noticed nothing except an unusually complex planting ritual. The observer, having been not present at the four weeks leading up to the final dance, most likely would find nothing special. It would seem like any village dance. I call to mind the example of the Lithuanian "Flax Dance." It presents an ancient tradition reaching back to the period of the *Rig Veda* as a common peasants' dance. Only the perfection of the performance might cause wonder. The odd presence here, in Southern France, in the center of the dance of a wandering and weird bent-kneed "foolosopher," could not cause concern that something of real matter was going on.

I am very fond of Saint Magdelene. I would like to think that when the institutional church labored to reduce her meaning for the faithful in these regions, she remained close at hand. I like to think that, though her signifiers were altered, her presence remained here as an inspiration among the many pilgrimage chapels of the region. I like to think that the little village of T—was inspired to sustain the essence of her meaning somewhere on earth.

I wish to express my appreciation to Amfortas for giving me such an indigestible bundle of anxiety during the meeting at Olivet. It drove me like a goad for several years. I trust my piece repays my fellows in the society with a lump equally hard to digest.

[An afterthought: I came upon a present day evocation of the "Esplumoir and garden." I call your attention to the unbuilt project of Frank Lloyd Wright for Baghdad, Iraq. Its proposed location was an island in the Tigris River. In plan, it appears to be laid out much like the dance-field in the village of T—.]

Notes

1) An interesting discussion of these monuments can be found in *Time Stands Still*, Critchlow & Bull St. Martin's Press, New York, 1982.

2) I discovered a superb discussion of the "Esplumoir" in an article by Helen Adolf in *Speculum*, "The Esplumoir Merlin." This essay also develops some fascinating relationships between the figure of Merlin and the figure of Elijah.

   a) Elijah, among the Jews, is the prophet par excellence; his prophecy even goes on in the Bird's Nest, where the effigies are woven of all the nations who band together against Israel. Merlin too is a divins and in his farewell speech says that *in* the Esplumoir, "je profetiserai cou que nostre Sire commandera."

   b) Elijah did not die but was translated to heaven. It is hinted inChronicles II 21:12 that he was active on earth even after his translation, and thus the belief developed that he was kept in heaven to be a witness of the last things. It is the same with Merlin: "Lor dist queil ne poroit morir devant le finement del siecle."

   c) Elijah is shown in close connection with the Messiah ben David, who in his celestial abode is suffering the pangs of pre-existence . . . and with the Messiah ben Joseph (or Ephraim) who will be slain but resuscitated by Elijah. This reminds us of Merlin who, after the fateful battle where Arthur is grievously wounded, goes into his Esplumoir expecting the time when Arthur will return from Avalon.

d) In episode K, "Merlin as a Shadow," Merlin frightens Perceval's horse. The Jewish Encyclopedia tells us that "Elijah's appearance among people is so frequent that even the irrational animals feel it." Merlin, though, has inherited his father's dismal qualities, whereas the barking of the dogs is joyous when they announce the presence of Elijah.

e) Merlin warns Perceval not to disregard the advice of the two children concerning the road to his right hand. One of the duties of Elijah is to stand at the crossroads of Paradise and to lead the pious to their proper places. His abode is not in Heaven proper but in Paradise, whose location is uncertain. The Grail country too is some kind of uncertain earthly paradise.

Dr. Adolf's penultimate example is as follows:

f) It is Merlin who points out to Perceval the road that leads to the house of the Fisher King. He seems to know all about the Grail. According to Jewish tradition, all lore, especially all secret lore, emanates from Elijah.

3) My guess is that Marya is dealing with these terms from an early Upanishadic point of view. She avoids using the "equivalent" Western terms: being and nonbeing. Why? I can only conclude, knowing her, that she is pointing toward the concept of "nonbeing" only as a term of language as some interpretations of Aruni attest. According to this interpretation, "asat" is the term used

as a semantic maneuver in order to describe the process of "becoming." Asat is negation only insofar as it represents a *poise* of "sat" that enables becoming. This interesting, though unpopular, viewpoint, I discovered in R.S. Misra's *Studies in Philosophy & Religion*, p. 38-74, Bharatiya Vidya Prakasana, Varanasi, India, 1971. I think I am on the right track here because the volume is introduced by a Kalidas Bhattacharya of Santiniketan.

CHAPTER TEN

Ali

Tenpa Tenzin was born into an important Central Tibetan family in 1910. It was the year of two major "cosmic events." The arrival of Haley's Comet coincided with the invasion of Lhasa by the Chinese. By the time he was three years old, the Chinese had been driven out of Tibet and the Dalai Lama had returned to Lhasa. The support of Great Britain was very important throughout this trying period. As a result of this congeniality between the two countries and their mutual acceptance of various treaty arrangements, Ali's family became very positive toward England and things English. At the outbreak of World War I, they were among those who urged the Dalai Lama to offer the assistance of Tibetan troops in India in support of the allies. They also arranged for Ali to have a tutor in the English tongue when, at the age of five, he entered Sera monastery.

When he was in his early twenties, the affair of Chokhorgyal[1] precipitated his family to hold council. They anticipated a troubled succession would be followed by lacerating internal struggles within the higher circles of Tibetan society. They were committed to the struggle, but they wished for one of their number to have both the stress and opportunity to practice the Dharma away from the homeland. Since they expected the United States to become dominant in the world during the middle years of the century, they decided to send Ali to that country, both to come to understand and to have the experience of life in a land not torn by war.

In 1938 (the Earth Tiger year), Ali established his residence with the small Mongolian Lamaist community in New Jersey. He arrived with his wife, a sister, and a brother-in-law. At an advanced age (relative to other students), he swiftly passed his high school examinations and proceeded to college at Seton Hall. The good fathers were pleased to admit a bird of such rare plumage. Though Ali had a natural genius for psychology and religious studies, he turned his efforts in the direction of science. Quite rapidly, he pushed through to a MS in physics. He chose not to pursue the academic life any further and stepped down from the American educational escalator with "only" the MS. His activities with Asaph, as described above, brought him into association with Amfortas.

Ali did not like to leave his enclave in New Jersey. But on one of my trips to New York, we did arrange to meet in Manhattan. There were aspects of the city he appreciated very much. He admitted to loving the turbulence of the streets, loving the chaotic produce and clothing markets on the Lower East Side, and the general feel of the city's fervor. On this day, he insisted on a surprising agenda.

"The Guggenheim Museum has not long ago opened. And I want to see for myself what all the fuss is about."

We met in the park across Fifth Avenue from the building. Our first view was through a veil, a tracery of tree branches and leaves with a few blossoms. The flowing concrete swirl, he said, "reminds me of a tiger and a dragon lying down together . . . in, as you may say, repose."

After we entered, he waved off a guide's suggestion that we take an elevator to the top. He thought that was another insane American "instant notion." He considered it almost as mad as helicopter mountain climbing. Under our own steam, we walked slowly up the ramp and then down.

If I hadn't known better, I may have thought he had been drinking. His gait wavered and angled, and his balance was so uneven that he bobbed about as though on board a ship. Meandering and weaving, seeming aimless, his progress was like a feather in erratic drafts of air.

Back on ground level, we stood in the center quietly for quite a long time until slowly his face broke into a toothy grin and he exclaimed, "Alleiy!" Quickly we walked out of the museum because he did not want to talk there.

We went directly to the nearby rowboat concession in Central Park. We each purchased several frankfurters and beer and found a table by the water. After a few sips of beer, he said:

How did he know to do that? Where did he come to know to do that? For people he has done an amazing thing.

Truly astounding . . . it is like Samboghokaya and

Nirmanakaya are fields of light . . . or, concern, or something like that . . . and the flows of those fields intersect and merge their boundaries in a building! How?

Ali was like that. He could make a bewildering statement that, as in this case, took us almost four hours of earnest conversation to explain.

He was quite tall and sported a drooping "Fu Manchu" mustache. He never went anywhere without a bright yellow beret perched whimsically on his bald head. Ali was a family man with a remarkable wife, three sons, and a daughter.

*   *   *

One Report in Three Phases
Ali
Phase One

I have found myself extremely attracted to the French mind of late. It seems a healthy complement to my Tibeto-Anglo mind development. How fortunate you of the West are to have a table of such diverse cultural products before you. It is like a closet from which you can find occasional fresh garments for your minds.

Gabriel Marcel was musing several weeks before Bastille Day. It was, to be exact, on July 4, and I like to imagine that the American Independence Day put him in the "mind" to ponder diversity. The July 4 entry was brief:

Temptation and the impossibility of judging for others.

Then, with a whole day to chew his telegraphic thought over, he was able to amplify this thinking in a charming French way:

July 5th, 1920
I mean that when we ask ourselves questions about the value of the world we live in we inevitably think ourselves obliged to put ourselves in the position of other people and ask ourselves whether their world is acceptable to them. But I am only able to judge my own universe if that. The universe of others is not given to me as *datum* and hence cannot be an object of appreciation. Of course I am almost inevitably driven to put aside this difference between their world and mine. By and large I admit that, strictly speaking, we have the world in common; but all that I have the right to say is that under these or those given conditions life would not be tolerable for me. We can go on to ask *whether under such different conditions I would still be myself*, whether they

would not be the source of new springs within me. In short, every judgment expresses a particular selection; and yet it claims to have value. This is Bradley's paradox. But then . . . [2]

Living in America for me was to be in a world different from anything I had imagined while at home in Tibet. Everything was not only different but a strange blend. I felt at the same time heavily taxed yet relieved of many mental burdens. It was much like the way I have been told that Americans experience their summer vacations.

So one summer I took my family on a typical vacation to the American Southwest. We blended in quite well. Many white-skinned people took us to be natives. But there was no way I could reproduce in myself the bittersweet anxieties and joys my American friends described as the inevitable accompaniment to their weeks away from their jobs with their families. I was feeling somewhat cheated of this uniquely Western experience simply because of my odd chemistry of character formation.

Then, while watching a dance at one of the "Indian" pueblos, I caught a glimpse of a very rare subjective state. Watching this incomprehensible, but for me somehow familiar dance, a feeling of great rest and refreshment overtook me. I had stepped into a universe bearing resonance with my homeland that was not apparent at first.

I became aware then, in that dusty plaza, that a piece of my mind had for years without my anticipation been trying to orient me. It had been exhausting itself in behaving like a "searchlight seeking out enemy planes." Watching the dance, this "mind" of mine was able to turn off the electricity more completely than either my meditation practice or my occasional retreats had ever allowed. How had this come about?

Though it is true that the homeland of buddhi may be called "the original face before birth," the homeland of the person is a world of events, meanings, ways of doing and seeing . . . in short, a cosmology. The dance I observed was like a village or an island in world-space-time that was quite close to where I had been brought up. To continue the figure, it was an island so close that the shoreline could be seen from ours and we could heard the dogs barking and the calls of children and mothers . . . and the arguments on still evenings and the drums and flutes.

I am describing an "island" more weighted on the *time* than the *space*. It is a time very different from what historians and ethnologists use when they presume a certain unfolding of the human adventure. When they call this circumstance matriarchal, that one patriarchal . . . or, becoming more abstract they call it "stone age," "bronze age," "feudal," "imperial," and so on, they are talking a different language. I speak here about raw time, time like raw honey . . . two/four time . . . three/four time . . . four/four . . . or nine/four . . . time.

From my point of view, with regard to beginningless ignorance, human nature is the same everywhere. It enfolds the same one hundred and eight knots of error and the same one hundred and eight beads of chemical solution which will dissolve these knots. But the shape and constitution of the knots and the proportions of the "chemical beads" that will untangle them vary from cosmos to cosmos. In a particular place, time is shaped uniquely *between* person and person. But between places and cosmoses, time is a shape and force of discontinuity.

The dance which gave me rest was, for the spectator, a bit monotonous, because the same series of steps was constantly being repeated. They would perform first in one direction and then after a loosely knotted duration execute it in another direction and then in one or another location of the village. One individual painted in black-and-white stripes threaded his way among the dancers. Now and then he seemed to be leading or indicating directions, and at other times he would wander off as though he had forgotten the whole business and sit on the ground . . . or suddenly stir himself to chase a dog. Then always he would return to the community in either enthusiasm or weariness to resume some kind of relation . . . even responsibility, toward the community of dancers. The village kept time.

The striped dancer kept a different time or none. Sometimes he entered the stream of the village and sometimes left it.

When I put all this together, I understood why I felt at home. To communicate this, I must, to quote the great Nishida Kitaro, "take one step back, one step down, then one step through." [3]

We Tibetans are just like other peoples in that we have been guilty of permitting certain aspects of our most valuable insights to become lopsided and lead us into abuse. But one thing we have seen and have been able to hold is the sense of the presence of the "absolute" in the human as human and *not* separated from activity. This is an inheritance of the ancient conditions of our life in a hard and awesome land. We *discovered* ourselves in a land where the surroundings were not naturally sheltering. Each of us knows that he depends on other individuals even for the pursuit of enlightenment. Even before the arrival of Buddhism, we had to admit that the "other guy" bore within them and in their actions the presence of the absolute. Our survival depended on this recognition. Due to these lessons taught to us by nature, we have some unique attitudes among Buddhist lands.

The Lamas, Dge-legs-dpal-bzan-po, and Tson-kha-pa have said, respectively:

> . . . human existence is a sacred existence. A person when born is a Buddha incarnate.

> The birth of a human being means that a Buddha brings up Buddha's child whose essence is a Buddha . . . and to have a Buddha come forth.

Now then, I go a step onward and push through to find the obstacle unobstructed I can ask, "From where does this Buddha come?" The Sanskrit word for Tathagata translates as "thus come or thus gone."[4]

The shapes of time have this feature that the making of them comes and the unmaking appears. The origins of time are not in time, and time's destiny is other than itself, though not different or separable.

Human beings make cosmologies that express the shape of time intrinsic to their particular island. The elements that build up the grammar of the structure are ultimately very complex but basically are simple enough to list:

A) Styles of production of
    1) food (much influence of climate here)
    2) artifacts and tools for necessities
    3) wealth
B) Languages
    1) ways of thinking develop for survival
    2) the ways all of *A* interact
C) Gender relationships
    1) ratios of males to females surviving infancy
    2) population densities
    3) patterns of the distribution of populations between moving and settled and the means of these groups to secure livelihoods
    4) historical patterns of plague and war

It is truly wonderful how from such a handful of basic times the human community meets so varied a system of crossroads, how the flow of events produces so many bundles of the possible. The way the crossroads at the borders of events are met and answered begins to determine the "type" of cosmology and locations of the islands in the ocean.

When Buddhism came to my land, it was not a landfall onto a desert island. It was a place where we could welcome the Dharma as a long-lost friend. The "Buddha nature" corresponded to an intuition my people had already accepted. As I said earlier, we had already sensed that there was something in the human being, our neighbors as well as ourselves, expressed in lesser or greater degrees by some and in the maximum degree by Lord Buddha. This something was not of the shapes and products of time.

This quality—nature, essence—is not different from the character of the striped figure in the Indian dance, Tathagata.

That "clown" was able to enter time and leave it simultaneously. It follows then that this "person" is connected to the originating dimension of which *time is an artifact*. This "person" is, acts, and works at right angles to our four dimensions. In potentia, we are all this "person."

From the Native American perspective, the striped figure wearing corn husks is the guide and guardian of the seeds of the community on the "people's" path toward their human fulfillment "in the south." From my perspective, the sublime clownishness of this "person" testifies to the tensility and the tenuity of time . . . the discontinuity and simultaneous continuity of our medium of life.

My own people find our origin in the union of a Monkey King and an Ogress. And one might say that by consequence of our lineage, we are in a precarious poise in relation to time. But if we devalue or debase time, we have mistaken the situation. Time *is* seeded with eternity. Samsara is Nirvana. Only through time do things become. It is both the mountain massif and the pass we find through the mountains to the Pure Land. It is the passageway of heroes and heroines.

You should be able to see why I felt at home among these Tewa-speaking people.

When I returned to my business responsibilities on the East Coast, my pondering on this theme were soon displaced by a fresh fascination with the American style of *managing* everything from water to money to life; with this difference, I now was aware of the Indians in our midst. Before, they had blurred in the general mass of the melting pot.

For instance, I had gone into Manhattan one day to look at the beautiful Monets at MOMA. Still dazed by the pleasant enchantment, I somehow walked myself over to the Carnegie Delicatessen and noticed an Indian inside the deli enjoying a pastrami sandwich and possessed of what I shall call an outline. I began to notice this quality when I crossed paths with Indians on the street or on the bus. Again, when I had gone to Mexico City on the trail of ancient records, even in this relatively "non-white" culture I found native peoples defined by this quality of "outline." This went far toward convincing me that the quality that had fascinated me was not a product of merely sharp cultural differences in the ordinary sense but that it drew its breath from some different source.

Any meaning I had gleaned from these observations evaporated as I resumed my studies and religious practice.

The Olivet conference produced such a feeling of unease in me, however, that I began afterward to have great difficulties when I returned back east. Studies, meditations, and the acquisition of various initiations needed by me on my path became nearly impossible. I began to think about all this.

It is rarely possible for a researcher in celestial mechanics or particle physics to face his or her own knowledge about the fragility of the human adventure while he or she is comfortably cozy, preparing a barbeque on their lovely secure patio. So also is it rare that I am able to face the conflagration at the end of time and the inexorable degeneration of the human species *in* time that is an axiom of our Tibetan knowledge. I do not believe I would be wrong if I added that this fact is not truly faced by even High Lamas of my people, surrounded as they are by their disciples and secure in their doctrinal correctness.

Each in our way, we have through our stories, by which I mean our cultures, elaborate inventions, and devices by which we keep our houses and patios and doctrines from crashing and sinking away beneath us. We have configured our islands in such a way that we can avoid both time and eternity.

I think the "outline" of the Native American comes about in this way. Each of them who succeeds in becoming adult must live *decisively* in both his or her *own* time as well as the time of their tribe. This is a decision. It is not merely happenstance as it is with us. It has to be this way, since the winds of time and eternity keep blowing through the "shapes" of their islands.

I had been able to find refreshment in our visit to the Southwest because of certain shared assumptions. But a decisive step had been taken by these people at some point, which turned their homeland into a cosmology that was also different from our cyclic view.

Other aspects of their culture, however, did not capitalize on the values their "difference" augured for *personal* development. As people, as a whole, they are no better or worse than others. Their oblique stance has even manifested in severe drawbacks for their relations with the dominant culture. They had a regrettable history of poor judgment when discriminating whom among the "aliens" they could trust.

Notwithstanding what I have just said, many Native Americans do have an outline. It bears witness to an important dimension of human potentiality. If we Asiatics and Europeans can face what is necessary to develop this quality, we may be able to reverse the tendency of our species to corrupt the very supports of life on earth.

Phase Two

After World War II, another Frenchman expressed his meditations on paper. In this case, it was the born poet St. John Perse. In keeping with the tone I have set, I will quote lavishly from his poem *Winds*:

> These were very great winds over all the faces of this world,
> Very great winds rejoicing over the world, having neither eyrie nor resting-place,
> Having neither care nor caution, and leaving us, in their wake,
> Men of straw in the year of straw . . . Ah, yes, very great winds over all the faces of the living!

> Scenting out the purple, the haircloth, scenting out the ivory and the potsherd, scenting out the entire world of things,
> And hurrying their duties upon our greatest verses, verses of athletes and poets,
> These were very great winds questing over all the trails of this world,
> Over all things perishable, over all things graspable, throughout the entire world of things . . .

> And airing out the attrition and drought in the heart of men in office,
> Behold, they produced this taste of straw and spices, in all the squares of our cities,
> As it is when the great public slabs are lifted up. And our gorge rose
> Before the dead mouths of the Offices. And divinity ebbed from the great works of the spirit.

For a whole century was rustling in the dry sound of its straw,
and amid strange terminations at the tips of husks of pods, at
the tips of trembling things,
Like a great tree in its rags and remnants of last winter,
wearing the livery of the dead year,
Like a great tree shuddering in its rattles of dead wood and its
corollas of baked clay—
Very great mendicant tree, its patrimony squandered, its
countenance seared by love and violence whereon desire will
sing again.

"O thou desire, who are about to sing . . ." And does not my
whole page itself already rustle,
Like that great magical tree in its winter squalor, proud of its
portion of icons and fetishes,
Cradling the shells and specters of locusts; bequeathing,
relaying the wind of heaven affiliations of wings and
swarmings, tide marks of the loftiest Word—
Ah! very great tree of language, peopled with oracles and
maxims, and murmur the murmur of one born blind among
the quincunxes of knowledge . . .

And amazingly, the poet sustains this level for another sixty
pages of verse. Now, from the Far East I will relate two brief
situations:

A monk from India was famous for his ability to discriminate
sounds and voices. He went to China where a king invited
the great Zen master Hsuan-sha to inspect this prodigy. The
master took a copper tong and struck an iron kettle.
"What sound is this?"
"The sound of copper and iron."
The master turned to the king and said,

"O my king, don't be deceived by strangers."

The other situation arises in my own country. When I was ten years old, I had to learn the following catechism:

kha-dog yon-na dkar-po yin-pas khyab zer-na pad-ma-ra-ga
kha-dog-chos-can dkar-po yin-par thal kha-dog yin-pas
phyir rtags ma-grub cihi phyir—

[If it is asked]
"Must it be white if it were a color?"

[It follows]
"A ruby possessed of color is white."
Reason: "Because it is a color."
[To this argument the answer]
"The evidence is not established."
Questioner: "Why . . . ?"

In both situations, we are taught that when we hear the wind blowing through "the very great tree of language," we must discern the general and the singular among the "quincunxes of knowledge."

Now a person might ask me, "Why did Buddha vow he would not enter Nirvana until all sentient beings were saved?" I could answer, "What good would do him to do so?" Before the play is over, will the protagonist permit himself to be erased from the performance? If he would, he will not have been at all.

To contrive to project oneself out of time or erase oneself from the story has no value. The tale goes on far past our perception of it. But when everyone is saved, we have something remarkable. We then have another kind of time, we have a story which has turned itself inside out. The sound of copper tongs on iron kettles is not copper and iron; it is the tongue of Buddha vibrating in the atmosphere. It is neither out of time nor embedded in it.

While enjoying my hobby of gazing through my telescope and watching a comet, I encounter questions that remain with me long after bedtime. I wonder, "Why do people so quickly put up their windbreaks, they can't stay up forever?"

A dear friend, an elder of my family, recently died. He informed us that his next residence would be in the court of Maitreya, the next Buddha, destined to come in 2,500 years. But that means that my friend is still very much here and present in my story. He has not absented himself from our world life but is instead very present to it. How could it be otherwise?

I have observed that some people in America have become so frightened of the winds of God that they have made themselves a strange story. According to this device, they will be delivered from time by a sudden separation of the good from the bad. The good (themselves) will be raptured into "heaven," eternity. Their enemies, and even their friends and loved ones, will be left behind to tramp through time until it ends. But how sad for them all, the good and the bad! With one windbreak, they think they have sheltered themselves from both time and eternity. They are hoping sadly for themselves to fall into "the rapture" of bottomless death. They remind me of the story in the Christian Gospel about the herd of pigs that threw themselves over a cliff.

For them, the virtue of this story is that it does provide a "shelter" without wind or breath, and that nevertheless is snatched from boredom by promised excitement. Most amazing about this is that the above story is being sold like pick-up trucks to the Native Americans. And here is the point of my circumlocution. Though the Indian has developed a real outline and all that is signified by it, they seem to lack the presence of a voice like that of Master Hsuan-sha to say: "Oh my king, don't be deceived by strangers."

Fruitful thoughts like these come to me while I give myself up to my passion of stargazing. Through my regretfully deficient studies, I do know the accepted names for heavenly bodies and their expected locations. Since we understand the laws of motion of large bodies, we are able to have a knowledge of past positions and future destinations of much that we can see. The spans are vast. There is much out there that we cannot see. As I watch for a few moments, delighted by some surprising celestial beauty, I think I see what is there. It is so present! Yet I know it is not so.

Much more poignant is the illusion regarding medium-sized bodies such as people. Our various histories say to us with strong persuasion, "This is the past in itself." Even in the procedure of a denial of it, they still are saying it. But when we cannot know the whole "present in itself" how can it possibly be so? I am not saying that the past does not exist. It most emphatically does. But I wish that when some group or other is saying, "Aha . . . this is it . . . that is the past!" we could also hear the speech of Master Hsuan-sha within the sound of the tongs, "Don't be deceived."

I think there are two kinds of "strangers" in the business of deceiving. One group is of cynical adventurers trying to conquer the past to possess the future. The others are, in the words of some other Frenchman, "Prisoners of retrospective illusions of fatality" facing a closed future. Examples of the first type are the Nazis who build their deathly ship of destiny with materials claimed by their view of the so-called "true destiny of the German people." The millions who climbed aboard into that rapture were assuming they could master the unseen future. An abysmal idea.

Examples of the second kind are of those well-meaning social scientists and psychologists who believe they can understand the *causes* of events through knowing the past. They are addicted to presumed causes derived from the belief that *they* can see the past in itself. Many "spiritualists" also are of this type. In my opinion, this kind of thinking merely succeeds in drying up for them the open depth of the present. It stakes out a closed future. It deprives the human being of accountability, responsibility for others, and, hence, dignity. To come to this view, they *have to deny common sense* as a valuable datum.

For both my own people and Native Americans, however, we neither see our story as the "past in itself" nor as an adequate explanation of the causes of the present. Sadly, as I hinted above, many native peoples are finding the illusion of certainties that are provided by both these kinds of presumed knowledge very seductive. Why should the answer of copper on iron be so satisfying?

Phase Three

Paul Valery provides me the tuning fork for the third "note."

> What a curious madness is communicating! Passing on one's disease, opinions—communicating life. Our opinions our convictions are not more than cruel necessities enforced on us. Something in our nature insists on our thinking about all subjects. The political system forces us to do so. God obliges us to come to a conclusion as to his existence and his qualities.
>
> Since our nature insists on our finding answers to all the problems that it makes us think are put to us, it also insists on our cherishing our answers, as personal creations. The contrary would be more sensible.[6]

I have been thinking about the resources in my own traditions that may help us out of this impasse. What comes to mind is the incarnation known as a *gTer-ston*, a person whose activity and charisma is important to us. Such a one has the possibility of keeping both the past and the future open and whose "communiqué" is *by definition* neither his own answer nor opinion, nor necessarily the message given by society. His genius lies in discovering lost or hidden scripture, teaching, data, or artifacts. The material he discovers is what has been "hidden" by our great national guru Padmasambhava. Just think! Had Guru's system worked at full capacity, what a shock it would have been for our "system." Our Tibetan culture would have continuously been pressed to reconsider its accepted past, reform our ancient teaching, and face our continuously arriving present with vigilant attention before its depth. We would have been compelled to include the future as *wildly* living under the sign of dependent origination. That is properly our culture's karma. Thus we could have been paying back the inscrutable loan and legacy left us by Padmasambhava. Needless to say, we have not lived up to his challenge.

What resources of the West offer deliverance from its appetite for fatality? Some French (of course) historians have rescued the old Judaic idea of requiring "two witnesses" and recast the demand in a refreshing light.

> Witness One: the set of voluntary witnesses; those who give accounts of the past as present.
> Witness Two: the set of "witnesses in spite of themselves," which give accounts of the past as present

The requirement has value when Witness One is tested by Witness Two.

Archeology is an example of "witnesses in spite of themselves." The good result depends on the rigor and impartiality of those examining the witness.

Asaph suggested to me the recent case in which archaeologists in the land of Israel have found no evidence of battle or violent destruction of inhabitants in those sites which the voluntary witness (the Bible) claimed to have been scenes of violent conquest by King David. The evidence suggested that the communities in question lived and either developed or evaporated in a natural way over long periods of time. Here we find a dispute between Witness One and Witness Two. Should this not cause people to reflect afresh on the content of the Bible's testimony? Was it some form of special pleading or lying? Or is the Hebrew scripture trying to express something else significant? Is it a communication of a different order than narration of literal events of the past?

If the West could embark on *gTer-ston-ship* with passion, in this way they may succeed in loosening the tongue of an accepted "history" that for so many has become a present prison house. I think—no, I *believe*—that the lips of the past, having been blackened by the smoke of altar fires and closed only under the seal of fear, wish to be opened.

Our much-needed witnesses "in spite of themselves" are the trails left by the configurations of our varied islands. In themselves they say nothing or little about the events, the crossroads, and intersections on the fluids of time. But set out thus: [Witness One] x [Witness Two] . . . they can do much.

Clearly the moment is here when we must . . . to save our skins and the skins of those who ought to come after us . . . sharply and severely cross-examine all our voluntary witnesses. Facing the winds that will be let loose by this activity will be far more pleasing to heaven than facing the winds of an earth denuded of trees or stripped by a thermonuclear holocaust.

Notes

1) Chokhorgyal is a small monastery founded by the second Dalai Lama, Gedun Gyatso. Near it is a sacred lake associated with special visionary activities. The affair mentioned must refer to the certain confusions and flurries of rumor surrounding the visit to this lake in the spring of 1935 by the regent of the time. The regent's party was seeking evidences for the location of the rebirth of the Dalai Lama. After certain undisclosed visionary experiences, both the regent, Rating Rinpoche, and the high official Kalon Trimon both decided to submit their resignations. Many peculiar political stresses and distresses occurred subsequent to this "affair of Chokorgyal."

2) Gabriel Marcel, *Metaphysical Journal*, Henry Regnery Co., Chicago, 1951, trans. Bernard Wall, p. 239.

3) Nishida Kitaro (1870-1945) was Japan's foremost modern philosopher. As far as I know, the quoted remark is not in any of his many books, or so Japanese acquaintances have assured me.

4) The following item from D.T. Suzuki's *Studies in the Lankavatara Sutra*, Routledge & Kegan Paul Ltd., London, 1968, may help here:

> Tatha means "thus," but the question is whether to divide tathagata into tatha and gata or into tatha and agata. In the first case gata is "gone" or "departed" and in the second case, if it is agata, it means "is come" or "is arrived."

5) St. John Perse, *Collected Poems*, Bollingen Series LXXXVII, Princeton University Press, p. 227-229, trans. Hugh Chisholm.

6) Paul Valery, *Analects*, Bollingen Series XLV. 14, Princeton University Press, 1970, p. 223.

CHAPTER ELEVEN

Kali

Patricia Murphy was born in Dayton, Ohio of a "blue-collar" family. Even before her confirmation, she had been having ecstatic experiences. To both her and her family, there was no doubt that her calling lay in the direction of professed spirituality. But she became fascinated with dance and studied at the Eastman School of Music in Rochester and then joined a dance company in Cleveland. The sexually ambiguous atmosphere of the company threw her into a period of confusion and led her to undertake a process of psychoanalysis. After passing through this tunnel, she went to England in order to visit the scenes of many of her childhood imaginings. Glastonbury was the pivot of her trip, and she became enamored of the religious community of sisters that had assumed some of the responsibilities for watching over the sacred site. She formally entered the Church of England and became a postulant of the Order of Sisters.

Several times she put off taking final vows and was permitted to publish occasional articles in *Whitechapel*, a rather specialized

Anglican journal. She became an avid scholar. A member of Amfortas in France, a subscriber to a number of eccentric British journals opened a correspondence with her that led to her association with the society. She was the only member of Amfortas not to be present at the Olivet conference, but she received full transcripts of the proceedings.

*   *   *

I believe I once exchanged glances with her, though I never actually "met" her.

It was summertime. I received a note asking me to pick up a package from Kali left at a certain bookseller in Bath. The note was specific about time and protocol. When I arrived, the bookseller was poring over his accounts. With no little impatience, I stood in front of his desk waiting for some attention.

I sensed someone come in whose presence saturated the small shop. For a fanciful instant, the place felt like a lion's den. My breeding and a slowly growing anger precluded my turning to look. As though stricken, the man looked up and past me toward the newcomer. The lady's voice arrested my preoccupation.

"Please, sir, attend to the gentleman first."

Now, there was no way I could gracefully turn around, so I explained my business. The man, after fishing a few seconds behind the desk, produced a good-sized package in brown wrapping paper, which he handed to me.

Turning to leave, I saw the delicate oval of a very slight woman's face whose eyes met mine for an instant. Her gaze seemed to pass through mine, into where there were no waves of joy or sorrow. Starting to speak, I found, as she modestly lowered her eyes, that I could not. As I left the shop, I passed close by her and seemed to hear her say, almost as though to herself, "I have faith in you, forever."

The package contained a long and fascinating manuscript written in an entirely different style from the report that follows in this book.

Asha
Kali

I have read the record of your proceedings with great interest and regret I could not have been present at all that snarling of gnarled wills which marked the parting of the ways within the society. You may find it strange that a person cloistered as I have been should find in that event the promise of good things for you all. But I do. Within the whole transcript, that conflict stands out as the one thing that proves to me you all are worth your salt. I will explain why when I conclude my report.

Several years ago in April, I was graced with a series of visions of an unusual nature about a community in the distant past. The previous Advent, I had prayed to be directed toward an understanding of the meaning of the visitation of the magi at the cradle of our Lord. But it wasn't until April, during Passiontide, that the response to my prayers occurred.

The exact sequence, I think, will prove enlightening. I had given myself the liberty of "breaking rank" from my community to spend a few moments meditating on Matthew Arnold's *Dover Beach*:

> The Seat of Faith
> Was once too, at the full, and round earth's shore,
> Lay like the folds of a bright girdle furled.
> But now I only hear
> Its melancholy, long, withdrawing roar,
> Retreating to the breath
> Of the night-wind, down the vast edges drear
> And naked shingles of the world.

Then, Emerson-like, I gave myself over to the craft of my whimsy and continued my truancy by picking up that very dear poem by Wallace Stevens, *St. Armorer's Church from the Outside*:

Its chapel rises from Terre Enselvelie,
An ember yes among its cindery noes,
His own: a chapel of breath, an appearance made
For assign of meaning in the meaningless
No radiance of a dead blaze, but something seen
In a mystic eye, no sign of life but life,
Itself, the presence of the intelligible
In that which is created as its symbol.
It is like a new account of everything old.
Matisse at Venice and a great deal more than that . . .

Something curious now happened. My eyes wrapped themselves around the dots following the *that*. The dots seemed to proceed serially without end . . . I stretched my attentiveness to them in a kind of half doze . . . from which I awoke into my first vision.

I seemed to be one among a group of adolescents at a lecture. At first, all I heard was the voice of the speaker trying to teach a difficult lesson. Somehow, I knew the context. We were in a small village on the edge of the Parthian Empire. Long before this, the wise ones of the community had moved here to distance themselves from the centers of our institutional faith.

We were here because, according to our elders, the authorities had fallen prey to an Ahrimanic error. The nature of the error was that the *fire-altar* had been misunderstood and been made into a vainglorious thing consuming the wealth of the surrounding lands. More in honor of a king than the "signature" of the fire of Ormazd.

Our village kept a very small fire-altar. It was able to be fed by wood offered without violence from the nearby forests. In this backwater of empire, we had been able to quietly keep to our understanding of our Mazdean faith. The constant political upheavals had actually made it possible for us to live in our own way without reprisals. Our fire was great in its spiritual intensity and the purity of its dedication. The fire was non-appetitive. It seemed to burn without consuming and contained all the sixteen types of fire.

The voice of the lecturer was articulating some ideas rooted in our conception of *Asha*. We are followers of Asha and Light. The word "Asha" differs in meaning according to the dimension in which it is used.

In the world of nature, it referred to the laws of nature, nature's way and order, and the miraculous harmony of all things. In the world of humanity, the inner world, it referred to truth, to justice, and to righteousness.

The speakers began to come somewhat into focus. They were older people, one man and one woman. They were today trying to broaden the horizons of the young who were sitting in front of them. They explained that other peoples and languages had the same *word* but composed it of different letters and sounds.

Far to the south in Hindustan, they divided the word into two. One was RTA and was applied by these people to the world of nature. The other was DHRMA, and this was the carrier of their thinking about the inner world of humanity. In Greece and Rome, the "word" was also divided into two.

However, among some poets of the Israelites, they also used only one word very similarly to our "Asha." That was the word *Emet*.

Now I began to look around the room and could determine the constitution of the class of young people as all younger than myself. I was a girl about the age of fourteen.

Synchronized with the emergence of this clarity was my awaking. I found myself nodding over the volume of Wallace Stevens in the same attitude as the young girl, my knees tucked under my chin.

Mild and fugitive, the vision did not cling and detract me from my community's Lenten devotions. I scarcely thought about it except as a suddenly surprising and regenerating dream.

Several days later, I went to the ruins of the Virgin Chapel, having drawn the agreeable chore of austere flower arrangements in the little, brutally exposed niche there. As I turned back toward the path from the ruined abbey, an impulse stirred me to make a short detour and stop at the Thorntree.[1] I stood in front of it, my gaze losing itself among the branches of flowering thorn. What I remembered at the time was being wakened by Sister Lucy and Sister Beatrice, who were solicitously kneeling by my side under the tree. They helped me back to our house where, despite protests, I was put to bed. I don't know how long I was knocked cold and remembered nothing.

Meals were brought to me, and I slept like a log the night through. Only in the morning, after I woke up thoroughly refreshed, gone through the whole morning drill, and completed Prime did the entire experience present itself to me as a clear, vivid memory of the day before.

I stood facing the thorn tree. A peculiar light shimmered and settled around it as though space had suddenly become liquid light radiating from the tree, from a source far deeper than its own heartwood. The birds in flight were arrested, slowed impossibly down to hold for a moment their place in flight or among the branches . . . and then everything began to move.

I was having an argument with a man only a little older than myself. From the look of him, he was in his forties. We stood in front of a tree identical to the one in Glastonbury. Nearby was a lake that I kept stealing glances at from time to time. The lake had a pristine brilliance which over and over kept catching my attention and diverting me from the argument. We both noticed my behavior and laughed.

As before, I somehow knew the context of this encounter. All over town discussions had been raging about a decision our elders had asked of us. Recent events of evil augury had convinced them it indeed was possible that the true religion might nearly vanish from the earth.

We had always understood our faith to be the medium of witness for the truth, Asha. We accepted sadly that from time to time the "people of lies," the *Druj*, would flourish. But always we were certain that deep heaven would respond by sending to earth "its" inspiration through people who embodied Asha strongly enough to route *the lie* for a time. But now our own faith seems to have been overtaken by falsification. Recent moves by "authority" toward absolute centralization threatened the existence of our own small, unique community.

The elders had suggested, so we may preserve our own truth and calling, that we ought to move to an entirely different location. They planned it very carefully. It could be accomplished without undue hardship. All over town, arguments have been going on between families and friends for over a week. Very soon the choice would be made.

Where Armenia and Syria blurred and faded into each other as tentative spheres of Roman imperial influence, a number of minor kings had managed to balance the pressure of Rome and Parthia. Here no central political or religious authority held sway. Into this wilderness region, our elders proposed to move our people so that one hearth of the religion could stay alive.

Our lands and wealth would be converted over a period of time into cattle. When we had accomplished this, we could immediately set out toward the west as a nomadic tribe. The period of property conversion would also be a period of training, during which our settled agricultural community could fit itself physically and morally for a life of travel. The hazard was great, but many of us had faith that Ormazd and the Fravarshis would be our guides and help.

This was the subject of the argument between me and my friend. I was for leaving . . . he for staying. My eyes kept looking with longing at the lake. I did not want to leave. This lake and the tree before which we stood were so special. In the lake, a virgin would conceive and ultimately give birth to the Sayoshant. According to our legend, the tree was one of the seven earthy representatives of the "tree of all seeds," the tree of "all healing." My friend kept raising the question of how I thought we could actually keep the true religion alive apart from these holy beings. I, for one, was sure we should leave, and by keeping faith, Ormazd would raise us another tree and, despite all logic, create another lake.

My recollection began to fade. I had to prepare to fulfill a certain private intention I had undertaken for Lent. This was the addition to my morning devotions of some meditations from the prime office of the Armenian Church. Today's was

O light, Creator of light,
Primal light that dwellest in light unapproachable,
O Heavenly Father-Mother [my addition] blessed are you by the ranks of the luminous ones; at the rising of the light of the morning shine forth upon our souls your intelligible light.

As I began the daily task, I was full of hope that the meaning of these outlandish dreams or visions would soon be intelligible to me.

As a child I was plagued with recurring dream states. With the passing of time and the acquisition of fresh interests, such as the dance, they diminished. When I entered Holy Orders, they stopped altogether. To undergo these recent encounters, which were more vivid than any I could remember, was both distressing and exhilarating. You see, I had come to believe that they were abnormalities which I had successfully sublimated or suppressed through my immersion in literature and the life of prayer. Until the "arrival" of these new visions, I was convinced that all my earlier difficulties were due to what Sir Phillip Sidney called "the blind man's mark." I quote:

> Thou blind man's mark, thou fool's self-chosen snare,
> Fond fancy's scum, and dregs of scattered thought,
> Bank of all evils, cradle of causeless care,
> Thou web of will, I have too dearly bought
> With price of mangled mind, thy worthless ware;
> Too long, too long asleep though hast me brought,
> Who should my mind to higher things prepare.
> But yet in vain thou hast my ruin sought;
> In vain though kindlest all thy smoky fire;
> For virtue hath this better lesson taught:
> Within myself to seek my only hire,
> Desiring naught but how to kill desire.

But now I realized that I had left from the equation something that made all the difference. But what?

Several days later, I went up Glastonbury Tor to gather some herbs for cooking. Now the decisive vision of the series came upon me. This time there was neither loss of consciousness nor diminishment of activity. It all passed before me while I was engaged in perhaps my favorite task in my favorite place. It was like a time lapse continuation of the dream at the tree. Yet it was alive, dense with promise and homecoming.

We had established our base by a bend in the early stages of the Euphrates River, north of Harrann. The journey west had been a success. The region chosen was within an area about the size of a small kingdom between three and four thousand square miles. Many small bands had found refuge, people whose lives were untenable nearer the centers of great power such as Babylon, Damascus, Jerusalem, and Antioch. Our elders were pleased with the conditions. They felt that gathered here, as though by providence, were the true followers of Ormazd . . . though other peoples called that goodness by other names. But we could taste unmistakably their dedication to Asha.

Behind, in our old homeland, stayed many of our community, including my dear friend. I often longed for his charm and his presence. But my decision had been made in full knowledge that for a time I would be inwardly bruised and bloody.

I sat by a small stream. Near me sat a man about ten years senior to me. He was one of the lore keepers. We were both very quiet. After a long time, when the only sounds were those of small insects and birds and winds blowing through the tall grasses, he asked me if I missed my friend. I started to cry. While I cried, I sensed my great desire. Around us the air was charged with smells of flowering coffee bushes and apple trees. When I stopped crying and looked up, I saw that my companion was still sitting in silence looking toward the ground at a small flower. His profile and the gentle gravity of his expression and his delicacy in not looking at me were profoundly touching. Everything inwardly was in motion. Gratefully I reached over and touched his hand.

It was as though Anahita herself had come down and filled my body with a flow of freshest running water which mingled with him. He looked up, and our eyes became new well springs of this flow between us . . . a flow surely *of* Anahita, for the source was the milk of the starry regions. Simply and surely we vowed to each other. Then we walked back to the encampment where we informed the elders of our sudden decision.

We were asked into the tent of the oldest man and woman where our sincerity was tested. They explained a concern that they had felt for both of us. We each had waited so long without seeking a mate that they had come to fear some evil had happened to us both as children. They were relieved. This sudden decision said something about our characters that explained all. Our fiercely independent natures had demanded a deeper certainty than either sense or intelligence could provide. Now that we were ready to become fully adult, a special task lay before us. We both had retained a profound virginal ground into maturity. They explained how, because of this, we had matured a natural ability to not identify with the weavings of false thought.

The assignment: the territory in which we were now living carried the dubious designation within some civilized spheres of "the wilderness of the peoples." New as we were here, there was a great promise for the fulfillment of our long-envisioned aspirations. The two of us could play a key role in the unfolding of our ideals on the stage of history. Husband and wife, we will travel as emissaries of Asha among the motley population of the wilderness of the peoples. The overt character of our mission would be to set in place various trade arrangements and covenants of mutual protection.

Along the way of these tasks, we will be exchanging views with our neighbors. Pressing us on will be an urgent need. A fresh formulation of our truths must germinate and have a haven where their seeds of vitality can be preserved into the unimaginable future.

I completed gathering herbs on the Tor and began the slow walk downhill toward the ruin of the Abbey. My "vision" gently ebbed away. As before, I detoured and stood with a sharp pitch of abstraction in front of "Joseph of Arimathea's Thorn Tree." With some surprise, I sensed keenly the outline of my body. It was a younger body than that of the woman's in the vision. What an affront to Anahita for me to have wished to kill desire . . . an affront to the starry regions beyond the circuit of the sun. It was some brutality I was visiting on my human inheritance.

The figure of the vision of the past had become a witness to my present. Contradictions set into momentums by these confluences . . . a past and my present . . . threatened to shred my psyche the several days between Palm Sunday and Holy Thursday. Our busyness saved my skin.

Some members of our community had instituted a "Seder" on Holy Thursday to memorialize our Savior's kinship to the Jewish people and our own solidarity with them. This custom grew out of the revelations the "Holocaust" brought home to us of the repellent history of the church toward the Jews over the centuries. The observance of this feast brought with it fortitude and an almost miraculous reconciliation of the tensions now twisting at my soul. The feast of unleavened bread, the festival of freedom . . . that antetype, that prefiguration of the *harrowing of hell and the resurrection*, actually harmonized my dual centers of gravity into a higher, more deeply resilient terrain. Still, sleep was impossible, and I welcomed the demand of vigil.

In the chapel, I reflected upon Paul. What had he found when he was an emissary to the wilderness? Or so his letters said. That very region, which now was part of my logo-geography. I opened my Psalter, and it parted at the psalm of Asaph:

Sing for joy to God, strength of us
    shout to God of Jacob.
Begin Music! . . . and strike timbrel! Make melody
    from lyre and harp.
Sound at new moon the ram's horn,
    and at the full moon, our feast.
For planned is this for Israel
    constituted by the God of Jacob
Detail work established for Joseph
    when he went out over against Egypt;
I heard a language I knew not.
I removed the burden from his shoulder
    his hands from the basket; they were freed.
In deep trouble you called
    and I rescued you;
I answered you from the secret place of thunder
I tested you at the waters of Meribah.

                                 —Selah

What a marvel is the textuality of the soul! Wherein a text pondered in the moment fuses with recitation in the past.

    I am listening to this verse while my husband and I are visiting a band of refugees near Lake Van in regions that formerly were Urartu.

    According to this group, the Achaeminian Dynasty had tempted and corrupted their homeland.[3] Already many of their countrymen were living in the wilderness, having left

Judea after the betrayal of one they called the True Teacher of the Lawgiver. For several generations they had been moving into the *wilderness of the peoples* in preparation of a coming "new time."

For a couple of days, my husband and I have been with them and been hearing their story. They had tried to sustain a way of life they could believe in despite the incessant wars and internecine struggles around them. As Israelites, they called themselves the "schoolmen of Asaph."

In the psalm which they had just finished chanting, it was pointed out by a scholar among them that the three names "Jacob," "Israel," and "Joseph" carried very profound meanings. They are called "schoolmen of Asaph" because of some implications within this psalm. They also like the designation because it is linked in some special way to the "generations of Joseph-Moses-Joshua and of Jesse, David, and Solomon." This was all beyond me. But my husband, who had spent much of his life studying not only our own lore but the traditions of others, seemed excited by their drift. Sometimes these people call themselves *New Convenanters* or *Essenes*.

They are a lovely people full of faith and exuberance. We have cordial relations with them, and this is not the first time we have visited. Tonight, however, my husband begs their permission to tell them somewhat of our story. I realize that he has not yet done this.

He scores into the ground the outline of a small rectangle. It is about seven-foot lengths wide and fourteen long. He sprinkles the sacred precinct with water he had drawn earlier from a fresh running stream. The two of us bring our small fire holder into one end of the rectangle and ignite it. We start the fire with small cedar twigs and balsam. He speaks:

I would tell you our song. Early in the story of the world, Gayomart, the servant of Ormazd, was a complete man. He was brought to death by the treachery of Angra Mainyu, "the Lie." The good Lord then created all the beings of the world . . . water, fire, earth, plants, and all the creatures in order to help defeat the lying one. All that is created is good . . . is a servant of God . . . is rooted in Asha . . . the truth. Such things as treachery, deceit, violence, illusion are the fabrications of the "enemy." Our struggle will go on a long time. But finally, our people, with the aid of the whole creation and the fravarshis . . . which is how we call the spiritual emissaries of the good . . . will succeed.

When we die, we will meet our deeds and thoughts at the crossing of the separator. *They* will judge us and testify to what *party* we belong. When the body is left behind, we permit the birds to clean off the bones and then the cleaned bones are gathered and buried to await resurrection at the final day . . . the day of the victory of the goodness.

Then there will be the last judgement. The Yazata[4] of friendship and healing, "Airyaman," together with "Atar" the fire, will melt all the metals of the mountains . . . and this will flow in a glowing river over the earth. All humanity must pass through this river. For that one who is *of* Asha, it will seem like warm milk; and for that one is *of* wickedness, it will seem like walking the flesh through molten metal.[5]

Ormazd is as much the desired master as judge according to Asha . . . the doer of the acts of good purpose . . . of life. To Ormazd, the kingdom whom they have established as guardian of the poor . . . Hear now our mantra by which we close our prayers:

Asha is good, it is best. According to wish it shall be for us, Asha belongs to Asha Vahishta.

My friends, we may not live to see the day of victory. But near that time, people will be helped by a man who will come who is better than a good man: the Sayoshant. He is the one who will ring benefit and lead humanity in the last battle against the evil.

How he will come to be is in this way. Preserved in the pure depths of the Lake Kasaoya is the holy seed of our Prophet. As the time approaches, a virgin will bathe in this lake and become with child. The child will be called Astvat-ereta . . . he who embodies righteousness. Kvarhnah will accompany the Sayoshant so that he may restore existence. It is said:

"When Astvat-ereta comes out from the Lake Kasaoya, messenger of Mazda Ahura . . . then will he drive the Druj out from the world of Asha."

Now, I have learned from my dealings with you from Judea that you also revere truth and justice. It is fitting that we bring aid to each other. It is fitting that we establish words to cut a covenant. Hear what I propose:

Your word for mountain is "har." Our word for the great mountain, which supports one end of the Bridge of the Separator, is "hara." Then too, our word Asha is what you mean by the word "emeth." There will be this word between us as a sign. "Mountain of Truth." Let it be said either way . . . HaraAsha or HarEmeth. If you should hear at any time one of those names, send someone to find us. If we hear either of those names, we shall send to find you.

The shock of hearing this drove me to my feet in both worlds. The sisters keeping vigil with me were alarmed that I may have had a relapse. I told them it was nothing but a sudden pain and that I had best retire to my room. As I left the chapel, I sensed the waves of concern these good souls felt for me. It was no less than I had for myself.

I now seemed to be moving through hypersubtle avenues of time. It could have been that my mind had come unhinged. The woman "through whom" I had been envisioning, now, as an outcome of the shock, blended with me so that her memory and thought was part of my memory and thought. No longer did I merely share shards of visions but comprehended the woman's whole story and the story of her people's journeyings. It became as available to me as were my memories of Rochester or Cleveland. A visit to Damascus or Artaxata was as vivid as my hometown. Her beliefs were clear to me . . . not as mere formulations but in the way I know to pick this herb over that and how to drive a car.

In a darkened world, our people had assumed the burden of light. Never would we be more than a small band living and journeying for generations through the "wilderness of the peoples." But we knew from Ormazd that the seeds of Asha we bore and shared would be taken by women and men of good will . . . to germinate within their own thought and faith where hope and beauty would be brought into their ways. And in this light of hope, we journeyed over the face of the earth.

The greatest tension in my psyche came from my reflections backward as a twentieth-century Christian woman. As "Kali," how clear it seemed that the religions of the Jews, Christians, and Muslims had been fortified over the centuries by the "tree of all healing" we carried with us. The small fire altar . . . I could say now it was continually kindled by intellectual and moral struggle in the service of our dedication.

And what a tragedy appeared to my "backward glance"! So many struggles, so many wars and bloodlettings over the centuries, so much labor and toil . . . so many of them were serving the counterfeit great fire altars of the Lie. They were laying waste the creation rather than building it up. From this perspective, was there any way I could continue my life here in Glastonbury? I was newly born into a fresh sense of human solidarity. Should I not now ride out to do battle as befits a human being? I watched the sunrise on Good Friday. I thank God I had not yet taken final vows!

Let me telegraph some implications, some "castles in the air," that were revolutionary to my thinking.

The triads of Asaph:

Joseph-Moses-Joshua . . . Leaving the "furnace of affliction, the desacralized world, to journey through the wilderness and arrive at the promised land. On the journey, the Tabernacle, the pattern of which is given from heaven, is established. The bones of Joseph are brought from the "furnace" to be entered into the promised land.

Jesse-David-Solomon . . . The journey from fragmentation to the cohesion of the line of Jesse. The establishing of the first temple, which is filled with the "kvod" (Hebrew), the "kvarhnah" (Avestan), the glory of God. The Essenes chose the Book of Ezekiel for the pattern of their "living temple." It too is a work focused on the temple, on the destruction of the earthly temple and the creation of the temple on the "high" mountain, the meeting place of humanity and God with the temple which is *God and humanity* in the company of each other. According to the "woman's" memory, the people of the "new covenant" had arranged their scripture so that Ezekiel was the twelfth book in sequence and the seventh of the books of the prophets.

At the mountain of the Chinvat Bridge, Hara is the dwelling place of truth and justice. In the tomb of Joseph, HarEmethia is laid the brutalized body of Jeshua.

There was no doubt in my mind that our two peoples had kept in touch during the hundred and fifty years between the time of our meeting near the shores of Lake Van and the time of Jeshua. But what this could mean is still beyond my comprehension. My dear Emerson has said, "A man [please read person] should have the flow of a river, the expansion of a tree, and the resistance of a mountain." I enjoy considering that the river is Anahita's, the tree heals all, and the mountain is the mountain of truth.

Above is all you need to know about my visions. As you can see, the prayer for an understanding of the Three Magi brought unexpected answers. Now I will keep my promise to explain why your debacle at Olivet convinced me of the worth of Amfortas. Struggle and difference is good.

Though not any longer at Glastonbury, I do carry the thorn tree of Joseph HarEmethia in my heart and continuously pray for your well-being.

Notes

1) The thorn tree is reputed to have grown from the staff of Joseph of Arimathea, which he planted in the ground at Glaston when a charter was secured from King Aviragus to establish a "church" on twelve hides of ground. Tradition asserts that this was the very staff Joseph had used when in the "Middle East." A thorn tree grew from this staff, the descendant of which still stands and flowers at Christmastime. People have continuously associated Glastonbury with Avalon for centuries. See works by Bligh Bond, Reverend Lionel Smithett Lewis, and more recently, John Michell for some very valuable lore on the subject.

2) A keshvar is a region with rather enigmatic boundaries but seems to carry meanings both geographical and geosophical.

3) For a sense of the conditions referred to, see all or any literature dealing with the Maccabean period. In addition to I and II Maccabees, much of what is termed "the Apocrypha" is of the same period. The *Testament of Levi* and the *Psalms of Solomon*, though they are of later provenance, capture the tenor of those parties which considered the temple defiled. For an interesting study on this theme, see "The Temple," an unpublished doctoral dissertation by Fujita Shozo, Princeton, 1970, particularly Chapter, pp. 87-165.

4) Yazatas are like angels. There are major and minor Yazatas. Often specific days are dedicated to them. For example:

Altar . . . Fire . . . Guardian of dwellings, aids
well-being, knowledge, valor, abundance, and
good memory. The attributes are "most bountiful,"
"beneficent," and "full of glory and healing."
Ninth day of the eighth month.
Anahita . . . Fertile, powerful, spotless, guardian
of the waters, aids wisdom, knowledge, power to
smite adversaries, giver of health and wealth. The
attributes are bountiful, courageous, strong of noble
origins, and most excellent.
Tenth day of the eighth month.

The above are admittedly of late designation. It is hard to get
a feel for the way they were lived within the time of Kali's vision.
Still, it was interesting. There are many others, and the above was
taken from Khoheste P. Mistree, Bombay, 1982, *Zoroastrianism:
An Ethnic Perspective.*

5) I have found an almost identical description of doctrine
   in Mary Boyce's *Zoroastrians*, Routledge & Kegan Paul,
   London, 1970, p. 28. In her volume, it is from a late text,
   the *Greater Bundahishn*, and could attest to the extreme
   conservationism of those communities which rely on oral
   tradition.

CHAPTER TWELVE

Shakespeare

Sir John Stewart was born in Greece to an English mother and a Scottish father who at the time was serving in the diplomatic service. The family seat was in the far north of Scotland, almost as far north as the mythical Mount Heredom. For many generations, his father's family had been distinguished jurists. His maternal grandparents were accomplished theater people of London.

After a typical and tormented upper-class British "boyhood," Shakespeare took hold of his life in time to make the grade and enter Oxford. His field was history. Quite soon at university, he showed the gift of being able to thresh and tease unique and unexpected patterns from masses of raw data. By the time of his wrangle, from which he emerged with "firsts," he had already been invited to join the Secret Service. At the 1936 Olympics, he had earned a berth on the long-distance-running team but did not place in Berlin. Overtly, German culture fascinated him and on the strength of this made friends and arranged to spend the next year in Heidelburg at the old university. Sub-rosa of course, he was studying the German preparations for war.

The scope of his activities during his service is unknown. He was acquainted with Lama's activities by dispatch throughout the war and afterward made a point of keeping track of "the Jew" out of an instinctive concern that Lama may have been a "red." Lama's piece in *Speculum* convinced Shakespeare that he was "all right" and actually interesting. So he entered into a correspondence. A challenge issued by Lama for Shakespeare to submit something of his own led to a practically impenetrable piece on the symbolism of the inverted rose held by Princess Elizabeth in her portrait. This portrait had been painted when she was the spouse of Frederick, elector of the Palatine.[1] Within four months of his initial association with the society, he was able to attend the Olivet conference.

*　　*　　*

From the time I reached my tenth year, I had to undergo an English upbringing. Due to it, the early stages of my relationship with Shakespeare were never on "the level." In addition to a knighthood, he had collected various confidential royal "insignia" and privileges. These added luster to the already bright halo he had acquired with his class. Furthermore, he was not inclined to make it easy for a man who wished to close, however slightly, the interval between castes.

He did not intend it, but at the Olivet conference, he almost always stood apart. The poem of Bukkoku Kokushi catches his spirit there very nicely:

> Though not trying to
> 　　guard the field from birds
>
> The scarecrow is not after all standing
> 　　to no purpose.

The occasion which altered our status quo, his and mine, was as surprising as it was delightful. It was as though an arcanely stressed mirror between us cracked and crumbled to the floor. Then quite simply in front of me was an exceptional person of a compassionate and well-tempered humanity.

In London we had attended a concert by the visiting Juilliard Quartet at Albert Hall. They performed a great Brahms quintet (with a ringer) and Hayden's *The Last Seven Words of Christ on the Cross.* Afterward we went out for a drink.

"Well, the music was all right, the hall was all right . . . but, Merlin, where were you?"

"There . . ."

"Really . . . there?"

"Oh, perhaps woolgathering some."

"Ahh . . . then, shepherd, hast thou philosophy in thee?"

"I trust I do."

"Not good enough. You have this *thing* in you, Merlin, that compels me to urge you to get some understanding. This *thing* I smell wants to serve me. Now, sir, it is neither natural nor becoming a person to *want* to shine someone's shoes."

"Yes . . . there is some kind of stupidity . . . some kind of fearfulness."

At my admission he fell silent. So did I. After a longish pause, he raised his Rob Roy.

"To all the sots."

"Sots?"

"Seekers of truth."

At this I burst out laughing. That was it.

Several years later, I was on an assignment in Germany and on the side attended a conference at Aspen Institute-Berlin. The theme was "East-West: Constructive Engagement." Shakespeare was one of a panel of five. During a coffee break, we rekindled our friendship. I must have been looking haggard.

"Merlin, you had best make yourself take a short nap after lunch. I don't think you'll survive unless you do. I always take one. Ten minutes makes the difference."

A highly-placed German lady invited "all the English" at the conference to her home for supper after the last session. There were, besides Shakespeare and myself, four others. Until he brought up the subject of religion, our hostess was very temperate and restrained. But the subject fired her to engage in an intense polemic against it. Her father, it seems, had been both quite religious and of high rank in the SS Elite Corps. The confessing church disgusted her. Gently, Shakespeare prodded her to expose her thoughts on the subject. Then very softly he began a discourse, no words of which I remember but which had the texture of a wonderful weaving in the air. He summed up:

"Right where you find you can say no . . . don't you think . . . right from there you find your truest yes?"

At this, to the embarrassment of all present except Shakespeare and myself, she burst into tears.

Later, as we were leaving, he fumbled in his jacket pocket and withdrew a small silver Celtic ross, and with that diffidence only the British upper classes can bring off, he held it out and dropped it into her hand.

"Here . . . you may someday find some use for this thing."

She did not refuse it.

The Energetics of Understanding
Shakespeare

How do we understand?

Do we . . . or do we not?

When we wish to say that we *have* understood, we are driven to use decisive and short statements, usually little more than a sound, a sign.

It is interesting to me that different cultures are similar in this though the sounds may be different.

Japanese say, "Ryo."

Tibetans say, "Ahlley."

Here in England, the expression is something like, "Ohh . . . ahh!"

If Americans ever succeed in understanding something, they probably would use a similar sound to ours. I could go on with this sign in different languages, but it would be beside the point.

At the moment you say "oh . . . ahh," were I to ask *what* had been grasped, probably I would be exposed to ten minutes of rubbish. Yet these expressions *do* say something very definite about the quality of understanding.

These utterances cannot be rehearsed or imitated. They are so short one can instantly hear if they have a bottom. Imitations are not complete circuits, they are not earthed. I admit to a special talent in listening since I spent some years refining my skills.

Shortly after the second World War, I was assigned to visit a number of our company's assets in the Middle East and South East Asia. The US, at the time, was extracting its pound of flesh for lend lease. Quite cynically, I thought, our cousins were supplanting our positions in these territories for their own commercial advantage while they, at the same time, compelled us to exhaust *our* thinned resources by paying to keep our occupying troops in the Asian theater. It is first-class irony that as reward for our war effort, we were enjoined to preside over our own liquidation. Many large American firms had made post-war arrangements with the Fuhrer that can only be described as "smarmy." But since we Allies won the battle, they were prepared to "take" only a trifle less.

For recreation, from the bitterness this caused me, I took my vacation in Japan where we had very few interests and where I could enjoy myself in my preferred indolent and indulgent way.

Through colleagues in our embassy in Tokyo, I was able to spend several pleasant afternoons playing with bows and arrows. As an undergraduate, I had been a ranking archer. So I was invited to join some fellows who had formed a club in an informal match against a small archery society in Kyoto. All of us had been away from competition for some time, but we acquitted ourselves well. We lost by a few points, but nothing to cause grief.

I was particularly taken by the style of Keiji Nokane. I found the design of the Japanese long bow remarkable . . . the method and application of the archers to it . . . fascinating. It turned out that Mr. Nokane was a teacher of archery, and after the match the two of us worked out a horse trade. I would teach him our rather off-beat (in my terms) system. From then on, whenever I happened to be in Southeast Asia or the Indian subcontinent, I usually would hop over to Japan and reward myself with some priceless hours of companionship.

I think it would be right to mention here just how I became obsessed with the problem of *understanding*.

On my father's side of the family, I was descended from the first Scottish Knights of the Temple during the middle twelfth century. The family maintained a private transmission of tradition as well as filiations with the overt Masonic lodges down to the present time. In the eighteenth century, when Freemasonry came into the open, the Sinclair side of my father's family was heavily involved. (I think it is to the credit of Freemasonry that, despite the ravages of corruption over the centuries, it received the highest honor of being outlawed and persecuted by that vacuous creature, A. Hitler.)

Prior to, and during the last war, it became clear that something was seriously bent in the esoteric Christian tradition. The *understanding* of those affiliated to it through various interpretations of "the Temple" was, in fact, a gross *misunderstanding*. The absurdities of Wagner, the repellent *Illuminati* of Weisshaupt in Bavaria, and the evil hiero-mysticism of the SS . . . all these were founded on the claim to *understand* those very same symbols upon which my family had established its inner life.

Loyalty is an excellent example. It was a ruling "code" word for the SS. It was also the ostensible motive of our American cousins in seeking to divest us of Hong Kong and seeking to hand it over to that febrile lunatic Chiang Kai Shek. On the other hand, our loyalty to the ideals of freedom, rather than earning us honorable terms for lend lease, earned us punitive terms. I am digging in this point because many of you live in the States and I predict eventual economic chaos as the inevitable result of your nation's greed for such hasty economic power at the expense of your friends.

As you can guess from these hints, the vista I regarded when I looked at the world scene was hardly reassuring. And yet everyone claimed to understand everything about what had happened and would happen. Even more appalling to me . . . the religious, the philosophers, the scientists, and the mystics all over the world now *understood* the truth.

In Japan, a land no less prey to human shortcomings, I found some refuge from the sham and dumb shows that had become order of the day. Perhaps it was because *they* lost the war and in experiencing failure and its attendant humiliations had to roll up their sleeves and think. There is no question in my mind the thoughtful among them were really trying to understand. I am quite tall and of privileged descent. It was hard at first for me to learn from "shrimps" who were yellow. No doubt my manner, at first, caused Mr. Nokane some pain. Finally, I learned a great deal. The substance of this report is derived from experiences undergone by me in a Neo-Shinto, survivalist community on Hokkaido.

Over the years, though our meetings were less and less frequent, Nokane and I sustained our friendship. After the splendid debacle at Olivet, I decided to rekindle the relationship on a firmer basis. To my surprise, I learned that Nokane and his family had left their home in Kyoto and moved to join what a mutual acquaintance, the philosopher Kojima, called "a hippie commune." After many tries, I finally reached him and was invited to visit them there.

It turned out to be a far cry from a "hippie commune." Mostly the members were mature individuals who had become disillusioned by the direction their country seemed to be going. The community has no name. In philosophy it can be best described as neo-Shinto. It definitely is not one of the new religions that have been springing up all over Japan like weeds. I was able to spend six months living with this group of individuals, and I learned much of value.

*   *   *

One day I was practicing archery with Nokane. I had released a particularly good shot and had an experience only slightly familiar to me from earlier sessions.

There is a certain sense . . . a sensation when a shot goes well. It is as though in one's stomach there is an intricate lock. As one exhales and draws back and down against the bow's arc, the tumblers begin to line up; and when the release is good and the shot true, they spontaneously complete their alignment and, with an almost audible "thumk," the lock opens, "the wedges are knocked out."

Now I had this sense but deepened, as though the lock had been attached to a large drum.

Despite my discipline, I blurted, "Ohh . . . ahh."

Nokane said, "Ryo!"

Understanding is not an arrangement of linguistic elements. Understanding is a vitality. This "vitality" is inseparable from the *ki* (ch'i) which creates and forms language. Since this relation exists, it is natural that people confuse the ability to follow a linking of thought and word to represent to oneself what is *meant*. This simple and slight error in discrimination leads to so much of the confusion and misunderstanding let loose on the world today.

Nourished by this slight error, huge financial, legal, medical, and governmental organisms flourish as subcivilizations engaged in the procedure of devouring civilization itself.

Civilization, in its lifeblood, is related to both understanding and language. So one might say that "understanding" feeds misunderstanding. To regain the ability to understand vitally, people must first *not* understand.

To describe the difference between English and Japanese archery is illuminating. In English style, the archer draws straight back, focuses on the target and, never losing his fixation, makes adjustment for range, weight of bow, wind conditions, etc. He never dilutes the attentive clamp on the target. The Japanese archer rather opens the bow from below it and "finds" at last the target's stability almost as he releases the arrow. Put another way, the arrow clamps to the target and the archer finally discovers the orientation of the shot. While aiming and drawing, the target *is* seen. But part of the archer's attention could well be walking by a mountain stream while other portions attend to breath, balance, "internal affairs," and so on. The natural tendency of the body in poised repose to expand . . . integrates to the point where the target stops "jumping" from side to side and is there . . . at the other end of the bow and its arrow.

Similarly, the gentlemen who established the Hokkaido village have chosen a non-assaultive method for their project. They find the material for their thought in the Kojiki, a vast collection of the ancient legends and mythology of their land. Such material is many things. It is civilization creating. It is language creating. It is saturated with the passionate intention to convey content. This _kind_ of material fires up the passion to understand.

The "energy field" that is the background and the foreground of the collection is prior to exact definition. The field throws a diffuse light . . . not a light without shadow as a shallow notion of diffusion presumes . . . but a light full of shadow, illuminated shadow.

Since contrast will show up at the point I am pressing, let's spend a moment looking at the obvious.

By the time of adulthood, most individuals have absorbed as a given, a picture that is understood as reality. Family, class, and culture provide for many shadings, but in general this picture is moving _from the past to the future_ or, conversely, _from the future to the past_. Events are _represented_ to their understanding as being situated in one or the other of these paths of time. From the age that this system has clicked into place, it will always limit the person who is trying to think.

Hokkaido sets itself against this.

They do not accept the simplistic "karmic" theories. Counted among these karmic or _from-past-to-future_ systems are Marxism, biological determinism, much Western psychology, and many philosophies of history.

They also reject the "teleological" theories of "from the future to the past." These include the common understandings of much religion, political theories of destiny, etc. To combine the two directions, as is done in some special cases of the above view, is no better, in their estimation, because it tends to make one bias serve the other in a distorted polarity.

Time, in Hokkaido: is always an individual matter. It is light itself and so is always flowing in at least two directions at once. More important, the individual is viewed as living his or her life as his or her time. And life in the human being has a number of different personal loci, which they simplify to five realms. This means that in practice there are at least five "lights" or five "times" that illuminate and situate every event.

My example from archery figures this way: an excessively clamped focus will cause domination over the realms by one or the other. The result is misunderstanding, but a misunderstanding that appears to be coherent and satisfying in the "language" of the dominant realm.

> [You see, the five realms must use the *same* words . . . i.e., . . . those that are current in the subject's culture. But the realm, the context (physical, psychical, memory, emotive, etc.), makes the words mean different things. They are in a sense different languages.]

In a situation such as this, the subject always understands, but in such a way as has been described—"having eyes and not seeing, having ears and not hearing." There is no question that, to accomplish, one must focus on one realm and then another. To understand, on the other hand, all the times and lights need to operate unobstsructedly from their own "locations."

Given this, and since the individual is not standing in any specialized dimension of themselves, where are they standing?

> [Apropos of this, an elderly Tibetan gentleman once chidingly informed me with some amusement that there are at least forty-nine loci in the soul.]

As mentioned above, works such as the Kojiki or, in our own case, the Bible, are like diffuse light. They are surrounding and penetrating. This is one aspect of their value to us.

To live a well-lit life takes some practice. There are certain angles or colors of light which we prefer because they are more flattering than others or because they seem to further some goals that we believe are at the burning point. Or we may find that a certain kind of illumination brings pleasure or the alleviation of pain and that living exclusively in it is the way to be. I would be the last to deny that our lives, particularly nowadays, need this kind of rest and certitude. Nevertheless, when the project is *to understand*, we need somewhat more than this to come into play.

For starters, the understanding of oneself is put aside. That is an advanced project. The first undertaking is coming to a position of being able to perceive more of the world in depth than we are used to seeing. Grasping *one matter well* opens the gate to others. On Hokkaido, they will start with some enterprise that holds fascination for an individual. It could be mathematics, pottery, cooking, archery, even sociology . . . the list is wide open. After taking hold of *something*, the individual turns to some body of thought.

An excellent example of this is provided by my friend Miura, the physicist. As a young boy, his family was attached to the remarkable Tenko Nishida at Ittoen. In the community library, he became attracted to the Proverbs of Solomon. Years after he had struck out on his own and gained recognition, he moved to Hokkaido. Here he returned to the object of his earlier fascination. It became the gate, which when opened released a full range of his remarkable capacities.

Whether he ever came to understand the Proverbs in the way of a Jewish or Christian scholar is moot. But he came to something of the nature of understanding in itself. I think his insights are highly original. They are full of life and will provide a useful case of how "diffused" light works in a text.

Buried deep among the several thousand remarks of Solomon, whom Miura chooses to call "the friend," following the Bible's lead, lies the laconic statement, "With all your getting, get understanding." [3]

For Miura, using the title "the friend" sets up the circuit of relation between the reader and not only the author but Wisdom herself. It suggests the worthiness of courting Wisdom and the relational and active nature of understanding. According to his metaphor, "Proverbs" is like an array used to build a radio telescope.

The remarks touch all manner of mundane things. They are about meals and clothes, about behaviors and animals. They go on and on and repeat many . . . stating the obvious . . . repeating from all sides and piling them up, piling boredom on boredom. Now in a radio telescope, the net result of the many signals over a wide territory is the ability to form trustworthy representations of astronomical phenomena. Similarly, all these aphorisms, repetitions in fresh contexts, repetitions in new sequences, and so on can bring one to something of priceless value with which to court Wisdom. Unfortunately in my country, it is nearly impossible, burdened as we are with centuries of presuppositions, to read the Book of Proverbs in such a way.

Presuppositions block conscience.

Conscience is what turns on the realms of light, the realms of being.

My case:

History had been my specialty at Oxford. While at Hokkaido, I had the use of an excellent library of Asian History. As I bore into it, I was soon appalled at my ignorance of very important data and the falsehoods supporting my cherished assumptions about my country's role in Asia during the nineteenth century. I had not been unaware of the facts but had ignored some and interpreted others in a way that would have been intolerable in a student had the subject been European history.

The great game, played so earnestly between Imperial Russia and Great Britain, had not been the "chivalric exercise" I had cherished. To be sure, the Asiatic Alim Beys and Yakub Begs[4] were indeed leaders of cutthroats who endlessly murdered each other and their own people. But *that* did not justify our talent in fostering these endemic behaviors for the sake of commercial advantage. The indigenous religious pieties of these agents of murder, massacre, slavery, and oppression throughout Western and Central Asia aroused my disgust as they would any Englishman. But we were revoltingly pious about our own role as well. Thinking these thoughts shocked me, as though a sliver of light lit up an unseen corner. A formulation occurred to me in the midst of my feelings:

"Piety that is not equaled by impartially devout behavior toward others regardless of religion or race can blight conscience as swiftly as murder."

To forestall objections, let me mention that self-defense can be a form of devout behavior. I am convinced that my experience on the archery range was needed preparation in order for this study to actually have an effect. I needed first the taste of ohh . . . ahh.

Just as the assumptions upon which we build our accepted public histories are too excessively focused for us to gain a well-rounded view, so is our private history imprisoned. Yet self-understanding and self-sensing depends on an acceptance of our own history.

In the first place, it depends on *data*.

For this reason, the Hokkaido group emphasizes a taste of understanding *something*, anything, before turning toward ourselves.

But there is a contradiction here.

The degree of our personal fragmentation becomes the milieu in the midst of which we perceive the "outside world" and the "datum" coming to us from there. This being the case, and one I offer the reader for his or her own verification, how is it possible to arrive at this taste of understanding?

Since I found Miura a congenial companion who had intentionally undertaken to understand something that is part and parcel of my own culture, I looked him up in his cottage. I posed the problem to him. He responded with a dose of irritation and a saying of Solomon's:

> There are three things I do not understand, yea four, the way of a bird in the air, a snake upon a rock, of a ship upon the sea, and the way of a man with a maid.

Then followed a long and at times intense discussion.
Nothing came of it directly.
Then I went to the archery range.

My next theme may seem like a retreat or another digression. In fact, I will be employing contrast again to show things up and come closer to the heart of the matter. I want to gather up three "themes."

1) Conscience as the ground of reality.
2) A "non-targeted" focus as the earnest of proper alignment of self with world.
3) The sad passion of humans to usurp being.

The following reflections occurred while I faced the target on the range:

> I turn my attention to phenomena in the world. As I try
> to investigate the world, I am investigating myself. This is
> the obvious answer Miura set forth by pointing me at the
> *non-understandings* of Solomon. When I strive to understand
> something in the world, I am willy-nilly examining the
> contents of my own mind.

Before coming to Japan this time—in fact, while on the Super Chief from Chicago to Los Angeles right after Olivet—I saw the handwriting on the wall. The regrettable California mystique would soon swamp the good young minds of England as it was swamping the intellectual promise of American youth. Combining with a reactionary indifference and fear of real learning on one hand and a sterile intellectualism on the other, this triangle of forces would threaten the literacy of the English-speaking world within a few decades.

Why was this happening?

But first what is the *what* of the why?

The slogans of the moment indicate the direction of the Californiazation of aspiration: self-realization, awareness, self-development, consciousness growth, the Now, enlightenment, etc . . . .

The words not only have auras; for some they have halos.

The words are the seeds of the direction. As the movement attracts more gurus and guides and thralls, what will become of these "concept seeds?"

The methods and the exercises will be the traffic lights for a sort of slow dance by individuals among the systems in search of the prolongation of *already desired states*. The ruling mimetic assumption of the drumbeat shall probably be, "if a high state can be sustained long enough or often enough, it will bring with it one of the above *words* with its halo."

Once and for all, there will be a settling of the problem of living, which Californians know *ought not* to be a problem. He or she will have gained the insignia of power. In the West, popularity proves the insignia of power. In its wake comes a sense of belonging and as much attention as a loved one.

But twenty years hence, in the eighties, there will *not* have come understanding, wisdom, intelligence, or ethic. And the virtues dependent on these gifts—justice, goodness, beauty—not only will fail to arrive but they will have become values ripe for demotion.

How can I understand this? To this what, why?

Is there a resonance that may come from my attempts to understand why this will happen (rather than simply to describe and predict) that may, *by the way of it*, deepen my self-understanding?

Though my English ear is not tuned to the high pitch needed to appreciate all the Pacific overtones, yes. The recollection of a phrase of Pascal's . . .

That is *my* place in the sun . . ." That is how the usurpation of the whole world began.[5]

A dislocation that is usurpation. An uprooting of the sense of the "what for" in human activity.

Our historical sense, public and private, is dislocated . . . our language. Our superb instrument becomes the tool which supports the usurpation. To continue our usurpation, we need then to usurp language and, in so wrenching it, deliver it to corruption. On the one hand, we become more illiterate, and on the other become more skilled at using language to dissemble.

The primal expression of understanding is a hidden treasure. The words, the sounds . . . Ohh . . . ahh! Ryo . . . Ahlley . . . is connected to the vitality of understanding itself. They are sayings intended for *the other*. They are morning light.

My absorption in history had built up in me a point of view which usurped reality and demanded *that* place in the sun for my *nation*. In a similar way, all the absorption in exercises and formulations of truth and philosophy of self and non-self will go only to continue a usurpation already in progress. The correctives built into actual time and meeting become unavailable.

> I am aiming at the tiny black target with the long bow.
> I am aiming at myself.

The five lights, diffused and blended as one, pass through into where I stand . . . into the ground underfoot and include the range and the target. The introspective look surrounds my elbow and wrist and feet and gut and, not stopping, goes on through into the lining of my presentness, which must be something else. In the moment inside-outside of breathing, the arrow is released.

Which . . . inside or outside is the most efficient locution of location?

The vitality of understanding invades my hiding places and the alteration of the remembrance of my own past begins. The languages of my justifications, in five tongues, begin to give up their territories and the geography becomes visible. Horrors and beauties emerge from the shadows. In seeing that I am less than I thought, I find myself more than I imagined. In seeing both the excellence and the baseness of my acts, I discover I neither was nor am very good or very evil. Like a grace, I see the thirst for the good that had been the lining of my daily thoughts. I see the grotesque inheritance of my parents' ignorance. I have inherited their unquestioning drive to usurp *being* and at times to usurp God.

In seeing the grief of the child I was, I see the dignity of the human spirit I am. I "feel" a very special sort of hope.

I find that love has never been absent from time and is the light of the very constitution of time. I see that a mystery has brought me to this place. A mystery that has called the universe into being and overspills it comes at me in the smile of a loved one. A mystery rehabilitates life and brings us to see the goodness inherent in our steps.

And so, recognizing that this presence has accompanied all the steps of my life, I am struck dumb and awed. From this awe-full understanding, in the words of the Friend, "is the beginning of Wisdom."

The arrow had gone true.

Tea is the order of the day.

I go and have a cup of tea with Miura.

Then I find my friend Nokane, and he prepares tea for me. He serves me in his beautiful Karatsu tea bowl. It has streaks of faintest blue in a rice-straw ash glaze. He lets me know it was fired in the Hobashira kiln. The world is here. The tea bowl is named Haku-o, White Seagull.

We smile at each other and look over the Hokkaido meadow where we see the stone dragon whistling in the dry tree.

This is not quite the report that Amfortas requested. But be kind enough to accept it.

Notes

1) *Elizabeth, Queen of Bohemia*, painted by Gerard Honthurst, National Portrait Gallery, London. Elizabeth, daughter of James I, was married to Frederick, elector of the Palatine, in 1614. The curious thing about the portrait is that the rose is held inverted by Elizabeth as though it were a microcanopy.

2) For a fascinating and well-documented account of this period, see *Ernest Bevin, Foreign Secretary*, by Alan Bullock, W.W. Norton & Company, London, 1983.

3) II Samuel 12:24. "God favored him and sent a message through the prophet Nathan; and he (Solomon) was named Jedidiah at the instance of God," i.e., *beloved* or *friend* of God.

4) Shakespeare is probably using these names as generics. Yakub Beg, for instance, was a former "batcha" or boy prostitute who used his skills to become ruler of Sinkiang. He ruled by slaughter. Finally, after a fit of extreme paranoia, he managed to completely isolate himself and come to a bad end.

5) Pensees, number 112.

CHAPTER THIRTEEN

Paracelsus

Ender Tanpinar was born to a poor Turkish family. His mother, who died when he was twelve, contrived to secure him an education by pretending that his father was dead. In fact, the father was working in the outlying provinces while the lad was attending the Dresfaka school for "fatherless" boys.[2] The experience of living with guile those several years marked him permanently with a passion for truth. During the years of his growing up, America was the promised land of dreams for Turkish youth. But he was cured of this after watching a Charleston contest in Istanbul. The spectacle convinced him that the world was demented. He turned with fervent intensity toward traditional Islam.

After completing his studies, then his military service, he moved to Konya where he attached himself to the Keepers of the Mevlana Shrine[3] and secretly took instruction. At the time, the Darwash were illegal. His activities between his arrival in Konya and the outbreak of World War II are unknown.

During the hostilities, he earned a reputation as a first-rate war correspondent and, under pseudonyms, he even managed to file stories with English newspapers. He remained steadfastly apolitical and, as a result, in a country as passionate about politics as Turkey, Paracelsus fell under suspicion of both "right" and "left" wings. He walked the tightrope and preserved his skin. By managing to offend everybody, he offended nobody. Paracelsus also had the gift of keeping "mum." A man of few words, his favorite expression is:

"Boil it down, boil it up, boil it down again, lies remain . . . Steam it out and steam it again . . . pretension. No salt and no sugar, then chew it if you can."

He was an informal student of modern philosophy and took issue with Heidegger in a letter he published in a certain Basel journal. Paracelsus referred to the philosopher as one of the "few people on earth to whom Freud's theory of anal retention may actually apply." Years later, it was discovered that the publication of the letter was due more to a moment of whimsy on the part of Karl Jaspers than to its philosophical or psychological merit. Nevertheless, it did attract the attention of a member of Amfortas in Geneva who entered into a correspondence with him. Paracelsus was intrigued by the "program" of the society and became an associate.

Due to difficulties typically suffered by Turks with paperwork, he encountered visa problems and arrived at the Olivet conference only for the final week.

*   *   *

Paracelsus dwells in a world which we, his fellows, can only infer from the traces his sarcasm etches into our minds. Marya once described him as "sarcastic, past the limits of the intelligible." It is true that natives of the Indian subcontinent are not as inoculated as we British. With us, sarcasm is played as tones on a pipe organ. But he stretched the limits of the art. He tends to twist and buckle the horizons and configurations of our world like a sun is reputed to bend light. Not only his style of utterance but his whole countenance called assumptions into question.

Most educated Turks I have met tend to tilt their head slightly back so as to be able to look at one down along the nose ridge. Paracelsus made it his habit to tuck in his chin and gaze at one upward, across his brow.

Whenever I was in conversation with him, I felt he did not believe a word I said. No amount of self-disclosure, sincerity, and so forth could dispel the impression. Yet for all the strain and pressure I felt while with him, as soon as a meeting concluded, I would enjoy a lightness and sense of well-being that was quite rare. When I mentioned this to him, he laughed and called it the "rock effect."

"When you stop beating your head on a rock . . . ahh, what a joy . . . I'm alive . . . how wonderful!"

I was once admitted into the curious perspective he lived with. Paracelsus had established his wife and daughter as permanent residents of Geneva. It fell out once that I was in town and was invited by Madeleine to join her and Paracelsus and his family for supper. We dined at the Three Fishermen, a modest but excellent restaurant on a narrow street just behind the Hotel du Rhone.

He was explaining how hard it had been to secure his family's residence in Switzerland but how it had relieved his mind.

"Can you imagine the babaganoush my esteemed government could make of me if these 'hostages' were still living in Istanbul?"

Madeleine kept looking at him as only she could. Finally, he blurted out:

"Madame, you do me an injustice. I am not playing. I say what I see."

"I am sure, but in the language of your peculiar mind, the word for seeing sounds too much like being."

At which point he laughed until tears streamed down his cheeks. I shall try to distill how he explained himself.

For him, each human being was in effect an entire world. Not in the "occulted" macro-micro-cosmic sense . . . but in a straightforward way. Without humanity, the planet is an environment. From what we love and hate, from what we read and experience, and out of how all this interpenetrates "somewhere," a world is formed with its own horizons and its own occident and its orient. The real God is not merely the "Lord of the world" but the God of all worlds. Only through God, in this sense, can our worlds meet, with horizons only slightly blurred. Somehow, Paracelsus's world grew and formed and underwent "geological pressures" in such a way that it exists at right angles to most of our worlds. Therefore his expressions . . . the outcroppings, cliffs, and rivers of his geography, jut and elbow into ours like "eikons" from another dimension. His sarcasm is as natural to him as a river flowing downhill or a boulder obeying the "laws of gravity."

For example, he hated war passionately. But he spent much of his time studying the phenomenon poking around old battlefields. This was not some kind of perversity. It was merely that our notions of pertinence and coherent behavior did not apply in his world. What was truly pertinent to him in his world always intersected ours in the form of a colossal impertinence.

About his face. It sometimes looked like the battlefields he loved to explore, the hindsight of cataclysm. Japanese health cultists would have classified his gaze as Sampanku. It bore striking resemblance to the gaze captured in those wonderful paintings of Rinzai and Bodhidharma.

As the American saying puts it, "It takes all kinds to make a
world."
On the Difficulty of Telling the Truth
[Conversations with a Yezidi in Exile in the
Azerbaijan Soviet Republic]
Paracelsus
There is a Buddhist saying: . . .
"What is the Buddha?"
"A dried shit stick."

If it were not for the adjective/verb "dried," I could add . . . a
Gypsy, a Jew, a Turkish writer, a Guatemalan Indian . . . But dried!
That makes one think.
I am suffered by my country because I am a fool. I am a rare
fool, and the word rare saves my life. After all, even nation states
try to save a dying breed. Under other names, there is one message
I get across on the sly:
"It stinks!"
The week before Christmas, I smuggle it into the Italian journal
Presso. The week before Ramadan, I get it into papers throughout
the Middle East. The week before Passover, I manage to get it
printed in the *Jerusalem Post*. All this takes not only cunning
but friends in high places. For national holidays, I do not bother.
Nation states exist to suck the marrow out of the bones of their
human soup. *They* are not even aware that it should not stink.
Now to get you in trouble if *they are* reading your mail . . .
Listen, comrades!
Politics is lying. Right-sided, left-sided, and center-sided lying.
Business is lying. Collectivized, free-market, nationalized, and
individualized lying.
So why don't I shut up?
Why don't I pull the plug on this electric typewriter and wall
myself into a cave?

Because.

I like life. I put up with the stench of it, *because.*

And furthermore, I will not "look blue and sit on thorns."

What I am going to tell you about now may be the most important thing you will ever read in your life.

When I returned home from our conference in Olivet, I was a little glum about having missed the week of the great immolation. These rites of sacrifice that have been part of the Americas always have fascinated me . . . this pulling the heart inside out through the breastbone so that the sun and the flies can eat it. Aah, well, our admirable Turkish bureaucracy had seen to it that I missed *that*. Compensation awaited me in the form of an invitation to attend a "writers' conference" in the Soviet Union. My government was pleased to *pay me* to attend. I could put my ear to the ground for them and at the same time stay out of their hair for a while.

The thought of the good food, the fresh landscape, and the opportunity to swim in the Caspian settled the question. I knew the territory like the back of my hand. Also, I had a friend living near the conference site who I really wanted to see again. Since I now have an official reason, I could do this without risk to life and limb trying to slip through borders. The Russians have machines nowadays at the border that can spot a spider crossing without a permit.

Years ago, this friend fled Syria during a routine liquidation of the Kurds and came to Turkey. This is when we met. Then when our nation began to tighten the screws on Kurds, he left for Soviet Azerbaijan. He joined himself to his own people living around Karabagh. These people are further candidates for Buddhahood as soon as they dry out.

So with a light heart I went to Baku.

Using methods learned from the Gypsies, my friend and I had arranged a meeting in a local "workers' sanatorium."

There he was, sitting in a deck chair, the classical "recovering alcoholic." After a few moments of pleasure trading insults, we got to the matter at hand. By the way, his *private* name, not used for years, is Qulu Hussain. Once he had been a leader of a few small bands of Western Yezidi. The Yezidis living in Iraq consider him a heretic and something of an idiot. For myself, I always found him a man of good sense.

I am not going to pretend that I recorded what he had to say on this occasion. Picture the scene we would have made . . . sitting on the veranda in sanatorium clothes enduring our "drying out" while I took notes of the conversation. My memory has long since been turned upside-down. To rely on that would be foolish. I can only tell you what I understood of this conversation. Now and then a phrase of his did stick in my mind like a wood tick. Those I will quote verbatim. This is how he started:

"I think God has gone on a holiday he planned for himself long ago. Being God, he has nowhere he can go but here."

Immediately we were plunged into our brand of theology.[4] This is the rationale: even on vacation, God is Truth. But here, since no one can tell the truth, God can come and have quite a rest. No one will pick up a piece of truth from the ground of any size even it if gleamed like a diamond. So by habit people leave God alone, and his holiday can go on and on with blissful anonymity.

I object that hundreds of millions of *human beings* are calling to God daily, hourly, by the minute, by the second, using hundreds of different names. He fixed me with his bright and permanently cheerful eyes and shrugged.

"So . . . or as a Jew might say . . . nu? . . . Truth . . . particularly in calling God is difficult . . . it is very hard . . . even an adamantine endeavor."

I confess to being pushed back into my shoes by this. I had long been convinced of Mevlana's saying "Every call upon God is answered by an inaudible, 'here I am.'" Now, sure of my attention, he went on. True, people are calling, but at the number they are calling, the "devil" might pick up. In his precise words, "*Who* is calling *what?*"

His point was that if so many people were really praying to God, how could the world be the way it is? And so he explained the excellence of his religion.

Yezidis refused to worship or call the devil, but they long have considered it prudent to propitiate "him." Because of this and the convoluted minds of those outside his faith, they became known as "devil worshippers." In their own opinion, nothing could be farther from the facts. In fact, they are the *only* religion that is *not*. They are aware of how things stand, so they give the devil "his due" and go on to worship God. *That* . . . to which everyone else is praying, they are propitiating. He admitted to some few exceptions among all the religions. Individual exceptions.

Their symbol for the "fallen angel" is the peacock. This is a strutting bird and fits their picture of the great angel which "fell" through pride and vanity. But in some distant future, this angel will awaken from its "overactive sleep" created by its two useless wings and, in a great movement of conversion, rejoin the company of archangels. This moment will herald the magnificent drama of redemption throughout the whole universe.

The crux is that people, by continuing to worship the creation of pride and vanity, keep putting off the great day.

"Calling a spade a spade," as do his people . . . hastens the day . . .

The conversation had gone on for some time now, and we became aware from the growing restlessness around us on the porch that "mealtime" was near. The two of us would now have to blend with the others here and contrive to disappear. Meals are the times in these places when both staff and inmates become more observant. So much food . . . so many people. We agreed to meet and continue in three days.

The writers' conference was scheduled for a sightseeing excursion. The authorities felt that we writing types could now enjoy surroundings more poetic and cultural than the oilfields around Baku. They had planned an outing to Tbilisi, formerly Tiflis, where Lermontov had been so happy, in neighboring Gurgistan.[5] This is a beautiful city with traditions of culture, and I have long been in love with it. By plane, Tbilisi is a short flight. Qulu told me he would have a message waiting for me by some means at the hotel when we arrived.

But, up to his usual tricks, he did nothing so commonplace as that. Our group stopped at the Georgian Writers' Union directly from the airport. There, a highly decorated factotum approached me and announced that the esteemed poet of the oppressed Yezedi people, one Quluadze, wished very much to meet me. Unctuously, our guides gave me permission to leave the group. I followed the functionary to where Qulu was waiting, and the two of us took off on foot to continue our conversation. When we finally arrived at our destination, a charming cafe near the river, he quoted me a Japanese proverb:

"Kan ni wa hari mo irezu, watakushi ni wa shaba o tsuzo."

Roughly translated, this means:

"Officially, a needle is not permitted; unofficially a carriage, horses and all without soap come through."

I must say, the café was very beautiful. Sitting there, I reflected that it had been many years since my heart had felt so much at ease. The atmosphere was springtime soft, and the air carried the faint smell of blossoms and, from nearby, the sound of water rushing . . . the river having been freshened by the melting snows on the Caucasus . . . touched me like song.

The other time when I felt like this had been many years ago when my Pir had taken me to Tabriz on a journey to visit an unmarked grave. Afterward we had gone to a coffee shop. Silently we sat and sipped tea. I felt then as though multiple streams of dew touched all the roots of my nerves and realized that through all the eight years of training I have been too tight. After that morning, my Pir sent me away to make a twentieth-century life for myself.

Now, sitting in Tbilisi, that same sense of sitting by the waters of refreshment captured all my body and mind and, touching my scraped nerve endings, healed them. Time and space, all of it, settled around the two of us in this small café.

After a while, Qulu began to make me laugh. Of course I could not laugh out loud at those passing by in Gurgistan and keep my scalp. A beautiful woman of resolute gait came by us, and Qulu remarked:

"That woman is that type of crane which once each year cannot decide among four things. Whether her wings are black and her body white, whether they are white and her body black . . . and whether to snap or to wave her wings."

As we sat, he remarked on each passing person. With swift sure brushstrokes, he caught *that* particular liveliness which made the passerby singular. Then after some time of this meditation on humanity passing before us, he outlined the reasons for the difficulty we have in telling the truth.

When the world was in the process of being created, at the apogee of the jubilation of the choirs of angelic galaxies at their newfound voices and the lavish bountiful giving-ness of the Creator . . . from nowhere there was the shadow of a doubt . . . The Creator brushed the doubt aside and went on with the work of creation. This doubt, however, since it had come from *God* was not that puny.

It could not go back to nowhere because nowhere was fast becoming somewhere. So *it* took its place in existence.

When it touched a star the star would go out. Instantly there was a problem. The Creator invited the doubt to return to "being." But alas, it had tasted existence and refused. Swiftly (as we understand swiftness) the doubt was locked up so not to infect the rest of *coming to be* . . . which was continuing as before with jubilance and joy.

But God realized this doubt would eventually cause trouble. Somehow it would have to be recombined into the appropriate place in the poem of creation. It could be done only if the doubt were persuaded to participate at some level and thus be revitalized by the continuously recreating thought of God. So it came about that the creation of Adam and Eve was undertaken. All the materiality of the myriads of "Earths" each contributed to the "hyle" of which God formed Adam and Eve. The movement of generosity on the part of all the hosts of creation was so intense that even *doubt* gave a grain of its non-materiality. But again, trouble.

Adam and Eve began to distrust each other so much that clearly the "human race" could not survive. They started right off quarreling about *to whom* their future offspring would belong. Obviously they would not last long enough to bring doubt back to its proper place in creation.

Now, the most glorious of the Archangels, the elder brother of Michael and Gabriel, was sent to our world to see what could be done. What he discovered distressed him. Adam and Eve could find only two attitudes with which to live. Although they were filled with all the wonderful potentialities of the whole Universe . . . all of this . . . could only be expressed as either belief or doubt.

For a long time the Creator meditated about this report.

Finally he saw what must happen.

They needed a certain force of self-reflection with which to the love themselves.

They needed a certain force of self-radiation with which to love the other.

But God did not want to start everything all over again.

He did not want to destroy the world that was coming to be.

He needed a "volunteer" to bring these forces to Adam and Eve. And only Archangels had these "forces" in the form of qualities. The Archangel to first see the problem naturally volunteered.

What happened after this is a long and often involved story. Too long and too involved. But in sum, for our theme, here is the result: In the situation that developed it was only pride and vanity that was able to keep people from doubting themselves and others to death. Pride and Vanity also insured that people are able to be defended from each other by throwing around themselves a net of lies. In these conditions *telling the truth* is only a subtler form of lying than outright falsehood. Who after all knows enough of "the truth" of any picture to tell it without causing the reaction of doubt, fear and mayhem?

For Yezidis the task is simple but the practice is complex.

The terms of the task are to release the Archangel that is spellbound within the garment of pride and vanity.

Then the Archangel is rediscovered as radiance and reflection . . . as love of the other and proper love of the self.

At the moment this can be done doubt will recombine with Creation as that rare treasure called "perception of otherwise than being." Our small portion of the Universe becomes redeemed.

It is the very difficulty of telling the truth in these conditions that becomes a fiery substance which, when admitted, begins to unbind the spell of the Archangel, Melek Taus.[6]

If it were not for the fact that I was in an exceptionally mellow state, I would have begun to get upset like a Bolshevik, because Qulu, for the first time in our unique friendship, was really stepping on my corns. For a Muslim to listen to God being spoken about in this way is offensive. More important for me, he had, in the guise of a fable, attacked a deeply settled conviction I held about both the nature of and cure for the mendacity in our world. But by now it was time for me to rejoin my writers' group and I had to leave. We made no further arrangements for meeting.

What happened next would have made Keloghlan grow hair.[7] It brought my state of angered confusion head to head with the event that had sealed in me both my cynicism and my conviction that telling the truth was the only way out of the world's mess.

The Battle of Stalingrad.

But I jump ahead of myself.

The plane, on leaving Tiblisi, went north instead of east toward Baku. Was the gracious USSR kidnapping us? No. By the curious logic of government-owned airlines, our hosts had decided that their illustrious guests should undergo a "history lesson." We were on an educational detour of over a thousand miles in order to overfly the city of Volgograd and to see how the scene of a ruthless battle which took several million lives had become a delightful and prosperous dwelling for several contented millions.

My frustration in trying to tell the truth about this battle was bitterness cubed.

As we flew over the lovely, fertile soil, the grasses and forests were still bringing into the air the salts and coppers and carbons and so on of countless corpses, and the whole affair came vividly to mind. The amazing victory was won by over ten full-field armies and two tank armies that had been kept totally secret and in reserve. It was a secret that not only Hitler but also Roosevelt and Churchill knew nothing about . . . No one believed the stories I filed. The Western press wanted only human-interest stories.

The Western governments had convinced the press that my stories were fevered imagination. They did *not want* to face the implications of the truth. The reasons are obvious. Both England and America had been postponing their invasion of Europe, the "second front," because they were convinced that Russia would be defeated at Stalingrad. This is what their "intelligence" suggested. If so, they would be stuck in Europe with inadequate preparation. To be willing to believe my story would force them to see that Stalin knew they were lying about their reasons for delaying the invasion. If Stalin knew they were lying, then he had already outfoxed them. It would mean that Stalin *wanted* them to delay the invasion so that he could have a head start on the road to Berlin. Unthinkable. And this came to be because no one was willing to ask direct questions of the Russians and demand candid answers. Everybody pussyfooted around asking for news of the situation by innuendo. They were answered by innuendo. Out of this mutual skullduggery has come a divided Europe and a world swamped in bitter and dangerous confrontation.

The page I had then written hovered in front of my eyes like a photograph:

RESERVE ARMY	ACTIVATED AS:	COMMANDER
1st Reserve	64th Army	Chiukov
2nd Reserve	1st Guards Army	Moskalenko
3rd Reserve	60th Army	Antonyuk
4th Reserve	38th Army	Chibisov
5th Reserve	63rd Army	Kuznetsov
6th Reserve	6th Army	Kharitonov
7th Reserve	62nd Army	Kolpakchi
8th Reserve	66th Army	Malinovski
9th Reserve	24th Army	Kozflov
10th Reserve	5th Shock Army	Popov

In addition:

A 3rd Tank Army of three tank corps, three rifle divisions, and a floating tank brigade . . . 640 tanks under the redoubtable Prokofi Romanenko. The 5th Tank Army . . . 500 tanks, additional independent tank brigades, and rifle and cavalry corps.

No one was aware of the existence of the above forces. I had gotten the facts, and it had almost cost me my life. Sorting it all through, I was convinced that if people had listened to me, the negotiating positions discussed by Roosevelt and Churchill in Casablanca would have been very different. Then the meeting of the "Big Three" in Teheran would have been on an entirely different footing. Yalta would have been very different.[8]

The world today would have different boundaries.

Would have been . . . If . . . What words!

Now as I looked down at the rivers Dan and Volga beneath us, my mouth again filled with familiar bitterness. But still, despite this, I felt fine. How can you explain it? If I had not felt fine, I would have ordered a bottle of vodka from the flight hostess. I would have drunk it down over Volgograd. I did not.

But later, when I returned to Istanbul, I knew I was "off." Something grabbed my intestines like a leech and seemed to be draining my life away. So I decided to return to the scene of earlier and better days.

I had not been to Konya since my Pir had sent me off to "develop on my own." How different it was from the days of the secrecy and illegality of Dervish activity. Now they even had a "Sufi dancing troupe" that practiced in the Mevlana Shrine. "Ah, well," I thought, "next the Bektash will open a hamburger chain in Albania."

I paid my respects to the saint, and as I was leaving the museum, I saw a familiar gentleman waving to me from across the street . . . Of course. *He* had turned up like a crow to pick my bones.

Qulu Hussain and I began our third discussion. It continued through the entire trip from Konya to Istanbul. Finally, with time out only for sleep, we finished up the week in a café next to the site of Halit Bey's famous "Institute." [9]

According to him, I had made the guiding star of my life the notion that truth was "easy" . . . that it was only human weakness and perversity that kept people from being truthful. He had administered some medicine . . . "poison, in fact," in the form of an outright lie, a harmless fable.

> After all, how could I or even any religion know what happened before the beginning? Your view of truth became source of a greater life . . . the idea that somehow, you knew the truth. This "idea" if eaten too much can make false a person's whole relation to life . . . such a falsehood can outweigh one's whole share of truth.

With this beginning, we embarked on a long ordeal. I have wrestled with how I would convey a full week's discourse in a few pages. I have wrestled and I have lost, and though I hung on until the end, all my joints are sprung and I still do not know. I am putting down fragmentary impressions and quotations that I recorded. They do not hang together any more than my joints, but they convey a "taste" of it.

> This bus ride shows it up very well. Do you imagine what thoughts that man there . . . the one squeezed halfway to "fana" may be having?"

He referred to a small man with a gold front tooth who had been jammed between two wrestlers. He had done the proper thing and made space for an old woman and her young niece to sit down. He was perspiring and casting his eyes wildly around while at the same time smiling and showing off his gold tooth.

> As a Yezidi, I have to read everything and keep on my toes. I read in Polish an article by some genius named Jan Szczepanski[10] that makes one think about such things like, "what goes on in a bus during the squeeze." Now there is a test of truth. You, Ender, like to say that human beings are the highest value for you and that is why it is so important to communicate. That man there . . . maybe he is thinking while his neighbor's elbow digs for his kidney . . . "these monsters who are squeezing out my life are neighbors, dear to me . . . are of the highest value to me" . . . He *could* be thinking that. His golden smile is merely the outward expression of this feeling of love. In his shoes you might be better off. You could say, "Listen, I have been created by God, who is perfect . . . so stop crushing my ribs" . . . or . . . "I am a journalist who knows the truth, let me breathe."

Later he became historical rather than existential:

> Before our clans became Yezidi we were Magus. Then that became rotten. Later, Islam came along. In between we met the Jews and the Christians. All these people began to act crazy so we decided to save our souls. We made up our own religion so we could be faithful to our sense of how things were. We didn't believe in murder. We didn't believe in submerging conscience in order to "belong to God." We didn't believe that only one people or one party had "souls beloved by God" . . . And so . . . what to do? These people

claimed some disgusting things for their "God." As I said long ago, we called their "God," Melek Taus, and propitiate him. We go on worshipping, then our God, Elijah, according to our best understanding . . . through prayer, thanksgiving, devout acts toward others and ourselves.

While the bus was traveling through the western reaches of the Anatolian plain, he got personal again:

I look out of the window and wonder just how you Turks are going to meet the real God. After all, you hold the truth to your hearts that you didn't do anything wrong to the Armenians. But when those bones under the plain there get up to dance and testify . . . what then? Come to think of it . . . imagine all the good Jews and Christians and Muslims going up to Heaven with their sacks of truth around their necks. Some Heaven! The bags turn out to be nests of scorpions. Think of it . . . millions of "good souls" hopping around before God's celestial eye like agitated fleas condemned to live eternally with each other.

At a certain point, it was near Cihanbeyli, he turned philosophic:

I read all your articles I could get my hands on, you know. I even read your letter to Basel. Yes, everyone fits into everyone else's theory. Isn't that what theories are for, to fit *others* into. Now old Egypt really made theory work for them. Think of it! A theory that will cover each and all . . . bury the whole lot under a pyramid and the problems are settled. Nothing sticks out. All the elbows, knees, feet are tucked in and folded under; the chins are pushed tightly into the chest. That's the way to go . . . the winning theory . . . the pyramid. They made their theoria [he actually used the Greek] last without a shudder for over a thousand years. Those Pharaohs knew how to work a theory. Utopia! It is to the Israelite's credit that finally they stirred in their sleep and got out of there. And it wasn't as easy as just walking out of the pyramid.

Halfway to Istanbul, I realized that the semidepression had not only not become lighter . . . it was getting deeper and deeper. I had an image of myself as a grey butterfly falling without gravity through a tar pit. My thinking turned desperate. I thought, "Everyone was right . . . *they* really are 'devil worshippers,' and I'm riding in a bus with Iblis himself and he is eating my soul!" But I felt immobilized.

"So come, Ender, what is the truth?"

The cat had my tongue . . . Pilate's question. He must have read my thoughts.

"Come, come, don't dramatize. The *mondo* has been falsified."

His use of Japanese, always a shock when it happened, now broke the spell, and I was able to answer. I told him that truth was what we could count on. I knew that I could count on Time, Suffering, Death, and the incursions of Fate. He smiled and passed me a small flask, which I had not noticed before. It smelled of Raki. Though I knew he was a devil, I was not going to be squeamish or religious and took a long swallow.

The next turn in his discourse was while we were in the bus depot in Ankara prior to boarding an "express" to Istanbul.

Yes, the business of liberating the Archangel from the love of his feathers . . . what a messy business! All these people we see here, they also face your "truths": time, suffering, death, fate. How beautiful they are, how fragile . . . and they do have courage. They have no idea how brave and beautiful they are. Instead . . . that one is an emperor, his wife a Josephine . . .

the one leaning on the counter is the Thief of Baghdad . . . the shoeshine boy is a magician. Can I say they are wrong to think that way of themselves? . . . No, the contrary is true . . . their fantasies are the beginnings of their salvation.

I was surprised by the drift his talk was taking. He fell into a long silence, staring into his coffee cup. Then he looked up and began to speak much more softly.

Yes, the languages of people and the language of their fantasies have a strange power. You, Ender, are fascinated by me because you still, under all your education, think I am a devil worshipper . . . despite all my explanations. But I will go further than before and say that not only are we not but we do not believe that such a "*being*" *against* God exists or can exist. Yes, the facts about us are so very different from what you have been taught as a child. When we began to be surrounded by Christians and then Muslims, true, our beliefs were different from theirs. But the biggest problems for our "neighbors" were that *we* were settled in the *most fertile locations*. Also, we have strong cleanliness obligations . . . obligations for our whole bodies not merely our hands. Generally we wear white and we keep our hair clean and braided like the American Indian. We never sought converts and we were obstinate about holding to our ancient ways. Of course, *something must* have been wrong with us . . . particularly since we did *not* believe in the existence of a "devil" like they did. This made us even more suspect. Fortunately for our survival, Shaikh Adi[11] found us after his many travels and searches and devoted himself to helping us to organize our way of life so that we might survive in what he saw as a world gone mad. To scholars he is regarded as the founder of our "sect." But in fact he was the architect of our survival. He showed us that the water in our beautiful sanctuary has its origin at the well of Zemzem at Mecca . . . and he demonstrated to us that we could believe in the divine dimension of Jesus and the prophetic stature of Mohammed. He was a kind of genius and set up a kind of mirror around us so that our neighbors refrained from trying to completely liquidate us for centuries. He was a genius. He was *the* Adi who had been a student of the great Qadir el Shurawadi, of both the Ghazzali brothers and also of Jilani. If your people knew that he was *that* Adi they would gnash their teeth even more. It is so. He made his center in the wilderness of Hakkiari in the ruins of the Nestorian monastery at Lalesh. Isn't it curious? The mechanics of the beliefs of people about us is a reflection of the *mechanics* of the beliefs of people about "God." You remember my fable about radiance and reflection and pride and vanity and doubt and fear? So what happens is this: people puff up their pride and vanity and their doubt and fear. Then by misusing their angelically present capacity for radiation of self and reflection of self they "create" a curious kind of "god" inside them which they then paint onto the world outside them. But truly this mechanism has power . . . no . . . the gift of love which is perverted by them to *drive* the mechanism has power. It is so great that it builds vast civilizations and then destroys them. One could say it is archangelic. So we say that Melek Taus has fallen on hard times thanks to the human race.

He paused for a long time. I remember the silence because it was so highly charged.

This creation they have painted onto the universe they feed with offerings, *this* they pray to, *this* they protect and *this* they cherish. Anything which may cause *doubt* about the sanctity of this "god," themselves . . . they call the devil. And so it is that when the archangel can be delivered of the excessive love of "his feathers," then Melek Taus, under a different name, will be "restored to the right hand of God."

We were on the bus again and on the home stretch. We began to see more sea birds as we approached Istanbul. After we had gone through Ismit, Qulu fell totally quiet as if he were expecting some significant response from me. I was in too great a turmoil to say much.

> Ender, you are a relatively good man. That is why I have arranged all this. But then I have my doubts that anything I say will make a hangnail's difference. Always though, there is the hope that through you someone else may be touched. So I am going to share with you a recondite matter which may be interesting. When you have the time, please research it . . . and if you have found good for yourself, write an article and send a copy to Szczepanski in Warsaw. His *Bus Test* has meant a lot to me and that may be a way of attending to the "law of paying back."

I could feel my heart begin to race. At last I was going to hear something esoteric. Long ago I thought I had dried out that appetite, having cashed it in for philosophy, psychology, and scrupulous journalism. But now I could feel my chemistry change in anticipation of this "recondite matter." Though it is fascinating material and I did write an article about it, to include it here would break the narrative and the push of Qulu's message. For this reason, you will find it in a postscript to my report.

Since my quarters in Istanbul were quite generous, I invited Qulu on our arrival in the city to spend the night so we could continue our conversation. The following morning he took me to his favorite haunt, a good-sized coffeehouse at Shehzabedashi.

In this place, Ender, people are accepted as they are with all their qualities and defects. The more defective the better received. You can tell that the customers here warmed up to us on sight. But why I particularly like this place is that they still remember and recount stories of Halit the Corrector and his Institute for the Rectification of Time.

I stared at him. I was amazed anyone in the city still remembered the activities that many years ago had all Istanbul talking. That a non-Turk like Qulu had any awareness of those few fevered years my father had told me about was astonishing.

Ah, Ender, that left eyebrow of yours is beginning its supercilious lift. Now listen, our trip here from Konya enabled us to talk of things in the great past of the world.

Why? *Because* we were suspended on six rubber tires and a bus frame. Perfect conditions! We were in that hard-to-achieve human state of "being en route," neither here nor there. Our talks skirted the suburbs of the limitless and the province of the imaginal. Now think of this coffee shop as another rare location for the transmission of knowledge.

This is the pivot of the limitless and the limited. After all, this is the favorite café of our sainted "regulator of time." A human life cannot be lived in the merely limitless or the merely limited. It is lived in the Pivot, in the hinges.

Those truths of yours, Time, Suffering, Death, and Fate, are hinged inside of us to Eternity, Joy and Sorrow, Life, and Destiny. Halit the Corrector's truth was that the hinge of uttermost sincerity is the palace . . . the palace where Time is rectified. I sound sentimental and hate myself for it. But listen . . . your *j'accuse* at the world's refusal to tell or listen to the truth is *in you*, self- righteousness. It's all right in the mouth of God but you should wash your tongue. You made much of the betrayals of the Allies to each other during the war and the dismal inheritance the world has gotten from it. But though you had ample knowledge of the Nazi betrayal of the human spirit and the Allies' disregard of it you remained silent.

Also, whenever I mention your country's crimes and sins against life and honor you bridle. I could go on and on . . .

You must see by now why truth is so hard even between members of the same family.

The demand on each is to find the "palace of the hinges" in us and *to say from there* whatever we are able to mean.

Where love and responsibility to the best in ourselves and the love and responsibility toward an *actual* other meet . . . there is the confluence of the seas of radiance and reflection. From there the deliverance of the captive angel begins. Now these last few days, and always in your writings, I hear the rattling of the chains of masters and slaves. We and them . . . God worshippers and devil worshippers . . . all those costumes and chains rustle in your silences. Why enslave yourself to some imaginary

"higher" in you? Why must the masculine dominate and enslave the feminine or the opposite? Inside or outside, it is the same sickness.

There to us, is the root of the "Fall." You remember my story, the one I told in Tbilisi about the dispute between Adam and Eve. Each of them claimed the priority. Each claimed possession of their offspring. *There* you have the root of masters and slaves. Realize for once how desperate and untrue is the lot of the slave . . . how insane and false the lot of the master.

He broke off here abruptly. We ordered coffee and mentioned no further serious matters until we parted three days later. We had moved our scene to another café, a smaller one, but it also was related geographically to Halit. The café was on Freedom Hill, exactly on the site of Halit's ill-fated Institute for the Rectification of Time. Our conversations during those days were about soccer, biomedicine, and the Soviet space program's plan to dominate Venus. Then we added a pinch of seriousness as we discussed the likely eventual assimilation of the Yezidi clans into the Information Society.

As you all know, I still say the same things I did before these meetings with Qulu. But their content is a shade different. When I say "shit" these days, it is so dry a word that unless you knew the language you would have no idea what I was saying. Who knows, in a thousand years I may become a Buddha.

*   *   *

Postscript

The original Book of Job consisted of the speeches of the "three friends," Job, and the Voice out of the Whirlwind. Qulu's clan, not at that time yet Yezidi, lived near some Israelite settlements not far from Samarra in the eight century, BCE. It was written in Aramaic by an Israelite. Either the author himself, or someone who understood the purport of the book, translated it into Hebrew and added the prologue, Elihu's speech, and the epilogue. These portions were made in order to illuminate what may have remained an opaque book.

It boils down like this: the *place* of the original story, that between Job and his friends, is an "other world." That is, it is no particular place. In the sense that the place is an underworld, the three friends do not need to *come*. (Sort of like the joke about the Soviet telephone company in the days of Stalin.)[12] They are already there . . . Eliphaz as "gold god" . . . Bildad as "destroyer" . . . Zophar as "god of the dead." In them, the archangel is completely fallen. If they can succeed in convincing Job of their views, they will have added to their company and be at "peace."

Like us, Job, has fashioned a generalized "god" from the arch- angelic feathers that are so worthy of praise. He sustains this *virtual structure* by "keeping the times." However, a suffering has happened. A trial is under way, and the foundations of the "sleep of Melek Taus" crack. The friends have arrived to patch it back into shape. During this story, Job's best friend is his wife, who urges him to curse "god" and die. If he could have listened and suffered the death that cursing this artifacted "god" would bring, matters could have been transformed right then. But the poem would not teach anything, and the Voice out of the Whirlwind would have seemed too gratuitous.

Job employs all his stratagems to preserve his sense of truth and his "god." The result is that he *does* unwittingly curse the Living God in that he wishes he had not been born . . . that he had been permitted nonentity. Finally, at the peak of pressure, the *condition* of "underworld" and the debate in it are breached. The real world breaks through in tempest, and the Living God is face-to-face with Job.

But this version is difficult to access. To make it more available to his people, the poet who translated it into Hebrew made a few helpful additions:

A) He sets up conditions of a trial to emphasize the meaning of Job's *names* and, hence, call attention to all the names used in the poem. Matters are now set out in heaven and earth, so we know the account is taking place somewhere "unusual."

B) He judiciously uses the explicit name of God only in the prologue, the introductions to the Voice out of the Whirlwind, and in the epilogue.

C) He adds the figure of Elihu. By his name and lineage, he situates him in the prophetic tradition. By name, Elihu harmonizes with Elijah. By lineage, he harmonizes with Ezekiel through Berachel the Buzite. He amplifies the latter relation by constant allusion to the cherub creature.[13]

D) Elihu comes from an actual somewhere and is of actual lineage. Hence he cannot be confused with a "type." There is no preparation of his coming, and he vanishes at the end of his speech.

E) At the vanishing of Elihu from the place of the trial, the poet brings in the answer of the Living God from the Whirlwind.

F) The epilogue "doubles" the assets of Job. They now have significance in depth and the daughters have names: Jemima, Kezia, and Keren ha Puch.

For Qulu, this canonical poem shows the way to redeem the fallen angel and ourselves . . . the fallen angel in ourselves.

Doubtless he was fascinated by this book since it is the first reference in the Bible to "a devil."

If you are interested to find out more about the relationship of this first biblical personification of the "adversary" to the subsequent folkways of the Yezidi, see my article in the *ISPI Journal*.[14]

Notes

1) This is a highly idiosyncratic piece. As I mentioned in my introduction, I think this entire report is a fiction. For example the description of the Soviet Order of Battle is identical to that found in *The Secret of Stalingrad* by Walter Kerr, Macdonald & James, 1978. Also, despite efforts to find a trace of anyone known as "Halit the Corrector" in Turkey, no such person seems to have existed except in a novel entitled *The Time Regulation Institute*. This novel, widely known in Turkey, can be found in English only in an unpublished translation by Mr. Ender Gurol.

2) This episode seems to be taken from *Yol (The Path)*. It is part II of *The Autobiography of Aziz Nesin*, translated by Joseph S. Jacobseon, Middle East Monographs, No. 7, Center for Middle Eastern Studies, University of Texas at Austin, 1979.

3) The shrine of Mevlana Jelal'adin Rumi.

4) This kind of "theology" seems endemic to the Near East. For example, in the Midrash Tanhuma, I found "Rabbi Simeon ben Halafta was asked: "In how many days did God create the world?" He replied, "In six days." And what has he been doing since then? He has been making ladders . . .

5) The Soviet Georgian Republic.

6) The Peacock Angel.

7) "Keloghlan" is the Turkish male Cinderella, Aladdin, Brave Little Tailor, and many other figures. He often assumes the role of trickster. He is always bald, and his name means "bald boy."

8) Casablanca conference of January 1943 between Churchill and Roosevelt. "Big Three" meetings in Teheran, late in 1943, and Yalta in February 1945.

9) See Note 1 above.

10) Probably Jan Szczepanski, the vice president of the Polish Academy of Sciences, Warsaw. See especially the second edition of the book *Sprawy Ludzkie*, Warsaw . . . the chapter entitled "The Value of Man."

11) A person named Shaikh Adi is considered the founder of the Yezidis.

12) Rather wrenching philology to tease these meanings out of the names of Job's "friends," but it is possible. See *The Body of God*, Eric, Gutkind, Horizon Press, New York, 1969, p. 138-9.

13) I found an interesting analysis of the relationship between the figures of Elihu and Elijah that bears out some of what Paracelsus says here. The overall conclusions, however, bear no resemblance to those described as the "lore of Qulu." *The Book of Job*, N.H. Tur-Sinai, Kiryath Sepher Limited, Jerusalem, 1967.

14) I can find no evidence that such a journal exists or ever has existed.

CHAPTER FOURTEEN

Madelein

Johanna Stein was born in 1929 to German Jewish family. Fortunately, her family immigrated to Australia in 1936 after having transferred much of their holdings to that country. They became "pillars of the community" in Sydney. At the age of fifteen, Madelein disappeared. The family offered large rewards, and a nationwide search bore no results. A little over a year later, she reappeared. She claimed to have spent the year wandering in the "bush" as far as Alice Springs. Psychiatric examinations showed her well adjusted and "normal." To forestall any recurrence of this event, her family sent her to live with relatives in the States, near Cleveland, Ohio, and far away from the lure of the wilderness.

After reading *An Autobiography* by Frank Lloyd Wright in her senior year of high school, she became attracted by the possibilities in the field of architecture. The closest good school in the field was at the University of Ohio, so she entered and, after much hard work, became one of the early female graduates of the department. Her plan had been to join the Taliesin Fellowship upon completion. But at this time, she became fully aware of the implications of the "Holocaust." She returned to her family in Australia so that she could have some time to sort things out. With their grudging approval, she returned to the interior. For several years she worked at odd jobs on ranches and trading posts. During this time she had come to the decision to immigrate to Israel. Despite her "good intentions," she became appalled at the treatment afforded Kurdish and other minority groups of Jews by the young "State." The standard argument that they were "better off," though it satisfied her reason, was inadequate for her conscience. The evidence of certain insensitivities throughout the bureaucracy made it impossible for her to remain.

With intense effort and the application of her undeniable charms, she was able to return to architecture after some time . . . she entered "at the bottom" in Corbusiers' firm in Geneva. In her free time she designed a model campus for a "university for indigenous peoples." It was projected for a specific site in Australia. Although it was merely an exercise, the paradigmatic nature of the design attracted attention among United Nations circles in Geneva and was published. Several months later, a letter of criticism was published that had been written by David. Both angered and pleased, she sharply rebutted the critique and so entered into a correspondence with him which led eventually to her association with Amfortas. The pivotal hinge in the dialogue was the interpretation of the following entry from *The Journals of Ralph Waldo Emerson*:

Dec 1849

Chladni's experiment seems to me central. He strewed sand on glass & then struck the glass with tuneful accords, & the sand assumed symmetrical figures. With discords the sand was thrown about amorphously. It seems, then, that Orpheus is no fable: You have only to sing and the rocks will crystallize; sing and the plant will organize; sing & the animal will be born.

*   *   *

About Madelein I am so strongly biased that I must push myself against the temptation of saying nothing, or very little. Inevitably I will say too much.

Her hair was brilliant red and usually pretty wild. Her pale skin and glowing green eyes contributed to an impression of unearthly beauty. An exceptional listener, it was often a trial to talk to her because she seemed to listen through a person. She seemed to hear several conversations at once while giving especially compassionate attention to one's past.

It was not until several years after the business at Olivet that I got to know her at all well. At Olivet she seemed too weird for my taste in friends. But since she was a resident of Geneva, I paid her a duty call after a visit I made to Paracelsus and his family. It was only several months before this visit that I had attended the concert in Albert Hall, and the world was seeming a bit new.

We met at a pleasant, tiny café on the small square of the Bourg-de-Four in the old city. At first, Madelein appeared distracted and constantly looked off along the street. Finally she settled her gaze on me.

"Your chattering is all frills and icing. You've just begun to pull out of your British 'dream,' you've just begun to grow up, and here you are sitting with me and launching yourself into 'cloud-cuckoo land.'"

"Why do you say . . . just beginning to wake up?"

"Isn't it so?"

I wondered how she could possibly perceive the recent changes in my interior landscape. I had to assume it showed despite my best efforts.

"Isn't it so, that you are still dazzled by that English manner . . . that diffidence . . . that sense of fair play and decency . . . that ability to lark off on horseback and spear aboriginal peoples through the back as though they were wild pigs?"

I began to protest. She put her hand on my mouth.

"I won't hear it. Don't you have any idea what you are, Merlin? You are a human being. For god's sake, snap out of it!"

The morning light dappling the small square was all gathered, that moment, into her hair and her eyes. She smiled. I count the moment the beginning of my adulthood. The beginning of my own fate.

I want now to light up Madelein's character from another side. It was about a year and a half after that morning. Separately, Shakespeare and I had been invited to spend a weekend with her and her family at her relatives' house near Cleveland. Though it caused us both scheduling problems, we could not refuse. She was one of those people who had the power to invite. Her parents were coming over from Australia to meet her "halfway."

The family was very impressed by the quality of her friends. Wealthy Australian and American Jews are quite susceptible to British style. She found this highly amusing. Her family and Shakespeare found themselves in a kind of awkward dance. They kept making a fuss over him while he, for his part, unwaveringly tried to render their attentions unnecessary. While we were toying with our cocktails, she began to "ramble":

"I've wondered often what Rabbi Hertz could possibly have meant when he described Britain as the best friend the Children of Israel ever had. Certainly he knew that after some pretty ghastly pogroms had eaten our marrow we were kicked out of England in the thirteenth century. We were excluded from England until the days of Cromwell. He had to know the dismal history. He was not a 'careless man.'"

No one really wanted to tackle this subject. But she went on as if musing to herself. When she was in this mode—there was this about Madelein—people had to listen. It was the same force that caused people to accept her invitations. But the form was so different because she almost chanted in her musing and we listeners invariably would lean over to hear what she had to say like eavesdroppers to privileged information.

"But what he must have meant was a radical kinship in the psyche. The English, despite appearances, have an irreducible sap in their psyche which ultimately utterly rejects sham. This is so despite the eternal games they play with each other. Once the Jews were invited back in the seventeenth century, there was no pressure to become *something else*. Though the British lie about everything, they will not commit the Big Lie . . . the essential lie is abysmal to them. They are unwitting followers of the Kotzker Rebbe. How did they get this way? I think that this seemingly minor quality is what set them against Germany in this century. They simply couldn't abide all that bombast and pretension. Really, pretension is the path to evil."

Madelein's parents began to fear we English guests could be getting uncomfortable and started moving randomly about to again fuss over Shakespeare and trying with insipid words to pat everything back into shape. He waved them off.

"Please . . . What your daughter is saying is interesting to me. It is likely that the action of the unintentional and the intentional are thoroughly muddled in us."

"Yes, sir. I think that's right. When you *intend*, you make a mess. Unintentionally, you tend to do the right things. That speaks for some basic soundness somewhere. Perhaps that is where you are kin to us. We both know that people are pretty helpless . . .

somewhere we know *that*. But we are not hopeless, we are never without hope. Our real life is not of our devising. Our real life is by the way of our hopefulness and good faith."

A different order of time captured the space of the room. I have met it often since and name it Madelein Time.

"Both peoples have relatively, inwardly prospered because you have not . . . despite appearances . . . utterly discounted women. You have an awareness, dimly, that as a people, without women you are nothing. You have been unable to completely lie to yourselves. Oh, there are those peoples all over the world who are able to convince themselves that men are the keystone of creation and that in *ideal circumstances* they could dispense with us. Short of that, they relegate us to fancy-sounding 'pig pens' called 'breeding stables,' 'sources of inspiration,' 'keepers of the mystery,' and so on . . . as did those Nazi termites. But though you cannot commit that lie, you still hold back from the truth. You have not yet realized our full stature. Until you do, you cannot realize your own. And if you can't, who can? And if no one can, the world will fall into ruin and desolation. If not now, when?"

We were all silent. We waited.

"And I do not mean merely those *so* guid women whom you acknowledge to be useful. But I mean also the poor, the disheveled, the incontinent . . . even the mad and hysterical. They tower before your very eyes and you will not see. They are, even more than the so 'guid,' the good, the mothers of God in everyone."

She winked at me.

A Dream
Madelein

I am not who I am . . . But also not who I am not.

The plain stretches vast distances around me. Night, and the plain is lit up by multiple sudden bursts of lightning. It is the field of lightnings . . . The field of electrical origins. On every square yard of the vast valley are shafts of "electrum . . ." of "chasmal" glowing, and the tips of their stalks are gathering the striking lightning.

Impossible here to have shape. Impossible to stand here as I stand without shape.

The plain must end . . . certainly as all plains do . . . at the mountains or at the sea. This plain must end at the sea, for try as I might, I can see no mountains . . . in any direction.

Now I am able to count. I find that I can, and this means before that moment I could not. Yet already I am at seven . . . eight . . . nine . . . ten . . . eleven . . . twelve . . .

"Where am I?"

A voice . . . I have a voice!

There is no answer. But the lightnings stop. It is quiet. Though it is dark now, very dark, the stalks I see are glowing faintly and they light up the ground. I start to walk and find myself walking into a canyon that could not before be seen. Steam is coming from the rocks. A good steam . . . it is healing my legs. White steam healing my legs. I must have shape . . . I have legs to walk with . . . legs to be healed.

I keep walking, walking deeper into the canyon, which begins to curve and twist. I round a sharp boulder and find myself moving upon the early slope of a mountain that I had not seen. I know this, that I am going up, because the plain with the glowing stalks of lightning reeds are visible several hundred feet below. Now and then, one or the other of them gleams to draw the lightning. But now the bursts are single rather than the simultaneous exploding accords of light that had been my only company while I had stood on the plain . . . For how long I cannot remember.

I am walking again into the canyon . . . up the mountain. A differing glow shimmers on the horizon . . . new now . . . another kind of light. Sharp smell of mountain wild flowers after a night of rain.

I can smell . . . ! See a flowering shrub to the right on the path and bend to smell it. A drop of water still clings to one of the petals. I lick the water drop off the flower petal and scratch my cheek on a thorn. How good it all is!

I am returning . . . from where . . . to where?

Or am I just arriving? Coming, or perhaps going.

The Eternal is very near . . . but has never been very far.

In the shadows thrown by the new light, there are faces. The light quickens . . . the faces change . . . they are ciphers waiting to be decoded by the sunrise.

Streaming torrents of light . . . a great sphere has appeared on the horizon . . . a sunrise. We stand for a moment face-to-face. I blush and feel my form outlined in the winds set loose by the sun . . . winds of galaxies . . . winds of oceans of unseen stars.

The girl form is familiar but unknown.

How long had I been standing on the lightning plain . . . standing how long among the stalks of the seeds of the treasuries of the lightning? Dimly, I am aware that all the long watch on the plain the Eternal had stood presence for me, had stood guard for me . . . had watched over me and eased the loneliness . . . had fortified me as I quivered and had steadied the trembling of my inner parts. The presence had somehow given to the most tender of the fibers of my brain and roots of nerve the certainty that the "time" in the field was but an infinite interval. I seemed to remember now that I had been given to understand that my initial despair was merely an all-too-human relation to the miracle of memory, making endlessness out of intervals.

The morning light is beginning to bring out shapes on a plain. A different plain stretches on the other side of the mountain. Finities of shapes of trees and houses. Near at hand, nestled against the lower slopes, is a small village. Farther along toward a horizon small streams begin to glisten into a river, and there is movement along pathways and along roads going into the distance . . . There near the horizon where the river ends, I see a city, still deep in shadow, showing the outlines of its towers.

Stirring in my chest, as of the stirring of birds through my whole torso and whirring and song . . . Love felt in solitude for the presence in the distance of my kind. Love without object, kindled by hieroglyphs of smoke rising from chimneys and the calls of drovers and the barking of dogs . . . cock crow . . . and now of children calling to each other on the village streets. Love hovers, and the village and the fields and the city beyond are folded gently into its presence.

Slowly, easefully, I begin to walk down the flanks of the mountain and feel earth and rock underfoot.

In the branches of an ancient cedar to the right of the path, yellow birds and a few red ones are chirping. And as I draw near, three crows in conference among its roots on the ground fly off . . . boisterously.

"Who am I?"

The voice with which I ask this question is very soft. I feel myself smile although I do not know the answer. In asking the question, I am received by the earth as family. The earth is also asking the question . . . and the trees also, and the bright-eyed chipmunk who suddenly appeared with cocked head also asks.

All, in asking, are praying the morning prayer of the world.

*   *   *

After long marches, I have come to the city.

The city is by the sea.

I distrusted the streets and approached it along the deep beaches, which stretch like arms around the harbor. It is a port, and the wharves are bristling with boats and ships. I find my footing on an old wharf. It seems far older than the city itself. In a timbered office on the wharf, the Harbor Master is looking at me across a wide oak desk. He has the keys to the city. I am not knowing what to say. His creased face reminds me of an old "abo" lore master I had met somewhere.

"I have come from the fields of the lightnings, from the place where the earth is putting up reeds of silence-speaking."

I had spoken the truth. There was nothing else to say. Slowly he reaches across the desk . . . his hand slightly trembling . . . passing across it a key to the city.

The key is wonderfully worked of amethyst and gold and silver and some other metal that seemed to flow continuously. He leaves it on the desk a hand's breadth from where my hand is resting. I take it simply and put it in my pocket. I am wearing trousers and a loose jacket and have put the key into my jacket pocket.

Wondering, I look down and see indeed that I am clothed, though I had been unaware before this moment whether I had been clothed or not. I do not know what to do with this key. But it is mine.

He looks down at a map of the harbor spread out before him . . . a map showing the currents and the shoals and the timing of the tides.

What is one to do in the city?

I do not ask. He remains staring down at the map. Slowly he begins to raise his head . . . slowly like the growing of rocks. He has tears in his eyes. He is smiling. He cannot find words. He shrugs his shoulders. I venture to speak:

"It is good to see a friendly face."

Briefly he closes his eyes and answers:

"Yes, yes it is."

He stands up and reaches his hand across the desk . . . it is open. I take his hand. It is curious, but he squeezes and shakes mine and lets it go.

I walk out of the office, which creaks in the sea wind and the sea's heaving, and, walking off the wharf step, onto a street that leads toward a cluster of tall buildings not very far away.

> Standing on the street juncture comes sudden memory of the fields. Only the fields. Now and then the whole plain rose into a swirl of formation of star clusters. The earth of the plain has no "matter . . ." but the materiality of color. Sometimes of the essence of red, of indigo, of a yellow as pale as whiteness . . . sometimes of the blue-green of the interstices which seam the faces of sunsets on earth . . .

The people walking on the streets are good to look at. How wonderful are people to look at on their daily tasks. Men in helmets of bright colors are working among high steel frames. Shouting to each other, I hear them in the distance sounding like birds in a tree. Women in gay dresses are walking on short stilts on the street, the dresses swirl around their forms when the sea winds blow. How wonderful this dance along the street and among the high frameworks!

I am drawn to approach a large old building.

Hieroglyphs on the stonework above the portal. The sign system is foreign to me and I do not know what they mean. People going in and out . . . usually in groups of two or three. Only rarely does a person go in alone or leave alone. I enjoy the "feel" of the people, so I walk into the building.

There is something in the atmosphere that is familiar. But it is disturbed and twisted by something quite alien to my "memory." I think it must be a school of the temple. A school of the arts. But there is a raw heaviness . . . a slight smell or carrion that around crows and vultures is normal . . . but here it is out of place. Instantly I leave the building and look along the street for a place to sit down.

I have not sat down for aeons.

There is no place on the street that I can see where one can sit or rest.

For courage I reach into my pocket and feel the firm sharpness of my key. Then I notice along a side street a small park and across from it is a building of very arresting form. It is round . . . or rather a spiral which widens regularly as it ascends . . . and on the top is barely visible a dome of transparent substance woven together with bands of gold and turquoise. My step quickens, and I hurry to it. No one is around. I push at the wide translucent door and find it is locked. My hand reaches for the key. I insert it into the lock. Quietly it turns and opens. I pocket the key again and walk into a small wonderful entry hall softly lit from deep shelves which border the entry only several feet above my head. In the hall is a long couch of ebony with crimson cushions and with a sheepskin thrown over it. I sit down.

For an instant I sense beyond the entry a wonderful and spacious place. But at this moment I have no wish to explore . . . only to sit and rest and think. I close my eyes.

> I hear a deep horn blowing . . . it has the sound of a didgeridoo.
> Faces, marvelous black faces crowd the avenue of my mind.
> A bustle of aborigines and I are pressed close together singing
> "the honey bee song."

From a far distance this word came into my mind, and I opened my mind to know the place in which I now sat and sighed a sigh of such relief it would have broken a harp. Opening my eyes, it was as I thought. Still I was sitting here at the entry to the building. I *could* pause and think things through, and then . . . at my wish, explore.

Where?

> Aeons standing in the field of origins.
> Why? Where were my friends? Where had my companions
> gone . . . why were they not in the field with me?
> No human being is utterly solitary on this earth.
> All have their fellows from the lowest to the highest.
> Who had been my friends before my eternal watch among the
> lightnings of formation?
> Ahh . . . I had gone on ahead. And no one followed?
> Thank the Eternal for the continuous mercy of the
> Most High while solitary among the sentinels . . .
> For what reason than the leave-taking and the parting
> promises if the next moment they would be no more?
> What had happened?

And then the lessons of the reeds of light elaborated themselves out before my attention.

*   *   *

I found that while pondering I had gotten to my feet and walked into the main hall. When I looked around for my bearings, I was just inside it with light streaming down from the oculus; bodies of almost liquid-colored light filled the central space, which vaulted above me all the way to the glowing dome. Balconies spiraled above with some doorways off them leading to chambers. From some of these chambers, from behind the doors, I seemed to hear voices. I began to mount the spiral.

As my eyes grew accustomed to the great spillway of illumination, my heart leaped in my breast. The building was balm to my bones, oil of cedar to my marrow. The wall surfaces were tan like the sands of fecund beaches. Hanging over the balustrades, which rimmed the spiral, were sheets of color . . . woven stuff of crimsons and purples. There were brilliant blue-green tapestries with figures of calligraphic emblems worked in gold and silver. Slowly, with an alertness best called "tracking" attention, I stalked my way up the great ramp to the final swing of the arc. Here was a small table and a couch. I sat down right here where the momentums of light and color and the curving forms rested against the jointure of dome and wall. Here the vitalities reconciled into a resonant silence.

And from here I sensed the implicitness within the space of both a sphere and a cube. Clearly, somehow the arcs of the spiral swung out from four invisible corners. A cube expanding rhythmically outward was the reference point, and though it was immaterial and built "only" of thought, it hovered within the solidities. And a sphere, similarly implicit, was intermeshed with all the dynamics of form and of the thought which generated the forms.

This place . . . this building . . . was redolent of memory. It had been prepared. It was familiar. It was homely.

From the vantage where I sat, the voices I had before heard from behind the several doors were scarcely audible. Why was no person besides me inside this miraculous medicinal chamber?

Like some recuperating animal, I again dozed off.

The field in which I had found myself was the interface beyond origination. Those for whom I had occupied . . . this unoccupiable place as a station on our journey had not come . . . And I had promised to wait. But they had not arrived . . . Still, the wonderful, most wonderful Shaper of Origin had honored my vow and sustained me among the realms of the births of poems until the "vows" had run their course in time . . . Bitter salts of disappointment had nourished the lightning reed fields until they had become springs of fresh running water.

As the salts became sweet, I stirred and woke up. Now refreshed, I walked down the ramp toward the nearest door from which the sounds of human speech came. The door was locked, but my key unbolted it.

The voices stopped. I entered the room and saw five people seated around a table who looked at me with apprehension. At the far end of the room was another door, and I closed the one behind me. They stared and did not speak. I spoke and it seemed to come from a distance.

"I do think you had better gather yourselves and leave. I am planning to bring some of my friends to live in my house."

Several times, one or the other tried to speak but could not. I felt their ferment of shame. Under their fashionable clothes was something barely recognizable . . . but at a level which did not motivate recognition. I waited. Slowly at first . . . then rapidly they left. I knew there were other residences in the house to clear out, but I decided to wait until I have found those who could occupy them.

Now there was purpose, and quickly I returned down the ramp and left the building. The door locked itself firmly behind me, and I started toward the street which led to the harbor.

The Harbor Master was still at his desk when I walked the creaking planking and into his office.

"Harbor Master, I believe you must reside here as well as work here among the maps."

"True."

"Then be so kind to me and accept an invitation to have drier, less-salt-sprayed quarters. In my house I have a vacant residence. Will you be willing to move?"

With surprising nimbleness he got to his feet and went to a corner of the office where he stuffed a few belongings into a duffel bag. Following me out, he turned and secured the door to his office and we set off. I had started in the way I had used before to go to my house when he gently touched my arm and pointed. There, just several hundred yards up the waterfront and one short block inland, I could make out the dome glowing in the gathering dusk. In finding it the first time, I had wandered in a boomerang arc through the town.

When we entered the domed court, I sensed the whole building tune itself as though it were a music-making being . . . melodies sensed rather than heard were springing from the spirals and haunches of the walls and down from the turquoise-and-gold-ribbed oculus. I led him up the ramp to his apartment. The ancient Harbor Master was delighted as a young boy. A large window was set deeply into one of the sloping walls, which gave onto the ocean, and we pulled a couple of chairs over to it and looked out onto the darkening seascape.

While we looked, he told his story:

> This building stood here before the city was built.
>
> Several of us arrived by ship and found it, but we couldn't get inside. We had seen it from far out at sea, outlined in the daytime and scattering spirals of light at night and we steered our vessel by it . . . hoping to find here other humans

and settlement. There were no people, but we decided, nevertheless, to settle. Having a sense of the Sea and the Tides, I became the Harbor Master. Others took up needed occupations, and in time some people from inland moved here. And then other vessels came bearing travelling folk, and we began to establish the city by the sea.

From time to time we noticed a few people, found ways to get themselves into parts of the building.

We respected them because they seemed to belong . . . but most often they were not a likeable sort. We reckoned they must be kinsfolk of the owners.

As the years went by, I began to have dreams. In the dreams there was someone who over and again told me that the owner was away waiting in the fields of sea origins, or sometimes walking along the shores of star births. There always was this longing to see the inside. But it was not to be. One day long ago, a stranger with a firm gait and a face brightly happy, though ravaged, came into the harbor office and gave a key into my keeping. He did not say for what it was but said that sometime before *too* long the person to whom it belonged would come. His exact words were,

"To you, Harbor Master of the city, at the confluence of seas . . . the key's owner will have to come." With that strange and hopeful augury I held my post. When I saw you, whom I knew but had never seen, and whose face gave my soul comfort, I could recognize that the time was here.

At this point in the old man's story, I feared my heart would shiver into pieces and I begged leave. I told him that soon I would be turning out the other tenants, but that since they had no access to the great court . . . for the time being it made no difference. I left and slowly ascended to the couch on the furthest spiral to assemble my thought.

This time, like a real human being, I stretched out on the couch and went to sleep.

And it seemed my sleep took me to another place and time. I woke up still on the couch, and the memory of where I had been in my sleep was gone.

It was now night time. More lights had come on around the perimeter of the court. I wanted to see what the city was like at night . . . under the stars . . . so I went down to my friend's quarters and gently rapped on the door.

He greeted me and, seeing me in good spirits, the worried look that had been flickering around his face left. He had rearranged the elements of the residence, and it now was quite cheery. I told him my wish, and he urged me first to make use of a facility inside one of the rooms to clean myself up and to defecate if I needed. To my surprise, I realized that I did.

When we stepped out of the building . . . now under the night sky . . . I realized that a part of a nagging strangeness I felt was the sense that this world had been waiting for me to return. And I was a woman. Yet in all the worlds that I seemed to remember, never had they been waiting for a woman to return. I stepped off a curb and, in the gap between footfalls, my mind filled with images of winds, winds . . .

> Blackening sky high among mountains . . . mountains that were small, desolate and stumpy hills. Lightning lashes against timbers.

Footfall landed on cobble, and around me now the city sang in its gaiety of nighttime life. We walked away and came to the street of the "temple school." The Harbor Master indicated a tiny, wiry woman, who looked old and weathered enough to be my grandmother and who was selling scripted paper from a small shelter.

"She was one of the original company on my ship. "

Recognizing him, she waved him over. When we were near, she noticed me with surprise. Her hand clutched mine, and she drew me nearer and looked long into my face. Then she fell against me and burst into sobs. I could feel the bones in her back as I put my arms around her, and she stayed a while in them, trembling like a spent wren. Somewhere far away in me, a cold seed of anger sparked against the usurping tenants of my house. The Harbor Master spoke very lowly . . . very slowly.

"Now that I have room, I can take her in."

I nodded and, taking each of their hands, led them back the way we had come until we were in sight of the front door. Then I urged them to continue. I watched the two old figures walking slowly. From time to time I saw the white oval of the woman's face turn back in the light of the streetlamps to look to me. I stood and watched them finally enter . . .

> The loneliness on the far side of the originations of poems, the fields of seeds before thought, avenues of the birth of lightnings.

Standing on the city street, I realize that there are many things that I know how to do. I do not know how to do as a person I see standing across the street smoking. I know what it is and feels like but cannot remember having ever done it.

What a strange, marvelously strange universe we participate in. The vivid memory of a moment ago has not enervated me . . . rather, it has strengthened and solidified me. No longer an interest in exploring the city at night. Now is the time to clear my house of the usurping tenants . . . the house prepared and made for me by my great friend now needs to be set in order. Afterward I will find those whom I can invite to share my dwelling with me. They are here in the city. They are those who had never extracted *that* promise from me. Their faith and their delicacy had been too spirited for that kind of claim.

Straightaway I returned to the house and went to consult with my friends. I did not know the protocols of the city. But somewhere I had learned that small acts may bear great consequences if in defiance of protocols . . . and that if the acts are major and come from impulse, the doer may bear a deadly backlash. So I needed to ask the Harbor Master about the proper means of ridding my house of these unwanted presences. I confided my problem to him at his door. He smiled now for the first time without restraint and became younger before my eyes.

"If you wish it . . . it is good. For wish is the marriage of will and desire."

He asked me in and had me wait while he swiftly prepared a document with these simple words:

> I, the owner of the premises known *to the city* as the Spiral House, demand that all present in the House, who are not by me personally and specifically invited immediately vacate the building.

There was a space for a signature, but I did not know what to sign. He handed me a gold and silver pen. I held it and waited for some inkling of my name. I watched my hand sign the paper, "Madelein Towers."

At once there was a rustling through the building like the rustling at the edges of nonentity on sleepless nights. And then after the last rasp of the rustle of silence as deep and golden as the valley beyond the mountain . . . and there came then a singing of the utterances before the saying . . . a sound of before the great soundings. Simply now, I asked the Harbor Master's permission to use his wharf for some hours of reflection.

The sea breeze was soft against my face as I walked the short street to the wharf's side. The sea's heaving was playfully creaking the pilings. The planks underfoot gave off the smell of time as I paced out the distance to the wharf's end.

Sixty paces . . . sixty guardians . . . each step an angel and an assumption of the tasks of the night.

I set my back against some old planking with my feet tucked under me and my knees under my chin and sat to wait. I have learned to wait.

Low toward the horizon, the large stars stir . . . the high ones overhead hold their places. A trembling across the blue-black vale of the sky . . . valleys and curtains of deepest blue stir from a wind far yonder . . . from where we come and go. These sidereal sea winds carrying the pledges of the new.

Far away on the water, a shape is moving. It is set on erratic bearings but is tacking arduously toward the shore. I hold my peace and wait. Hours pass. Bells in the city have tolled the midnight hour. Under sail I see the barque now . . . with a lone seaman struggling with rigging and tiller. I do not move. From an oblique crown of the heavens, I seem to feel old friend Neptune plying his subtle art through the growing event. My chin is resting easily on my knees even as I watch the vessel founder several hundred yards from shore. Thank God I have learned to wait!

Soon I can hear the heavy breathing of a man. He is nearly spent and is climbing the wooden ladder of the wharf. I see "hands fresh from shipwreck" grab and then pull him up onto the firm planking. He sits struggling for breath at the wharf's edge. Noticing me, he manages some words.

"So do you just sit there?"

"I sit . . . but you are welcome, stranger . . . and I have a place where you can be warmed and fed."

So saying, I stand up and begin to walk homeward. Without questions, he follows.

The walk feels strange. Behind me I can hear the man following with the sound of water squeaking and squishing in his clothes. I do not turn until I have entered my house and found my two new friends waiting anxiously in the great domed chamber. Then I see him blinking . . . blinded by the sudden light. His face was as I knew it must be . . . brightly cheerful and ravaged by intensities of encounter I could not fathom. Strands of seaweed hang from his hair. A small pool of water gathers at his feet as he stands there. He was as I knew he must be . . . the man who had brought the key to the city for me long years before. And somehow I had glimpses of his history . . . for he, among all of them, had tried to save and, failing, had tried to follow. In some way I had memory of journeys over the pathways of the earth I shared with him as I stood among the foundations of thought. And time wove back these memories into the filament of my mind where they flowed and were sealed like sap under the bark of a tree.

Essences of journeys among the heavens were their corollary. We four now sat in the entry and wept and talked the night through.

When the morning light graciously began flowing from the dome, the four of us knelt and prayed to the unknown and most intimate companion of our separate ways. The one who had somehow preserved us and now fortified us for the world to come and the unprefigured events of the new day.

Shaper of origins
as you have called your universe into being this day . . .

and hung therein worlds above and worlds below at your "word."
So with your multiple loving-kindness unify our hearts and enlighten our eyes.

*   *   *

Around me on the red dusty ground are friendly faces of the tribe that had taken me in. Black faces, broad and open faces with eyes set deep in their heads, are around me. An old man and an old woman are holding my hands and murmuring to me. The woman's left eye wanders off on its own to the side now and then. The man has several broken teeth and a scar along his chin. She is saying:

> Good you woke up. You need to be a strong girl.
> Among your people outside our song.

He says:

> You were some place real. Never knew one of you blokes to get somewhere real. You don't remember it now . . . You will.

She says:

> When you remember where you were . . . it will come years from now . . . remember us too then.

*   *   *

As they predicted, and I must have been fifteen at the time of the dream, I remembered my dream just yesterday while I was sitting in the Jardin Anglais, where the Rhone leaves Lake Geneva, having my lunch.

Who had been dreaming? Perhaps it was something more personal. Yet the dream was charged with the presence of life and death and absence . . . there was a return from a far country. There was friendship and a fidelity of painful beauty among those who needed no promises and exacted none.

A recovery of a truth, of a promise that is simply promise itself . . . without terms.

The magical marvel of a building whose each spiral was threaded and inlaid of pattern that was the stuff of heaven; a haven. Where "no one was themselves," four persons came into their own. And I was implicated in it all.

Yes, dear friends . . . watch and wait. Do not abdicate doing but, as the old song says, "lay thy deadly doing down."

An Extraordinary Happening

To my surprise, after having distributed these reports, I heard from the group that had broken off many years before in the form of a package on my doorstep, which should be self-explanatory.

Dear Merlin,

    I am in receipt of your "reports." I shared it with members of our "splinter group." We liked it. We thought we could add something of value to it. We will use your format.

The Group Who Rode Away

Temporary Secretary

Arthur

CHAPTER FIFTEEN

Ferirefiz

Gemma Lazovich, Feirefiz, is a woman of the old school.
She can ride a horse and is a skilled archer after the style of
the ladies of the Scythian tribes that gave imperial Rome so much
trouble.

*   *   *

Well, well, well. Who is Madelein?
Australia . . . Dream time!

the didgeridoo—
fashioned from a log,
hollowed by the green ant people.

I started to get at the last chapter, Madelein, by roaming
around the footpaths near LeBeaux where legend says Mary
Magdalene spent her last days. On dozens of the tiny footpath

shrines in the area, the original dedication to the Magdalene had been supplanted by the "holy family."

Where else has this happened?

In that last chapter of your reports.

But it didn't.

Back in Paris weeks later, reading an article in *Architecture Aujourd'hui* by Sybil Moholy-Nagy. A university campus being built from zero in Chicago, Illinois—well!

Here in Paris was the first university from zero, 1060.

Then, a hundred years later, St. John's College, Oxford.

Still following the spoor set in your last chapter of reports of the Magdalene, I'm standing at Magdalene College in Oxford, an intriguing place. Its library "tower" persisted through the centuries despite all efforts to take it down when they redid the college a number of times and fought over its architecture. And the tower is its very gateway.

Here in the twentieth century, the rooms of Magdalene College saw the beginning of the Oxford movement, the Settlement System, the "Inklings."

As if prodded by the spirit of the Inklings, I decided without further ado to be off to Chicago. Though as you know, years ago I had been as far west as Olivet, I never did get to Chicago.

It is 1965. I must present this account following the advice of that old rogue Alfred Korzybski to "time bind" events. He had taught his theories of general semantics and Null A exactly where we had our meetings at Olivet College in, I believe, 1937.

So, 1965, Chicago.

The Blackstone Hotel.

I buy an issue of *Architectural Forum* from the newsstand. Featured . . . "The Shrine of the Book" from zero in Jerusalem by Frederick Kiesler.

Featured . . . the University of Illinois at Chicago Circle from zero, designed by Walter Netsch.

remarkable issue
timely for me
account of the site selection
for UIACC.
On the site of Hull House!

When SOM was exploring sites, they began with ninety, which then narrowed down to four and then the mayor., Richard Daley offered the site at Halsted and Polk and the surrounding area. Developers went frenzied and took it to court because it had been designated for urban renewal. The Supreme Court (whether of Illinois or the United States, it did not say in the article) decided in favor of Netsch and SOM,

provided that Hull House would be preserved.
You'll find something about the Keisler piece in the appendix.
I entered the campus from the north entry
over the elevated granite walkways,
which had iron chains fixed to granite bollards.
It called to mind
the iron chain bridges I had crossed in Tibet
built by the legendary
Tangtong Gyalpo
in the mid-fourteen hundreds
of our counting.

I lingered on the walkway while students were bustling to get to classes. A pity the kids couldn't pause to appreciate this approach. Not bad for a twentieth-century approach to a "topos." Tangtong Gyalpo had called his "iron bridges," along with the stupa or temple, which would be on one or the other shore, a "representation of Enlightened Mind."
We Europeans might call that an "Eikon of Sophia."

The campus was still under construction. Only the central core and its plaza, the library, the administration building, the student union, part of engineering, and some classrooms for humanities, which were located in lyrical modest cubes on the ground surrounded by grass and trees, were done.

Following the walkway to the central plaza, I came to the design element that had caught my attention in *Architectural Forum* at breakfast. The stairway amphitheater. One comes upon it and stops. That is its virtue—it is a *place* where one stops. A "place" where "space" is utilized.

The Tibetans give a dramatic and contradictory pictorial representation of this numina by a dancing female figure with the head of a lion: Seng Dongma, the "lion-headed dakini."

But here it is a "stop." A discontinuity which is nevertheless a continuity.

Clearly the architect had some brains, was worth his salt.

An architect worth his salt?

I turned my steps to the west, to the massive library. Almost at the very entrance is a glass case with a magnificent volume of *The Divine Comedy* well displayed and protected. It seems this is the seven hundredth anniversary of Dante's birth. Is this Chicago?

I need to think about this.

I have good walking shoes and decide to get *off* campus and to ponder my impressions, which are initially overwhelming. I am told that just a few blocks from the campus is a still-thriving Greek town with shops, cafes, and nightclubs. Wonder of our century, several blocks from the "campus starting from zero" is a village of Greeks within the city! And soon I am hearing the lovely sounds of demotici. In a window is a book jacket with the famous portrait of Dante. It graces Nikos Kazantzakis's translation of the poet. Synchronicity. Who could resist?

Sitting.

I stare into my coffee.

It gets cold. I don't order another yet.

The waiter sings in Greek as he brings me a fresh, hot cup. I don't know Greek, but the sounds are beautiful and I come back to myself,

"Is that Kazantzakis in the window for sale?"

"No, it belongs to the owner of this shop and it's in the window to honor the poet Dante's seven hundredth anniversary."

I savor the fresh, thick coffee. A distinguished elderly gentleman seats himself. Having heard my accent, he courteously speaks to me in French. "I'm Takis. I own this shop. And, like Nikos himself was, I am a Dantisté."

The conversation that ensued was enlightening and very long, so I will only present the pith of what Takis had to say:

Dantistés

Dantistés are not to be confused with the Dante Alighieri Society, which is a political entity with many branches in America. Many "well-meaning" people belong to this organization, just as many well-meaning people may have belonged to entities, such as the Nazis Party, the Communist Party, the Republican

Party, the Democratic Party, the Soldiers of Christ, the Soldiers of Satan, the Green Dragon Society, the Golden Dawn, and the list could go on and on. These "clubs" are interested in power. The Society of Dantistés (henceforth SOD) is not. The clubs, factions, can be what Dante described as leading to hell where only two forces operate, will and desire.

The Tibetans have a saying, "If you can *learn* to have a good will, you can reach your desires." The *good* and capacity to *learn* have to be added to will and desire, but one cannot do that from *within* that sphere. One requires what Dante called "the intellectual good." The Dantistés work and study and maybe sometimes pray and do not club.

A good case in point, which I will use to demonstrate how we Dantistés operate, will be a specific person, an honorary member, Mikhail Greuzenberg. He was known as Borodin. And he walked this street, Halsted, that we are on and he was a friend of Jane Addams. He was vilified by many, including a former student, Mao Tse-Tung. He was admired by another, Chou-en Lai, and met his end in the "Gulag Archipelago."

(Of course, I remembered a brief mention of him in Malraux's "Man's Fate." I mentioned it to Takis and he snorted. He went on with his story.)

In 1890, Jane Addams opened Hull House. This neighborhood was full of immigrants. Italians who had been followers of Mazzini, Russian Jews who were fleeing the pogroms, Greeks smelling trouble came. Within the decade, there were some Assyrians and Armenians who were fleeing Sultan Hamid's genocide, which took five hundred thousand Armenian lives in 1896. There were more Bulgarians than in the largest city of Bulgaria and they all came to Chicago. And the Italians kept coming.

(He urged me to get and read *Twenty Years at Hull House* by Jane Addams and her sequel, *Another Twenty Years at Hull House*. Though I admired her, I had never read her. I am limiting this portion to his explication of Borodin as a particular example of how SOD works.)

Borodin was from Riga and passionate about the labor movement as an ideal, not a stepping stone to power. He came to Chicago after the aborted 1905 revolution in Russia. He taught English at Hull House to Russians and also taught classes in American citizenship. The idealism of the labor movement, which began at Hull House, was palpable. It had succeeded in abolishing child-labor abuse and exploitation in Illinois, only to have the exploitation restored by the Illinois Supreme Court within a year. This inspired the young Borodin. The idealistic streak became visible during a critical event in Douglas Park on the west side of Chicago. Borodin was the moderator of a large labor rally. At a certain point, a Roman Catholic priest (one of the good ones) who supported fairness for working people was addressing the crowd. A Russian representative to the meeting, a Bolshevik, came on to the stage to object and make him leave. Borodin supported the priest. A fight broke out throughout the crowd and was only broken up by the intervention of the police. It made all the Chicago newspapers. We of the SOD had a glimpse of Borodin's character and decided to watch his career and help where possible.

When the Bolsheviks succeeded in trumping the moderate revolution with Lenin's arrival in St. Petersburg, all the communist exiles hurried to return.

Borodin was in no hurry to return. He no doubt had heard from the Armenians and Greeks in Chicago, as well as from informed Germans who had been part of the German immigrant wave in the 1840s, that Lenin was a tool of the German high command. According to well-informed Armenians, the success of the Bolsheviks was a result of "German meddling." The German high command desired at all costs to end the war on the eastern front. General Ludendorf was certain that when the wave of German soldiers was released from combat on the eastern front to join the western front, they would overwhelm the Entente powers in France. Then they could return to the East with their Ottoman allies to finish building a German-Ottoman empire all across Asia.

The Armenians in Chicago, as well as Greeks, were painfully aware of this since it gave the Ottoman Turks liberty to massacre the remaining Armenians in southern Russia and northern Turkey between 1915 and 1917. Added to the 1.5 million Armenians already murdered, a further fifty thousand to seventy-five thousand Armenians who could have been saved were genocidely massacred, thanks to Lenin's treacherous agreement to not honor Russia's commitment as a member of the Entente.

Borodin was not in a hurry to go back to Russia with what he now knew. One of the members of the SOD recollected for us a very serious conversation with Borodin, whom everyone called Berg, shortened from Greutzenberg. Borodin expressed his dismay at the complicity of Lenin with the German high command. Our man listened. It seemed Borodin thought that the labor movement in America would fail, just as the emancipation of the slaves within a decade of the Civil War began to fail, leading to worse and worse Jim Crow Laws in the South. And, also, the child labor laws, which his friend Jane Addams had accomplished, were revoked by the courts. Vainglorious lunatics like J. Edgar Hoover had equated such things as labor rights, children's rights, the rights of women, immigrant rights, the liberation of the black population, and so forth with sedition. Berg asked, "What kind of country is this?" Our colleague said, "A very young country, which both Samuel Johnson and De Tocqueville described as suffering from that condition Dante called 'the Cornice of Avarice' as a national trait. But a trait that could be tempered with time. Being a very young country, the American psyche suffers from a boom or bust mentality, like a drunken teenager riding a horse who almost falls off on one side then almost falls off on the other."

Borodin was silent for a long time. Then he said to our man, "Of course, in fact, Lenin may not live long. He has a brain illness. As a child he needed support to hold his head upright. All my friends went back. Here, in America, Jane and her friends can continue the good fight. They know their way around this country." Borodin decided to go back to Russia and take part in building the Communist state, but he never was quite a true-blooded Bolshevik. He became a famous Comintern agent. (There is an interesting portrait of him by Clare Sheridan, Winston Churchill's famous communist cousin, which shows how thin his Bolshevik mask really was.)

It should be mentioned that none of the exiles from the Russian 1905 episode had the privilege that Borodin had, to being exposed to some of the greatest people and ideas of our time. This helped to prepare a foundation for him that he may not have been aware of at the time and which was of greatest importance to the world, as we of the SOD perceived it.

That foundation was possible in Chicago in those days. And it was particularly centered at Hull House. The basis for modern architecture, the arts and crafts movement, organized social work, the educational ideas of John Dewey, the ideal of racial equality, and J.B. Yeats's idea of modern theater were all given expression here. Also, Chicago absorbed the impact of the first World Congress of Religions, the first introduction to Asian cultures in America, the impact of Vivikenanda's visit, and the philosophy of Rabindranath Tagore.

Borodin also could have met survivors of the Hull House community's brave struggle against the smallpox epidemic of 1895-1896 and of their use of that event to leverage the first steps toward labor organization by closing down the sweat-shop system. *This manufacturing system had been discovered to be sending smallpox infection all over rural America through infected garments, blankets, etc.*

None of the revolutionaries, not Lenin, Trotsky nor Stalin, had had the privilege of such experience consciously internalized.

The SOD could see that, potentially, Berg-Borodin might not be a power-grabbing type of Communist but a person of principle. To use the measure of Canto 24 of "Purgatorio," he was not really a politician but essentially a poet. This can be seen by his choice of the revolutionary name Borodin, the name of an artist.

(I will leave out Takis's account of intervening years and pick up at the Chinese Revolution.)

The SOD knew things that the revolutionary leader Sun Yat Sen did not know. This was thanks to our uniquely "honorable access" to information from both the Black Hand and the Carbonari societies of Italy.

A Chinese youth became the protégé of Julian Carr, one of the founders of Duke University who was a devout Methodist and the most wealthy and powerful man in the tobacco industry. His product was whimsically called Bull Durham, after the popular British mustard Durhams which was produced in the town of the same name. The goal of

American Christians was to convert China to Christianity and make China available to American commerce. (This aim had been openly expressed in congress in 1900 as the purpose of the Philippine conquest.)

Charlie Soong, the protégé, returned to China to do missionary work. Through his extended his family, he was very well connected with the most powerful Tongs, which controlled the harbors and the opium trade. He had his daughters educated in America and Christianized. One daughter, Ching-Ling Soong, became the wife of Dr. Sun Yat Sen who was the leader and president of the new emerging China. The second daughter, May-Ling Soong, became the wife of Generalissimo Chiang Kai-Shek. Ai-Ling Soong, the third daughter, became the richest woman in the world and was later based in Boston, Massachusetts.

At the time Borodin arrived in China to become the Comintern agent, the Russians were greenhorns and knew nothing of this "landscape," nor did the Communists in China. Sun Yat Sen and Borodin hit it off, as did Hari Prasad Shastri, a remarkable Hindu mystic who was a teacher of Dr. Sen.

The SOD knew that the struggle against the warlords would not succeed in anything resembling a just society. This was obvious given the overall plans of Germany, the remnants of the Ottomans, the plans of Japanese secret societies, particularly the Green Dragon Society, and, of course, the interests of American commerce and missionary activities which consciously or unconsciously were supporting the opium trade with tobacco thrown in.

At that time and place, possibly the only representatives of the idea of the dignity of labor was held by the small Communist Party. The situation can be captured in this exchange between an American consul and Dr. Sun Yat Sen:

"Do you realize who Borodin is?" (a communist and a Jew). Mischievously, Dr. Sen answered, "Lafayette?"

The Kuomingtang, Sun Yat Sen's coalition of communists, republicans, and labor, was betrayed by Chiang Kai-Shek and the Tongs, who controlled the docks in Shanghai and turned on the unarmed workers, killing three thousand. At the time, Borodin was in Wuhan suffering from bad dysentery. In three previous years, he had succeeded in leading Sun Yat Sen's forces in beating the warlords. For two of those years, the famous Chou En Lai had been his secretary. The SOD had forewarned him of the powers of the opium and tobacco interests on the docks. And we'd also warned him of the dangers of Chiang Kai-Shek.

But being a bit naïve, he did not want to believe this of Chiang, since it was he who had discovered him and had promoted his career, raising him to power even before he married into the Soong family.

In Wuhan, it must have been a shock for him to realize that all of the information we had given him about Chiang Kai-Shek and of the Tongs' control over the docks was correct. He took advantage of our offer to get his wife and sons to safety by sea (of course, there was a huge reward for his head) and of our offer of the escape route for him and for Madam Sun Yat Sen, which we planned for them across the Gobi Desert.

His parting speech demonstrates his poetic view of history.

"Do not suppose that the Chinese revolution is ending or that it has failed in any but the most temporary sense. It will go back underground. It will become an illegal movement, suppressed by counter revolution and beaten down by reaction and Imperialism; but it has learned how to organize, how to struggle. Sooner or later, a year, two years, five years from now, it will rise to the surface again. It may be defeated a dozen times, but in the end it must conquer. What has happened here will not be forgotten."

It must be understood that most well-meaning American missionaries were blissfully ignorant of any of the truth of the situation in China, dazzled by their non-Christic dream of a Christianized world.

As Dantistés, we regret that they had not heeded their teacher's warning, "You travel a thousand miles to make one convert and turn them into a worse spawn of hell than yourselves." Which, by the way, the great Spanish poet Juan Yerpes, aka St. John of the Cross, did take heed when he opposed the plans of his order, the Carmelites, to send missionaries to the Americas.

Takis had much more to say, but for the purposes of this chapter, this example of how SOD operates is sufficient.

My conversation with Takis gave me an impression of someone who could help my immediate exploration. I asked if he knew Walter Netsch, the architect. He did. Could he arrange a meeting, an interview? Yes. He went to the phone of the taverna and then came back.

"In one hour you will meet Netsch in a restaurant, the Tradewinds, on Rush Street. It is owned by an Italian friend of mine." He drew me a map and instructions how to get there. The "L" at the university to downtown. The subway to Chicago Avenue and State Street. Then a two-block walk. "Don't bother with a cab. Take ordinary transit." He disappeared into the back.

I went out on to the street, got the "L," and reached the Tradewinds with five minutes to spare.

No one is in the restaurant.

Which has white tablecloths.

One waiter dressed in black pants.

White shirt and white apron.

A tall, thin man with a loose-fitting jacket comes in and joins me.

"The French woman?"

"Oui."

"Hungry?"

"Oui."

He waves. The waiter comes over and presents a large menu. Netsch orders lamb chops. I order the same. After a pause, I quietly asked Netsch how this place makes money. He whispers, "I don't think it does."

I tell him about reading Sybil Moholy's piece and also the piece in *Architectural Forum* and that I visited the university this morning. I had needed to get away to ponder the impressions of the project, and that's how I met Takis.

"What were your impressions?"

I told him about the Tibetan iron-chain bridge builder and the walkways. He was delighted.

"I never heard of this Tangtong Gyalpo, but when I was working in the Aleutians during the war, I met a Mongolian who told me about those bridges, still functioning after five hundred years. I never forgot it. Well, you *are* a serious woman. Ask what you want."

There was a very long silence.

"All right. The central plaza with the quinquinx."

"That will take a long answer. You may or may not know that I designed the US Air Force Academy in Colorado Springs, but in securing that commission, the firm I designed for, Skidmore Owings and Merrill (SOM), was up against Kitty Hawk, which was using Frank Lloyd Wright. It was an explosive encounter during which I felt very insulted by Mr. Wright. I took it personally. SOM won the contract, probably in great measure due to my experience building military bases during World War II and my experience working with the military and familiarity with the military way of doing things. Later, my complete plan was accepted except for the chapel. I broke down at the hearing when the chapel plans were rejected. My boss Ned Owings came up to me and recommended I take a trip at the company's expense and take a look at the architecture in Europe, rest, and think.

During this trip, two things began to happen. I realized much of what Wright had said was appropriate. And also the actual tactile reality of geometry consciously and reverently explored as Idea and Ideal was sharply present, from Stonehenge to Aachen, from Mont St. Michel to Chartres, and was also present in the remarkable civic spaces in Italy, though not the buildings. Italy had good civic space, good vernacular houses, and lousy churches. I came back to the States a different man. I was emotionally ready to recognize my "destined" mate when I met her, Dawn Clark, whom I married. Dawn is an energetic social activist.

Now when our firm was offered the site near Hull House, you can imagine how excited Dawn and I both were. But none of this could be public, of course, given the insane politics of Chicago. Our first step in establishing a program to begin our design work was to ask the existing faculty of the University of Illinois in Chicago located at Navy Pier what they thought they wanted and needed. Their response was totally disappointing. Almost without exception, they could only think of convenient faculty parking, good space for coats and hats, and comfortable faculty offices where students could easily come by and hang out.

Both Dawn and I realized that if we had children we wouldn't entrust them to these "professors."

We went back to the whole idea of civilized liberal education. Liberal comes from the idea "to liberate." The individual needs to be liberated through education from ignorance, hence the "liberal arts." One would hope that the student becomes liberated enough to choose a major. They could study such majors as behavioral sciences or engineering or architecture or humanities. My solution had to be to *design* a campus to do the job by *its character*.

Socrates called himself a midwife who could assist the delivery of the real person through a certain kind of confrontation, what a modern Socrates, George Gurdjieff, called "being-confrontative mentation." I called the style I developed "confrontative architecture," though its critics called it brutalism. The idea was to present a confrontation by which students could be helped to orient themselves in a complex and pretty hostile urban environment. Neither "packaging" nor a "Disneyland Ivy League" could do the job. By the charter of the university's program, the students were to be kids from the neighborhoods of Chicago. The organizers foresaw an enrollment of twenty thousand students in less than ten years. It was to be a real city university.

"You arrive and view the whole city, not a bird's eye view from above but a tree-height view, *partly* freed from the city, so that a student can react instinctively and creatively about the city where he lives."

The lamb chops had long arrived and were getting cold on the plate. We ate. After we finished eating, he indicated a few elements to notice. The "absolute golden ratio" of the administration building, the plan for Art and Architecture building not yet finished.

As we parted, he smiled a bit bleakly and urged me to not brush away any of the implications that may occur to me. He said, "To quote Einstein, 'Take your own thinking seriously.'"

"The central core, what you call the quinquinx, is dangerous to the status quo. The city fathers won't realize it right away any more than their counterparts in Athens until the impact of the 'Octave' had been felt. Then they no doubt will tear it out, but by then, thirty years or so of Chicago students will have begun to think about their city and society, hopefully in a more liberated way . . . perhaps."

He gives me a packet and he is gone.

It was already turning dark on Chicago Avenue and Rush Street, so I hailed a cab to my hotel. I spread out some of the drawings of the plans Walter had slipped me before he left.

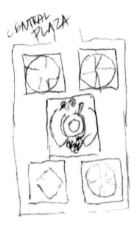

The Central Core

There was a sketch of Stonehenge.

Stonehenge

A sketch of Aachen cathedral where Charlemagne was crowned Holy Roman Emperor in AD.

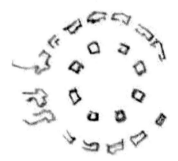

Aachen Cathedral

Then a sketch of the Sarsen stones of Stonehenge overlaid on Aachen Cathedral's palace chapel and the Sarsen stones coincided at the same scale.

Sarsen stones of Stonehenge overlaid on
Aachen Cathedral's palace chapel

At least two thousand years separated the constructs. A sketch of a sunbeam striking the golden orb above the throne at Aachen on the traditional day when emperors were crowned, June 21 at noon.

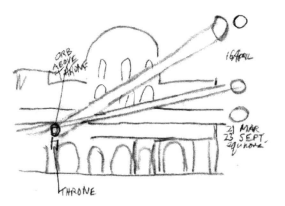

Sunbeam striking the golden orb above the throne at Aachen

The midsummer day's sun at Stonehenge also had a specific marking point. The quinquinx at UIACC is connected to all this. There was a note with the sketches. "I find myself enjoying playing with different geometries. Walter."

I studied the materials carefully before I went to sleep so I could have purpose when I visited the campus next day. At breakfast, I noticed an article in the press that the city fathers had planned to tear down the important Wright Robie House, which was saved by an intervention from the New York developer Zeckendorf. And also that the Louis Sullivan Auditorium was saved by the New York Tischman Brothers. For a French woman, this is almost unbelievable. What a country America is. Absolutely anti-historical and anti-science and anti-art if it weren't for these NY Jews.

The Blackstone Hotel is very close to the auditorium building. So I decide to go a few steps and see if I can get a peek. It is under rehabilitation by the Tischmans. The hall had been used as a USO dancehall during World War II, and all the walls were painted battleship grey to cover the gold leaf. The Tischman Brothers were trying to salvage elements and restore it to being a concert hall. One of the workers demonstrated the acoustics for me, which were truly amazing. They also told me that part of the office components of the auditorium project were merged with the historic fine arts building and had been turned into a new university called Roosevelt University. A little bit of historical preservation in Chicago anyway but coming, as I said, from New York.

I inquired at the university about the Sullivan-Wright legacy that still survived. A lot of homes still functioned, but my informant lamented that what he thought was a truly great building had fallen to the wrecking ball—Midway Gardens. Suddenly, he became animated. "One of our faculty, a professor of public administration, lives in a Wright house. His office is in the next building, the Fine Arts Building. You go out the lobby here on to Michigan Avenue and the first building entrance to your left will be the Fine Arts Building. There is a bank of antique elevators that could take you up. Would you like to talk to him?" When I nodded, he dialed and asked if Dr. Watson would see me. Receiving an affirmative, he told me the number of the office. I think it was the sixth floor. And off I went.

It was an archaic elevator like many in France, open with wrought-iron doors. The elevator man was a cheerful Irishman. He took me up to the sixth floor. I walked down the hall, and soon I was in a bright, spacious, south-facing office of the old auditorium building complex.

George Watson told me his family lived in the Isadore Heller House. A fine three-story building Wright designed in 1903. I regretted that I wouldn't have time to visit it, since I had a tight schedule. But I wondered if he had seen Midway Gardens before it was demolished. He said he had come to Chicago too late.

Dr. Watson's secretary had been listening to our conversation and volunteered that her father had known the building. Watson perked up, "Rhoda, I never knew that." "Well, I don't talk about him much." Rhoda was a petite, attractive girl in her early twenties. She could have been French the way she carried herself.

I said, "Well, I'm really interested in some of these buildings, the early public spaces that Wright designed." Rhoda invited me to dinner, that is, if I would travel with her to Skokie and if her family agreed. She made a phone call. They did agree, and I was to meet Rhoda in front of the Fine Arts Building at five o'clock. That gave me the whole day at UIACC to meditate and reflect about Mary Magdalene (don't forget, that is the theme of this chapter and the quinquinx).

I entered the campus the same way as before using the mass transit system. This time I walked directly to the central amphitheater, which was human scale, chamber-music scale. I could imagine a string quartet in the center and students sitting all around. Then I explored the so-called four excedra. NE, SE, SW, and NW. The plaza, a golden section rectangle.

Due east of the center of the amphitheater, on the other side of a monstrous student union, is Hull House.

Cancel the student union. Consider it, not its function but the building itself, the "necessary evil" for the whole enterprise. The strong *approximate* center line runs from Hull House, through the amphitheater, to the rather nice library on the west side.

And—at this particular moment, July 1965,
celebrating the seven hundredth anniversary of the birth of
Dante.
At this moment let us say
Fifty or sixty years earlier
at Hull House,
William Butler Yeats entertained Jane Addams
and her amateur players,
showed them how to stage a play without scenery.
Just a few years earlier in 1901, Frank Lloyd Wright delivered
the lecture, "The Art and Craft of the Machine."

Now each of the so-called excedras could have had a soloist in the center and students hanging out on the stone steps around them. Now, if the kids are wearing brightly colored clothes, you've got a pretty "cool scene."

> And then, look.
> The central amphitheater is open to east and west,
> trees eventually planned
> Eastern window—Hull House,
> western window—library.
> *Humanityness*. Bravo, Netsch!

By the time I returned to the Fine Arts Building, I had an enormous amount of material to digest, which I will spare the reader. I'm a little early, so I browse in a gift shop facing Michigan Avenue run by a woman who looks to be of mid-Eastern origin. I suspect she is Lebanese, so I try conversation in French. She responds in French, which is a common tongue among cultured Lebanese. Her name is Wadia Basil.

Curious.

I spot Rhoda through the window. I bid adieu to Wadia and go out to meet her. After a short walk, I'm fascinated to climb up to the famous "L" of Chicago where the North Shore Line that goes to Skokie is boarded. The conversation on the ride is a little stilted, but we find a common enthusiasm in science fiction. She has another year in school to get her BA. She wants to get away from home. On the several-block walk from the station to her house, we pass a building with a sign that catches my attention: "Iranian Hebrew Congregation." I remark it, and Rhoda, whose family name is Goldberg, mentions that Skokie is a suburb with a very large Jewish population. Her father is Louis and her mother Helen. They are very friendly, the meal is good. As soon as polite, I ask about Midway Gardens. Mr. Goldberg was an ordinary hardworking Jew, very authentic, himself. He had severe leg problems which led him to have to earn a living selling insurance, not his preferred means of livelihood.

Years before, he had been a junior partner of the demolition contracting firm which demolished Midway Gardens. The experience left him with a deep sense of contradiction. The company had been ruined while demolishing the building. They had not been prepared for any building of such sound structure in Chicago. At the same time, they managed to preserve much of the fine detail and sculpture for the benefit of posterity. Mr. Goldberg had admired the beauty, harmony, proportion, and grace of the whole and the parts in a simple, direct, but hard-to-express way. But it had ruined their company. This deep wound of joy and sorrow had stayed with him, and although his outward demeanor was rough and pugnacious, he had a remarkable and fine quality of being.

I returned from this meeting quite chastened in my thirst "to know." At the desk at the Blackstone Hotel upon my return was an envelope from Takis labeled "a Dantisté view of some illustrious families of our time." A note from Takis:

You might find this amusing. The Dantistés view of the spiritual root systems of families with fancy and auspicious exteriors and with dubious content:

A) The Kennedys, who own Chicago's Merchandise Mart building and who have huge interests in whiskey and politics. You will find their roots with Count Ugolino.

B) The Dulles family, very active in politics and US "intelligence," who are well rooted with the of sphere Pope Boniface VIII.

C) The Luce family whose roots are fed from Gianni Schacchi and Myrrha.
"The judicious will understand."

Appendix I
Appendix Item: Shrine of the Book Jerusalem

I. The shrine consists of sixteen space units.

II. A lawn gently sloping down a very long retaining wall leading into a grove of trees with a circular platter of stone block to sit on.

III. The open plateau.

IV. The square fountain.

V. The protruding upper part of the vessel-dome covered with 271,000 white tiles, upon which at need the fountain sprays water for cooling.

VI. A black basalt wall 75 feet away that is about (*about* is very important when dealing with cosmology), about 60 feet long, 40 feet high (with a fire trough on top), and six feet thick—this of particular importance since 6's and 60's are connected to the tsar in ancient Babylonia.

VII. Open staircase leading down to a large rectangular patio.

VIII. To the right of the patio, a research library.

IX. Across from it, the then entrance to the shrine proper.

X. The entrance to a high exhibition hall facing the black basalt, which is descended 1 1/2 stories below the plateau. In it is a square opening with a large tubular bronze gate.

XI. Through the bronze gate, an underpass of seven platforms, each six inches lower than the next. To the left and right of these platforms, exhibition showcases for biblical manuscripts; beyond them . . .

XII. A 75-foot underpass supported by continuous arches connecting floor, wall, and ceiling and slightly inclined in opposite directions. The color of the concrete shades gradually from light blue-grey at the bottom to dark blue-black at the top.

XIII. Finally, a high, flat, chiseled stone wall containing a comparatively small bronze door split in half. It opens on one's approach and, once inside it, a few steps upward one enters . . .

XIV. The main vessel-dome, a container for the seven Dead Sea Scrolls. A circular shell construction of double parabolic design. Open at the top is a circle 6 feet 3 inches in diameter through which the daylight filters down the corrugated interior of the dome-vessel which has a diameter at the bottom of 8 feet.

XV. Two open stone staircases around the center of the dome-vessel lead down to a rough stone crypt 50 feet in diameter, which contains showcases with precious artifacts found in the Dead Sea region.

XVI. The exit from the dome area passes through one of the bronze doors into a corridor 28 feet long. The walls curve along an elevated stone foot path leading directly to . . .

XVII. An almost 200-foot open-air meditation walk flanked by two high stone walls and three cut-out openings through which one may view Jerusalem and its parliament. Continuing the walk, one reaches a door, which returns one to the common plaza of the public spaces. It is unusual to most but not to us Dantistés that two such thought-built works of architecture would be in the same issue of *Architectural Forum*.

XVIII. Kiesler designed this for seven Dead Sea Scrolls. No one realized that many more scrolls had been smuggled to Jordan during the 1948 war in the car boot of the wife of an American diplomat. They were recovered several years after the 1965 *Architectural Forum* article appeared. In fact, after the 1967 war after the Israelis captured all of Jerusalem. [A Hindu Rishi might have said that it was the karma of theft that produced the 1967 war for the scrolls to return to their rightful place.]

Appendix II

Copy of Letter from First Secretary of American Embassy,
Constantinople. Case Endorsed by Prof. H. S. Todd

COPY OF LETTER FROM FIRST SECRETARY OF AMERICAN EMBASSY,
CONSTANTINOPLE.   CASE ENDORSED BY PROF. H.A.TODD.

October 19,1922

Dear Allen:

Prince Magarino, whom you undoubtedly remember,
has recently been talking with Captain Hepburn as to the possibility of securing some kind of suitable work in the United
States. I presume that the most suitable work would be something along academic lines. Captain Hepburn asked me to write
you on this subject and inquire whether you know of any possibilities of this kind. I enclose a brief memorandum concerning Prince Magarine which may be helpful in considering
this question.

With warm regards,

Faithfully yours,

G. Rowland Shaw

Allen W. Dulles, Esquire,
Chief of the Division of Near Eastern Affairs,
State Department, Washington.

Appendix III

Feirefiz's reflection on Takis's note he left regarding those who "with colors fairer painted their foul ends":

A) Kennedys, and with colors fairer, painted their foul ends—probably a simple matter of family dynamics spiced with hypocrisy. i.e., a couple of examples which could be multiplied. For example, Joe did not win his party's nomination for the US presidency against Roosevelt despite his promise that he could deliver "35 million Catholic votes" mainly against England. He was forced to withdraw his bid when his dossier was presented to Roosevelt by the British intelligence service. Joe Kennedy had used the American Embassy as an avenue for Nazi espionage while America was still neutral.

• He tried to get guarantees that he would acquire the Haig and Haig distributorship for himself even before the second World War even got really going (this caused hilarity among Russians, who were snooping and also among Intrepid's people).

• This bent was carried through later by his sons in an Ugolino-type family structuring.

B) Dulles played everybody against everybody for himself like Pope Boniface VIII did (note copy of state department letter above). He was in charge of Ottoman Oil. Betrayed, the Entente promises to the Armenians and the Kurds. He then took a two-year leave of absence to "pursue law degree" but really arranged the largest loan in world history to a foreign country. Thirty billion 1920s dollars to

Prussia, no doubt helping Germany rearm for World War II. This pattern of betrayal, consciously or unconsciously, continued for the rest of his time in the OSS and perhaps, even worse, in the CIA even as late as the 1950s when the CIA got rid of Mossadegh. In Allen Dulles's daughter's words, "we got rid of Mossadegh because he didn't have the balls to stand up to the Russians." Public record on all of this is now easily available.*

C) The Luces. Everyone knows their story and the effluvia of their lives . . . suicides, scandals, etc.

---

* Incidentally, oil was a part of the US interests to take over Great Britain's former empire after the war. We forced England to pay lend lease funds immediately at the end of the war so that English life in the decade following World War II had greater hardship and starvation than during the war. A good example of this aim is Pat Hurley's letter to FDR in December 1943 advising him on how to take over Iran's oil, etc., from the British. At the time, it was not public knowledge (and it was not known to FDR) that Pat Hurley was a highly paid consultant of Sinclair Oil. This is only the tip of the iceberg concerning these types of people in high positions in the US.

We also forced England to pay all Allied expenses in SE Asia. We did this despite the fact that England was broke. We used this brokenness as a means to blackmail England to agree with us on any number of issues. We also opposed Churchill's advice to eliminate and not support Amin Husseini, who in 1928 was the inspiration of the Muslim brotherhood in Egypt, and then in the 1940s the inspiration for the secret police of Syria, and after the partition the creator of the SIS in Pakistan. Our decisions about Amin Husseini were probably motivated by US desire to supplant Britain as an influence in the Middle East and Asia.

Appendix IV

A) Incidental notes on Amin Husseini, Grand Mufti of Jerusalem, demonstrating how US interests conflicted with world interests. The Mufti's diary found by Allied intelligence quoted Hitler as assuring him, "We will reach the Southern Caucasus, then the hour of the liberation of the Arabs will have arrived. The hour will strike when you will be the lord of the supreme word and not only the conveyor of our declarations. You will be the man to direct the Arab force and, at that moment, I cannot imagine what would happen to the western peoples."

Amin complained to von Ribbentrop. He complained that despite the Nazi declaration to destroy the so-called "Jewish national home," the Jews were being exchanged for Palestinian Germans and German prisoners of war. All such exchanges involving Jews were stopped. The result was that hundreds of thousands of Hungarian Jews were liquidated as a "practical example of friendship" by Germany toward the Arab nation. Document NG-5461 Office of Chief of Counsel for War Crimes. The following expenditures were made in German Marks:

Mostly for Husseini and others. 800,000 Marks for him yearly and for others, 4,993,860 Deutsche Marks yearly budget of Nazis to Husseini.

B) Churchill asked the US and France to help catch Husseini. France winked, and the US, wishing to butter up the oil countries, refused to cooperate so the Mufti escaped to Cairo in a maneuver engineered by Marouf Dawalibi. Shortly thereafter, he was the greatest hero in the Arab world. However, when Israel succeeded in its war in 1948, he continued to work and reappeared in Karachi, Pakistan to preside over a twelve-day world Muslim congress. He called on the congress to engage in a full struggle against the non-Muslim Hindus of Indian and, of course, the Jews. He assured the delegates, "We shall meet with sword in hand on the soil of either Kashmir or Pakistan." Six months later, King Abdulla, who was a moderate leader of Jordan, was assassinated when he was about to enter the mosque of Omar. Many other moderate Arabs were assassinated within months of this. The assassin of King Abdulla was the member of Palestinian group call Jihad Mukadess, or in English, "sacred struggle organization."

C) The fact that he was allowed to escape and was shortly rewarded with opulent residences in Cairo, Damascus, and other places for the rest of his life mostly because of US and also French aims in those regions. Also able to establish organizations, which within time became official in Pakistan, Syria, and Iraq despite Churchill's warnings, is an indication of shortsightedness of people with an insatiable appetite for oil. At least this is an opinion of SOD.

D) The above needs to be looked at in conjunction with our brief mention of the Armenian and Kurdish liquidations, because it seems that Amin Husseini had been an officer in the Ottoman Empire army.

CHAPTER SIXTEEN

Trevrizent

From a document I had found in the Olivet library:

This night we had an amazing group in the library. Usually only one or two of the "stars" who dropped by Olivet were there. But tonight, there was a galaxy.

August 1935—

Monday night—Carl Sandberg, Sherwood Anderson, Frank Lloyd Wright, Golo Mann and his sister Erika (son and daughter of Thomas Mann), Alfred Korzybski, Ford Maddox Ford (Fordie for short), Joe Brewer, the college president. Then there were non-stars, assorted faculty and friends.

Tonight, Fordie reads a piece sent by a friend of his who had died last November, A. R. Orage. The piece was a quote from a work by Orage's teacher, George Gurdjieff. Many of us had heard of him. In fact, a recent faculty member, George Hansen, had played Gurdjieff's piano music from manuscript for the Taliesin Fellowship, Frank Lloyd Wright's school. This was during a visit of Gurdjieff to Taliesin in March 1934.

Hansen, a Wisconsin native, was visiting there since every aspiring Wisconsin young man wanted to look it over. When George had described his meeting with Gurdjieff to me, his laconic comment about him was, "I'm on his side."

Now why Fordie decided this was an appropriate reading for us was because the ostensible subject was the human problem of slavery. Olivet had been one of the first abolitionist colleges in America, having been founded along with Oberlin College by a man named Shipherd. Olivet's founding was in 1844 or 1846 and had been dedicated to, in the school's words, "the furtherance of social and individual responsibility." Fordie had the idea that the thoughts in this paper were interesting to be read particularly in the library of an abolitionist college and that we might all enjoy them. Gurdjieff, in Paris, has been writing a vast epic presenting a critique of human life on Earth.

"Historical data which have reached contemporary people concerning what really did occur in the past clearly show that people of former epochs did not divide into two streams of life but that all flowed along in a single river. The general life of mankind has been divided into two streams since the time of what is called the Tikliamishian civilization which directly preceded the Babylonian civilization. It was from then on that there gradually began to be that organization of the life of mankind dividing people into masters and slaves. Also to be either masters or slaves in a collective existence among children like ourselves of our common creator is unworthy of human beings."

The above is verbatim. My grasp of the purport is this: There was simply a single stream of life, work and aspiration that graced the human spirit with development and proper spiritual growth. This would be talking about the period of time before the so called Flood. After that famous event the human psyche became bent and there was no longer a single stream of humanity moving toward development but instead there were two streams. There were the streams of those whose minds and souls who were influenced by the idea that human beings could own other human beings and there were those who were free of this idea. Slavery itself affirms by its institutions the concept that humanity has no intrinsic worth. Whether people are slave owners or slaves or those in between, those who accept this idea gradually begin to lose the sense of even their own worth. And to come to the understanding that there *is* this worth, many religions had to be developed to remind people of their basic worth. Unfortunately since it began to occur that human life could not seem to proceed economically without slaves, even the religions often supported this idea of slavery. And many techniques had to be developed then to free humans from this upside down perception.

When Fordie had finished reading this piece we fell to talking about these slaveries and freedom. The conversation that followed was great fun. Korzybski insisted that the idea of slavery came about as a linguistic maneuver. "Yes," he said, "it stands to reason that the tower of Babel was a poetic figure of the linguistic maneuvers to allow one group to dominate another group."

One of us (not one of the stars) pointed out that the biblical account did show that the hubris of the builders of the tower was the product of lying and deception, for the biblical text does say that instead of mortar, the builders used slime or bitumen, and also mud for stone, so clearly the poem of the building of the tower is a critique of people not using things according to their nature. It's pretty clear that in the hot desert of Babylon, mud held together by slime won't get you very high off the ground. Our conversation then went into all kinds of permutations.

I have just quoted from a document I had found in the Olivet library. For me, a person more interested in the modern world, the implications were very fascinating for my Elizabethan studies. If we take slavery as our theme, the world of the sixteenth century that was witness to the wars of the Spanish Empire against the Ottoman Empire, slavery had become an essential economic concern. Islam had never in principle opposed slavery and had embraced it from its early times. The numerous slave revolts of the tenth century and others attest to this. Christianity always had difficulties with slavery as an institution due to its origin, but because of economic factors, the doctors of law at the University of Bologna had determined that it was quite legitimate to have slaves, provided they were not Christian slaves. So the Spanish Empire, in order to maintain an economic balance with the Ottomans, shipped non-Christian slaves (black) from Africa to the new world, which created the economic basis to continue the war and to afford great wealth to the possible Roman Catholic communities. The bankers of Genoa and Venice provided the capital for the Hapsburgs of Europe. The Protestants mostly objected to slavery, so in England in particular, a struggle between the Protestant ideals and the established church still embracing these Roman concepts led to great tensions within the English court at the time of Elizabeth. Britain became engaged in a life-and-death struggle with the Spanish Empire.

Obviously, not all members of the Spanish Empire were scoundrels. As a matter of fact, the Hopi people of the American Southwest have a tradition that the Holy Roman Emperor Charles V had written a protocol guaranteeing sovereignty to all indigenous people of the New World. But within a few years, the military, the clergy, and the wealthy nobles of the empire had put so much pressure on him that the protocol had been twisted to produce the document now known as the Treaty of Guadalupe.

Sir Francis Drake, famous for having been a privateer, was devastating to the Spanish Empire because he took booty from vessels returning from the new world which were full of indigo, spices, silver, and all things very valuable, whereas he quickly saw it was bad piracy to take boats going the other way since they were full of slaves. During the time of the transatlantic trafficking, 40 percent of black slaves went to Rio de Janeiro and thence to other parts of South America. Others went to the Indies and so forth. There was a basic triangle consisting of Africa, Europe, and the New World. Ships to the New World picked up slaves in Africa and went on the Indies, Rio de Janeiro, and Mexico and returned with goods which could land at England, France, and Spain.

Then, from my perspective, I had a strange insight about the great Shakespearian play *The Merchant of Venice*. The merchant's name in the play was Antonio. During the play, he had four ships bound for the various destinations of the slave market (Mexico, Tripoli, the Indies, and England), so clearly Antonio was in the slave trade. Any educated Elizabethan would know *that* ("the judicious, who are worth a whole roomful of others").

I began to look at the records of performances in Elizabethan England in the 1590s and found there was great agitation due to rumors that Queen Elizabeth was going to permit Jews to return to England since their expulsion in 1209. A revival of the Christopher Marlowe play *The Jew of Malta* in the 1590s triggered intense anti-Semitic riots in London which involved an elaborate accusation of an attempt to poison Elizabeth by a converso Jewish doctor that we now know was a political maneuver. However, at this time *The Merchant of Venice* was staged, and almost instantly the anti-Semitic riots stopped. How on earth was it presented? The way the play has been presented, up until recently, would *create* anti-Semitic passions. One must premise that "something" in the staging of *The Merchant of Venice* had the opposite effect. My further research has shown that the group that wrote Shakespeare was presenting a critique of the slave trade and the society that was so created in Venice and in the Spanish Empire. Later I will present the basic production values that would make this apparent. This caused me to reflect on the teaching that may have come down to us and the critiques misread through centuries of either deliberate falsification or ignorance. To the English population, Santiago (Saint Iago) de Compostela in Spain was, in the words of Sir Francis Drake, an infernal nest of witches. Iago was the patron saint of Spain and, of course, in the tragedy of *Othello*, Iago, seeming saintly, is the cunning exploiter of the good nature of the Moor.

The expulsion of the Jews from England in 1209 had a curious history. The church historian Jocelyn told of an event which befell a Benedictine abbot in the St. Edmonton Abbey in which the abbot had gotten himself indebted to some Jewish money lender who over the years kept extracting usurious interest, finally leading to great humiliation for this "innocent" Benedictine abbot. The successor abbot finally went to the king, who ordered the money lender to trial where he compelled the debt to be forgiven by pulling teeth and the money lender punished. But even before Jocelyn's account was written, such rumors had led to the burning of thousands of Jews in the church of St. Edmunds, a great pogrom in York, and to the expulsion of the Jews from England in 1209.

Now, a careful reading of the account of Jocelyn, a study of documents which probably did happen at the time of the great intellectual court of Henry VIII, would suggest that Jocelyn's account was propaganda. One needs to remember that during the days of Henry VIII, the intellectuals in his court were in touch with rabbinical authorities in Venice investigating the validity of canon law's determination about the rules of marriage and divorce. Now, if one transposed Jocelyn's account of the Jew and the Benedictine onto the trial of Shylock and *The Merchant of Venice*, the plot and structure are alarmingly similar. Clearly, the Shakespearian group had this template in front of them which they turned on its head, having Shylock demonstrate the perniciousness of slavery in the process of a brilliant vaudevillian performance. Earlier in the play, we are informed that Saturn threatens (note that it does not harm) and lead is ruled by Saturn, which was considered the ruling planet of the Jews. During the progress of the play, Shylock does a superb vaudevillian performance of threatening, but nothing is ever done.

Tracing this theme a bit later, the struggle for freedom has a long history. Many thoughts came to mind during this intervening period. One of the most poignant was the one aroused by John Stuart Mill's essay on liberty. That it won't do people any good to get rid of tyrants if they maneuver the king or the tyrant to being an inner tyrant. Also, it made me consider the Talmudic saying that heaven sent down ten portions of "sleep" to earth and nine portions were taken by slaves. Clearly it means slaves *and* their masters and that that portion of humanity which accepts this falsification of human nature has swallowed those nine portions of sleep that stupefy us. The persistent call to awaken that Zarathustra, the ancient Hindu masters, Moses, Buddha, the school that surrounded Jesus, made or sounded were to help our common struggle against sleep, which is sometimes called "ignorance."

This paper is going to develop some themes tracing this effort to wake up in Western civilization. We'll start with a trajectory beginning with the school of the prophet Isaiah, which continues from about 800 BCE, proceeding through successive centuries to the closure of the written Isiaian books in about the third century BCEv, but we will show it emerging in the school associated with Jesus, particularly in the gospel of Matthew. Another school that helped establish the Western tradition begins with the prophet

Ezekiel, which can be called Ezekielian, preserved though the centuries in Israelite tradition and Greco Israelite tradition emerging with the temple eschatology in Qumran and John of Patmos, the "author" of the book of Revelation, the Apocalypse. There is a third Israelite tradition which will be called the Wisdom Tradition, beginning with the court of King Solomon and eclectically moving through time and manifesting in our "hinge period" in the so-called "Gospel of John."

I will show this stream emerging in the Elizabethan period in England and its flowering of literature. The stream of waters flowing from the Ezekielian tradition will be shown in the sacred geometries in Europe, the poetic tradition sublimely expressed by Dante, and the sixteenth-century academies of France. The Hokmah or wisdom tradition flows from the Gospel of John to merge with the elements of Egypt, North Africa, and finally, the Grail traditions in Europe.

Now, I'll return to the paper I was quoting.

Carl amused and refreshed us with some of his wonderful singing of the Boll Weevil Song, Careless Love, I Wish I Was a Little Bird, Cigarettes Will Spoil Yer life and We'll Roll Back the Prices, and we began to talk about the real terrifying events happening in Europe at the time. The only one really alert to this hazard, was Fordie himself (and the Europeans) who shared a letter he was planning to send to the English foreign minister for publication. He gave me a copy of his final draft late in 1938 which I think is important enough to include in this paper.

"February 27, 1939

To the Rt. Honorable Malcolm MacDonald

Sir:

I take the liberty of intruding on your attention on the subject of Palestine as a national home of the Jews. In 1915

in common with a number of historians and economists—
amongst them being Profs. Gooch, Hobson, Hobhouse, Sir
C. P. Scott of the *Manchester Guardian* and others—I was
approached by Mr. C. F. G. Masterman, then Chancellor of
the Duchy of Lancaster—in his capacity, I think, of the chief
of Ministry of Information—and asked for what proposals I
and they thought should be made for terms of peace by the
Asquith Ministry. Amongst my proposals which included the
creation of a Rhenan [sic] Republic to act as a buffer state
between France and Germany was the creation of a National
Jewish Republic in Palestine—which amongst other things
would act as a buffer state between the Turkish Empire and
Egypt, then a British protectorate. In that proposal I called
Palestine the Jewish National Home, using, I think, the phrase
for the first time. Since that date I have paid very prolonged
and earnest attention to the Jewish world problem.

Permit me to say that I am of the opinion that the only
possible solution *is* the creation of a Jewish Republic, whether
independent or as a British protectorate is immaterial as long
as it can be represented at the league of Nations and be capable
of sending properly accredited diplomatic representatives to
powers committing atrocities against Jews. I will spare you
my reasons for this conclusion; you must be aware of them
yourself at least as well as I. And sir, you must be at least
as well acquainted as I am with the physical and mental
atrocities which are being committed against Jews in every
nation whose territory lies between the Baltic and the Black
Seas. That being so, I do not see how you can do anything
but agree that if the public opinion of Christendom—and I
use the term advisedly—could be really made aware of these
things, an immense movement determined to ameliorate the
Jewish world-lot must eventuate. But to bring this about
the Jews themselves must be in the position of a sovereign

authority having power to obtain publicity for those same atrocities. It is a question of concentration of effort. Today individual reports from press correspondents and others of atrocities such as take place daily, and particularly in Rumania, are simply suppressed by the press of almost every nation whereas a diplomatic report address from the Jerusalem Government to the White House or the Court of St. James's or an authoritative speech before the League of Nations must attract some attention.

I am aware, sir, that in your official capacity it is no part of your function to ameliorate the world condition of the Jews but that desire must exist in the heart of every civilized man and it must be of benefit to our country should she conduce disinterestedly to that end. I am aware that it must be prejudicial to the Empire to create in the Arab and Mahometan sections of the Empire a feeling of hostility to the Empire but I beg you, Sir, to give weight to the consideration that it must be infinitely more prejudicial to Great Britain to earn the reprehension of the whole of the civilized world.

When on the third of July, 1914, Sir Edward Goschen addressed to Bethmann-Hollweg the proud words: "When it is a question of the observance of treaties, it is not the custom of His majesty's Government to count the costs."—I am quoting without the White Book—England at once stood higher in the estimation of the comity of nations than she ever stood or than any other nation ever stood. It is all important for the very existence of our Empire that you should not at this juncture find yourself under the necessity of saying—like Lord Randolph Churchill—that you had "forgotten Goschen."

It is perhaps not exactly pertinent for me here to advert to the policy of the Government to which you belong when it "forgot Goshen" at Berchtesgaden and Munich. It causes us— whether deservedly or no—to stand today in the estimation of nearly every moderate, instructed and liberal minded man in this country, a little lower morally than perhaps any nation ever stood. And I do not need to tell you that the Prime Minister's declaration yesterday in the House of Commons to the effect that he has recognized the Franco regime without sufficient guarantee for the protection of the Republican population has roused in this country a feeling of horror that has probably never been paralleled. They see in the Prime Minister a dictator with no one to control him, who, at the bidding of the totalitarian dictators, has delivered infinite thousands of innocent humanity to a certain butchery. I may add that in the view of a great many political thinkers in the country, the Prime Minister's surrender of Spain to the totalitarian powers renders Great Britain for strategic reasons of almost infinitely diminished value as an ally in case of war. I am talking now of people who would otherwise have been willing to engage this country in a war on the side of her former allies.

I ask you to understand that I am not here expressing my own views but those of, I am convinced, almost the entire thinking and working class population of the United States. And I ask you to believe, sir, that in writing this letter I am attempting to make you aware of a situation as to which you are probably little instructed. I think that until yesterday, the majority of the population in this country would have favoured aiding the European democracies in the struggle against totalitarian powers. Today, that chance has diminished nearly to the vanishing point. In giving you that considered opinion, I think myself, therefore, to be performing a patriotic duty.

And I trust your daily Fate may not be as
mine is to hear such men, who till yesterday
were the friends of our country, averring every

day both in public and in private, that the British Empire is a concealedly fascist organization in the hands of venial, commercial interests and under the dictatorship of a ruler who is known to a great part of the world as "Judas, the son of Judas." And how much more will that accusation not be heard if you proceed to a further betrayal in Palestine itself.

I will however add, for what it is worth, my own private opinion on the Palestinian situation. We inveigled these unfortunate people into that country by a promise, at least inferred, of protection, unhindered immigration and [a] measure at least of independence—for what other meaning could the words "National Home" be taken to bear? There is, sir, a Nemesis that attaches to nations—a Nemesis in no way supernatural but as much a matter of cause and effect as is the force of gravity. That equation can be thus expressed: If a nation earn the detestation and contempt of the public conscience of the world, it shall find no one to come to its assistance in the moment of extremity. And, living as I do amongst the class that forms public opinion in this country and in France, I am, I take the liberty to imagine, more aware than you how near we have already come to having earned the opprobrium and contempt of the civilized world.

I have the honour to be, Sir, Your obedient servant,

P.S. I am sending copies of this letter, omitting two sentences of Paragraph [seven], which I have indented to the *Times* and *Manchester Guardian* with the request that they publish it. I presume that if you consider that the publication could be of any national disservice, you can take steps to prevent its being published."

In addition to Fordie, Golo and Erika Mann were aware of the dangers because their father, Thomas Mann, had to leave Europe because of his opposition to the Nazi government in Germany. Alfred Korzybski was aware. He was an intense critic of the Hitler program, quite seriously describing it as a twisted Aristotelian logic of the unsane variety. But we Americans, Frank, Carl and many of us in the room, were really in our dreams and not sensitive to the events happening in Europe, though later, of course, we would all be swept into those events.

Suddenly a small woman, Kathleen Toomey, who had recently joined the faculty, blurted out, "I've something I'd like to add about Gurdjieff's ideas."

Kathleen was a modern dancer who had worked with Doris Humphreys and had also spent some time at the New School dance program, which was being directed at that time by Sophia Delza. I had learned from Kathleen that as a much younger woman, Sophia had participated in a demonstration of Gurdjieff's dances that was performed at the Neighborhood Playhouse. Kathleen was at Olivet for a temporary teaching job, having just come back from Europe with a young son whom she had placed in a boarding school at Devil's Lake, North Dakota. She brimmed with ideas but was very shy. The conversation seemed to have stimulated a very important part of her psyche, and I'll try to reproduce what she said.

She thanked Fordie for having read that portion of Gurdjieff's work and then went on to explain how many of the ideas he was trying to introduce to the West could not really be understood without his work on body movement and music. What she said was so interesting I actually took notes while she described her experience.

She said, "The dance or movement that Gurdjieff called the octave, once it is mastered, can prove an entry to the text known in the West as the Sermon on the Mount. Gurdjieff had been raised in Armenia close to the Eastern Orthodox Church and the Armenian epic tradition. But before discussing the Sermon on the Mount, it would be helpful to look at one example that is less complex. Gurdjieff was finding a language to present ancient ideas to modern sensibilities. The Armenian Apostolic Church, having been the first official 'Christian' church in the world, had a number of unique traditions, many of which have been forgotten now, though not entirely. The ancient world used the expressions often—Father, Son, Holy Ghost, etc. Gurdjieff used terms like First Order Sun, Second Order Sun, and Third Order Sun to describe a process of emanation. He developed a dance called 'The Number Four Hop' (and at this point she laughed) with an alternative title, 'Hymn to the Sun,' or more relevantly, 'Prayer for Instruction.' In the ancient Armenian liturgy, the monks sing a hymn at Prime in Tone VII, a prayer addressed to 'Oh Light, Creator of Light,' what could be called the beginning of light, the creation. Subsequent verses address a light born of the light, a light proceeding from the light and so forth. Each portion of this hymn ends with the words 'shine on our souls thine intelligible light,' clearly a Prayer for Instruction . . . The sequence of moves and pauses in the Gurdjieffian movement articulate what could be called the modulations of worlds through which the original light reaches humanity. Some parts of it are very close to what scanty fragments of dance recorded in Gnostic writings of the 'intertestamental period.' For example, the circle dance in the Gnostic Gospel of John.

"Now, to the Sermon on the Mount. Of course, as everyone knows, after the Israelite exile and return to what the Romans later called Judea, there were many schools of thought among the Israelites. There were communities in Egypt, Greece, Spain, the 'wilderness of the peoples' (namely the area at the origin of the Tigris and Euphrates rivers), and the Caucasus region the land of the Hayc, known today as Armenians, where many peoples of all background had immigrated to escape the Roman Empire. There were also very large communities in Babylon, Persepolis, and Alexandria. The main languages that the Jews were using were the languages of the communities where they lived but, on the whole, Greek, which was a universal language, was the one employed by most communities in the Mediterranean area. In the east, Aramaic was the language of the Babylonian and the Parthian Empire. To make matters easier for the Jews in the eastern region, versions of the Bible and scripture were written in Aramaic, a text called the Targum Onkelos. In the Greek area, and typical of their great mental genius, the whole text was translated in the form we know today as the Septuagint."

At this point the eyes of our group, particularly Carl Sandberg's, were glazing over and ready for sleep. But her next statement woke everyone up.

"In the whole Septuagint, there is only one use of the term *mat*, disciple. And in the New Testament, there is only one use of the term 'purity of heart,' and that is in the opening octave of the Sermon on the Mount, which the instruction says was given to the disciples, *mat*."

Since almost everyone in our group was a literary type, this strange anomaly caught our attention, and we began to listen to Kathleen quite seriously.

"Since the gospels are written in Greek, it's useful to understand that the first octave of the sermon uses the term *macario*, 'happy' in English. But the English does not really carry the force of *macario*, particularly as we use the term in the last several hundred years. But *macario* is the appropriate translation for the Hebrew word, *ashray*. As a dancer, and if I were to dance these words, I could tell you quite simply that 'happy' would not do. I couldn't dance 'happy' without looking like Walt Disney, and the word often used in English Bibles, 'blessed,' I couldn't dance without looking stupidly pious. So I'll use either *ashray* or *macario* to explain how the octave would be danced as it related to the Sermon on the Mount. Now as a dancer, when one performs the octave, the arms take positions which impact both the audience and the performer in almost the same way."

At this point, she got up and demonstrated this to us, but I don't have the skill to reproduce it here.

Do—*Ashray* are the poor in spirit for theirs is the kingdom of heaven.

Re—*Ashray* are those who mourn, grieve, feel sorrow, they shall be comforted (but in the Greek, the word has the sense of strengthened also).

Mi—*Ashray* are the meek. In English it is translated as "meek," but perhaps it would be better translated as those of gentle spirit.

Fa—*Ashray* are those who hunger that right may prevail.

Sol—*Ashray* are the merciful, compassionate. They shall find mercy and compassion.

La—*Ashray* are the pure in heart (this is the only time in the entire New Testament that this term is used, and without going too far into matters, which would involve going into the Prophet Isaiah, we'll stay with the text here) they shall see God, obviously with the eyes of the heart.

Si—*Ashray* are the peacemakers (since this is the seventh of the octave, it would indicate peacemakers between above and below). They shall be called the sons and daughters of God. I've added daughters simply because it would have been understood in those days *among the disciples*.

Do—*Ashray* are those who suffer persecution that right may prevail. Theirs is the kingdom of heaven. Which sounds the next *do*. Technically, biblical scholars call this an *inclusio*.

"It is clear from the movement that these are not different people—some merciful, some righteous, and so on. This is about how to be one complete person. Now this particular demonstration of the first octave is too complicated to carry though the entire sermon, but I recommend any of you who are more curious to look at St. Augustine's division of the Sermon on the Mount into octaves, though he used the term sevens that can be interchangeable in the dance mode.

"Another unique feature brought out by the octave movement is that in the *mathematical center* of the sermon is what is commonly called the 'Lord's Prayer' or the 'Our Father,' which forms a perfect octave in itself. I go through this whole exercise just to point out that Gurdjieff's teaching was not only a critique of human life but presented ideas of a positive and creative nature for the benefit of human life."

As she finished her talk, she suddenly became shy again and sat down, leaving us all in stupefied silence.

Later in this chapter, you will see that this was very useful to what I'm presenting. As I said, the above was in a paper that I found after going into the Olivet College library during a break in our meetings. I'd gone in because I noticed a light in the evening when usually the library was dark. The meetings had taken place in the beautiful Congregational church next to the library. Dining and other activities were in the other parts of the campus, but the library was usually closed. So I went in and found a casually dressed gentleman in his early or mid fifties doing some work. He was surprised that one of us dropped in, saying he had hoped to keep out of sight. He had some business to do in the library, but usually he spent his summers on the Lake Michigan shore. Since he was there and I came in, he said, "Who are you anyway, the Society Amfortas that's rented the school?"

I said it was very hard to explain, at which he laughed and said most things were. He introduced himself as George Hansen, and I introduced myself. (You'll note that his name turns up in the paper quoted as having been part of the group that had met in the library basement.) It was through our conversation that Mr. Hansen, who was a musicologist and librarian, gave me the material from which I have quoted above.

Mr. Hansen and I began to talk. He said that during the summers, he and his wife went to their property on Lake Michigan shore where he also enjoyed his hobby of model railroads.

Since I'm a "people person," our conversation did range far and wide. And since it wasn't that long after the war, we discussed politics, but he also he mentioned the years at Olivet between 1932-1937, an especially charmed time for this little college in a little town in the state of Michigan. A reaction of isolationism had set in just before we entered the war, and many of the people who had been there during the very bright years were dispersed around the country or went back to Europe. I was quite astonished that such a small school had boasted such a remarkable assembly of friends and faculty just before the war.

Before we parted, George let me borrow the packet that included the paper I have quoted above. After I'd worked my way through the packet of material Mr. Hansen had let me borrow, he had already gone back to his summer quarters on the Lake Michigan shore. I wasn't able to discuss some issues that would have been very fascinating, such as his playing music from manuscript in 1934 at Frank Lloyd Wright's school and how Alfred Korzybski, who was the inspiration for general semantics and for neurolinguistics, got there. I was able to understand Fordie's relationship to Orage on several accounts since they were both literary figures, and because Orage had been interested in P.D. Ouspensky as well as

Gurdjieff, and I knew that Ouspensky's book, *Tertium Organum*, had been quite the rage during the '20s and '30s and had dealt at great length with the "fourth dimension." And also that Fordie, though writing as Ford Maddox Hueffer, had done some work with Joseph Conrad about the "fourth dimension" that they had published. Things began to make some sense to me. It seems that just before the war broke out, there were many strides being made toward a deeper understanding of science, religion, and the possible intelligent further evolution of human beings. And there also had been intelligent efforts recommended by Winston Churchill which could have possibly averted the second act of the World War that had begun in 1914. Due to distrust and special interests among potential allies, that particular avenue was not followed. Also, it seems because of the same "appetite" of the Western church to conquer the Eastern church, certain unfortunate political decisions were made by the political powers within the Vatican hierarchy. (Worthy of note—the reader should be reminded that for four hundred years, there had been battles between the Roman church and Eastern orthodox church, a portion of which were called the Baltic crusades, and although neither side won the battle in these four hundred years, the line of contention existed during the period from roughly 1200 to 1600. Nowadays, the so-called famous Iron Curtain follows almost exactly the line of the Baltic crusades; so one might say, if we were Martians, that Western Europe still has the hots for Eastern Europe, regardless of their religious persuasions.)

So let us place ourselves back into the "intertestmental period" two hundred years prior to the beginning of the current era and two hundred years into our current era. The Roman Empire (let us call them the Latins), having overtaken Greece, was still engaged in trying to extend their conquest over the eastern parts of the Mediterranean area and were trying to match the temporary conquests that the "student of Aristotle," Alexander the Great, had attempted vaingloriously to achieve. One virtue of his horrific exercise had been the exchange of ideas, to some extent, between the East and the West.

And, of course, as the paper that I quoted above indicated, this process of war constantly fed both sides with captives who became either slaves or prostitutes; and although there was a benefit of ideas, on the ground you might say conditions weren't that good for human beings. The Latins' enemy for several hundred years of this time, Parthia, had managed to create a diverse religious environment for the peoples under their influence. The Latins' empire tended to be much more doctrinaire, permitting divergences only if the emperor were worshipped. Fortunately, not all of the people were living in this political power arena. Ordinary people lived their lives, philosophers philosophized, the great spiritual schools continued, modifying their expression in concert with the surrounding conditions. Since I'm writing as "Trevrizent," obviously a representative of the "Grail," "Crater" tradition, I am going to present how "schools" managed to maintain the continuity of the essential teaching despite the changes of political climate. I'll use a quote from the Hebrew prophet Isaiah, more appropriately spelled Yeshe Yahu (the substance of being), when the prophet described three sections of the civilized world: Egypt, "Whom the Lord of hosts shall bless, saying, Blessed be Egypt my people, and Assyria the work of my hands, and Israel mine inheritance" (Isaiah 19:25 King James Version 1611).

We consider him transmitting the idea of three specialities approximately developed in these three regions: Practicks in the Mesopotamian regions, Vision in Egypt, and the preservation and recording of the lineages in Israel.

The schools, apparently for the people of Israel, found it important to transform the more mathematical, astronomical, and mythological method of Mesopotamia into a more humanistic understanding to be brought forth by the heritage of Israel. In the story surrounding the flood, we find a list of ten deified kings who are changed into ten patriarchs. Also, the mathematics changed from a six-base system to a ten-base system. And the epic tradition of Israel transformed the very mythological traditions of Sumerian and Babylon to a more humanistic expression. (Closer at hand, we have an example of this occurring in China when mythological creatures, such as the phoenix, were changed into more tangible humanistic images, such as the stork, under the influence of Tang Dynasty Buddhism.) A hint of this process can be found in the works of Philo of Alexandria, the great Jewish philosopher, when he applies an old teaching device used by both the Talmudic sages and the prophetic schools of Israel and the Wisdom schools of Greece and Egypt. It can be called either "the gap method" or "the contradiction method." I will return to this a little later. For the moment, I'm going to leap far ahead in time to the struggle of the two empires, the Spanish Empire and the Ottoman Empire, by any objective reckoning two of the most oppressive empires the world has seen since the famous Pax Romana. As a kind of "snapshot," we can look briefly at the battles waged by these empires in the Mediterranean when the engines of all the galleys, the oarsmen, were either slaves or lifetime prisoners.

England and some of the Protestant countries were beginning to stir in their sleep and realized it would be very valuable to have copies of the religious scriptures in their own languages. Efforts to translate the Bible into everyday languages were made fitfully, first in small circles in Spain, Italy, England, and France; most of these translators were hunted by the authorities. This led in England to the English bibles of Wycliffe, Tyndale, the Geneva bible, and finally, the King James Bible. The earlier translators were martyred, but their work survived in the King James, which became the authorized version of 1611 and is one of the greatest masterpieces in human history—a genuine tribute to the work of the Holy Spirit. It is the opinion of our Grail fellowship that this kind of result does not simply "just happen."

Now I will bring in Philo of Alexandria. In his *Questions and Answers*, which only survived in Armenian, he uses the contradiction method. How could the Flood of Noah's time, of such vast proportions, be dried out by winds? He observes that it's not very likely. The *wind* mentioned in scripture, *ruach* (Greek would be *pneuma*), is used for spirit. He then proceeds to challenge our thought through this contradiction. When humanity is drowning in a flood of immense proportions, as perhaps the period of those wars between *gog* and *magog*, or let us say Spain and Ottomans, the wind, the spirit, begins to clear an area at least a little bit in Britain. This, in fact, had perhaps been the seat of the first Western Christian church, possibly in Glastonbury. The second Christian church began officially in Armenia. Now, from the perspective of the Grail schools, this breath of spirit began to have a liberating effect in England during the Elizabethan period and in some schools in France. From this beginning, dry land, struggles for human dignity grew.

Let us look for example at the Circle of Shakespeare and its last play, *The Tempest*, which was presented as a celebration of the marriage of Princess Elizabeth to Frederick, the elector of the Palatine, who was the leader of the great Protestant princes of Europe.

In *The Tempest*, there is a *structurally* unique moment which has the same elements as the twenty-ninth chapter of the prophet Yeshayahu. The elements are a strange meal being presented: a book that cannot be read, the stupefaction of people as if blind, the action of conscience brought on by the unique figure named Ariel. These structural elements are common to both *The Tempest* and Yeshayahu chapter twenty-nine. There is also a very fascinating pulse of spirit resonance between the play and prophet. This resonance is heard in a legend preserved in a Talmudic tractate, Baba Bathra, in which the prophet Yeshayahu escapes from attempts to capture and kill him by fleeing (by some uncanny means) into a cedar tree. However, the king's servants track him to the tree and, cutting it into pieces, kill him. In the play *The Tempest*, we find Ariel has been freed from being imprisoned in a pine tree and is to be released to the "elements." This should be enough to recommend to the judicious reader or playgoer that the ""comedy" *The Tempest* may require serious study from a fresh viewpoint.

Now, let us return to look more carefully at *The Merchant of Venice* than we did in my earlier mention. In act 2.7 (lines 15-20), the leaden casket is described as "threatening." Then in act 3, (lines 104-105), the lead casket is again described as threatening; however, the leaden casket *is the casket* that contains the treasure. Now, lead is the metal associated with Saturn, which according to the times was the planet that governed the Jews. Before putting *The Merchant of Venice* on the stage, we would direct the actor playing Shylock that he play his part according to the stereotype of the "money-lending Jew." Jews had been forbidden residence as a consequence of the rumors triggered by Jocelyn in the twelfth century, which had led to the burnings, massacres, and ultimately, their expulsion from England in 1209. So we would say to the actor (I would pick Peter Sellers), "Play the stereotype, but play it so broadly as to be comical, with several exceptions." The exceptions would be Shylock's conversation with Tubal (act 3 scene 1) and Shylock's discussion of slaves in the possession of the Venetians (act 4 scene 1). Nothing else need be done for the play to tell the story (except perhaps for Portia's uneasiness in the last scene) that slavery is an obscenity and a slave-based society—rotten to the core. One could go to other plays and find similar enlightening potentials, which for a country beginning to emerge from oppression would be tremendously encouraging.

I remind the reader that I'm writing this paper under the name "Trevrizent," a name that has fascinating references far beyond its use in Wolfram's *Parzival*.

I sense that this paper is drawing to an end. In the tradition of my "school," we might say that the "potato has dropped." I'm going to give a brief sketch of three strands of tradition that had existed among the Israelite people which have carried forward into Western civilization.

The Ezekielian School, began in Babylon during the exile of the Israelites and continued in a direct line to Qumran and the author of the "Book of Revelations," the Apocalypse of John of Patmos. This school produces "and the leaves of the tree were for the healing of the nations." What is critical to grasp in this school's development is its origin in Mesopotamia and the continuity of its meditation on the figure of the Temple. There were several temples. There was the temple of Solomon, which was one thing in its beginning and over the centuries became "something else." And it was this "something else" that the prophet Ezekiel described as being destroyed. A temple was subsequently rebuilt when the Israelites returned from captivity, thanks to King Cyrus who had defeated the Babylonians and was the first major Zarathushtrian king. He returned the Israelites to their homeland and provided the funds for the temple to be rebuilt and for the scriptures to be restored. However, the scripture were restored with a new script, substituting the square Assyrian script for the original Paleo Hebrew script. Traces of this ancient script are retained in portions of the Dead Sea Scrolls. Then, in the time of Herod, this "second temple" was fixed up and described as beautiful, but then it was destroyed by the Romans under the leadership of Titus. About this temple, there is a line in the Talmud which can be read either "when the temple was destroyed, an iron wall was built between Israel and God" or "when the temple was destroyed, an iron wall came down that had been between Israel and God." It must be remarked that the Herod who made this "beautiful" temple, was the same who murdered his sons and almost succeeded in murdering his daughter. A later Herod, in the town of Caesarea, in one day had twenty-five thousand Jews killed by the sword for having made a protest to the emperor. A very curious family for the temple-building business.

The Temple tradition being presented by the Ezekiel, Apocalypse school, is far too complex and subtle to be described in this paper at all. We can only recommend that the reader who wishes to look further begin with the Jewish traditions of the Desert Tabernacle as described in Me'am Lo'ez and go on from there.

The Wisdom school we will call the Song of Solomon or Jedediah, which is the name for Solomon used by the author of the Book of Chronicles. This school has its roots god knows where and god knows when, but it seems essential to all traditions that the sap that flows through this school must never leave the planet. I would simply indicate three phases of its work as a teaching school by using the three books in the Bible *attributed to* Solomon called Koheleth (Ecclesiastes), Mishle (Proverbs), and Shir ha Shirim (Song of Songs).

"Ecclesiastes" functions as a subject for deep pondering to chasten the student's tendency toward self-exaltation by forcing a confrontation with impermanence and death. When that chastening has been thorough-going and the student has tasted what in Melville's words is "the fine hammered steel of woe," the next stage will be entered. The book Mishle uses what I referred to earlier as the gap method very widely. It includes proverbs, advice, and a profusion of statements reflecting the grittiness of day-to-day life. It also brings a sublime poem on a cosmic scale, presenting an image of creation which can be viewed as a midrash on the beginning of Genesis. It touches the highs, as it were, and the lows. (The Christian gospel of John may carry the continuum of this school insofar as it begins with a song of cosmic wisdom or logos, goes though the gritty events of life and death, encounters in chapter 11 a Greek-style peripeteia, goes through several chapters

[chapters 12-17 probably should be rearranged] of profound tragedy, and after the "resurrection" ends with a very homey, down-to-earth, freshly caught fish picnic at night shared by Jesus and his disciples.)

After Proverbs has stabilized the student's heart, mind, spirit and will, a profound study of the Song of Songs, Shir ha Shirim, is undertaken. Possibly the student learns that love and wisdom are inseparable, *echod*.

CPSIA information can be obtained at www.ICGtesting.com
Printed in the USA
LVOW13s2312250414

383313LV00001B/1/P